Praise for *The War Nurse*

"Tracey Enerson Wood achieves two particularly difficult things with this novel: a fictionalization of a real person's life, which is always a challenge—and the feat of writing a character from a century past who is accessible to a modern audience but still entirely of her era. In *The War Nurse*, based on the true story of pioneering World War I nurse Julia Stimson, we are transported to early twentieth-century France, where a band of medical professionals struggles to meet the ever-changing demands of a war zone. You will smile, shed a few tears, and learn alongside Julia in this impeccably researched, well-drawn, based-on-a-true-story tale, written by a former RN. As our collective interest in World War I is reawakened, *The War Nurse* shines an important light on a woman whose story was, until now, lost to time."

—Kristin Harmel, *New York Times* bestselling
author of *The Book of Lost Names*

"*The War Nurse* is a vividly rendered, moving tribute to one woman's determination to make a difference in the world. Tracey Enerson Wood sets us down in war-ravaged France and immerses us in the lives of a band of courageous nurses braving battles both physical and moral. A riveting and surprisingly timely story of courage, sacrifice, and friendship forged at the front lines."

—Kelly Mustian, *USA Today* bestselling
author of *The Girls in the Stilt House*

"*The War Nurse* is a fascinating, intimate look at the true story of Julia Catherine Stimson and the incredible work she and her nurses did to save lives during World War I. Through careful research, this book shows the incredible bravery and compassion of women who find themselves in extraordinary situations."

—Julia Kelly, international bestselling author of
The Last Garden in England and *The Light Over London*

"*The War Nurse* is a rich, gripping history of one woman's lifelong battle against systemic prejudice. As Tracey Enerson Wood's heroine says of herself, 'I wasn't a man, for whom the things I wanted to do would have been easy. I was meant to break down the wall in between.'"

—Stewart O'Nan, award-winning
author of *The Good Wife*

"Once again, Tracey Enerson Wood, with her impeccable research and evocative prose, kept me glued to the page. Wood has a talent for bringing strong, yet lesser-known women from history, to life. Her fictionalization of World War I nurse Julia Stimson, as well as the supporting cast, transported me back in time, had me smiling, crying, and learning. Fantastic!"

—Linda Rosen, author of *The Disharmony of Silence*

"If you, like me, are a voyeur of historical drama that unfolds as if the kitchen window flew open and the characters were caught in action, then *The War Nurse* is for you. Tracey Enerson Wood's storytelling verisimilitude—the detail, persuasive dialogue, and twinning of history with a hidden love story—prove her skill at immersion, but also that rarest of traits: a big and generous heart that roots for the unsung heroines and heroes of the time. This author shines a light for us all to see our past anew."

—Diane Dewey, author of *Fixing the Fates*

"If you've read *The Engineer's Wife*, Tracey Enerson Wood's debut, you are already aware of her talent for merging fact and fiction into a story that will make your heart hurt and hold you captive until the very last page. She doesn't disappoint with *The War Nurse*."

—Barbara Conrey, *USA Today* bestselling
author of *Nowhere Near Goodbye*

"Based on a true story, Wood's latest highlights Julia's quick thinking, organizational skills, and endlessly caring heart, bringing life to a brutal era. Fans of Patricia Harman will love Wood's treatment of medical expertise in a historical setting."

—*Booklist*

"*The War Nurse* is an incredibly well-researched historical fiction novel with a sympathetic heroine... Any readers who enjoyed the mix of romance, intrigue, and medical accuracy of *Call the Midwife* would love *The War Nurse*."

—*New York Journal of Books*

Praise for *The Engineer's Wife*

"Well-researched with great attention to detail, *The Engineer's Wife* is based on the true story about the exceptional woman who was tasked to build the Brooklyn Bridge. Though the great bridge would connect a city, it would also cause division and loss for many. Tracey Enerson Wood delivers an absorbing and poignant tale of struggle, self-sacrifice, and the family transformed by the building of the legendary American landmark during the volatile time of women's suffrage, riots, and corruption. A triumphant debut not to be missed!"

—Kim Michele Richardson, *New York Times* bestselling author of *The Book Woman of Troublesome Creek*

"*The Engineer's Wife* is historical fiction at its finest. Tracey Enerson Wood crafts the powerful and poignant story of Emily Warren Roebling, the compelling woman who played an instrumental role in the design and construction of the Brooklyn Bridge. This is necessary fiction for our time—paying tribute to women's overlooked contributions and reminding us of the true foundations of American history."

—Andrea Bobotis, author of
The Last List of Miss Judith Kratt

"Who really built the Brooklyn Bridge? With its spunky, tough-minded heroine and vivid New York setting, *The Engineer's Wife* is a triumphant historical novel sure to please readers of the genre. Like Paula McLain, Tracey Enerson Wood spins a colorful and romantic tale of a storied era."

—Stewart O'Nan, award-winning
author of *The Good Wife*

"Tracey Enerson Wood raises Emily Warren Roebling from the historical depths, bringing to vivid life the story of the woman who saved the Brooklyn Bridge."

—Anne Lipton, MD, PhD, contributing
author in *Putting the Science in Fiction*, and
Harlequin Creator Fund recipient

"The writing meticulously evokes the sights, sounds, and smells of 1870s New York...Wood spares no detail in showing us what led up to that first stroll across the great bridge—by a woman."

—*Kirkus Reviews*

"*The Engineer's Wife* is just the sort of novel I love and—I hope—write. Against all odds, a dynamic, historic woman builds a monument and changes history as she and her surrounding cast leap off the page. What a life and what a beautifully written and inspiring story!"

—Karen Harper, *New York Times* bestselling
author of *The Queen's Secret*

"This important work of historical fiction brings to life the strength and resolve of a nineteenth-century woman overshadowed by men and overlooked by history books."

—*Booklist*

"Wood's satisfying historical feels true to its era yet powerfully relevant to women's lives today."

—*Publishers Weekly*

the WAR NURSE

the WAR NURSE

A Novel

TRACEY ENERSON WOOD

sourcebooks
landmark

Published by Sourcebooks Landmark, an imprint of Sourcebooks
P.O. Box 4410, Naperville, Illinois 60567-4410
(630) 961-3900
sourcebooks.com

The Library of Congress cataloged the hardcover edition as follows:

Names: Enerson Wood, Tracey, author.
Title: The war nurse : a novel / Tracey Enerson Wood.
Description: Naperville, Illinois : Sourcebooks Landmark, [2021]
Identifiers: LCCN 2020051811 (print) | LCCN 2020051812 (ebook) |
   (hardcover) | (epub)
Classification: LCC PS3623.O6455 W37 2021 (print) | LCC PS3623.O6455
   (ebook) | DDC 813/.6--dc23
LC record available at https://lccn.loc.gov/2020051811
LC ebook record available at https://lccn.loc.gov/2020051812

Printed and bound in Canada.
MBP 10 9 8 7 6 5 4 3 2 1

To the heroes, both long gone and with us today,
who fought for freedom and safety in our world,
and to those who cared for them in their hour of need.

CHAPTER 1

April 1917
St. Louis, Missouri

P erhaps God made a mistake, and meant for me to be born
a man. Certainly he gave me a man's height, a jaw like an
anvil, and shoulders fit to carry the world's burdens. But I am,
through and through, a woman, with all the sensibilities and, I daresay,
strengths that includes. And I needed all of them, every ounce of courage, every fiber of muscle, every memorized detail of my profession.

On occasion, I shamelessly used my impressive stature when it
suited my goals. In fact, that fateful morning, when the bespectacled Dr.
Valentine barged into my office, ranting about the actions of one of my
nurses in training, I rose from my desk chair and stood next to him, the
top of his balding head even with my chin. Somehow, this seemed to
even the playing field between the chief of medicine and chief of nursing.

My office was a handsome space, and I was proud to have earned
it. A huge walnut desk the size of a dining table imposed its bulk in
the center, and bookshelves lined all four walls. There was something
empowering about it, and watching Dr. Valentine's eyes flick around
the room, taking it in, pleased me.

He waggled his pointer finger at me. "Miss Harriman is the most obtuse nurse I've ever had the displeasure of working with. You make sure she doesn't come with us."

"Come with you? Where are you going?"

His eyes widened behind his thick eyeglasses and his mouth gaped, as if he had just witnessed a ghost. "Oh, no, not my place to say. Better it comes from the powers that be." He looked up at the ceiling, as if angels were the higher power. "Well, ta-ta, then." He backed away, creeping out of my office like a guilty schoolboy.

I quickly forgot about his strange comment and unreasonable complaint about the nurse and returned to my huge workload. After three years in St. Louis at Barnes Hospital, organizing then leading the medical-social work unit, I had been promoted to superintendent of nurses and head of nursing training at the affiliated Washington University. As superintendent, I was responsible for every aspect of nursing at the university hospital, from recruitment and training to policies and procedures. I frequently coordinated with the heads of other departments and worked feverishly to stay up to date on new treatments and practices.

At the same time, I was handling all the duties of a dean for the nurse training program. Without the title, of course, as nursing wasn't considered an academic major but more of an on-the-job training program.

I had nearly two years as superintendent, and it was a most rewarding experience. With the possible exception of Dr. Valentine, Washington University had the finest doctors and was on the front edge, especially for dealing with cardiac and facial surgery.

Despite all that, Dr. Valentine's strange remark reminded me that it was probably time for me to move on. There was change in the air, something I sensed the way the rustle of the leaves and birds taking flight told me of an oncoming storm. Even before the huge proposition that was about to land in my lap, I knew I would be leaving my beloved St. Louis.

I was teetering on a rolling ladder, adding new textbooks of medical-surgical nursing to the top shelf, when tall, muscular Dr. Fred Murphy, the chief of surgery, dropped by my office.

"Good gracious, Miss Stimson, get down. We have people to do that." He brushed back the locks of light-brown hair that continually fell upon his forehead, which along with his oversize eyeglasses gave him a boyish look. But he had been a star football player at Harvard and seemed to fill the room with an aura of power and authority.

I'd had a bit of a crush on him since we both had arrived in St. Louis back in 1911. I had to be careful, because gossip was the fuel that fed too many of the doctors, nurses, and other staff. At nearly thirty-six years old, I was considered a spinster, so any eligible bachelor was eyed as my potential suitor, despite my many denials, claiming the truth, that I simply didn't have the time for one. So I had to steal a glance at Dr. Murphy when no one was looking, happy to have this opportunity alone in my office with him.

Not only was he tall and strongly built, he was bright and amusing, yet totally unassuming. He was charming in a most sincere way, opening a door for me in a gentlemanly fashion or offering his umbrella in the rain. But he was never condescending to women or dismissive of them as so many men were.

Dr. Murphy held the ladder while I climbed down. From the chest pocket of his crisp white lab coat, he produced a yellow paper.

"Is that a telegram? For me?" I held out my hand, but he wasn't offering.

"Do you have time for a chat?"

Hearing those seven words, I had a premonition that my world and the position that I had worked so hard for were about to be upended. I sucked in my stomach and braced myself. Dr. Valentine's slipped words came back to me. Clearly, upheaval was in the works.

"What is it?" Again, I held out my hand for the telegram.

"You might want to sit down."

In a small act of defiance, I sat on my desktop. "Is my position here in danger? I know I've upset the applecart a few times, but the changes I've made are justified."

"In a way, yes." He cleared his throat and used his fingers to rake back his hair. "As you may recall, our School of Medicine was identified by the Red Cross as a base hospital, to be activated in the event of an emergency."

"Yes. An honor, to be sure." My mind reeled. I had been placed on some Red Cross committee, but the meetings were rather an old boys' club affair, with much drinking of whiskey and smoking of cigars. At some point, someone would read a short update from the Red Cross, then they would adjourn to play golf or meet their wives for dinner. Minus me, of course. "Has there been a fire? A tornado?"

"No. But seems the emergency they were really preparing us for has arrived." Dr. Murphy took a deep breath and blew it out slowly. "War. This is from the surgeon general in Washington, DC." He read from the wire. "'Can your unit go to Europe and how soon?'"

My hand clapped to my mouth as I gasped. "Will you go?" Of course, I knew him well enough to know the answer to that question.

He nodded. "The unit is the entire medical staff of the university, plus supporting personnel."

"What about the 'how soon' part? We don't even have troops over there yet. Surely we have some months to prepare while they are still getting trained."

"I've been told the Red Cross's answer to the surgeon general was that we would be ready in six weeks' time." He took his pipe out of his pocket and rubbed his thumb across the carving on the bowl.

"Six weeks! What will that mean for the hospital? How will it run without the medical school staff?" I felt my list of options diminishing by the second. "It's going to shut down, isn't it? Is this my termination announcement?" With my recent wanderlust, I had been toying with the idea of returning to my native New York. But still, I didn't want my hand forced.

"Not at all. The hospital will hire medical staff from elsewhere and will continue on."

"But you will be leaving." His words hardly comforted me. I had grown quite fond of him. "I will miss you."

His voice softened. "You don't have to miss me." He sat next to me on the giant desk. "You see, the idea of a base hospital unit is that they take a well-functioning group who have trained together, know one another's quirks and strengths, are bonded in a way that fosters good communication and dedication to one another, as well as for their mission.

"Central to all this are the nurses. We can't run a hospital without them." He turned and looked straight into my eyes, no doubt wanting to judge my reaction.

My mind was still spinning with the obstacles we would face with a complete change in medical staff. I was already forming a transition plan in my head. "Don't worry. We will carry on."

He scratched his temple. "I'm not sure you understand. We want to take you and your nurses with us to Europe, or wherever we may be sent."

My mind continued to whirl, even as part of me had already accepted the challenge. Dr. Murphy chattered on, with numbers, deadlines, and names. One of the names was Dr. Valentine. I began to sort out nurses and other support staff to consider taking with us. Dr. Valentine needn't have worried about Nurse Harriman. Although I disagreed with his assessment, she lacked the years of experience we would need in every nurse we took.

Dr. Murphy patted my shoulder as he rose. "So lots to think about. Let me know what you decide." He headed out, then stopped, silhouetted in my office doorway. "We'll need to find sixty-five nurses willing and able, with no return date in sight." He gave a knock on the doorframe, then stepped away before I could voice the hundreds of questions in my brain.

⇛

Before moving to St. Louis, I had spent nearly my entire adult life in and around New York City, which tended to see itself as the center of the universe. Moving out west in 1911 had seemed an act of courage, but once I was there and met the lovely people, I realized how foolish a thought that was. I had lived there as a child, and I felt welcome and accepted as if I had never left.

I had landed my dream job, training women to be professional nurses, right next to the medical school. We had the finest equipment and knowledgeable and dedicated staff. I had set up a challenging curriculum, too challenging according to some, and my nurses, both in training and my instructors, continually impressed me. Envisioning a steady progress from untrained help maids to vital members of a health care team, I thought the future of nursing was in my very own grasp.

But the forefront was still in New York, and I was beginning to think it time to go back, to leave the comfort of St. Louis and find new challenges to conquer. I had pursued the field of nursing after my family wouldn't support my dream of becoming a physician. Now, with a decade of experience, I had already reached the pinnacle of my profession. I was about to complete a master's degree, and with it, I could return to New York and push the boundaries of what nurses could achieve. And maybe a small part of me had wanted to return to rub my father's and uncle's noses in my success.

But it no longer seemed the right time to return to New York. The thought of Dr. Murphy leaving without me caused a surprising pang. Perhaps the war, not New York, was the best next step for me. It felt like I was hurtling forward on a train, and the track had suddenly switched directions.

❧

Europe was in the midst of the Great War. After much heated debate and valiant efforts by President Woodrow Wilson to avoid U.S. involvement, we were heading into the conflict. I had followed the news with trepidation, fearing my younger brother, Philip, would be conscripted. My oldest brother was already serving in the army, and Phil had asked to join units in New York and St. Louis. Never had I ever envisioned being part of the war effort myself, except perhaps to nurse the returning wounded.

When I was a student at Vassar College, I spent a summer volunteering at a camp in Montauk, at the very eastern tip of Long Island, which was being set up for soldiers returning from the Spanish-American War. It was an eye-opening experience for me, just as I was trying to imagine my own place in the world. I still had a copy of a letter I had written to my sister:

October 1898

My dear Elsie,

How I wish you could have come with me to Montauk. My classmates and I are assisting the men building all manner of huts and encampments for the soldiers returning from Cuba. Rumor has it we will house close to thirty thousand in this sandy, soggy place. We have set up a chow hall for the workers and serve them porridge for breakfast and a chipped beef gruel for nearly every dinner. They don't complain, and neither do we when we see the ragged, sickly troops pouring out of the ship transports.

Some are suffering from typhoid or yellow fever; others seem healthy but must be screened before returning home. Can you imagine that? Victoriously fighting a war on foreign soil, only to be held almost like a prisoner for fear of contaminating our citizens. They keep us students well away from the soldiers, but one can't help but see their forlorn faces, begging for a kind word, a thank-you for bearing the weight of our nation's battles. I give a wave from the distance, but it pains my heart not to do more.

Your loving sister,
Julia

Although my experience there was limited by the need for isolation from infectious diseases, it taught me the tremendous sacrifices made by those who care for the most heroic of all, those who fight our wars. Indeed, Reubena Walworth, the nurse who had recruited us from Vassar, lost her own life to the typhoid she acquired there.

The memory of losing Reubena both pained and frightened me. Rationally, I knew that as a nurse, I was more exposed to deadly contagious diseases, but we took measures to protect ourselves, and it was an unavoidable part of the job. But perhaps irrationally, my instinct was to flee to safer ground. I admitted only to myself that my drive toward a leadership role was partly an effort to distance myself from contagion.

Yet I knew I would go with the unit. I had no husband nor children to miss me, and although my rather privileged background wouldn't hint of it, I was raised to have a purpose, to serve with whatever gifts and grace God had given me. I was strong, physically, emotionally, and spiritually. There was a reason I was given these gifts and entrusted with this responsibility. But how would I find sixty-four additional nurses? How could I ask them to leave their families, risk their own safety?

One thing I felt sure of was that all the nurses we recruited must be fully aware of the risks and of the open-ended commitment. I grabbed my plan book. First task: identify prospects, both to help me recruit and to join the unit. Second: plan the necessary training. Third: order the necessary uniforms, equipment. Raise funds? Surely that wasn't my task as well. I started a list of questions to ask Dr. Murphy.

The quest was on. We invited most of our qualified staff, but that wouldn't be enough. Newspaper advertisements and posters were placed all over the city. Pleas were made in ladies' magazines. We concentrated on the St. Louis area but put out some announcements nationally as well. A flyer placed in markets and post offices proclaimed: "We need Nurses! Qualified Trained Nurses needed for the War Effort. Full room and board, uniforms, and competitive pay."

For days, I alternated between worry that we would never find enough qualified nurses willing to give up their lives and embark on an unknowable journey, and fretting about recruiting such women and offering them the hope of a new, exciting life, only to crush them with overwork and dangerous conditions.

Each day, I awaited the mail carrier with both anticipation and anxiety. And each day, I was met with a few invoices and a shrug. "Sorry, Miss Stimson," the mailman would say. "Maybe tomorrow."

Perhaps we faced an impossible task. How far would our recruitment efforts need to go to find so many qualified and willing nurses? They would have to be risk takers, as so much was unknown, as well as dedicated to a cause that still seemed rather vague. Indeed, President Wilson, as well as the rest of the country, had been very hesitant to enter the conflict that seemed to have so little to do with us.

Fretting didn't get the work done, and I proceeded, ordering supplies and arranging for transportation and uniforms for those I could only hope would come.

Another obstacle to recruiting we faced was that we didn't know if, when, or where our unit, now known as American Red Cross Base Hospital 21, would be sent. It was possible we would remain in St. Louis and become a treatment and recuperation center for returning veterans. How could I ensure the nurses were informed of the risks if no one knew what they were? I would need to earn their trust, and I would need to be worthy of it. This was the mantra I wrapped myself in, the rod of steel that became my backbone.

⁓

Whenever I needed uninterrupted thinking time, I walked through Forest Park. It reminded me of my cherished Central Park back in New York City, and seeing the trees and ponds and birds always brought me a sense of energy and renewal.

I pinned on my hat and wool cape, there still being a chill in the early spring air. The park was just across the street from my office, and I grabbed my sack lunch to enjoy there.

Once inside the park, I waved to a gentleman whom I had seen many times, sitting on his usual bench, pigeons circled about his feet. I walked briskly down a gravel path, hoping my favorite park resident was up and about. Up a slight hill and beyond some cherry trees just beginning to burst with pink buds, there she was, Miss Jim, the park zoo's recently arrived elephant.

As I grew closer, I saw she had benches strapped to her back. They looked large enough for six adult riders, and this saddened me. The benches were empty, and she trotted around, bobbing her head and raising her trunk, not seeming to mind at all. A handler came around from behind her, and she trumpeted her approval as he hosed her down.

I found an empty bench and tucked into my lunch. Miss Jim was an Asian elephant and former circus performer. She was as out of place as my nurses would be in a European war. She was captive, not free, and had been so her entire life. I struggled with that, enjoying seeing the animals so but at the same time wishing they were freely roaming in their natural habitats.

But Miss Jim seemed quite content. She never had to struggle to find food. She feared no attacks from tigers, and she had shelter if she wanted it. Indeed, an entire elephant building was being constructed just for her. She had traded, or rather had been given, safety and security in exchange for her freedom. She also had a purpose to her life, giving rides to her enthusiastic fans. Thousands of schoolchildren had collected pennies to purchase her, and she ran up to see the little ones when they visited. Surely an elephant was intelligent enough to know she was loved and able to resist if she didn't want to perform?

My nurses would have more of a choice. I would be as forthcoming as possible as to the risks they were taking, the possible austere conditions, and the difficult work. But like the captive elephant, they wouldn't be free to roam around as they wished. Their daily lives would be working long hours, with limited opportunity, perhaps none, to explore wherever we were sent. Of course, when I recruited them, I would also share with them the tremendous contribution they would be making to our country and its allies. Whether I could recruit one or one hundred nurses, they would know as much as I did about the possibilities.

Next, I headed over to the aviary cage, which was always alive with birds from around the world. Their squawking, trills, and chirps could be heard from a hundred yards away. *What advice do you have for me, my dear feathered friends?* Some ducks waddled up to me from inside the cage. They cocked their heads, as if asking me what I wanted. Or more likely, wondering if I would feed them something. Other birds flew at the cage and hung on to its webbing, peering at the sky above. Peacocks strutted, searching for grubs or seeds, or flapped their wings to warn others away from their special find.

Birds were going to be birds. Soldiers would be soldiers. Nurses would be nurses. There wasn't much one could do to alter the nature of animals, human or otherwise. One could provide opportunity for growth, challenges to meet, and the freedom to choose another path. Like Miss Jim, the birds seemed to be telling me to drive on with my task at hand. To trust individuals to know their own limits, and give fully of myself.

It was time to get back.

I stepped quickly down the polished hallway, my boots clicking on the tile floor. I had much to do, so I was chagrined to see a delivery boy with a cart stacked with overflowing crates outside my office.

"Can I help you?" I asked.

He was no more than nineteen years of age, with short blond hair and terrible teeth. "I'm looking for J. Stimson."

"You have found her." I took a packet he offered and regarded the remaining boxes. "But I'm not sure she wants to be found."

"Uh, yes, ma'am. Where should I put these?"

"You must be new. The supply room in the basement. Come along. I'll show you, Mr. . . . ?"

We had been ordering supplies and madly tucking them away like a community of squirrels. Everything from bandages and medication to tinned meals and shoelaces was to accompany the hospital unit wherever it was to be sent.

"You can call me Ned. But these aren't supplies. It's interoffice mail, all addressed to you."

My heart sank to that special place below the rib cage. "Surely this all can't be for me." I unwound the red string securing a large envelope. It contained applications, ten of them. All seeking nursing positions for Base Hospital 21. I opened another envelope, and another. Each contained ten or so applications. I did a quick calculation. There had to be more than a thousand applications on that cart.

My sunken heart rose again, my spirits lifting as if the sun had come out on the dreariest of days. I startled poor Ned with a loud squeal and a hug, then helped him push the cart into my office.

After several days of plowing through the reams of applications, with more arriving it seemed by the hour, I realized I needed an assistant if I was to get through them in any reasonable amount of time. I was loath to ask any of my nursing staff; they were already working long hours. So when Ned appeared with yet another load, I asked if he had any extra time.

"For you, ma'am, absolutely. I've got nothing until the four o'clock delivery."

Ned and I sorted the applications, first separating out the clearly unqualified, too young or too old (the age requirement being twenty-five to thirty-five), then arranging the remaining ones by availability and training. Soon, we had about two hundred hopeful prospects.

The application form asked for a short essay on why the person wanted the job. The answers were both heartwarming and distressing. I quickly realized I had been looking at the challenge through the rosy lens of a privileged upbringing. These women—the applicants were overwhelmingly female—were by and large not seeking a great adventure nor driven by a need to do their part for the country. They had other motivations.

For example, a Rebecca V. wrote:

I take in ironing and mending, which I tend to after my twelve-hour shift at the hospital. I have to straighten my right hand out with my left before I can dress myself for bed.

Nora W. said:

I was orphaned in London and sent to Canada to work on a farm at age seven. After eight years of hard labor and vile punishment if my chores weren't done, I escaped to Ohio and worked my way through nursing school. I don't want to say how.

Not all were seeking an escape from a life of drudgery, or worse. In fact, one reminded me a bit of myself:

I have a good life. My parents are good to me. I have a nice beau. But I am capable of so much more. They thought I was crazy to go through nursing school and act like it was a silly phase. Now they want me to chair the social committee of the art museum. I would rather die.

It occurred to me that the Great War would be throwing together people from different backgrounds and cultures like never before, and my nurses were no exception. It was a grand experiment of human nature. I hoped and prayed that the finer side of our humanity would show through, and in the end, the horrible, horrible war could have something positive come out of it.

CHAPTER 2

May 1917

After a flurry of correspondence, checking of credentials, and interviews, both in person and on the telephone to candidates with access to one, we had recruited all the nurses we needed, plus a few backups. Next came the grueling training.

Since many of the nurses already worked at Barnes and the doctors were all local, it naturally became the center for training. But our war assignment (the precise location was still unknown to us) was unlikely to have the modern equipment and facilities we were accustomed to. So I requisitioned an unused dormitory that lacked modern heating and full electricity to simulate our future working space.

It was dark and dank, perfect for my purpose. There was a coal stove for heating water and one electrical outlet. There were eight cots, separated by muslin curtains, in which we cycled volunteers. A combination of medical school students and off-duty interns, clerks, and orderlies, they were happy to help the nurses out of patriotic duty.

Of course, the nurses didn't need training on basic care. But they needed training for injuries they would have had less experience with, such as severe burns and amputations and shell shock.

I stocked the area with some supplies, being careful to leave out some commonly used items and adding some substitutes. Then I gave my volunteer "patients" descriptions of their injuries and symptoms.

The exercise was going along swimmingly, with the nurses making excellent substitutions (a roller bandage for a sling, a glass syringe for all sorts of things, like cleaning wounds or splinting a finger), when Dr. Murphy stopped by for a visit.

He stood in a corner, arms folded across his chest, silently observing my nurses in action.

I gave him a briefing on the various imaginary situations the nurses were coping with, from shrapnel wounds to concussions. "Each case has a list of doctor's orders, but how they carry them out is up to them."

I tried to gauge his response, but his face gave nothing away.

"They're doing quite well, don't you think?" I said.

"Do you mind if I throw them a few challenges of my own?" He pulled some index cards out of his pocket and was already jotting notes on them before I could answer.

"Certainly you may. The more realistic the better."

He filled out eight cards, and I held out my hand to review them.

"Not so fast, Miss Stimson. I'll assign them directly."

If I didn't know him or trust him so much, I would have been incensed. But he had his ways, and this was new territory to chart. But still, a line of responsibility had been crossed, and a twinge of irritation fluttered within me.

"Ladies, if I could have your attention." He waved the cards in the air. "For those who don't know me, I'm Dr. Fred Murphy, and I'll be heading up the medical side of our intrepid little group."

The nurses stopped their tasks and grouped around him. The volunteer patients joined as well.

"I thank you all for putting your own lives aside to join us on this mission. I truly believe it will be the experience of a lifetime for all of us. But it will not come without unimaginable challenges. You will see things no one should see, face uncomfortable conditions with little time for rest and recreation. But you will be giving a most precious gift to those who bear the brunt of the hardship of war. You will be seen as angels, even as you perform painful treatments. You will be the last face many will ever see and the first voice some will hear after a terrible battle.

"I know of what I speak. I spent some time with a French unit in theater. So if you have questions, I'm happy to answer. The responsibility is great; the challenge, real. But we will try to prepare you the best we can."

The nurses, now in a semicircle around him, clapped politely. He was a natural at this sort of leadership. I imagined him cheering on his football team at Harvard or waxing eloquent in lectures to his surgical residents.

These were skills I needed to further develop. It wouldn't have occurred to me to slip an inspiring talk like this into a training session. So I studied how he varied the pitch and volume in his speech and used his facial expressions, hand movements, and posture to enhance his message. I watched him focus on each person in turn, holding their attention, because none would want to be caught looking away. And I made a mental note to write and rehearse encouraging words, so they would come as naturally as they did to Dr. Murphy.

He waved the note cards again. "Here I have written a scenario for each of you. You are to imagine you are the first person to come upon the particular situation, so there are not yet doctor's orders to carry out. Just you, your training and judgment, and the materials you have at hand."

The nurses murmured among themselves as the doctor handed out the cards. Only some of the discussion was on their assigned tasks. I noticed one nurse elbow another and say, "You know why he came, don't you?"

The other nurse responded by glancing at the doctor, then me, and tapping her index and middle fingers together.

Clearly, despite my efforts of hiding any indication of my affections, gossip had made its way to this new unit. It wasn't that I minded being fodder for their entertainment, but I didn't want to damage my or Dr. Murphy's professional reputation. In any case, it was better to ignore the innuendo.

I was dying to get a peek at what Dr. Murphy had written on his cards but had to be satisfied with the looks on the nurses' faces. Some stared at the cards wide-eyed; others, like my hard-edged Nora, the one who had escaped servitude on a Canadian farm, just nodded. She favored black dresses, matching her straight black hair, which was parted down the middle and pulled tightly into a bun. A natural leader, she was as tough as her difficult upbringing might suggest. I had heard the younger nurses refer to her as a "battle-ax," even as they soaked up all the wisdom she offered.

Meanwhile, Charlotte Cox, a petite young nurse with wavy blond hair, scratched her head and showed her card to the nurse next to her. If Nora was a battle-ax, Charlotte was a butterfly. Pretty and slight and undemanding, no one would ask her to lift a patient, but she'd be the first one to go to if you needed a sympathetic ear.

While the nurses reviewed their cards, Dr. Murphy was chatting with the volunteer patients, apparently giving each an assignment of their own. I heard him say things like "you're unconscious" and "you're a terrible flirt." To another, he said, "You have to pee real bad." They nodded, and some of them chuckled in response.

"Now choose a patient and share the card with him," Dr. Murphy said to the nurses. "Do what you need to do, and report back to me in ten minutes' time."

I ground the ball of my booted foot on the floor. This wasn't sitting well with me, but there didn't seem to be much choice. One

THE WAR NURSE   19

of my biggest fears was losing good nurses before we ever set sail, but my other fear was sending them into situations without the best training and preparation we could give them. While part of me was insisting I needed to have firm control of every aspect of training, my more reasonable side knew that allowing the input of trusted others was beneficial. I took a big breath and bit my lips as I watched my nurses scurrying around their patients and the supply cabinets.

Ten minutes later, Dr. Murphy announced, "Time's up." He waved the nurses over. "Report."

Nora piped in first. "My patient had debris in his eyes from a mortar explosion. I carefully washed his face, then rinsed his eyelids with saline. I held his eyes open, rinsed with more saline, and looked for imbedded foreign objects to report. Finding none, I taped his eyes closed to prevent further scratching of the corneas."

"Very good," Dr. Murphy said. "And what would you have done if you saw a foreign object imbedded?"

"Instructed the patient not to touch his eyes and reported it at the first opportunity."

"Excellent. Next?"

Charlotte stepped forward. In her soft West Virginia drawl, she said, "My patient is a double leg amputee who is complaining that his feet hurt, and he kept trying to get up to urinate. I check his bandages for bleeding, reposition him and elevate his stumps. Then, I reassure him that he is having phantom pains. They are to be expected and will fade with time. I would also check to see if he was due for his morphine, but, uh…first I gave him a urinal."

Everyone laughed as Charlotte colored with embarrassment.

The next nurse reported an arm injury with pulsing blood loss, an arterial bleed. She said she applied direct pressure, but that wasn't enough and no help was on the way, so she used rubber tubing or something similar as a tourniquet above the injury. "I talked to him the whole time, even though he couldn't talk back."

Dr. Murphy nodded. "Fine work. And you?" He pointed to Dorothy, a tall, lanky, highly experienced nurse, who I was surprised hadn't volunteered her report first.

Dorothy cleared her throat and studied her note card, scratching her neck and hesitating a beat too long.

"Something wrong?" I asked gently.

"It says I've come upon a soldier in a field with a mouth and jaw injury. Due to the bleeding and swelling, he can no longer breathe through his mouth or nose."

"And what do you do?" Dr. Murphy rocked back on his heels while the other nurses paid rapt attention.

"Well, I… He needs a tracheotomy."

"And I repeat, what do you do?" He began to pace. "He's gasping his last breath. His eyes bug out, pleading with you."

"I've seen the procedure a hundred times."

"You have a sharp knife and a syringe. What do you do?"

"I… It's just a small incision."

"He's lost consciousness, nurse. There is no one else around. It's up to you. Can you save him?"

The nurses covered their mouths, waiting for her answer.

"Between the ribs of the trachea. The syringe could be used to suction blood or as an airway. But…"

"Yes, nurse?" Dr. Murphy stopped his pacing and stood in front of her, hands on hips. "He still can't breathe. Do you perform a tracheotomy and save his life?"

"No, Doctor." Dorothy stared at her shoes and wiped her eyes with the back of her hand.

The room shuddered with a collective gasp.

"Explain," he said.

"I am not qualified to perform the procedure. There are limits to what we can do, and we must accept them. To do otherwise would open a host of new problems."

"As sad and frustrating as this may be, she is right." He looked around at the bewildered nurses. "We medical professionals must adhere to the limits of our training and licensed authority. To do otherwise would create a chaotic system with no standards and unreasonable expectations."

"Thank you, Dr. Murphy." To the nurses, I said, "We will discuss further tomorrow. You are dismissed for today."

The nurses gathered their books and notes, and they and the volunteer patients filed out the door. Dr. Murphy and I lingered a moment.

He turned to me, a look of concern in his eyes. "Was I too harsh?"

"It's a difficult but important lesson."

"I sense some reservation."

I winced. "I wish you had apprised me of your plan. I could have prepared them better."

"That's rather the point though, isn't it?" He stepped toward the door. "One of the most important skills they will need is how to think on their feet in stressful situations. They will never know what's coming at them. If they can't handle a surprise test question, how will they cope in the midst of war?"

"I understand. But it appeared to me that you didn't assign the tasks randomly."

"What do you mean?"

"For example, Charlotte, who is my most empathetic nurse, had the patient with phantom limb pain. Dorothy, the most experienced clinically, got the most challenging ethical and medical dilemma. I suspect you've learned something about each of them. If so, wouldn't it have been better to have switched them around, or at least randomly assigned the tasks?"

"I'm flattered you believe I had that much forethought. I assure you
I didn't. But I think it worked out well anyway. The goal is for everyone
to learn, and since the best possible person answered each question, all
learned from them."

I stepped along with him, extinguishing oil lamps on my way out.
He had a point. And I knew that part of my resistance to his method
had more to do with my own territoriality regarding my nurses' training. I had to push that aside for their own good.

❧

Later, Dr. Murphy's lesson gnawed at me. In the face of certain death,
was it really inappropriate for a nurse to perform a procedure she knew
full well how to do? It wasn't merely an academic exercise; in fact,
with nurses traveling the countryside between duty stations, it wasn't
unthinkable that they could come upon a similar emergency.

I decided to bring my concerns to Dr. Murphy. I invited him to
tea in the nurses' lounge during the quiet morning hours. As I poured
steaming water over a small metal ball filled with tea leaves, I asked if
he thought Dorothy's answer was truly the right one.

"In actual practice, I believe a nurse would do all she could to save
someone from certain death. But there is a difference between what we
teach as policy and what an individual decides to do."

"Our professional guidelines hold that as long as a nurse performs
as a *reasonable* person would, then there should be no repercussions."

"Exactly. She would be protected in this case." He folded his long
legs under the small chair.

"Then why not teach that?"

"That is where it gets fuzzy. You see, if we teach a physician that it
would be appropriate to perform procedures for which he is not trained
or qualified, then we are failing in our training. He must know that
he is protected from being disciplined if he does all he can within his

scope of practice. The moment I or anyone in higher authority tells him otherwise, we would be complicit in leading him down a dangerous path. Where would it end?"

I poured the tea into our cups, enjoying the sweet aroma. "Biscuit?" I offered him a shortbread cookie, which he popped into his mouth whole. I was making a point of using British wording for things, thinking it would somehow help my nurses adapt to the British system once we arrived in Europe.

"I'm afraid our scope of practice is a little fuzzy as well. We are allowed to do tasks as assigned, which can cover quite a bit of ground. Our profession is still sorting out what nurses should and shouldn't do."

He scooped two spoonsful of sugar into his cup. "Well, then this is a good time to develop protocols. Add training for things that it would be beneficial for nurses to do. Remove responsibility for tasks that are not reasonable."

"That's easy to say. But our nurses were trained in several different states, each having their own protocols. And they're bound to be faced with new procedures there, ones we never saw at home. For example, I've read they are now transfusing blood not directly from person to person but from stored containers. I imagine that might lead to it changing from a medical procedure to a nursing one." I popped a biscuit into my mouth and washed it down with the hot tea.

"It's new territory for all of us. We'll train for as many new situations as we can think up."

"How do I incorporate the training from seven different states? Who decides what our nurses can do when practice at home is different from or behind what's happening in the field?"

He sipped his tea, purposely allowing it to steam up his glasses, then wiping them off by swiping them like the windshield wipers appearing on automobiles. He helped himself to another cookie. "That would be you, my dear."

I smiled behind my teacup, amused at his antic. He had a way of hitting just the right note to ease my prickly sense of authority. And now I was a "dear." I allowed myself a moment to muse that the rumors of a romantic relationship were true but kept my eyes off him.

✑

One thing I had learned back when I became a supervisor at the Harlem Children's Hospital was that I couldn't both lead all the nurses under me and simultaneously attend to the myriad personal and professional problems that inevitably popped up. I couldn't both stay on top of the demands from the local community, the changes in science and practice, the continuous need for training and retraining, and listen to the sobs of a new nurse who found her work too difficult. Not that I didn't feel for the nurse or think that a few moments with her wouldn't be beneficial. It was simply a matter of managing a finite amount of time if I was to do anything at all but work. For even with a steady habit of twelve-hour workdays, it couldn't all be done.

The system I was developing for Base Hospital 21 was rather like the military, with units broken down to fewer and fewer numbers until the smallest unit someone was responsible for had about eight people, much like an army squad. So I determined my sixty-four nurses would make eight squads of eight each. Each squad would have a squad leader and seven members.

The next question was how to choose those leaders. I had my own ideas of potential leaders, nurses who had shown strength, good judgment, and reliability. Margaret, Dorothy, and Nora came to mind. But considering we had all volunteered for this mission, I thought the nurses should take part in the decision.

At lunch one day, I handed each of them a sheet of paper. On it, I asked them to name the nurses, excepting myself, whom they would go to for advice. Whom would they go to for questions about nursing but who could also be trusted to maintain their confidence and give sound guidance?

As I had hoped and expected, the three nurses I had in mind were on nearly all the completed papers. The other five I chose from recommendations that sometimes surprised me.

Assigning my nurses to their squads, however, was not in the least democratic. I knew there were certain cliques I wanted to break up, a few personality clashes that were better off with a little separation. All in all, I think my system worked and freed me from having to count to sixty-four all the time. My eight little hens took care of this and so many other details for me.

I suggested the squads come up with monikers for themselves, like combat pilots named their planes. Serious or humorous, I thought it would give them a spirit of belonging and pride. To my surprise, they all decided I should simply number them, Squads 1 through 8. Apparently, they weren't as enamored of the quasimilitary structure as was I.

CHAPTER 3

Mid-May 1917

S

ix weeks had flown by. We had recruited and trained to the best of our abilities and were all pawing the ground to begin our new adventure. It was time to say goodbye to our comfortable American lives. A series of train rides took us to New York City, but sadly, we had no time to explore. I had written to my family that I wouldn't have time to see them, as we would be transported directly from Grand Central Terminal to the pier.

The huge railroad terminal building had been completely rebuilt since I had moved to St. Louis. The new building was impressive, even to a city girl like me, with high arched windows and an immense barrel ceiling, painted like the night sky, over what was likely the grandest indoor space I had ever entered. I let the nurses wander around a bit, with instructions to meet at the big four-sided brass clock that dominated the space. I headed over to the fresh market to pick up a few of my favorite treats for the long trip ahead.

When we met up again, the nurses were bubbling with enthusiasm, and I myself felt two feet off the ground. I liked to pretend my impressive stature, booming voice, and somewhat feigned aura of competence—after all, I knew little more about what we were about to face than did they—had helped fill them with the necessary bravado. There was no hint of cold feet; everyone was ready to go.

As the ship sailed from the port of New York City, the nurses lined the rails and waved to the hordes of people who came to bid us farewell. The boats in the rivers tooted and blew their whistles, and their passengers cheered and waved as we passed by. Then, there was a quiet moment as we passed the Statue of Liberty. She was now mostly green, her former copper color having been painted by the winds. For most, she served as a welcome. But her *beacon hand*, as poet Emma Lazarus had dubbed it, also seemed to be wishing us a fond farewell.

The weeks leading up to that moment were filled with myriad details of planning. But now, we were off on a great and important adventure. *We are making history.* The words ran through my mind over and over again. What an honor it was to be leading this group of women, the first to be called to serve for such duty in the U.S. Army. We were being sent to aid our allies in the Great War, in the front ranks even before our troops were ready to go.

That evening, after ensuring all our trunks and supplies were accounted for and everyone was settled into their cabins, I made one last check before retiring. I made my way to my own cabin by first knocking and peeking into each of theirs. Maybe that seems strange; they were adults after all. But many had never ventured out of St. Louis before, and only a handful had ever been on a ship. They had been advised they could lock their doors whenever they desired privacy, but it gave me a bit of satisfaction that not a single one did. They were all so comfortable with one another and, I assumed, with me.

My nurses slept bundled into the cots stacked like cordwood against the bulkheads. Two or three women shared each cabin, the sealed portholes and blackout curtains eliminating any sense of traveling on holiday. The air was thick with their breath and the scent of soap from scrubbed faces and hands. There was also the subtle note of sweat, an undercurrent of excitement and uncertainty running through the ship like an invisible stream.

The SS *Saint Paul*, a lovely if aged ocean liner in peaceful days, had been stripped down and refitted to return to a previous mission: moving troops and support to war. The ship leaned gently from port to starboard, each cycle one minute and fifteen seconds, rocking my dear ones in peace. I hoped the last months of training had given the nurses the confidence they needed to face our enormous task.

As I passed through the narrow corridor, the sound of retching came from the head. I rapped gently on the elaborately carved wooden door. They couldn't strip the *Saint Paul* of all her glory; she let slip some of her charms like a coquette baring an ankle.

"Yes?" The faint reply came through the slightly cracked-open door.

I recognized the voice and was not surprised. "Miss Cox? Are you unwell?"

Charlotte appeared in the slit of the doorway, eyes downcast in her pallid face. "It's nothing, ma'am. Must have eaten a bit too much dinner."

"I'll get you some towels to refresh yourself." Oh dear. We were not yet on the open seas. How would this delicate flower be of any use in a stinking, bloody field hospital? She might require more assistance than she could give. Perhaps I had been too hasty in the rush to recruit such a large number of nurses. There were bound to be failures, but we could ill afford to lose them so soon.

During the day, the men assigned to the ship held drills on the deck, practicing marching and shooting guns out to sea. They fired artillery cannons, still on the ship from the Spanish American War, each round rocking the ship with a loud *BOOM*. Most of the nurses cheered at the sound and laughed at the shudder in the walls of the cabins. But my dear little Charlotte curled into a ball on her bunk. I patted her like a baby during the exercises while wondering how soon I would have to send her back home.

As we were "invited," so to speak, by the British, they would be supporting us throughout our assignment overseas. In fact, they were already much in evidence, as most of the stewards and stewardesses on the ship were British. And how well they treated us! I had only to glance this way and that before a steward in a sharp blue uniform appeared to ask if I required assistance.

As chief nurse, I was grateful to have a private cabin, where I whiled away the hours checking and rechecking supply requisitions through the obtuse British system as well as reviewing the bits of information and tips mailed to me by one of the current chief nurses. Or rather a chief matron, as the British called them.

On the second evening on board, I had a visitor to my cabin. It was Miss Dunlop, the chief nurse of the Philadelphia unit, the other group of nurses on board. They were Base Hospital 10. I had corresponded with her in recent weeks and found her to be very knowledgeable. She was perhaps in her midforties, with a streak of silver making an elegant statement in her tightly wound brown hair.

The American Red Cross had provided all the nurses with nice dark-blue serge uniforms, but I was not having my nurses wear them on the ship except for official functions. Miss Dunlop was wearing hers, and it was as crisp as if it had met with a hot iron just minutes before.

After introducing herself, she looked me up and down, taking in my ordinary civilian travel clothes. "Did you not receive the uniforms?"

"We did, and there will be time enough to wear them. I thought my nurses might as well enjoy a few more days in their own clothes."

"Hmph. A coddler."

"I am no such thing." I belatedly invited her into my cabin. We were not setting off on the right foot. "Will you join me for some tea?"

She pulled a flask from her pocket and waggled it. "That depends."

I didn't really enjoy the taste of alcohol, but the situation seemed to require imbibing. "Why, that will be a nice addition," I said.

As we chatted and sipped our spiked tea, she softened her attitude. She was experienced with the American Ambulance Corps and had served overseas. I was tempted to take notes as she shared stories of adapting to other cultures, but it didn't seem proper at the time.

One of the challenges I found in leadership was the lack of camaraderie I had enjoyed in the early days of my career. Although I wasn't one to share gossip, it was sure fun to hear it. And having a group of people to share daily triumphs or shed a tear with when things didn't go well was an incredibly important support.

Now, aside from Miss Dunlop, with whom I was not yet comfortable, I really had no peer. I did have an assistant, Miss Taylor, who was quite dedicated and competent but had made her feelings regarding personal chatter quite clear.

Before we left St. Louis, I had invited Miss Taylor to my office for a chat about the training session with Dr. Murphy. Petite and rather frail-looking, she sat bolt upright in the chair like a frightened cat and answered all my queries with "yes, ma'am," "no, ma'am," or "I don't know, ma'am."

I suspected she was hesitant due to hearing and believing that I had a particularly close relationship with Dr. Murphy by the way she pressed her lips together every time I mentioned him. When asked indirectly about the delicate issue, she squirmed. "If you don't mind, Miss Stimson, I like to keep my feelings and opinions to myself."

I wasn't sure if she was intimidated by me or if it was just her nature, but I respected her request. I treated Miss Taylor as if she were any other of the nurses under me, that is, with a certain professional distance. Even though I craved what they had with one another, I knew I could never be part of it.

↪

In my lonely moments, I turned to my stack of personal correspondence, running my finger along the smooth blue satin ribbon that bound it. When I moved to St. Louis, I didn't bring a stick of furniture or even so much as a spoon. What I did bring were important family letters or carbon copies of some I had sent to others that were particularly meaningful. It was a rather lazy way to keep a journal; why write the same information twice?

During my summer in Montauk, my first away from home, I was so homesick, I wrote and wrote in order to get plenty of letters back, which I read over and over. It was then that I had the first inkling of what I should do with my life.

Dear Mother,

After hearing you go on for years about your acquaintance, Emily Warren Roebling, I can finally say I have met the fine woman. She was here at the invitation of Reubena Hyde Walworth, the nurse and Vassar graduate who also requested my classmates and me to volunteer here. Miss Walworth is nothing if not persistent!

Mrs. Roebling was invited by Miss Walworth, since "if she can build the Brooklyn Bridge, she certainly can build a campground." The difficulty of building a "campground" that is to be a field hospital for thirty thousand very sick soldiers and their caregivers and built on sand and swamplands seems to be understated.

Mrs. Roebling is impressive, both in physical stature and message.

She stands just a few inches shorter than me, which, of course, is still rather tall. She arrived by train, alighting without any assistance and carrying her own bags. I was appointed as one of her escorts, and she rapidly and instinctually took in a mass of information that tumbled from the mouths of our doctors, builders, and local leaders.

The next day, she met with the camp officers with a detailed plan for future construction. I watched their eyes widen and jaws drop as they reviewed them. Apparently, they didn't expect much from this unofficial engineer, and a woman to boot.

Later on, Mrs. Roebling delivered an inspiring speech to the staff. She impressed on us the importance of doing such. "It will be incumbent on you young women to carry the message forward. Learn to speak with authority."

I wish I had written it all down, even though her words were enhanced by her powerful delivery. She spoke of duty, of dedication to a cause. She thanked us all, even though we volunteers have not done much to merit her high praise.

Afterward, while I was escorting her to the train and we were chatting about the great plans she had laid, she abruptly stopped walking. I asked if she needed something.

"Yes, my dear girl." She stabbed my chest with her finger. "You. You represent the future of women. I have seen how you carry yourself, seen the intelligence behind the veil of modesty."

My cheeks grew hot as she went on, and I wondered why she had singled me out of many.

"Miss Walworth tells me your marks are tip-top. I understand you have some physical difficulties." Her eyes dropped to my scarred and now shaking legs. "All that means is that you can face the challenges that you will surely meet. I expect much of you."

I managed a feeble "Yes, ma'am" before she yanked up her dress and stepped up into the train.

Oh, Mother, what am I to think of this? Am I to believe she gives this little speech to every young woman she meets, or do I have a higher responsibility because of my fortunate circumstances?

Your loving daughter,
Julia

I teared up, rereading my own letter. Not long after I had graduated from Vassar, I read of Mrs. Roebling's passing. It was as if someone had thrown a direct punch into my gut. As I tucked the letter back into its envelope, it occurred to me that I had never written to her to thank her for her words of encouragement. I had been so flabbergasted at the time that I neglected the opportunity. Emily Roebling had set a course for my life, and she would never know it.

A deep tone sounded in the ship, like a foghorn on a lighthouse. Maybe it was a signal to the other ships in our convoy or perhaps some signal for the crew. I was curious to learn more, to see the captain's bridge, the engines, the galleys, and so forth. I liked to know how things worked. But I was a guest on this voyage, my duties strictly limited to the well-being of my fellow passengers, my nurses.

It turned out the tone was a signal for the crew. Soon after, there was a knock on my cabin door. I and the other nurses stumbled out, some yawning and rubbing their eyes, clearly roused from an afternoon nap. We were ordered to find our life jackets, then head to the top deck.

I knew it was a drill, but others didn't. This helped me identify more about their individual characters, as some calmly found their jackets and helped the others who weren't quite so quick to respond.

The drill was a practice session to learn about how to evacuate the ship in an emergency. It was one of the required changes that had come about since the sinking of the RMS *Titanic* five years earlier. Each and every person had a life jacket and an assigned lifeboat. During the drill, we practiced going to our assigned stations, where we were to climb onto the lifeboats swinging from davits should an emergency evacuation be necessary.

The crew endeavored to make the exercise as realistic as possible, using megaphones to pass along messages. "Now hear this. We are four hundred nautical miles off the coast of Newfoundland, not far from the resting place of the *Titanic*, may she and her fallen rest in peace."

I watched my nurses. Some acted as if it were quite the game, patting at their life jackets and making swimming motions. Others elbowed the clowns, scolding them to pay attention. Still others had hands to their foreheads to block the bright sun as they seemed to scan the water for icebergs. The terrible tragedy was still quite fresh in everyone's mind, and we were on nearly the exact same route, during spring, the same time of year as the ill-fated ship had sailed.

A helpful boatswain in a blue uniform and white hat came over to reassure them:

"Don't worry, ladies. We have an ice patrol out here around the clock now. And much better communications."

Back in my cabin, I carefully restowed my life jacket. It wouldn't do if I, of all people, were to misplace it.

I lit my electric lamp and debated whether to read more of the letters. They were ones I had sent to my father, during a time in our relationship I did not wish to relive. I adored him, and although he made his decision out of some sense of duty, it confounded me then and confounded me still. It went against all he had professed to me since I was a little girl. And yet, when the time came to live by the words he had preached to me, he instead went with the wind of the times.

One letter had irregular fold lines from being crumpled, then straightened again. It recounted my uncle Lewis's visit to me at Montauk, which had convinced me that I was destined to follow in his footsteps. He was a rather prominent surgeon in New York City.

He was a hero in that military camp, having developed innovative treatments for battle wounds and preventing infections. As I led him around the grounds, the physicians and military officers would come up to him, fairly gushing with their thanks and admiration. I wanted that.

Oh, how hopeful I had been, with the sparkling clear vision that only a twenty-year-old could possess. I had been quite spoiled, for I had been taught that not only was I expected to go out and make a difference in the world but that the opportunities to do so were boundless.

The next few letters in my stack dripped with sorrow and confusion as I railed against the two men I held in most esteem, the two men I thought would support my ambitions. The two men who denied me financial and emotional support because "women are not suited for the practice of medicine."

A familiar twist in my gut caused me to stop reading. After graduating from Vassar, I cast about, taking several unfulfilling jobs, and managed to scare away the few interested suitors my sisters sent my way. I liked to blame my height as the reason they never requested a second date, but I feared it was my own failure to provide any sense of fun or interesting conversation that disappointed them.

Taking poor care of myself, an old skin affliction on my legs had come roaring back. The cause was unknown, but once it started, it was difficult to treat. My legs became so covered with open sores, I had to be hospitalized. But there was a silver lining, for it was there that I met Annie Goodrich.

I was in my hospital bed, unravelling a row of knitting that was supposed to be purled and cussing up a storm, when Miss Goodrich marched straight to my bedside. She introduced herself as the head of the New York Training School for Nurses.

"Oh, I'm sorry. I didn't think anyone could hear me," I said.

"Hear what?" She crinkled her brow in confusion, but I was sure she had heard a few expletives. "You're Julia Stimson?"

I nodded.

"A surgeon I know asked me to talk to you. He thought you needed some career guidance."

She didn't have to say his name. "No doubt that was my uncle Lewis."

She sat on the chair at my bedside, and we chatted a bit. She reviewed some of the new developments in her field and how nursing was as much a profession in its own right as law or medicine. She said, "We need to encourage bright, educated women like no time before."

As we grew comfortable with each other, she asked why my uncle Lewis had been so solicitous of her help.

I folded the top of the bedcovers and smoothed the crease over and over as I pondered answering a delicate question without insulting all she stood for. "All my life, I was told 'to whom much is given, much is expected.' It wasn't enough in my family to follow the rules, get good marks, be kind to others. As you know, my uncle is quite well known for his advances in surgery, and my cousin is a high government official. And some time back, a very special woman told me that I had the wherewithal and duty to do something important with my life."

I paused to see her reaction. Her face seemed open and interested.

"I don't want to seem conceited, but rather, driven. And my drive has always been to a career in medicine. So I did all the steps. Graduated with honors a year early from Vassar. But when it was time to apply for medical school…"

"Your uncle didn't help."

"Worse. He and my father were actively against it, saying it was not an appropriate career for women. So without the financial support or the blessing from someone close to me who was so prominent in the field, it was hopeless."

"I'm truly sorry this happened to you. And if it is still your dream, you should look for a way to attain it. But I'm a believer that things happen for a reason."

"I believe that. But so far, I haven't figured out what that reason is."

"If you really want to do something with your life and the medical field is your passion, then you should consider nursing. They are the ones who actually give the care. They are the ones the patients count on and who know what needs to be done. Physicians don't have the time or the inclination to really get involved in the healing process. From what Dr. Stimson told me about you, it seems a perfect fit."

We talked some more, but the idea was rapidly gaining my interest. What did I have to lose? I asked her, "What if, later on, I still want to become a physician?"

"That happens sometimes but not often. But for those who choose that path, what better preparation could they have?"

"First, I need to break out of here. Do you know about this?" I pulled the bedsheets from my bandaged legs.

She rose from her chair, not even glancing at my legs. "Training starts in two months. You'll be fine by then. I'll write a letter of recommendation to any school you choose, but of course I hope you choose mine."

I was excited about something for the first time in ages. But I couldn't accept favoritism due to my uncle's influence. "If you don't mind, Miss Goodrich, I'd like to apply on the strength of my own academic and personal record."

She turned to leave. "As you wish."

So I became a nurse both because of and despite the influence of my father and Uncle Lewis. But it had been my decision, and it saved me from a downward spiral from which I might never have recovered.

❧

Tearing up the last two letters, I vowed to never ponder those what-ifs again. I glanced around at my cabin. *My* cabin. Beautiful wood inlaid walls, stacks of books and personnel records. A desk with an extra lamp to make up for the blacked-out porthole. I straightened myself in my chair, the chief nurse on a very important mission.

Aside from my Achilles' heel, or rather in my case, Achilles' legs, I was healthy and fit. With the possible exception of Charlotte, I was backed by dozens of well-trained and dedicated nurses. Most of them had had a much tougher upbringing than did I. I needed to let go of the hurt and embrace the challenge ahead of me.

I retied the blue ribbon around the letters, saving the rest for another day. But their lessons—of hopes and dreams, of visions and disappointments—stayed with me. Even so, I couldn't calm the tumbling in my stomach, couldn't ease my mind to a restful state. All I could hear was the pounding of the engines, their vibrations a constant hum through my body. I couldn't see out the sealed porthole, but I knew there was nothing but the black sea and sky.

A sense of panic crept within me, like being squeezed by a python. *What on earth have I done? Why am I leaving the world I know, the job I loved and worked so hard to attain?* I pushed those thoughts out of my mind, forcing the python back into his cage.

At dinner each night, I shared a table with several of my nurses and an accountant who was conscripted as an orderly, and sometimes a doctor or two joined us. For some reason, it was never Dr. Valentine. I wasn't sure how I had managed to get on the wrong side of his acceptable people list, but I was fairly certain it was because I stood up to him, both literally and figuratively. But there would be no hiding behind heavy office doors in this assignment. We were bound to knock heads.

Our group liked to discuss what we would be doing back home in St. Louis. One of the men kept his watch set for St. Louis time. One of the days on which we were sailing was the graduation day for my student nurses back home. Oh, how it pained me not to be with them. At the appointed hour, we gave a toast and signed a card to send to them.

I only had to look around at the eager and dedicated faces around me to realize we were headed in the right direction. To unselfish service, to something bigger than all of us.

We arrived in Liverpool and spent a day there as our belongings and supplies were sorted from the ship. Something we learned to get used to was the people of the town rushing up to us, pressing gifts of sweets or books or flowers upon us. They grabbed our hands, sometimes even kissed them.

They called us sisters and angels sent from heaven. And we Americans did seem to be from some heavenly place of abundance compared to the Brits. They were, without exception, very thin and pale. Perhaps not quite at the brink of starvation but not too far from it. I felt conspicuous with my robust frame, and it seemed wrong to accept their gifts of food yet impolite not to. I had only a few crackers left from my purchases in Grand Central Terminal and wished I had thought to bring tasty treats to share with them.

My assistant chief nurse, Miss Taylor, was both quite overwhelmed and moved by our reception. "But we haven't done a thing!" she kept saying. As a small woman, barely five feet tall, she sometimes disappeared in a crowd. I, at over six feet tall, was generally head and shoulders above the rest and could spot her, whereby I would drag her by the elbow to safety. This seemed comical to my nurses, who likened us to Douglas Fairbanks and Mary Pickford. I laughed it off as a compliment. After all, I would tower over even the swashbuckling actor.

⌘

Next was nearly two glorious weeks in London, where we stayed at the luxurious Waldorf Hotel and were treated to theater, concerts, fine food, and lovely teas. Mixed in were lessons on what to expect once we arrived at our duty station. After rumors that we were to be sent to Russia, Africa, or Mesopotamia, we learned our unit was to serve in Rouen, in Normandy, France, to replace the staff of British Expeditionary Force, or BEF, Hospital No. 12.

If ever I was in doubt regarding the need for our country to come to the aid of our allies in Europe, that came to an abrupt end after speaking with a major in the Royal Army Medical Corps, or RAMC. He was impossibly thin and hollow-eyed and perhaps four or five years older than me, which is to say about forty. At first, we made small talk, some lighthearted ribbing about the Brits about to hand the Yanks a hell of a mess they'd gotten themselves into. As he grew more comfortable with me and the five or so other Americans at the table, he shared his experience as a prisoner of war.

"I was captured in early 1915, then spent three days crammed into a train with hundreds of other prisoners. We had no food or water. I watched helplessly as dozens died of thirst and dysentery, trying my best to stay away from their fetid corner. Every so often, we would stop in a German village. Women dressed in Red Cross uniforms held up cups of water or milk to our lips, only to snatch them way, shouting *Schweinhund!*" He told us that was a terrible slur and translated to *pigdog*.

This didn't ring true to me. "Are you sure they were from the Red Cross?"

"German Red Cross, German army in disguise, who knows?" The major shrugged. He went on. "Upon arriving at the camp, our warm overcoats were taken away, and we were left to freeze in our uniforms, which by then were reduced to rags. We slept on sacks of hay without so much as a tent to protect us."

He plucked at his blue uniform sleeve, removing something I couldn't see. "Order was kept by severely beating any prisoner who made an attempt at escaping or who, like me, tried to write letters in code, telling the truth and begging for help." He stared straight ahead, his tone emotionless and matter-of-fact.

"So many died. Malnutrition, Typhus. Dysentery. Torture." He looked me dead in the eye. "I don't know why I survived."

One of my nurses asked, "How did you escape?"

I was glad for the question, for I could bear no more and could sense the rising level of anguish among the others as well as they shifted in their seats or fidgeted with their hands.

"After nearly a year in hell, I was released in an exchange of prisoners."

As if that experience wasn't horrifying enough, his new assignment was also harrowing. "I was put in charge of a hospital ship. In one trip across the Channel, we left in a convoy of two hospital ships, a destroyer, and a few others. The other hospital ship was about five hundred yards behind ours when it struck a mine. As it sank, the destroyer pulled up alongside, and the doctors, nurses, and crew aboard tried to leap onto it, with all but three of the nurses making it."

We all sighed in simultaneous relief and horror.

"But shortly after they were rescued by the destroyer, it too hit a mine."

There was a collective gasp.

"And your ship, did you pick up all of them?" I asked.

He slowly shook his head. "The destroyer was blown to smithereens." He looked about at our stricken faces. Perhaps at that moment, it occurred to him that we were all about to embark on a Channel crossing ourselves.

"But we were able to rescue the three nurses in the water, yes we did. They were none the worse for wear."

We sat in stony horror still.

"And no worries about mines now, mates. This was back in early 1916, you see. Since then, there's been nonstop patrolling by the Flower ships."

Now we sat in silent confusion.

"You know, the herbaceously named minesweepers. Leave it to the British to name heavily armed triple-hulled warships after flowers."

A few chuckled a bit.

Nora asked, "Where is your hospital ship now?"

"Well, uh…" The major hesitated. "It's under repair. Hit by a torpedo."

There were a few more gasps.

Nora got up and pushed in her chair as the stewards were clearing tables. "There isn't any use worrying about the submarines. If the Germans are going to kill us, worrying isn't going to prevent it. If they do kill me, I'm going to come back and haunt the whole German army." With that, she marched off, head high.

The major continued to try to ease the minds of the others. "I assure you, your passage will be nothing like that. The worst that will happen is a tummy ache from a light sea roll…or the British rations."

On our last night in London, Dr. Murphy gathered the whole unit in one of the hotel dining rooms. Like the rest of the hotel, it had high ceilings and crystal chandeliers. But this room was lined with burled wood panels. We had had our high tea in it each afternoon. It was so sophisticated and proper, the nurses said it made them feel uncomfortable. They would stiffly hold out a pinkie as they sipped their tea in a small act of humorous mockery.

Dr. Murphy had told me that he wanted to give a sort of pep talk, so I made sure that every last one of my nurses was in attendance and in uniform. A few of them were still wary of him after the harsh training experience, but having come to know him better, they knew his tough lesson came from a place of respect for nurses as professionals.

It was a rather tight fit in the dining room, with eighty or so nurses, orderlies, and others seated in chairs or standing against the wall. The flowery wallpaper and elegant wall sconces seemed out of place for our apprehensive mood.

Dr. Murphy cleared his throat and spoke softly and earnestly. "Ladies and gentlemen, you are about to begin a part of your life like no other before. The days ahead of you will be the most trying, the most difficult, the most painful of your lives. They will also be perhaps the most memorable and the most important.

"You are likely to see things a person should never see. You will be doing more for your fellow human beings than you ever thought possible. You will witness pain and sorrow seemingly beyond endurance."

He paused, the room quiet, all eyes fixed on him. Then, in a stronger voice, he implored, "There is only one way of bearing such close contact with human suffering and with whatever discomforts we must ourselves bear, of working out our own problems and antipathies and antagonisms. One way to keep our souls serene and maintain the strength to go on. And that is to do it with the deepest religious motive and utter devotion to service. We have come to serve in whatever way we can and as long as we are needed."

I looked at my sixty-four nurses. They were young, fresh faced, and eager. Certainly, many came from difficult circumstances, but were they really prepared for the situation we were about to be thrown into?

They nodded as they listened intently to Dr. Murphy and didn't wince a bit when he mentioned the likely cases they would see: burns, horrific wounds, and amputations. They didn't look away when he talked about living in cold, wet tents for a year, or two, or who really knew? My heart was lifted with their bravery and spirit, while another part of me, a nagging, doubting self, wondered if I had led these women down a path fraught with danger, physically, emotionally, and psychologically. Not a one of them, nor I, would be the same person when we returned home.

This was a responsibility I was to shoulder for the rest of my life. I vowed to protect them as well as I could while still ensuring their heroic sacrifices would not be in vain.

The room was dead silent for nearly a minute after Dr. Murphy spoke as his words took hold in the minds of the assembled. Then, someone clapped. Then another and another, until the whole room erupted with clapping and cheering. I felt lifted up by their wondrous spirit. It seemed we could do anything indeed.

The German U-boats were sinking large numbers of ships, and we were all apprehensive about crossing the Channel, despite the RAMC major's attempts to reassure us. But we needn't have worried. We would sail in a large hospital ship, clearly marked with huge red crosses and surrounded by warship escorts. As we left Southampton, the skies above us were guarded by buzzing airplanes. Even the Germans wouldn't dare to attack.

CHAPTER 4

After the overnight sailing, we arrived at Le Havre, France, and following the now familiar English breakfast of fried eggs, baked beans, and smoked and blood sausages, the nurses disembarked from the ship and loaded onto a train that took us away from the coast and alongside the Seine. We were met at a station just outside Rouen and transferred onto ambulances. These were the same trucks that had just delivered wounded Tommies for their trip home to England and still smelled of their iodine and bandages. These were familiar, but they reminded me that we would have many more unpleasant sights and smells to get used to.

I was fortunate to ride in the front of the ambulance with the driver, a chatty British chap named Benjamin, with arms too long for his sleeves and legs that nearly doubled up in the driving position. I worried about the nurses in the back as we bumped, sometimes violently, along a country road. Now and then, I got a peek at the Seine. It was mid-June, and the river was swollen within its banks and rather muddy-colored, but it flowed serenely between rows of flowering trees. It was hard to believe a terrible war raged less than a hundred miles away.

After a short drive, we arrived in Rouen just after lunch. My stomach was already rumbling by then, and I hoped I wouldn't have to wait until dinner to eat. How spoiled we had gotten in England.

Benjamin must have heard my protesting stomach. His accent was so strong, his phrases so unfamiliar, I had a hard time understanding him. "Gettin' peckish? 'Alf the hour more, I should think. You like bubble and squeak?"

"That will be lovely. Are we in downtown Rouen now?" We had entered a denser part of the city, with many stone and half-timbered buildings. We drove along the wide and gray Seine River that bisected the city. Long barges and other supply boats drifted up and down the river.

"You're in luck. We have an extra minute to see something special." Benjamin turned down a side street, and a couple of blocks later, we were in an open plaza with a Gothic cathedral looming over it. It had double rectangular spires and three magnificent arched entryways. It rather reminded me of St. Patrick's Cathedral in New York City but was certainly far older.

"That's beautiful. Somehow, it seems familiar," I said.

Benjamin braked the truck to a stop but kept the engine puttering. "I present the Cathédrale Notre-Dame de Rouen."

"I think I've seen a painting of it."

"Only one? Dozens of paintings have been done of it. Every one of them by Monet." He laughed.

"As in Claude Monet? Yes, of course. I should have remembered. I love his art."

"Well, more lucky stars. He lives just down the river. Maybe you'll run into him." He wiggled the throttle about until it found its place with a crunch, and with fancy footwork on various pedals, we lurched ahead. "And Vincent van Gogh lived and is buried not far from here. This little corner of the world attracted quite the artists."

My eyes took in the beautiful city, with women pushing carts laden with fruits and flowers, the tidy cobblestone streets. And to think, Monet. But I shook my head to clear such thoughts. I wasn't here on holiday.

After leaving the heart of the city, the buildings grew farther apart, and the roadway worsened. I placed my hand on the ceiling of the truck to keep from falling into Benjamin or out the door. The ambulance rolled over several deep ruts, causing us to veer sharply side to side. My satchel flew off my lap, and I bumped my head on the doorframe.

"Sorry 'bout that, ma'am. But here we are." Benjamin sounded the horn. *Ah-ooh-gah*.

The scene could not be more different from the charming small city. We were now somewhat outside the city, at a racecourse. We drove past a low fence with a broken gate and stopped at a row of wooden buildings with peeling white and green paint and loose and hastily tacked-on boards. It must have at one time been the grandstand. I caught scents of grass and flowers, with not a whiff of anything to do with horses.

I crawled off the seat and went to open the back for the nurses, but Benjamin got there first. They came out, some rubbing their heads, others rubbing their eyes while yawning. If they could sleep through that ride, they should be well suited to life a hundred miles from a war front.

"Just there are the offices." Benjamin pointed to the grandstand. "Beyond that lies the hospital and the racetrack, should you feel the need to stretch your legs."

The setting reminded me of a state fair, with tents and paths through the grass and many people milling about. The dirt racetrack circled the preponderance of the tents, with a few tents on the grass outside the loop. Surrounding the huge, flat complex were thick hedgerows and stands of grand trees, sycamores and oaks, which were fully leafed out and magnificent.

A middle-aged woman in a dark dress and white apron approached from the offices. She fanned her ruddy face. "Oh, you must be the Americans. We are ever so grateful to see you. I'm Matron Lipton. Come, let's get you settled in."

Matron Lipton, who was the British chief nurse, my counterpart, gave us the grand tour. The hospital was rows and rows of tents, the rows labeled *A*, *B*, and so on. Each tent had two to four rows of beds, about fourteen in total in each row. There were smaller, connecting tents between the long rows. Some tents had their sides rolled up, and some didn't. In the ones with open sides, we could see rows of beds; maybe half were occupied, the empty ones made up with sheets and a blanket. Our unit consisted of about twenty doctors, sixty-five nurses, and about the same number of clerks, stretcher carriers, and other assistants, enough for a five-hundred-bed hospital. I counted the tents and estimated the number of beds in total. There had to be far more than five hundred.

"Matron, if you please, how many patients are you equipped for?" I asked.

"Well now, we don't have nigh as many as before the Australians came to help us."

"Australians?"

"Why yes, they run a smaller hospital at the other end of the racecourse. Then there's the prisoner unit, just over there next to General 9, which is also being taken over by you Yanks. We're the biggest of the three, of course."

Three hospitals, all on one racetrack. And prisoners? Mostly all in tents from what I could see. The only permanent structures were the grandstand, a few wooden huts behind it, and some open pavilions. "And how many beds does BEF Hospital 12 have?"

"All told, thirteen hundred. Sometimes more."

I blinked, stunned by the number. As I stood there, managing staff numbers in my head, Matron Lipton had moved on, my nurses swarming about her like a group of children eager for story time. I double stepped to catch up with them. But I bit my tongue. It wouldn't be fair to them or the matron to discuss my concerns at that moment.

"After we get the nurses settled, perhaps we can have a chat alone," I said.

Matron Lipton and I met in a set of rooms that she had already vacated for me in the back of the grandstand. It seemed to be part of a more or less permanent structure, made of thin wood rather than canvas like the patient tents. It was formerly a room for the jockeys, the matron told me.

My office included a sitting area, which I paced out to be about eleven by fifteen feet, with adequate furniture: a table covered by a blanket, some bookshelves, and a desk. A soft yellow light shone from the electric floor lamp, and an oil stove heater stood in the corner, a teakettle on its flat top.

She also showed me my own private rooms sectioned off in one of the larger huts for nurses. There was a metal cot with a thick mattress in the sleeping quarters and a sitting room with several chairs and scatter rugs. Each room had an electric lamp and windows to let in natural light. The rooms that would serve as home for my nurses were barely large enough for two cots and a small table between them, with trunks for their belongings at the foot of each bed. I hated having both an office and better living quarters than did they. But my work would require long hours of administrative work, and it would be beneficial to have a private office.

"Fancy a cuppa?" Back in the small office under the grandstand, the matron tested the temperature of the kettle on the heater with a tap of her finger, then poured the steaming water into china cups.

I smiled. Tea was a religion to the British. Lunch could wait, and probably would wait until dinner, I told my rumbling belly.

"So now, what are your questions?" She slid a porcelain cup in front of me. "Sugar? We've been lucky to score a wee bit."

I shook my head. "No thank you." I stared at the dark, loose tea scattered at the bottom of my cup. No tea balls here. I asked some basic questions and complimented the work they had been doing for three years. Straightforward things that seemed safe while I worked up to the hardest question. "I guess my next question involves the patient load. I'm not sure you're aware, but we were advised that we were replacing all the personnel of your unit. But we are staffed for five hundred patients, not thirteen hundred."

"I'm aware."

I sipped my tea, waiting for a further response.

"We've learned to work shorthanded. You are no longer in the world of 'staffed for five hundred.' Right now, we have just short of two hundred patients, and that's what we're, as you say, 'staffed for.' Our precious doctors and nurses aren't cutting out paper dolls, waiting for casualties to come in. We run at full bore, and when the inevitable deluge comes in, we do double shifts or task a prisoner to help or, in the worst cases, send for help from Blighty." She took away my half-empty teacup. "We've worked our arses off. Now don't bodge it up." Her glare was half pride, half threat. "Anything else then?"

I bit my lip. I needed to speak to our unit commander, not cause a rift with the person I was there to relieve. "Not just at this moment. Thank you for the tea. Tomorrow maybe a more in-depth tour, if you have time?"

At dawn on the fourth day of our tutelage by our British counterparts, I heard the distant boom of the cannons. It was a deep vibration, more felt in my bones than heard. On and on they thundered. I dressed hurriedly and pinned up my hair without first brushing.

Matron Lipton was already at breakfast, pouring coffee from a tin kettle into a teacup. She glanced my way, then touched her own neatly arranged hair. "Blimey, there's no need for you to be up so early. Take your rest now. You will be glad for it after we've gone." She pulled a dainty teacup, embellished with pink roses, from a shelf. "Coffee? Or of course we have tea if you want to be civilized about it."

"Coffee will be fine, thank you. How does one sleep with the cannons so close? Don't you feel you need to be ready to evacuate at any moment?"

Matron Lipton paused after filling my cup halfway and cocked her head. "Cannons? Oh, one gets quite accustomed. And they're not close. Just depends on how much the wind carries the sound. Now the casualty clearing stations, or CCSs, are much closer. Twenty kilometers or so from the front, not far out of range of the Big Berthas. We're lucky to be assigned here."

"Indeed. Are there nurses at the clearing stations?"

Her face took on a pained look. "There weren't at first. The units provided medical officers, and soldiers took turns being orderlies and such. But as the war drags on, they're too shorthanded, so nurses have been helping to man the stations. It worries me greatly." She looked at me with watery eyes. "My own niece serves in one."

"That must worry you so. Do you know whereabouts she is? Maybe I can check on her now and then."

Matron Lipton shook her head. "Not exactly. The war has been stuck in those same trenches for years now. One side lobbing whatever evil contraption they've come up with at the other side, then the answer back with something bigger and more deadly. A war of contrition is all. Here, we will pick up the pieces until one side gives up or runs out of sons and daughters to sacrifice for the moment." She picked up a crumbly triangle from a tray. "Scone?"

I grabbed a plate from the shelf. "Please. So you feel safe here?"

"I think the hospital has moved once in these three years. Anything can happen, of course, but there is little time to fret about it."

I sipped my coffee. I longed for a bit of milk in it, but there was no way I would ask for it. "I see. It seems the hospital has been fairly quiet since we've arrived."

Matron Lipton chuckled. "You've been fortunate to arrive during a lull. But judging from our morning greeting, things will be a-hopping tonight."

Matron Lipton was right. By four that afternoon, an ambulance arrived with four wounded. My nurses were so excited, after months of training and waiting, to actually have something to do. They flew into action, the British nurses stepping back upon seeing them at the task. With sixty-four nurses and four new patients, there was much elbowing and many a "pardon me" before I sent most of them out of the ward.

At five o'clock, three more ambulances arrived. At six, an entire unit of sixty soldiers marched up in a ragtag formation. Some carried stretchers of men wrapped in bloody bandages. I called for ten more nurses. The British nurses assigned the soldiers to beds, which they crumpled into, filthy uniforms, dirty bandages, and all. There was no apparent system. Their nurses then went down the rows of beds, taking notes and changing them into blue hospital pajamas.

I heard a nurse cry out and hurried to her. She was standing next to the bed of a patient with the fixed gaze and gray, mottled skin of death. I pulled a borrowed stethoscope from my pocket. "What happened?"

"I'm sorry, ma'am. But look here." She pulled back the brown blanket, revealing the soldier's fully intact right leg lying in a pool of blood. "He was chatting with me, said he walked in here and was going to walk out again."

I checked in vain for a heartbeat. He had bled out while the nurses took temperatures and offered tea. If his injury had been properly identified, we could have saved him. "It's not your fault, dear. I'll summon the doctor to confirm, but I'm afraid he's gone."

My blood boiled. We had to create a better system. But how to impress this upon the British, who had, after all, been dealing in this theater for three years, was a delicate question. Meanwhile, the beds continued to fill up. I had to summon more nurses.

The next day was quite the same, with early morning cannon volleys followed by a trickle, then a deluge of wounded men walking, crawling, and being carried into the hospital. Throughout the day, I would hear a sound like that of distant thunder. It would grow closer and louder until I could tell it was the sound of hundreds of footfalls. Then, I would hear the singing or sometimes whistling of the men as they marched by on the street on the other side of the hedgerow. When I peeked out my window, I could see the helmeted heads as the units marched by. Sometimes they were followed by motorized artillery or tanks, the squealing and creaking of the wheels and tracks drowning out the songs of the men.

My nurses made me so proud, tackling one difficult situation after the next, my group leaders assigning them to shifts and areas of responsibilities. After three days, the guns became silent again, and I saw my chance to voice my concerns. Not with the British, as was my first instinct, but with my own chain of command.

Dr. Murphy, now a major, was the American head of the medical unit under Colonel Fife, who was the overall commander. I was considered active duty but held no rank, so in the absence of a normal chain of command, I went to Major Murphy. He also had a small office in one of the jockey rooms, not far from mine. The door was open, and he sat at a small metal desk, filling out paperwork.

I cleared my throat, but he took no notice. "Major Murphy, may I have a moment to speak to you?"

He looked up, a grin spread across his face, and he motioned to an empty chair facing his desk. "Miss Stimson. Lovely to see you. What can I do for you?"

"It's about the intake system, sir. Or lack of one, I should say."

He put down his pen. "Go on."

"It's only been a few days, but I already see a pattern. We're losing patients who we shouldn't."

"This is war in a foreign country, not a peaceful day in St. Louis. We can't save them all, Miss Stimson, or should I call you Matron?"

"Either will do." I traced a pattern of circles onto my dark-blue uniform. "But still, there should be some order to the process. Patients should arrive having already been assessed for urgency. And to put them to bed, still in their filthy uniforms, flies against all rules of sanitation. How are we to best use those first precious minutes?"

"Again, Miss Stimson—"

Apparently neither title suited him. "Matron, yes. I think I prefer that," I said.

"I don't think you comprehend the horrors of the battlefield. The units are doing well just to get them here alive. In the beginning years of the war, they had quite the system. The injured were first examined by a medic in the unit, then passed back to a collection area if they needed more help. Then, they were screened, and some went to a CCS, where most got the treatment they needed, or…they succumbed.

"But as the stationary hospitals developed and the units started moving more quickly, the patients started pouring in the hospitals at a much higher rate. Now they are sorted, mostly by nurses close to the front. And they have nothing but their eyes, ears, and hands to decide if a man has a chance to be saved. Once they get here, it is up to us."

"Then we must have our own way of sorting them."

"That is something you can do without my approval. If you want to manage intake, I give you the authority." He picked up his pen. "Anything else?"

"When, sir? I feel rather like a guest here. It is still a British hospital."

"Not for long. Two weeks at most. I advise you to learn all you can from them, as we will be on our own when they leave."

It was good advice. There was plenty to learn, and I needed to develop a system that would work before trying to make official changes. One thing I struggled with was the complex British supply ordering system. Everything needed to be explained and noted in four different places, in four different ways. Depending on the item, its cost, and where it came from, there could be any number of requests and permissions to gather. And we would be stuck with the system, because even though the British were pulling their doctors, nurses, and other medical staff, they would remain responsible for our supplies. I was eyeing some of the better clerks, planning to ask for them to stay on.

Meanwhile, the issue of how to sort casualties arriving en masse concerned me. A surgeon was heading to a nearby French base hospital to learn about skin grafts and other new ways to reconstruct faces and also to track the care from the time of injury. I decided to accompany him to observe how they handled intake of mass casualties. Thankfully, the surgeon spoke more French than did I and was able to translate what I didn't understand.

The French hospital was similar to ours, nothing more than a series of tents, lined up lengthwise along the river. Ambulances delivered their wounded to the first three tents, which were called *salles de triage*, or sorting rooms. For most, it was obvious what the issue was. Those whose injuries were less apparent carried a tag with a word or two of explanation if they couldn't speak for themselves. Here, basic information such as assigned unit, registration number, and family location was taken. At the same time, a surgeon did a very quick check and assigned them to either an urgent or nonurgent salle.

I followed along through the tour of operating suites and recuperation tents, making mental notes for how we could implement the best ideas into our hospital.

When I returned late that night, I found that every one of my nurses had been on duty for twelve straight hours. The Germans had fired artillery shells filled with chlorine gas, and hundreds of soldiers had poured in, coughing and choking on their own fluids. Their clothes and skin had been decontaminated in the field, but I worried how thorough that was.

Many of the soldiers had difficulty speaking and swallowing, their throats were so raw. I helped one British soldier into his bed, and he politely asked for water. He was achingly thin, his cheekbones too prominent, the bony orbits of his eyes plainly visible. He was short of breath and quite filthy and had some burns on his arms that appeared to be partially healed, but he was in no immediate distress.

"I could drink and drink, but it doesn't put out the burn," he said as he gratefully accepted a glass.

"Do you want to tell me what it was like?" I hesitated to ask, but his voice seemed strong, and I knew having someone listen was important.

"We weren't prepared like we should have been. The winds were blowing from west to east, and the bloody Huns don't like gassing themselves. But they've gotten more clever, using the artillery shells instead, depending on the wind.

"Anyway, we were in the trenches, and there was a faint sweet smell, not at all like you would expect. Like a peppery pineapple. Then the greenish-yellow cloud rolled over us. By the time we got our masks on, it was too late." He shook his head.

"I did better than most. When they jumped into the trenches, I climbed out. That gas is heavier than air, so the trench is the last place to be."

"Then why did they go in them?" I pulled a bedsheet over him, careful to avoid the burns on his arms.

"Instinct, I guess. Different gasses act different ways, so it's hard to remember anything but getting that mask on during a panic."

I moved on, helping to give oxygen and breathing medications and doing whatever I could to make the injured comfortable so they could rest. That, after all, was the only true cure.

I sent the weariest nurses to bed. If they themselves had no rest, they would be of no use the next day.

I had failed in my duty to properly schedule my dear nurses, allowing the Brits to determine their duties. I set up a system of a day shift and a night shift, with leaders for each. I then assigned nurses based on their experience, strength, and compatibilities. Since the evening hours were the busiest with surgeries and arrivals, I assigned the older nurses to nights, with my most senior nurse, Dorothy, in charge. This would prove to be one of the best decisions I made.

We had a small area past the last ward where the nurses could gather between shifts. It became a tiny refuge where they could talk about their struggles and triumphs of the day. It was also where they got to know one another better, sharing treats and stories from home.

I mostly left them to themselves, as they needed a place without an authority present. But occasionally, I would join them at their invitation.

It was a few weeks after our arrival, just before the British staff were to leave, when Charlotte beckoned me to meet with them.

I plopped down into the luxury of a padded chair they had saved for me and accepted a cup of tea. "Yes, my lovely ladies?"

They giggled, and Margaret, at age thirty-two one of the eldest, piped in. "We decided we needed to know more about you. Where you come from, your dreams, your worries. What you did for fun before all this merriment."

"What if I prefer to keep that a mystery?"

They giggled again and sat forward in their seats. So much for mystery.

"I grew up in an intensely competitive family in St. Louis and later upstate New York. We children were expected to attain perfect grades, play a musical instrument flawlessly, dance acceptably, but otherwise be unseen and unheard." I pursed my lips. "The boys were to become doctors, lawyers, or pastors, like my dad, while the girls…"

"Were to run a home and have babies," several said in unison.

"Well, yes. But I had the misfortune of the expectation of doing something with my talents, like many in my family, while at the same time adhering to what was acceptable for girls."

"So you became a nurse."

"Eventually, yes. But I wanted to be a physician, like my uncle. But that was not to be."

My nurses grew quiet, seemingly sensing a still raw point.

Charlotte's sweet, gentle voice broke the silence. "What did you play? What instrument, I mean."

"Oh, the violin. Not exceptionally well, but one might recognize a tune if I worked hard at it."

"I'll bet you were wonderful," Margaret said.

At that, Nora elbowed Dorothy next to her. They both rolled their eyes. I could imagine they were silently saying *teacher's pet*. I flashed a little glance at them to let them know I saw all.

"I do miss it." I had not played since a time back in St. Louis, when I became overwhelmed with my work and studies. I closed my eyes and imagined the violin under my chin. I tilted my head and played with an imaginary bow. Even that made the tension in my forehead melt away.

"Is there anything else you want to know?" But I had already said quite enough.

In the next few days, I made notes of procedures and skills I thought would be beneficial and appropriate for my nurses to learn. This was a delicate dance, as we didn't want to step on the doctors' toes or overwhelm the nurses. But it seemed that having a bit more training in some things would save time by not having to fetch a doctor and save lives by more timely action.

I thought skills requiring lots of practice, such as suturing, were best left to the surgeons. But the field of physical assessment seemed a logical place to start. So I asked Drs. Murphy and Valentine to hold a series of clinics on things like a basic neurological exam and using a stethoscope for lung and bowel sounds. For the most part, the nurses were eager to learn new skills, but my older nurses, Nora and Dorothy in particular, had reservations.

They came to my office together after the first session, which happened to be on lung auscultation.

They were quite the pair, these two, delighting in late-night sharing of shots of whiskey. As they were both team leaders, they rarely worked together, but here they were, visiting me during precious whiskey time.

"We'll get right to it," Nora said as she pulled out the chairs facing my desk for Dorothy and herself.

I reached into my desk drawer and pulled out a full bottle of

Jameson that had been gifted to me and a couple of glasses. "No need to rush."

"This won't take more than a double." Dorothy filled their glasses. "We just want to clarify some things. This new training, I mean, it's good for the girls to learn all they can. That's why they came. But I worry…"

Nora filled in. Seemed they had worked it out beforehand. "We worry, when is it too much? The girls are nearly overwhelmed each day. Sure, we've had a few slow days, slow weeks, even. But that's not the normal situation, and it seems the pace is ever increasing. There's rarely a shift when I could say, gee, the nurses had time to do so much more…"

"I understand your concern. That's why I've selected topics that I thought would help the nurses in their everyday duties, not add to them. For example, a nurse might check a surgical patient for bowel sounds and, finding none, hold back on his dinner until he could be checked by the surgeon, thereby saving the patient from vomiting and herself a lot of cleaning up. That's just an example off the top of my head. What I'm hoping for is better and more efficient patient care, not more duties."

Nora twirled her glass. "Who gets to decide what they're ready for?"

"As team leaders, you do."

"One more thing." Dorothy pointed to her tall, stiff cap that was part of the nurses' uniforms. "Can we get rid of these godforsaken things?"

Nora chimed in, "Amen."

"What's wrong with them?" I despised them myself, as they were impossible to keep clean and never seemed to stay straight in my hair, no matter how many pins I used.

"The genius in Washington who picked them never worked in a tent hospital, that's for sure," Dorothy grumbled.

Nora added, "I knock mine off seven times a day, going through the low tent entries."

"I see." I always had to duck under the entries anyway, but that would not be so for the shorter nurses. "The caps are important for patients to identify us. But I'll ask about something more practical."

The stack of requisitions on my desk seemed to grow unchecked, despite me spending at least two precious hours each day processing them. I was tempted to lay my head on top of the stack for a moment, but a gentle knock on my door prevented any respite. "Come in."

Charlotte flitted in and alighted like a butterfly on my extra chair. "So sorry to disturb you, Matron, but—"

"You're not disturbing me, Miss Cox." I couldn't resist a peek at the watch pinned beneath my right shoulder.

"It's regarding my room, for which I am tremendously grateful." She tucked a blond curl behind her ear.

I sighed and responded rather irritably, "What is the problem with your room? Would you prefer one of the tents?"

"It backs up to the X-ray room."

"I see. A busy location, especially at night, but isn't the entrance on the opposite side? I scarcely think we can find you something quieter." I pulled the next requisition from the pile.

Charlotte stared at her fingertips, which were beginning to tremble. "It's not the noise, ma'am. It's the X-rays. I can feel them coming through the wall."

"Explain." If this were anyone else, I would dismiss the notion as just another minor complaint, like the lack of proper shoe polish. But Charlotte had proven to be extraordinarily perceptive. She often gravitated to a patient just before they passed, even ones who weren't expected to die.

"Well, I don't know how to explain it exactly. It's a sound, but not one I can hear. A vibration, sort of, that I feel in my gut."

"Our hearing detects a range of frequencies. Dogs, for example, can hear frequencies that we can't. I suppose it's possible that the machine makes sounds that you can detect while others can't."

"Yes, Matron. I'm sure you're right." She tapped her fingers together and made no move to leave.

Pushing aside my stack of paperwork, I gave in. "Shall we check it out together?"

Her face brightened. It must be a lonely world for her, with no one to understand her sensibilities.

We went to her tiny, sparse room, not much bigger than my closet at home. Most of the nurses were quartered in huts or tents behind the grandstand, but when our desperately needed additional nurses arrived, we had run out of space, and a few nurses were squeezed between the X-ray room and laboratory. Charlotte's and her roommate's cots were neatly made, and a small braided rug warmed the floor between them. A single light bulb hung from a ceiling wire. A lit candle flickered and provided a warm vanilla scent, no doubt an effort to cover the dank odor that pervaded the camp.

"Are you feeling the vibrations now?" I asked.

"No. Nothing."

I made a show of knocking on the thin walls, nothing more than sheets of plywood. The light bulb blinked and dimmed a bit, but Charlotte seemed not to notice.

Instead, her eyes widened, and she spun toward the back of the cabin. "There, do you feel that?" She held up her hands. "A little tingle." She ran her finger lightly across her lips, then ran it down her chin, chest, and belly.

"No, I don't feel or hear anything at all." The timing of the light dimming, which happened whenever there was a surge in electricity demand, and her noticing some sort of change was too close to be a coincidence. "Wait here a moment. I want to check something."

I hurried out of the hut, around the corner, and to the entrance of the X-ray room. Captain Ernst was helping a patient from a makeshift examination table, a stretcher lying across two sawhorses, onto another stretcher held by two orderlies.

Tall, with dark, wavy hair, he wore an air of indifference as he set about his work. But I knew differently. He was immensely proud of his work, often offering lectures regarding new developments. On one such occasion, feeling sorry for him as he addressed a smattering of patients and doctors who had wandered in, I secretly bribed a few nurses to attend.

"Knock knock. Are you just getting started, Captain?"

"Yes. One done so far. I'll be done shortly if you need me."

I nodded and headed back to Charlotte, having confirmed my suspicion that the X-ray machine had just come into use. Intending to address both of our concerns without frightening Charlotte, I came up with a plan.

She was standing in the middle of her cabin, eyes closed and arms crossed over her belly.

I cleared my throat so as not to alarm her. "Miss Cox, now that you mention it, I think I do hear something. And Captain Ernst could sorely use this hut for his supplies. I'll see about assigning you and, uh—" I looked at her roommate's cot, embarrassed to not recall who was assigned to it.

"Rebecca. Yes, thank you so much. Rebecca doesn't hear it, but I'm sure she'd be fine moving with me."

Changing cabins was the easy part. How would I convince the dedicated Captain Ernst that his X-ray machine was leaking something that might be harmful?

Several days later, I had secured Charlotte and Rebecca a new hut, far from the X-ray room. But Charlotte's sensations during the X-rays continued to haunt me. I read everything I could find regarding X-rays, which wasn't much as it was a fairly new technology, and there were few textbooks lying around.

In my research, I found that X-rays were discovered and developed mostly in France.

It was time to approach Captain Ernst regarding my concerns. I picked dinner time, early in the evening, before the casualties arrived. He was sitting alone in the mess tent, scooping ham out of a tin.

"Have you a moment, Captain?" I said in a bright, cheerful voice.

He motioned to the bench across the table from him. "Please."

I slipped onto the bench and set my tray on the table. Gelatinous ham, cubes of what appeared to be potatoes, and a slimy green vegetable I couldn't quite identify. At least the bread looked good.

"You'll need this." He pulled a label-less bottle of brown liquid from his pocket, and I eyed it suspiciously.

"Don't ask, or I take it away."

I shook a few drops onto my finger and tasted them. Salty, vinegary, and slightly sweet, with a hint of tomato. And maybe vodka. I sprinkled my food with it. "Can you bear some shop talk? Questions, mostly, just between you and me."

"Fire away." He took the bottle and stuffed it back into his pocket. "There are only the two of us in the Sacred Trust of the Brown Bottle."

I started with a tip I thought might ease his work. "I see you transfer patients onto a stretcher for examination. Is there something special about the exam stretcher?"

"Not really. We have to change it out often, as it gets quite soiled, as you would imagine."

"I see. I was wondering, wouldn't it be easier for both you and the patient if he remained on his own stretcher? Moving must be quite painful for some and difficult for you to manage on your own."

"That would require two stretcher carriers to stay for each exam. Interesting point though. We shall have to try it out. Any more advice?"

"As you know, I've reassigned the nurses who occupied the hut behind the X-ray room."

"Thanks. Didn't know I needed the room till I had it." His face scrunched up, then he put his serviette up to his lips, evidently spitting something out.

"Tell me, do you feel safe, doing X-rays all day?"

He raised his eyebrows. "From what?"

"The rays themselves. Hasn't radioactivity been shown to be harmful?"

"In much higher doses. And I wear a lead apron."

"How do you know that's enough?"

He wiped his mouth with the bunched-up serviette. "Because I've had the best training in the whole world. From Irène Curie herself."

I looked at him blankly.

"You know, the daughter of Pierre and Marie Curie."

I knew Pierre and Marie Curie, who had jointly won a Nobel Prize for discovering radioactive elements, had lived in Paris. "Of course. How fortunate for you. And I'm sure she's eminently qualified, but I still have some concerns."

The captain rose and collected his dishes. "Why don't you join me in the lab and show me what's bothering you?"

❧

Captain Ernst placed a key in the flimsy lock securing the X-ray room. Equipment stood on a table next to a pair of sawhorses. "It's quite simple, actually. We center the stretcher across the sawhorses.

Photographic plates are slid under the patient according to the target body part. Electricity is fed to these coils and then runs to the cathode tube."

"A Crookes tube, in which the air has been evacuated." I couldn't help smiling at my little bit of knowledge.

"Precisely. The electricity excites the atoms in the remaining air, and electrons are attracted to the positive anode. This releases an electromagnetic pulse, a very short-waved beam we cannot see. These are the X-rays. They go through skin and muscle but are slowed down by bone or metal. The plates capture this, and voilà." He held up an X-ray picture of a rib cage. "We have a view inside."

"Perfectly amazing. And you can control these rays' direction?"

"Not 100 percent of them, but mostly, yes."

"And do they bounce around once they hit bone or metal or wood, for example?"

"Hmm, I would imagine so."

"Have you heard about the researchers with burns and worse? Clearly, the rays disturb tissue."

"Right you are. But those were people exposed for hours on end, for months, even years. It wasn't unusual to expose a researcher's arm for hours to get a picture. Now we can do it in mere seconds. Even so, we take the precaution of a lead apron and shielding.

"And radioactivity isn't only beneficial in X-rays. The Curies have discovered and isolated a radioactive element, radium. They've experimented with using its radiation to destroy cancer and other diseased tissues. In the future, radiologists like me will be doing much more than taking pictures of people's insides. We'll be curing them."

"That would be a miracle." But I was more focused on our current issue. How to bring up Charlotte's vague complaints, in the light of all this science, percolated in my mind. "So the rays can go through skin and muscle and are slowed but not stopped by something as thick and dense as bone. When they hit something dense like lead, they stop. Or perhaps bounce."

I measured the room: three paces. "On the other side of these thin walls are people, coming and going, sleeping and working. All being exposed to X-rays, many hours a day for months. You're protected by your apron, but what about them? And what about the parts of you that aren't protected?"

The captain replaced the X-ray picture and presented a folded shield. "I also have this. And I do appreciate your concern but believe I know my business."

"I don't mean any disrespect."

He nodded. "What is driving you to ask?"

I bit my lip. "Under the Sacred Trust of the Brown Bottle?"

"Of course."

"One of my nurses, Charlotte Cox, can detect the rays. Her former hut is now your supply room."

"I know the one. Little blond girl. Quiet, afraid of her own shadow." He shook his head. "I hear she also senses the souls fading from our fallen soldiers."

"That's what they say. But I validated this claim during an X-ray procedure." I described the earlier incident.

"Interesting. I will write to some folks in Paris. Meanwhile, collect all the lead you can find."

Where would I find lead? Then I remembered the sound in the busy operating tent, the clank of extracted bullets and shell fragments hitting metal buckets.

❧

Letters from my family arrived just a month after our arrival in France. What a joy it was to read of my sister's education and Mother and Dad's pride in everything we were doing abroad. I smoothed the vellum over and over, hoping to ease my homesickness. Even though I had lived away from them for quite some time, the ocean between us and the war made me feel farther away than the moon.

I was folding a letter back into its envelope when there was a knock on my door. Instead of yelling for them to enter, as was my habit, I opened the door to find three nurses spread across the frame: Charlotte on the right, Dorothy in the middle, and Margaret on the left. Smiling like Cheshire cats, they were obviously hiding something behind their backs.

"My dears, what can I do for you?"

"We were all missing home and thought you might be the loneliest of all."

It was as if they had sensed my feelings through the walls. Tears sprung, quite unbidden, from my eyes. I had not cried a single time since leaving St. Louis, and this show of emotion would not do. I turned to wipe them away, unseen. "Why, what a lovely thought. Now, what do you have there? A biscuit to share? Oh, I do hope so."

The women laughed. "Even better," said Dorothy. She nudged her thick eyeglasses up her nose while keeping her other hand hidden behind her back.

Then Margaret, the shortest of the three with light brown hair tucked into a neat bun, produced sheaves of yellowed paper with thick lines of markings across them.

I accepted the paper. "Sheet music? Whatever for?"

"Voilà," the three said. Dorothy produced a horsehair bow and Charlotte a slightly battered violin.

My hand clapped over my gaping mouth. "But where? Who?"

They all chattered at once. "We went into town…knew you played…had to look it up in French…did you know it is *violon*?"

Dorothy held up the bow. "And this is an *archet de violon*."

"You did this for me?" Again, those darn tears intruded upon my vision. I set aside the sheet music and took the violin Charlotte offered, ran my hand across its smooth grain. It was obviously well made but in need of some polishing. I tightened the strings.

"Go ahead. Try it." Dorothy handed me the bow.

"Oh no. I will need some time to get it in tune. I am overwhelmed, ladies. Thank you so much. But…" I hesitated, not wanting to hurt their feelings after such a magnanimous gift. "You must promise me this. You must not spend your hard-earned money on me. I will accept this gift and will find a way for it to benefit all. But otherwise, your work, your dedication, is the only gift I will ever want."

Dorothy elbowed Margaret. "I told you."

"Now leave me be." As I closed the door, I longed to join them in the common room or for a chat in one of their huts. But lines had to be kept between us if I was to maintain any semblance of authority. Somehow, my loneliness grew.

I found some clean rags and wiped the violin and bow. There was too much rosin in the horsehair, but otherwise, it seemed to be in fine shape. I tightened the bow hair, then tucked the violin under my chin and played a note. Oh, the sound of it thrilled my ears. As I continued to tune it and play some simple songs, I could feel my spirits lift as if by magic.

CHAPTER 5

S oon, the time came for our British counterparts to leave. We had been working alongside them for a few weeks. Mostly, it was a congenial relationship, but we all knew it was to be short-lived. As their remaining days with us drew to an end, small scuffles broke out over the silliest things. Arguments about how and where supplies should be stored. The proper way to make a bed (British: cover loose over feet to promote good circulation; American: tucked in to keep out the germs). But eventually, compromises won the day. After all, we were on the same side.

Plans were made for a gathering to bid them farewell. I was nervous that it would coincide with a rash of new patients, so we chose early afternoon, which was usually quiet, and had several backup times scheduled just in case.

Parting was bittersweet. We had enjoyed their company while at the same time longing to do things our own way.

The night prior to the event was a busy one. Two hundred wounded soldiers had arrived. Although we didn't lose a single one, it was a marathon of surgeries, blood transfusions, and dressing changes. Some of the patients had wounds too large or too deep to be closed, and they had to be irrigated. We were using the new Carrel-Dakin method, which required a delicate balance of chemicals in the disinfectant solution. Too strong, and it would injure the tissue further. Too weak, and it wouldn't kill the germs. It also required a complex arrangement of tubing that had to be carefully filled, drained, and monitored.

The next morning and afternoon, the staff filtered into the dining tent for the farewell ceremony like walking dead, so complete was their exhaustion.

The tent, although my nurses had made some effort at decorations, with fresh flowers on the tables and a few lit candles here and there, seemed too somber for the celebration we had planned. After all were assembled, some sitting at the tables while others crowded into every available space, the ceremony began. The British unit commander and Colonel Fife each made brief remarks. Major Murphy and his British compatriot, along with the other doctors, nurses, and other staff, clapped politely at the formal goodbye speeches.

There must be a way to warm up this solemn affair, I thought. Then, I remembered my violin, which I had finally gotten shipshape, even if I didn't have much of a repertoire. I fetched it from my room and asked Major Murphy for permission to play. Permission was granted, and with an audible sigh of relief, he faded back into the crowd.

I played the few songs I knew from memory, mostly silly little tunes any child would know. We had a small upright piano, and Dr. Gross, a young surgeon with a bad hip, started to accompany me, making it a bit more pleasant. Then I had an idea.

Slowly but strongly, I played the first few notes of a patriotic song. Dr. Gross nodded, and we began to play "My Country 'Tis of Thee."

Dorothy stood tall and sang along, then egged on her fellow nurses. Soon, all the Americans were singing loudly "Sweet land of liberty, of thee I sing." After two verses, we stopped to much applause. Then, Matron Lipton rose. She sang "God Save the King" to the same tune. Soon, all the Brits had joined in, louder and stronger than had the

Americans. The last time through, the Brits and Americans sang their own versions simultaneously at full voice.

When the voices faded, I put down my violin and sang the British third verse a cappella:

"Not in this land alone,
But be God's mercies known,
From shore to shore.
Lord make the nations see,
That men should brothers be,
And form one family,
The wide world o'er."

The crowd was silent, then roared in approval. They hugged one another and cheered. Someone started a chorus of "For She's a Jolly Good Fellow," and Major Murphy raised my arm as if I had just won a boxing match. For once, I was proud of my low contralto. Truly, I had taken up the violin because I had been embarrassed to sing with the men in the church choir. But here, none of that mattered. Music was reminding us of our common mission, of strength and togetherness.

I had played with passion; I had sung with joy. It was a glorious moment that I shall never forget.

❧

My family and friends back home were so dear in their letters and sent me whatever I wished for that could be shipped. How much to share with them was always a matter of consideration. I wanted to be as honest as possible while at the same time not worrying them unnecessarily about problems they couldn't do anything to fix.

I tried to sound upbeat, as indeed I was generally well and happy.

But one evening, even as my stomach rumbled due to not having enough time to eat properly, I wrote the following letter:

Dear Family,

We are well settled into our routine here; our new system is flowing like the Hudson to the ocean. Yes, I still long for home and to see all of you, but our task here is great, and I am honored to be part of it, in whatever small way.

The food is nourishing and plentiful, so you needn't worry about that. Although the fare does become rather monotonous; the ginger treats you've sent were well received by all.

For example, we have eggs, sometimes powdered, sometimes fresh, and flapjacks for breakfast. Also a dark, strong-tasting sausage made from pig blood that takes some getting used to. Dinner is typically a jelled ham from a tin, dried beef, or salted fish. Our provisions come from England mostly.

Now here we are, in the midst of a country with a rich history of enticing foods, and we eat tinned gray meat from London! I've made up my mind to see what I can bargain and barter from the locals. If for nothing else, it will make my nurses so happy and raise morale during the long work days. Do not worry one tiny bit about me. I am doing what I love and wouldn't have it any other way.

Cheerio for now, and hope all is well there.

Lovingly,

J

Although more or less true, I could only hope my family didn't see my words for what they were: the ramblings of a hungry person.

After the British left, we once again became American Expeditionary
Forces Base Hospital 21, at least to us, as we were still officially No. 12
in the British system. This simple thing raised the spirits of my nurses
to no end. Perhaps it was also due to me declaring one of the spaces
vacated by the British as a nurses' lounge. Now the nurses had a more
comfortable place to gather and chat among themselves about the day.
We moved the piano into the room, which was about the size of a large
American bedroom, and they had sing-alongs as well.

Of course, I gave them their privacy. After all, what they wanted to
complain about could very well be me! But I would poke my head in
occasionally, and usually they would invite me for tea.

On one such occasion, some nurses were discussing what they
would do after the war. Dorothy said, "I am a nurse. I will continue to
be a nurse, wherever I'm needed."

Another said, "No, I will go back to a normal life. Get married, raise
a family, work on the farm."

"Yes!" another agreed. "Isn't that what the war is about? To have
freedom, just to live your normal life?"

Margaret said she wanted to go to school, to become a "real"
professional, a doctor or lawyer, maybe. She dreamed of going to the
University of Pennsylvania.

"Isn't nursing a profession?" I asked.

There was a long silence, then Margaret answered, "How can it
be when it's only for the duration? A profession is a career. You do
it for life."

"Then women don't really have professions," Charlotte said. "Unless
you consider motherhood a profession. But even then, your babies grow
up and no longer need you."

"Matron, what do you think?"

I contemplated all their ideas. Things I had often thought about myself. My goal was always—and still was in many respects—to become a physician. That seemed my true calling, a profession I had a proclivity for since childhood. That door had slammed shut in my face, but I hoped that with my nursing and war experience, it might just pry open again. But was that what I still wanted? I started thinking out loud.

"Are you not a mother once your children are grown and not in your care? Is an author not an author when she merely stares out the window, dreaming of characters? Is a soldier not a soldier when he holds no gun in his hands? A nurse is a nurse in every fiber of her being, whether she comforts the mother of a baby with a fever or holds the hand of a dying neighbor. Some choose to make it their only career; some move on to other things. But nursing is in the heart forever."

Shortly after, a conversation with Major Murphy gave me more insight. We were preparing the operating theater for the arrival of the ambulances. He was so good about helping out in that way, and I learned much about instruments and new techniques during these quiet times. For example, he showed me paraffin-coated sterile bottles he had procured from another hospital. They were to be used for blood collection—the paraffin and the addition of citrate to coat the interior helped prevent the clotting that had been a tremendous problem.

I noticed a supply of gas masks on a shelf and asked him how they were used in the operating theater.

"We're still sort of experimenting with them," he said. "There have been studies on giving concentrated oxygen for lots of different things. Miners, divers, and people who have lost a lot of blood, among other things." He showed me a large metal tank, which looked for all the world like a torpedo. "We've been working with a British doctor, John Haldane, figuring out ways to get the oxygen into the patient. One of the most promising is, believe it or not, through a gas mask."

He briefly explained how it worked, the importance of the seal around the face, the valves and filters and such. It was quite the contraption. It seemed much more effective than our current practice of holding a tube, connected to a coated silk bag of oxygen, in the patient's mouth. This could be strapped on, freeing the nurse for other duties.

"What a fascinating thing for a doctor to do. At one time, I desired to be a doctor myself."

"Why, when you are clearly suited to nursing?"

"Some don't see nursing as a profession. More of something to do while you're waiting for your life to happen. Even the men that do it only stay with it for a short while. I have a feeling marriage and children are not in the cards for me, and I can't see filling charts and changing dressings my whole life."

"First of all, don't rule out starting a family. Some smart, sophisticated, and worthy man will eventually wear you down, and you'll allow him to marry you. Next, I am shocked that you dismiss all you and the other nurses do. Why, we physicians couldn't function without you." He set aside the gas mask and moved on to a table heaped with instruments ready for sterilization. I adjusted the flame on the oil stove to bring up the temperature of the vat of simmering water.

I accepted instruments to drop into the boiling water, the splash burning my hand. "Ouch." I shook the water off my hand. "They wouldn't want to anyway."

He grabbed a cool, wet rag and placed it on the burn. "Here's how I see it. The nurses run things, sort things out, so we doctors can make the final diagnosis. Which, of course, the nurses already know, but they like us to feel important. Then we are like the mechanics of the automobile. We take out the bad bits, shine up the muddy ones, tighten this and that, and"—he swiped his hands against each other—"pronounce her fixed. Then it's up to the nurses to get her back on the road."

The idea stuck with me. My dreams of becoming a physician began to fade that day, not because I thought I wasn't able or it wasn't possible but because a new, brighter dream was taking its place.

After the instruments had boiled, we both donned sterile rubber gloves. I moved a set of scalpels from a pot of cooled water to a cloth-covered tray. "Mechanic. Ha! I will have to share that with my nurses. And I shall have to share it with my uncle Lewis. That will redden his face."

"Uncle Lewis?"

"Dr. Lewis Stimson. Surely, you've heard of him. The first surgeon to operate in the United States using Lister's aseptic method. Also operated on Ulysses Grant."

"And founder of one of our top medical schools. Of course I've heard of him." He folded a sterile towel over the instruments. "I didn't realize you were related. No one at the university ever mentioned it."

"I was careful not to. Nor my grandfather, a president of Dartmouth, my cousin, high up in the State Department, or my aunts and uncles who are inventors and philanthropists. My family doesn't believe in riding each other's coattails." I puffed up like a peacock. "'Pick something important, and be the best at it' is more our motto."

The nurses all adored Major Murphy. He was not only a great supporter of me, but he spent every moment of every day doing for others. If a hut ordered twelve eggs and only six appeared, he would commandeer the telephone to fix it. He found coal stoves when there weren't any to be found, and oil for our lamps. When the roller bandages or surgical supplies didn't arrive as expected, he would hunt them down.

And they gathered like smitten schoolgirls when he told tales of his days at Harvard. His very favorite concerned a certain football game, which he proclaimed to be "worse than any day I'd seen in the war."

It was a game of the two famous rivals, Harvard and Yale. The game disintegrated into an all-out brawl, with teeth knocked out, heads smashed to the ground, and plenty of kicks to the kidneys. The major himself spent several hours unconscious after a bad blow to the head. "We weren't allowed to play each other for years after that!" he said, somehow ebullient over the whole thing.

This was all in addition to his duties as a surgeon. When he could escape the office and no patients were in need of him, he played baseball with the enlisted men. Heaven only knows when the man slept.

I heard complaints from some of the chief nurses of other units, who weren't so fortunate to have this type of support. For example, they made rules for their nurses, only to have them reversed by doctors in charge with no good reason or explanation. I counted my lucky stars daily to have Major Murphy looking out for us and the whole hospital.

How different things would have been if Dr. Valentine had been in charge. It seemed he was more interested in keeping nurses in check than in letting them rise to their full potential. For example, I had authorized my team leaders to go directly to Dr. Murphy when I was not available. He burst into my office late one afternoon, carrying what appeared to be a tray of surgical instruments. His face was reddened; I braced myself for a fight.

"I never authorized nurses to use these on burn patients." He rattled the metal on metal.

"Dr. Murphy did."

"You need to see me about these things. And your nurses shouldn't be consulting the chief at all."

I shuffled papers on my desk. Signed something random, just to be ornery. "I authorized them to."

"You're circumventing the chain of command," he blustered.

"What would you have them do? I can't be on duty twenty-four hours a day."

"Well, I... You have to figure that out. But stop taking advantage, just because Dr. Murphy is sweet on you."

I had the distinct feeling that Dr. Valentine was operator in chief of the gossip grapevine. "Thank you, Dr. Valentine. I'll keep that in consideration."

CHAPTER 6

July 1917

With the exception of a few admin persons and a straggling officer or two, the British were gone, and our dietician and head cook were finally able to plan and prepare meals that were more familiar. They saved a few of the favorites from the British menus, such as bangers and mash and Yorkshire pudding, but the baked beans and black blood sausage at breakfast thankfully faded away. The supplies still came from London, so orders for things like jelly or bacon met with some strange results. Alice Stedman, our head cook, told me the "jelly" that was sent consisted of a box of cherry-flavored powder, to be used to make a jiggly, sweet gelatin dessert, and the "bacon" was a salty ham.

We generally ate family style, the food presented on large trays that we passed around each table, taking a reasonable portion, of course. The nurses had their own mess tent, but the rules weren't strict, and sometimes orderlies, doctors, or even walking patients would sometimes join us.

There was plenty of food, but it had to be ordered, prepared, and budgeted for, and we were all very conscientious about not wasting anything. We saved scraps for stray cats and dogs, and inedible things like eggshells and bones were put in a compost heap or sometimes saved to make stocks.

All my life, I had a healthy appetite. When I saw the tiny portions the nurses at my tables took, I started cutting back what I served myself. But I found myself getting hungry between meals. I was relieved when we started getting packages from home, as they sent me some of my favorite food treats.

Still, with the long active days, with miles and miles of walking the wards, I was getting a bit thin. Late one evening, having run out of my private provisions from home, I wandered into the kitchen tent, hoping to find a snack. I was also hoping that no one would be there, to avoid the embarrassment of seeking extra rations between meals.

But Alice Stedman was there, drying some stock pots. I turned around in my tracks and tried to sneak back out without being seen, but it was of no avail.

"Now, where you be off to, miss?" She followed after me. "Is that you, Matron?"

Alice was a short, stocky woman, who seemed to have a bad hip and walked with a limp. She was from either Alabama or Georgia, and her accent was so thick it sometimes seemed she was speaking another language.

"Oh, didn't mean to bother you, Miss Stedman. I'm sure you're all closed up for the evening."

"You're a tall one, aren't you? From the look of you compared to a month ago, I don't think you're eating enough. Don't you like my food?"

"I like it just fine. Much better actually, since the Brits left."

She laughed. "Well, I tend to a more southern style, which might not be to your liking. It's how we make it back in Alabama."

Alabama. I made a mental note.

"I was just about to fix myself a mess of beans. Like to join me?" she asked.

"If it's no trouble."

She made up two big bowls of green beans, which were cooked down very tender and flavored with bits of ham and some browned onions. I wolfed it down faster than was polite, and she scooped more into my bowl.

"So why you gettin' so skinny?" She loaded a huge forkful of beans into her mouth.

I looked away, feeling heat rise up my face. "I try not to take more than my share. But it seems I'm accustomed to quite a bit more than others."

"Now, you listen to me. You're a big woman. Ain't nothing to be ashamed of. But there's not a scrap of extra on ya, and a woman needs a little extra to keep healthy." She wiped her mouth with a kitchen towel. "I understand you're in a fix, dining with those tiny slips of things and wanting not to look greedy. So I'm gonna make you a little something in the evenings and leave it in your room, if that'd be okay with you." She winked. "Just between us."

She scraped back her chair, and I did the same and rose to leave.

The image of gobbling up extra rations in my room like a feral dog gave me a moment's pause. But only a moment, because my now satiated self declared, "I would love that. And if there's something I can do for you…" I reached to collect my bowl.

She waved me off as she collected both bowls. "Don't tell nobody."

The British had wanted the hospital to be as cheery and homelike as possible, for both the patients and the staff. They planted all sorts of flowers in the greenway in the center of the racecourse, and the track itself remained mostly free of tents and buildings. Red geraniums, blue delphiniums, irises, and fragrant sweet alyssum created a riot of color against the tender green grass.

As Rouen was notoriously rainy (the French called it *Le Pot de*

Chambre due to the resulting muck), the flowers grew profusely, even spreading to areas between the huts that hadn't been planted.

One day, gray with the constant drizzle, a mongrel dog showed up, shivering and cowering in the greenway. Underneath a covering of dirt, he was light tan in color. The nurses fed him, washed him off, wrapped him in a blanket, and placed him by a warm stove. We couldn't keep him, of course; how would we prevent him from wandering into the theater or instrument rooms? But they named him Sam, and once you name them, they're yours.

Sam seemed to mostly attach himself to Major Murphy, perhaps due to the scraps that the major suddenly was unable to keep on his fork.

The dog would sit by Major Murphy's side at all meals. Never begging, just performing cleanup duty. The major also enjoyed taking Sam for walks in the morning and midday. He invited me to join him, and despite my objections of being too busy, I did. Soon, this became a habit, then the habit a necessity.

On our walks, we talked about everything and nothing, from how to handle difficult cases or how to improve administrative routines to the more personal. I learned he had been married to a woman named Cornelia, then widowed at a young age, and now had a sweetheart back home. Then I learned the sweetheart was breaking his heart.

We were halfway through our route, on my favorite part along the river. Tall and full horse chestnut trees grew in a line, providing shade over our path. The flowers had fallen from the trees, and the clusters of spiky pods were just starting to form. We spoke of the beauty of the area and discovered we both adored the painter Claude Monet.

"Benjamin told me that Monet lives not too far away. One of these days, we must escape upriver and see his gardens." The trees thinned out a bit, creating a frame for the river view. "Wouldn't this be a lovely spot for him to paint?"

He didn't answer, and we didn't speak for a few minutes. We were so comfortable with each other by then that this was not unusual; indeed, they were pleasant moments. But this silence went on for longer than usual. Finally, I broke it, cheerfully asking if he'd had a new letter from his beloved.

"Why yes, I have." His voice was tight, and he looked away.

"Is she—is everything all right?" I lightly touched his hand.

"Oh, she's fine. Just brilliant," he said, his words clipped.

He picked up the walking pace, and I stepped with him. Simultaneous feelings of dread mixed with a lightness and joy, which confused me to no end. Why did I feel lightness when something was clearly upsetting him?

"Well, that's lovely. Perhaps you'll be able to meet in London soon." I couldn't let it go. My inner self chided me, while its evil twin pushed me on.

"Here, read how brilliant she is for yourself." He slipped a letter from his pocket.

I scanned the loopy, feminine script. It was short, just a few paragraphs.

Dear Murph.

Yuck.

I had been faithful for all these long months, now nearly a year, waiting for you, worrying ever so. I'm afraid the worry has gotten the best of me, and my health has suffered. I'm not strong like you. I can't bear the strain.

I must let you go, lest you waste your time pining for a girl who no longer deserves you.

I have found another, someone who is here and takes care of me, so you needn't worry for me at all.

I wish for you much happiness for all your days.

Love, L.

I gasped. "Oh, Major, I'm so sorry." I hoped my words sounded as perfectly sincere as part of me meant them. In truth, I was feeling a stirring in my heart every time we were together. I looked forward to our walks not only for the chance to escape our duties for a moment of distraction but for the sound of his voice and the occasional brush of his fingers across my hand.

Which he did—and more—when I gave the letter back to him. He took my hand in his and said, "Julia, will you do me the biggest of favors?"

"Of course." I couldn't think of anything I wouldn't do for him.

He pocketed the letter and motioned for us to sit on a park bench. After we were settled, he reached down to pet Sam while I waited to learn of his favor. Conversations with him took patience. He was not one to speak without carefully considering his words—a trait I admired and could use more of, but still found frustrating.

Just as I was about to ask about it, he said, "Would you please call me Fred? I think we're past the Major and Miss Stimson stage."

"Certainly. But not in front of the others. You must have heard there are rumors about us. And we should be especially careful around Dr. Valentine. It seems he's the self-appointed chief of the rumor mill."

"So what?" He waved my accusation away. "Let them have their fun. But I agree, only when we're alone together, which I hope will be often."

"Agreed," I said in my most professional manner. But inside, I was as giddy as a girl at her prom. "Is that the favor? Or are you just warming up to that?"

He laughed. "That's all I ask for now."

CHAPTER 7

The trains arrived in Rouen each evening and were met with ambulances. The British practice was to bring the stretchers from the ambulances straight to a bed. There, the soldiers lay in their filthy uniforms and wouldn't see the surgeon until morning.

Through the night, the nurses went from bed to bed, changing bandages, giving baths, and injecting morphine to those who needed it. When they found someone having trouble breathing or with heavy bleeding, they would summon a surgeon or internist. On nights after gas attacks, the tents seem to shake with the sound of hundreds of men violently coughing and gasping for breath. These nights were the hardest for the nurses.

In addition to the coughing, there was the difficult task of changing the clothing of the men who had been exposed to mustard gas. Normally the easiest bit of admitting other types of patients, it was traumatic for both the patient and the nurse. First, she had to carefully remove the crisp-with-dirt uniform, using gloves due to the contamination. Most of the men gritted their teeth and bore the pain silently, but some screamed as the fabric was removed from their burnt skin. They usually tolerated the hypochlorite solution poured over them and being wrapped in bandages, but being dressed in the heavy blue pajamas caused another round of yelps.

Worst of all was to come upon a patient who had been quietly bearing his pain. A nurse came to me in tears. "Matron, I just can't bear it."

"What is it?"

"My patient with the burns across his chest and back. We put him
on his stomach, because that side is a little better."

"It's difficult to deal with patients in pain. But know that you are
easing it as best you can," I offered, my words seeming pathetically cold.

"It's not that, Matron. I can accept that. It's the singing. The poor
man just keeps singing, right through his gritted teeth, and I can't bear
it."

The positive attitudes of the wounded men continued to amaze the
nurses. Not a one would complain about some discomfort or incon-
venience when they worked with men who had experienced the vilest
things yet carried on as if it were another day on the farm.

We continued to serve mainly British soldiers, with some Canadians
and Australians and the occasional American. The combination led
to humorous rivalries and practical jokes. I saw an American sur-
reptitiously pour out a Brit's tea and replace it with coffee, which was
spit out as if it were poison. The Brits loved to mock the Americans'
accent, which made everyone laugh. A multinational group of amputees
gathered each day for a card game, sometimes placing a prosthesis on
the table to up the ante.

With Fred's blessing, I convinced Colonel Fife, the unit commander,
to allow us to rearrange the patient receiving process. We had waited
long enough; the British were gone, and it was time to implement
our own methods. I proposed we take the most critical cases straight
to the X-ray room, with those walking or not needing X-rays going
to the bathhouse. Once they were medicated for pain, cleaned up,
and treated for vermin such as lice, we dressed them in blue pajamas

and transferred them to the *salle de triage*, which soon became known simply as triage.

In triage, as I saw in France, the surgeon would do a quick examination, then the soldier was either assigned a bed, sent to the operating theater, or transferred to another hospital. This prevented much of the disruption of the wards and, more importantly, ensured the most critical patients were seen sooner.

This worked rather well, but still the process took too long, and we sometimes lost men whilst they waited for the surgeon. We had five surgeries in process in the theater and three more surgeons working at bedsides. Nearly half needed to be resting or seeing to their own needs. This left only three to do triage, and with sometimes hundreds of wounded men arriving in an evening, they were quickly overwhelmed.

I attended a weekly medical staff meeting chaired by Fred, who headed up the medical side, Colonel Fife, the overall commander of the unit, and the chief of surgery, Dr. Valentine. They were all quite a bit older than me and of course physicians, and they seemed to politely listen to my ideas, even if they didn't value them as much as those from someone with an MD after their name.

"Let this meeting come to order. Miss Stimson, ladies first." Tall, slightly balding Fred was of course my favorite. He made every effort not to show any undue emotion toward me, barely looking up at me as he opened the meeting and invited me to speak.

"Our first concern, as we complete the transition to wholly American staff, is how best to utilize their precious time. I have come up with a plan, therefore, to that end." I passed around a diagram I had drawn for each of them. "Gentlemen, our triage plan is a great improvement and has no doubt already saved lives."

"Here, here," Dr. Valentine said. The short, robust man with perpetually smudged eyeglasses banged his coffee cup.

"But I think we can do better," I continued. "In my diagram, you'll see I have moved some of the process to staging areas in the field."

I shifted in my seat in discomfort as the silence while they reviewed my diagram went on too long to be good news. There was some coughing and throat clearing, but it seemed no one wanted to be the first to throw darts at my idea.

Colonel Fife tapped the diagram. "As the only regular army officer here, I need to point out a few things. Miss Stimson, you have good intentions but perhaps not the first notion of the situation at the battlefront."

The other doctors stifled a chuckle.

"Are you aware that the first persons to treat our wounded are often under fire themselves? Do you understand they may be working with shells exploding only feet away? Their vision is half-blinded by gas or even just by the gas mask covered with the splatter of dirt and blood and who knows what. It is all they can do to get them to a train or ambulance without getting shot themselves. And now you want them to play doctor as well? One of the gravest mistakes the British made was sending their physicians to the front."

I stood, thankful for my excessive height and booming voice. "I'm asking no such thing. What I suggest is enhancing the staging areas, out of the range of artillery, where we can give further care and assessment before sending the wounded on to the hospitals. The medic who delivers the wounded to the transportation area would pass on just a word or two regarding the injury so that a tag can be made for each man. Something like 'right arm, tourniquet' or 'mustard gas, no mask.' Maybe some color-coded tags would make the identification easier and quicker. Then the medics can get back to their units, and the station takes over."

"Bottom line, Miss Stimson, is we don't have control over the battlefield," Fred offered in his quiet, calm way. "Nor do we want it."

"I concur." Colonel Fife tapped a finger on the diagram. "We cannot control where we have no jurisdiction."

"Then maybe we need to go where we are needed. A team, say a doctor, a nurse, and an orderly, rotating out to staging areas. These areas exist already, no? The CCSs, and also the points where the trains are loaded. From what I have heard, a tremendous amount of responsibility is laid upon a single nurse, who must decide in an instant who gets evacuated and who is beyond help. I think we can do better. And I propose to be the first nurse so assigned."

"Have you lost your mind completely? Do you have too many nurses and orderlies on your hands? Our surgeons are extremely short-staffed as it is, and you propose having them traipse out to within miles of an ever-changing front, taking up more time and, dare I say it, exposing them to all sorts of hazards?" Colonel Fife tossed the diagram aside.

"We have asked for reinforcements." Fred tapped his pencil. "Miss Stimson may have a point here. We have three surgeons, who could be operating, tied up in triage. With quicker evaluation, we could further eliminate the cases that come here that should go elsewhere and perhaps treat them in the field instead of making the long trip to the hospital."

"You'll never get the field commanders to agree."

"Soldiers returning to battle after a quick stitch-up? Medics able to rejoin the units more quickly? I should think the commanders would welcome the idea." Fred broke from his usual formality to give me a wink.

Colonel Fife, if hardened by years of fighting wars, was still a thoughtful man. "Very well then. We'll send the proposal up the chain."

The answer from the field was something along the lines of "What are you waiting for?"

Benjamin, the ambulance driver, hailed from Manchester. He was to be on the last trip back to "Blighty," as the Brits called their homeland. He came to me the day before the transport, his hair trimmed and neatly parted down the middle, dressed in a fresh if two-sizes-too-large uniform.

"Allo, Matron, could I have a word before I go?"

I was explaining to an orderly how to sort units of blood by type and date but excused myself. I held back a sigh. It seemed I was forever being interrupted with a million small things and barely had a chance to do anything useful. But Benjamin had proven a trustworthy helper, somehow appearing just as he was needed and always wearing a gap-toothed smile.

I led us to the nearly empty mess tent, where there was always a pot of coffee. "So you'll be heading to Manchester in the morning. Whatever will we do without you?"

"That's just it, ma'am. I don't want to go back." He poured us both a cup of coffee. I was becoming rather fond of the robust aroma; it was fresher and stronger than the watery stuff brewed back home.

"I admire your dedication, Benjamin. But it wouldn't be fair to keep you here longer. It's been what, two years already?"

"Three, or nearly that long. But I've got nothing to go home to and hope they'll let me stay on with you Americans. My life is here, and I've never felt better or more useful."

That saddened me. I couldn't imagine a life where wartime duties seemed a better alternative than home. "Why have you come to me? It's not my decision."

"Was hoping you'd put a word in. Several of us limeys will be staying back."

"True, but they're supply chiefs and administrators and such. And we've already sent for a new driver from St. Louis." Although I had always enjoyed Benjamin's company, I knew his replacement. In fact, I had requested Ned, the ever-helpful clerk, and he had readily agreed.

"Please, Matron. I can do anything. Carpentry, plumbing, electric. I built my own house, I did. What's one more bloke left behind?"

All those skills would surely be useful. We frequently used German prisoners for construction and repairs, which always made me uneasy.

I stood up and gathered our cups. "I'll see what I can do."

The next morning, I was barely dressed and still shaking off the nightmares of a restless night when there was a knock at my door. It was Benjamin, holding a steaming cup of coffee in one hand and a wool coat in the other.

"Top of the morning, Matron. Thought you'd want a cuppa. Seems we have an assignment."

"Am I going back to Blighty with you?"

He chuckled as he set the coffee down on a table. "No, ma'am. You're stuck here with me. And I've a request from the commander to take you to town. Part of the bargain."

A week earlier, I had requested and was granted permission to go into town. "I planned to take a bicycle. We certainly can't spare a truck just for me and my errands."

He took my coat off the hook next to the door and held it open for me to slip into. "Orders are orders, ma'am."

There was something about his bright cheeriness so early in the morning that annoyed me. But I donned the coat, grabbed the coffee, and followed him out to the truck he had left running.

We bumped along the country road in the Ford until we reached Rouen proper, where the cobblestone streets were smoother.

"Have the roads always been this bad?" I asked. As far as I knew, we weren't in an area that had been attacked.

"Road maintenance isn't high priority. And this area is pretty good by comparison. When I was up in Belgium, I saw soldiers get hit and fall over face-first in the mud because of the heavy pack on their backs." He glanced at me. "We couldn't get them out, because we'd get stuck ourselves and shot to pieces. Those guys didn't die from being shot. They drowned in the mud."

Horrified by this, I remained silent for several minutes, just staring as the countryside went by. Finally, Benjamin broke the silence. "You'll never guess how I managed to avoid trench foot."

"Do tell."

"Where I grew up, there were quite a few pig farms. Outside the slaughterhouse, we could pick up all manner of offal for free. A favorite thing was pig bladders."

"Of course they were." I laughed. Benjamin seemed to have a story for any occasion.

"They're like tough balloons, you see. We'd blow them up and tie them off. Then use them to play football."

"Oh, like our pigskin football."

"Nah, way better. Lighter, but water- and airtight."

"And this helped with trench foot?"

"Back when there were still pigs in the area, I collected a few bladders, just like I did back home. Cleaned them out, then stretched them over my socks before putting on my boots. Kept my feet nice and dry."

"Quite the ingenious use. Did you share it with anybody?"

"Nah, not enough to go around." He stared at his hands. "Guess that wasn't right of me."

Oh no. Now I had made him feel badly. "No, it was perfectly right to do."

Whatever regret he had was short-lived, and his mood suddenly brightened. "What's your pleasure, Matron? A little nip?" Benjamin mimed taking a drink as we passed a café-bar.

"I wouldn't mind, but my first task is a patisserie. Or whatever they call a bakery."

"That depends on what you want. A pastry? Then we're off to the patisserie. Bread? I know a boulangerie just on the next corner."

"How about croissants?"

"Ah, then I suppose either will do."

"Then let's go to the boulangerie. The nurses say the dark bread the British served was once used as the struts on a carriage wheel."

The baker, after Benjamin's introduction and my flailing attempts at speaking French, insisted on kissing both of us on each cheek, a thorough handshake, and for me a lingering, teary hug. Knowing flour was strictly rationed, I kept my order to the minimum, so that each of my nurses and orderlies would get one half of a croissant and a nice slice of bread.

But the baker wouldn't hear of it, filling a box with twice as much, then heading into the back room for what I presumed was his special stash.

Benjamin shared my description of the British dark bread, and they both had a good laugh. Then the baker wrote down what appeared to be days of the week and the hospital location—Champs de Courses.

"What is he saying?" I nodded toward the notepaper.

"He will begin deliveries next week."

My eyes widened. This was sure to set the dietitian in a tizzy. But she now reported to me. It might mean less budget for tinned meat, but I was willing to make that sacrifice. I took a bite of a croissant, which melted in my mouth like a cloud in heaven, the buttery flakes no doubt coating my lips. When I could manage to speak again, all I could say was "Lovely."

CHAPTER 8

August 1917

T he nurses had water pitchers, basins, and buckets in their huts for washing up. But the only hot water came from an oil stove in the mess tent. We would fill hot water bottles for our beds on cool nights, then use the water from the bottles for washing up in the morning.

But for convenience and time saving, I kept a towel and bar of medicinal soap in a supply tent near the mess tent. As it was near the oil stove, it was warmer than my bedroom, so I did my tidying up there.

Just in case someone had time for the luxury, at the end of the supply tent was a cast iron bathtub, its white enamel chipped and one foot missing. It looked rather like an old, listing ship, and one of the Brits had dubbed it the HMS *Old Sorry*.

Sometimes, if the line at the men's bath hut grew too long, we would give a patient a bath in it, filled pitcher by pitcher from the mess tent tank. This created a moment of slightly panicked confusion when a patient heard he was going to Old Sorry.

I avoided special treatment due to my position but made an exception for my stowed towel and special soap. I hung a board with my name on the door for privacy when I was using the hut for a quick wash up.

One evening, undressed and wrapped in a blanket, I arrived at the supply hut only to find my soap was missing. I fumed and uttered a few expletives probably heard in half the camp.

Afterward, I announced at evening report that the soap needed to be returned in the blink of the eye of a newt, or that was what they would be having for dinner.

What the nurses didn't know and I hadn't the nerve to tell them was that I needed the soap for medicinal purposes, as I feared a relapse of ulcers on the skin of my legs. The condition that caused me to be hospitalized when I met Annie Goodrich was always a threat and worse during conditions of stress. I had to maintain strict antiseptic procedure if I wanted to keep on my feet.

෴

The following day, the cake of strong-smelling soap had returned, only slightly the worse for wear. Along with it, my name board had been replaced with the one for HMS *Old Sorry*. I laughed it off, but it made me think. It was a challenge, in this leadership position, especially in this far from home and difficult environment, to know how much of myself to share with my nurses. Too much, and they might lose a certain mystery and respect for a superior. Too little, and it could breed an emotional distance that hindered a good working relationship.

I decided to keep my old, scarred legs to myself and let them think I was just a bit batty, if not mysterious.

෴

Captain Ernst rushed up to me during dinner, a letter flapping in his hand. I had started to take my meals in the officers' mess under the grandstand rather than with my nurses. More to give them some privacy from me than any need of mine.

"She's coming!"

"Who?" I wiped my hands on a serviette before accepting the letter.

"Miss Curie. Oh, isn't it wonderful? She taught the classes in Paris. Just a young girl, really, but whip smart. You will love her."

"I think someone here already does." I winked.

I thought I saw just a hint of color warm the normally stoic man's cheeks.

"She's half my age. Tease all you want, but she's coming, let's see…" He pulled at the paper in my hand and pretended to look for something. "Ah yes, the eighth of August."

"Well, how lovely." I glanced at the letter. "She wants to 'review the mobile X-ray techniques and is most interested in the captain's ideas of shielding workers.' Hmm, isn't that interesting?"

He snapped the letter out of my hand. "Well now, we'll explain how that all came about when she's here, of course."

"No need. How are the new walls coming along?" We had carpenters build a new wall around the X-ray room, with a space between the front and back of them. I was collecting extracted bullets and shell casing fragments from the operating theater, cleaning them up, and giving them to the captain. He then used them to supplement the pieces of lead shielding he could get from supply to pour into the wall space.

"Filling up nicely, I should say. I can't wait to show her. And your idea of keeping new arrivals on their own stretchers was brilliant. Much more comfortable for them and sped up our process considerably."

"I'm so glad." Mentally, I put a check mark on my side of the favors column.

As promised, Irène Curie arrived early on the morning of the eighth. We had been alerted by wireless and rushed out to greet her. A rather large truck pulled into our compound. It was a panel truck, with the words "Service de Voiture Radiologue" painted on it, along with the Red Cross symbol. A young woman popped out of the driver's seat, wearing a white dress with a white cap, rather like a nun's.

"That's her!" Captain Ernst hurried over to the truck.

They double kissed in the European fashion and expressed a string of rapid French I had no hope in understanding, although it was clear they were happy to see each other. While they went on, another woman appeared, having apparently come around the truck from the passenger's side.

Miss Curie took the arm of the older woman. "Captain, look who I have brought along. Meme, meet Captain Ernst, and—" Miss Curie finally noticed me.

I gasped, recognizing the older woman from photographs. The wiry, unruly, graying blond hair, the deep, closely set gray eyes that seemed to hide the world's secrets. It was Madame Curie herself.

I lost all sense of decorum and rushed over to the trio. "I am Julia Stimson, the chief matron here. Welcome. Oh, thank you for coming. Can we help you with your things? How was your trip? I'm sorry my French is not worthy to speak." I couldn't seem to stop gushing.

"No need. We speak perfect English," Madame Curie said with a distinct Eastern European accent.

"Or Polish, German, Russian—" Irène added.

"Hush, child. We do not speak Russian. You—" She pointed a chapped finger at the captain. "Get the box from the back. Be careful. It is heavy."

This was going to be interesting. Madame Curie had a reputation for being cold; indeed Einstein was quoted as saying she had the emotions of a herring. But Irène was warm and pleasant, chattering on as she took the captain around to the back of the truck.

I traipsed behind when Captain Ernst led the Curies to his X-ray lab.

He took on a formal tone as he demonstrated his moveable X-ray tube. "With my foot, I can press the lever and move the equipment precisely ten centimeters. In this way, we can triangulate the object, determining its exact location in the body. Of course, not as sophisticated as the moving pictures you perfected, Irène, but this works well for our purposes and saves on photographic plates. We do a double exposure, so one plate per object."

"Before this, the surgeons were causing more injury with their explorations," I said.

Madame Curie gave me a withering look and a bit of an eye roll. Of course, she would have been well aware of this, having brought X-rays to the battlefield. *I must be more careful of what I say to her*, I chastised myself.

Then, the captain showed the ladies the additional shielding we had put into place for the machine operator, the patient, and anyone else nearby. To my surprise, Madame Curie dismissed it all with a wave of her hand.

"If you do your job quickly and efficiently, there should be no need for all this. Why, my Irène has performed thousands, perhaps tens of thousands of these types of procedures. Burns from radioactivity are evident within fifteen days. And see for yourself, she is perfectly fine."

"But, Meme, this will not be so with the new radon gas cylinder. The half-life—" Irène said.

"Yes. This is so. Perhaps the doctor is a man in front of his time." Madame Curie nodded toward the wooden box that the captain had set on a chair.

He had looked silly as he staggered under the weight, despite it being smaller than a bread box. "That must weigh eighty pounds. Lead lined, I presume," said the captain.

"Indeed. We have brought you a most precious gift. Radon gas," Madame Curie said. "I have captured this with great care over time from naturally radioactive rocks. It will replace the air in the cylinders. We have found this obtains much clearer pictures, with far less exposure time." To me, she added, "I hope this will put your concerns to rest."

I glanced at Captain Ernst. It seemed he communicated more than he had let on.

Soon, Madame Curie tired of the lesson and requested a quiet place to rest.

"Of course. Sorry for not offering this sooner, after your long journey." I led her to my room, it being the quietest and most private available.

I pulled out a chair for her, but Madame Curie promptly stretched out on my bed, adjusted the pillow to her liking, and covered her eyes with her arm. I was a bit taken aback by this but soon recovered. This was a Nobel Prize–winning scientist after all. She could lie wherever she wanted. I was just about to step out of the room so she could rest when she spoke.

"Miss Stimson, isn't it?"

"Yes, Madame. But you may call me Julia."

"Miss Stimson, why are you here when you could be riding horses in Arizona?"

"I do not ride horses, Madame. I am a nurse. From New York."

"I thought you came from St. Louis."

So she knew. Was this some kind of game? As if in answer, she removed her arm from her eyes and laughed a rueful laugh.

"Ah, I love my adopted country more than my life. And we are grateful for the Americans coming to save us from the Boche. But somewhere, deep in the pit of our stomachs, is the fear of what we must pay in return." She turned toward me. "Is France to become an American colony, like India to Great Britain?"

"No, Madame. Americans are not the British. We do not take unwilling territory as colonies. We fought two wars against them for this very reason." Now my hackles were up. I could feel my arms prickling. "And the British are fighting for their own country, on your ground. I think your fears can be put aside."

"Thank you, my dear. Now I'd like a rest."

Dismissed from my own room, I wandered out, hoping I hadn't stepped on international relations or insulted a national treasure.

I did a quick round of the wards and checked in with Miss Taylor and my team leaders.

Miss Taylor fussed at me, scooting me out of the office like a misbehaving child. "Really, Matron. All is well here. Get yourself back to Madame Curie."

I didn't have the heart to tell her that our important guest was presently napping.

A quick look at my timepiece told me that Fred should be off duty. He had wanted to meet Madame Curie but had been in surgery all morning. I hurried over to his hut and knocked on the thin door.

"How did you know I was thinking about you?" He greeted me with a warm smile.

"Because you think of everyone, all the time. But I come with news."

"Good, I hope."

"It is. We now have radon gas for our X-ray machine. It is supposed to give us clearer pictures. I'm sure that will be of benefit to you for surgical cases."

"Interesting. And from where did this magic appear? It's not something we can order up from London on a whim."

"That's the best part. It was brought here by the Curies—Marie and her daughter."

"They came already? Why wasn't I informed?" His grin faded to a scowl.

"You were in surgery, but you haven't missed them. In fact, Madame is napping upon my bed at this moment."

"What? Is she unwell? Take me to her."

⟿

When Fred and I arrived back at my rooms, Madame Curie was up and helping herself to some biscuits from a tin sent to me from home. How excited my sister would be when she learned who had enjoyed her baking.

Madame Curie had apparently combed and repinned her curly hair into its bun. The nap seemed to have boosted her energy, as she flitted around like a little sprite. I introduced her to Fred.

"I'm most honored to meet you. And I hear you have brought a most wonderful gift of radon gas," he said.

"The pleasure is mine, dear sir. I only ask for a report of its usefulness every so often." She bit into the biscuit and nodded approvingly.

"Of course," Fred said.

"Yes, of course," I echoed him, then we looked at each other awkwardly. We both seemed to be rather awed by this little firecracker of a woman.

"So the two of you run this hospital now? I came when the Brits were still here. They built a fine reputation."

The way she narrowed her eyes at us, it seemed like we weren't quite measuring up. My feisty inner being couldn't resist a protest. "Major Murphy and Colonel Fife are in charge. And I assure you, that fine reputation will continue. In fact, we've made many improvements. For example, we're sending medical teams out to the CCSs..."

I was immediately sorry I had brought that up, having still not been allowed to go to a CCS.

Fred seemed to understand without me mentioning the sore point. "Soon, Julia will go herself," he said more to me than to Madame Curie.

"Of course, my dears." She looked from me to Fred and then me again, seeming to calculate something. "So tell me, how long have you known each other?"

Fred jumped in. "Oh, we go way back, Madame." He clapped me on the shoulder. "I've known Julia for what—six years now?"

Uncomfortable with his hand on my shoulder in her presence, I shrugged away.

"Hmm. I see." Madame Curie started packing her few belongings. "I'll be on my way. No need to see me out."

We bid her farewell, as she seemed in a sudden hurry to leave.

"She's a little odd, wouldn't you say?" I asked Fred after she was off.

"She has every right to be as odd as she desires. Most brilliant scientists tend to be."

But odd wasn't quite the right word. Something about her visit left a lump of lead in the pit of my stomach. I couldn't quite figure out why.

~

Our sweet and now official driver, Benjamin, had eyes for Charlotte. Somehow, this didn't sit right with me. I felt as if they were my much younger brother and sister. He and Ned, who had recently arrived in the country, had also become fast friends and were always eager to set off on errands together.

They both appeared in my door after a trip to the rail station to pick up mail and supplies. Ned, the American, in his olive drab uniform, and Benjamin in the British green khaki.

"A letter and a telegram, Matron," Benjamin said.

I opened the telegram first, a dispatch from London.

DOCTOR PHIL STIMSON CONSCRIPTED US ARMY

My younger brother. He had followed me to St. Louis and now

to the army and, inevitably, to war. I had encouraged the first but not the latter.

I hurried over to the office to see what else I could learn. I was able to use the telephone to gather a few pieces of information. It would take several months, but Phil would be joining the fight.

But things were further along than Phil had let on. The next morning, a "shave and a haircut" knock awoke me.

"Just a moment." I scurried to put a robe over my pajamas, run a brush through my hair, and scrub my teeth. Then I answered the knock. "Two bits."

Fred ducked his head through the door. "Sorry so early, but I thought you would want to see this straightaway." He waved a telegram ahead of himself.

"Do come in. I'm halfway decent."

"Good enough." He slipped through the door and into my sitting room, which was really just a sectioned-off part of my room with two upholstered chairs.

I lit the kerosene burner under my coffeepot. "Who is it from?"

"Dr. Philip Stimson. Your brother, I believe?"

"Phil! Yes, my younger brother." I rushed over to grab the telegram and ripped it out of the yellow envelope. "Oh God, don't tell me something terrible has happened at home."

I felt a warm hand rest on my shoulder.

J STOP ARRIVED LIVERPOOL STOP ON WAY TO FRANCE STOP
EXACT LOC UNK STOP P

"He's coming! Oh, I hope he will be close. Of course I wish he were staying safe at home. He's a children's doctor, so he must have volunteered."

"A family trait?" Fred turned toward the door. "Well, I'm glad he finally found a way."

"What do you mean?"

"Oh, uh…" He looked down sheepishly.

"A way to do what?"

He scratched under his nose. "Well, as he may have told you, he wanted to join Base Hospital 21, back in '16."

"He said he changed his mind. I'm confused. Why didn't he come with us then, instead of being assigned to a combat unit?" I felt anger rising in me, at both my brother and Fred. No doubt Fred foresaw my anger, which explained his reticence.

"I turned him down. We couldn't spare another resident. And he's a pediatrician, for God's sake."

"You? You made the decision yourself?" I shook the telegram in my hand. I had a strong feeling it was going to be followed by another telegram, with much worse news.

"I did. And it was the right one." He slammed his fist into his other hand. "We don't get to favor certain people, even when they have a tiger for a big sister."

Suddenly feeling foolish, standing there in my bathrobe and at the same time angry for no good reason, I bit my lips before I uttered words I'd later regret. Instead, I opened my door and waved him out.

❧

I received just a handful of letters from Phil as he was settling in on the Continent. He couldn't share where he was but assured me he was safe and happy. He had arrived in mid-August, and from the hints in his letters, I concluded he was not far away, probably up near Cambrai. In early September, we heard of a bombing at a CCS just north of us. Thankfully, I was too busy with the incoming wounded to spend very much time worrying about Philip. Otherwise, I would have done nothing else.

CHAPTER 9

September 1917

E ach day, I received a pile of mail with a combination of hope and dread. It was always a happy sight when a package arrived, whether intact with brown paper and string or in a broken heap inside a canvas bag. We had started to encourage all our benefactors to send their precious gifts inside some muslin, as the long journey wore straight through cardboard and paper.

But I always sorted through the most likely happy pieces, searching for any word from Philip. On the morning of September 8, I found not the letter from my brother that I was hoping for but a letter from a chaplain from the No. 3 Canadian General Hospital. I held the envelope a moment, hoping it contained happy news regarding the ongoing recovery of patients we had sent there. But something about it seemed ominous.

Then I spied another letter from that unit. This one's return address was for a lieutenant colonel. My heart started thumping, and I eased into a chair before reading.

Dear Miss Stimson:

This note is on behalf of your brother, who was admitted today into this hospital, slightly wounded in the muscles of the back by shrapnel.

There is no cause for alarm. He will be sent on to the base after a short treatment...

Hurriedly and with my vision narrowing into a tunnel, I opened the letter from the lieutenant colonel. It provided a bit more detail:

...the piece of shell entered his back just below the right scapula in a slanting direction. I sent him on to a CCS and am advising him to try to get down to your hospital.

Yes! It seemed he was well enough to travel, or would be soon. Of course, he must come to our hospital, where I could look after him personally and ensure he got the best of care.

I adored my younger brother. I had encouraged him to become a physician when it was clear I could not. He had both a wacky sense of humor, subject to performing practical jokes, and a tender heart. When he thought he might have hurt someone's feelings with one of his antics, he apologized profusely.

Oh, how I missed my talks with him. He had a way of breaking through the clouds of complex issues and seeing a clear path ahead.

The colonel concluded with:

He has proven himself a good officer whilst with me, and I am very sorry to have to lose him, as we rarely get them back once they go to the base. I greatly regret that this has happened.

The breath went out of me as if I had been punched in the stomach. *Oh my God.*

I grabbed both letters and sped out the door toward Fred's office. I burst in without knocking. He was filing paperwork into a briefcase.

"Julia! Come to see me off? I don't leave until—"

"Oh, must you leave? I've just gotten word." I offered the letters. "It's Phil. He's been injured in a raid on his hospital."

"That's quite disturbing. How badly is he injured?" He continued to pack his bag, which seemed uncharacteristically insensitive to me. Finally, he stopped and took the letters.

Fred shuffled between the letters. "This is normal protocol. He's injured, that's all."

A small wave of relief washed over me. "How bad do you think it is?"

"Not life threatening. He was hit by shrapnel. I don't have to tell you how common this is and how well the men usually do."

"But it went down his back. What about his spine?"

"I presume he's moving arms and legs. They'll have to open him up of course, to remove the shrapnel and drain the channel. It will be a long, painful recovery."

"Where is this hospital? Can we bring him here?"

"Up in Étaples, near the Sick Sisters Hospital."

"I must go at once."

"I don't advise that. There's been some unrest up there, riots in fact, and that's in addition to an enemy attack. I wouldn't be surprised if they send him to Blighty."

"Then I'll go there."

"Julia, you can't just run off like you're going to save him."

"Miss Taylor can run things for a few days. Certainly, you understand that I need to be with him." I was already packing my bags in my head.

"Of course she can, but that's not the point. We have to wait for him to be dispositioned appropriately. Let them get him through surgery, wherever that might happen, in the best and most timely place possible."

"The best place is right here, with the people we know and trust. Not somewhere else, where he is just another casualty."

"Again, I'm sorry it didn't work out for your brother to be assigned with us. But now, you need to have more faith. He's going to be fine. Do you give inferior care to patients you don't know personally?"

Chastened, I relented. "Fine, but when he is stable, I want your word that you will help bring him here for recovery. How many others have the opportunity to convalesce with loved ones nearby?"

The next few days were spent chasing down where exactly Phil was and finding a way to get him to us. The commander of the Cleveland unit was very helpful in locating him at the No. 20 General Hospital in Étaples.

I was able to get through to No. 20 by telephone but was distressed to learn that they were preparing to send Phil back to England. With every fiber of my being, I knew I must have him there with me. He had the sort of wound that could easily be ignored as non-life-threatening among so many that were. But it was also the sort very likely to get infected without careful observation, and it extended dangerously close to his spinal column.

I badgered poor Colonel Fife until he agreed to work on bringing my brother to us if he was well enough to travel. He was also gracious enough to allow me two days leave to travel up to visit him, along with a doctor to evaluate and treat him if needed on the trip. This was especially considerate of him, as he had steadfastly refused my requests to go to a CCS due to my critical duties in the unit.

But those were tense days in the coastal area of northwestern France. I sat in the telegraph office as cables came in. They were calling for all available military police to rush to Étaples. Then there were orders that no one would be allowed to enter or leave the area from

Boulogne to Camiers. I asked the young soldier manning the telegraph machine what this was all about.

He shrugged his boyish shoulders. "Some sort of riot goin' on, ma'am. That's a bad place up there. They say if they don't kill you in the hospital, they'll be sure to kill you the next day on the training grounds."

"You mean the prisoners? Are they treating prisoners that badly?" I thought back to the horror stories regarding the German camps. "Surely, the British are better than that."

"Oh, it's not the prisoners that are bad off. It's the new recruits that get sent there to toughen up, and the wounded, fresh out of the hospital, being readied for battle again. They run them ragged, double-timing on the sand dunes while firing shots over their heads. I hear they beg to be sent back to the front.

"So a few got mad enough to stage a protest. Then the police came in and started shooting. Killed a French woman, I hear. Or maybe just wounded her." He shrugged his shoulders again.

His nonchalant tone confused me. How much was true and how much was rumor, I couldn't fathom. But I did know I had to get Phil out of there.

Colonel Fife appeared in my office door. "Good news. We have a man who needs to go up to the British Hospital for Chinamen."

"I'm not sure that's good news for him." Word had spread that Egyptians and Chinese were not being treated as well as soldiers with lighter skin. It was disturbing to me that soldiers on the same side would be treated poorly. As if fighting this war against a ruthless enemy weren't bad enough. "Why would it be good news for us?"

"Because he needs to go in the direction of Camiers. That's where—"

There was no need for him to explain further. I was on my feet in an instant. "Phil. We can get past the road blocks and rescue Phil!"

"Precisely. You, one of the doctors, and a driver can get going tomorrow. I'll let you choose who."

Of course, my first choice was to travel with my favorite doctor, Fred. But as he was off with the traveling surgical team, it was Dr. Valentine who accompanied me. Our relationship had not started on the best foot, and I thought we could get to know each other better on the drive. And of course, I chose Benjamin as our driver for the trip, totaling nearly 250 miles.

We dropped off our Chinese patient, then had a lovely drive up to the coast. Dr. Valentine proved a delightful conversationalist. He was enamored of Philadelphia, where he had trained, and insisted we stop and visit with the Philadelphia unit. I was only too happy to meet with them, as I had kept in touch with their chief nurse, Miss Dunlop, since sailing with them on the *Saint Paul*. Dr. Valentine, Miss Dunlop, and I teased one another over which was the better city to live in, Philadelphia or St. Louis. For every park or museum I could mention, they would name two.

After the quick visit, we were back on the road, continuing our spirited conversation. It seemed surreal, speaking of grand American cities while motoring through France, passing green pastures and intermittent peeks at the Atlantic Ocean. If it weren't for the occasional bombed-out village and too-skinny people guiding too-skinny cows, I might have imagined I was on holiday.

Upon entering Étaples, it was clear that something had changed. There were military police at every street corner and barricades blocking off many roads and hospital entrances. When we were stopped, Benjamin showed our authorization papers, and we were let on our way with warnings of possible escaped and dangerous soldiers. Carefully, we picked our way up to Camiers.

It was dark by the time we arrived, and if it hadn't been for Benjamin's excellent eyesight, we would have never found the hospitals.

"The Boche, those bastards, bombed the hospitals. They have airplanes that can fly at night now. So no outside lighting is allowed," Dr. Valentine said.

Without a lantern, we had to hold hands and thread our way down a narrow path to the hospital tents. We arrived at a hospital that had been taken over by a unit from Chicago. The chief nurse insisted we join them for dinner, and we could hardly refuse. They were eager to show us around, but I rudely kept inquiring as to my brother.

It turned out he was in the British hospital next door, and we were taken to him by the commanding officer himself, once again stepping into the forbidding darkness.

"Watch your step now. Crater on the left."

There was no crater to be seen in the black velvet air, but I imagined it a huge, gaping hole in God's earth, created by a force of evil in an otherwise peaceful place.

Phil was in a tent with other doctors who had been injured in the attack on his unit, along with some who were injured in the aerial raid on the hospital. He was sitting up in bed, pillows carefully arranged about him so as to avoid his wound.

"There's my girl," he said, as cheerily as if I had just popped over to watch him play baseball.

Joy and relief at once filled my heart. He had not the hollow-eyed look of the typical men who came to No. 12, but then, he had only been in theater about a month.

I leaned over to kiss his cheek. He was clean shaven, and I detected no fever.

"I've come to kidnap you. We're quite short of pediatricians at the moment."

"Well, you've got me." He held up his pale, freckled hands. "Sorry not to be a surgeon like your friend here." He nodded toward Dr. Valentine. I was sure Phil was using the term *friend* facetiously. I had complained to him in letters more than once about how Dr. Valentine was a thorn in my paw. "But you know I'm becoming quite the expert on infectious disease," Phil said.

This piqued Dr. Valentine's interest. "Are you now? With any luck, maybe they'll let us keep you."

"Well, I don't get to decide these things, but I wouldn't mind an assignment where I can check up on my big sister."

"After you recover, of course," I broke in. "Are you up for a road trip? Your medical officer says you are clear to travel if you choose." I hesitated, trying to frame my face and voice in as neutral tone as possible. This would need to be his decision. "That is, if you want to go and can bear the pain." I had noted him wincing with each small movement. I was beginning to doubt that a long, bumpy drive would be the best thing for him. But certainly, our hospital was in a safer area, and he would be with me. "We can make you as comfortable as possible, but—"

"They have treated me splendidly here. No question. But I'm ready to go with you right now."

Dr. Valentine tried to gently dissuade him, seemingly wanting to ensure he really wanted to go. "We'll be staying the night. Take the time to think about it."

"Yes, sir, but if you know my sister at all, you know what the answer will be." He flashed a grin at me. Oh, how wonderful it was to see that.

⚜

The next morning, I hurried to see Phil first thing. He was already up in a chair, and an orderly was helping him to dress. His bed had been stripped and his belongings neatly arranged on the floor.

"So I take it you haven't changed your mind?"

"What the hell. You could probably use some supervision."

I took his hand. It felt cool. "No fever this morning? Has the medical officer released you?"

"They've already called for a stretcher."

Indeed, two men were carrying a stretcher toward us. It took another orderly and myself to get Phil onto the stretcher, as he could barely support his own weight. But soon we were off in the ambulance, headed back to Rouen.

⌐☛

We arrived at suppertime, and thankfully the hospital had not been too busy in our absence. Colonel Fife had a bed for Phil ready in an empty tent. He was well settled with many pillows to keep him comfortable and books and puzzles to keep him entertained. It felt like a weight had been lifted from my shoulders, having him safe and where I could keep an eye on him. If I did nothing else in this war, I would see my brother through as best I could.

CHAPTER 10

October 1917

O ur lull of admitting injured men did not last long. In the waning days of September and early October, we started receiving one hundred to two hundred injured each night. During the day, I worked in the office with supply requisitions, communications, payroll, leave approvals for my nurses, and on and on. We had a secretary assigned to us, and this was a most welcome relief, as she could type like the wind. My assistant, Miss Taylor, had been with me all along and could perform all these tasks in my absence.

After supper was when the ambulances usually showed up. The receiving tents were now well ordered, and I no longer needed to supervise there. But on many nights, there were dozens of men needing surgery. Most of it was minor, the removing of shrapnel from every imaginable body part. I would scrub up and assist when the caseload was especially heavy. Although new nurses had arrived, we also had several away at the contagious hospital with diphtheria.

As the caseload increased and the nurses became more experienced, they took on more and more tasks. In surgery, they were no longer simply handing over the sterilized implements. After much observation and practicing on fruit, my nurses were inserting drains and suturing as well. This meant the surgeon could move on to the next piece of shrapnel much more quickly.

On nights with heavy arrivals, the problem became what to do with the patients who were awaiting surgery. Dr. Valentine came to me while I was making rounds in a tent with our postoperative patients. Each tent had from fourteen to thirty beds, but not all of them were occupied.

"We need to start using these beds for the men in receiving. We've run out of beds there."

"You can't bring them here. They are still in their filthy uniforms, they are unstable, and we are not staffed to take care of their needs."

"Well then, get staffed. Do you want us to put them two or three to a bed because you're fussy about pajamas?"

"This is not about fussiness. This is a clean, postop area. And if you fill it with preop patients, where will they go postop?"

"Back to the same damn bed."

"Doctor, we have a logical flow here. If you disturb this, it will cause confusion and contamination." I knew by instinct that his plan wouldn't work. But I couldn't just refuse to help the situation. "Let's go together to the receiving area. I'm sure if we put our heads together, we can figure something out."

❧

A quick look at the overloaded receiving area and I could see Dr. Valentine's point. There were patients lying on stretchers on the cold ground outside where the ambulances left them when they had to move on. There were patients sitting on the rough wooden floor, some sitting back-to-back to support each other.

But I could readily see a solution. There were connecting tents that led from the receiving area to the operating tents. We could line the floors with blankets to keep out some of the cold and dampness, then file stretchers along the floor on either side. We could tag each position so we could readily find the patient when he was next for surgery. Excited to have a clear idea, I went to explain it to Dr. Valentine, but he had already departed. Just as well. Now I could implement the idea without hearing his objections.

The next day, Miss Taylor and I were running up and down the lines of stretchers, checking the identities and conditions of each of the men, when Dr. Valentine marched up, his face reddened, and the worst sign, a vein on his forehead bulging.

He reached Miss Taylor first. "Who did this?"

"Good morning, Dr. Valentine," she said pleasantly. I needed to learn how to keep him from getting under my skin like she did.

She attempted to show him her clipboard. "All is in order, as you can see—"

But he was having none of it. He looked squarely at me. "Miss Stimson, why are our patients strewn about like pieces of litter?"

"You would rather have them outside in the elements? Or sent to the hospital for German prisoners? Because those are our alternatives."

"Oh indeed." He bent down to check the tag on a nearby soldier, who was somehow sleeping through this. "And who has given approval?"

"Let's see. Major Murphy, London, and oh, I just got this dispatch from Red Cross headquarters in Paris—"

My evil twin was once again in evidence. The Red Cross dispatch was received before we had started the new system, and they were actually requesting ideas to help with the crowding problem, not approving it. But I knew Dr. Valentine, who had had many trips to Paris for meetings, would be swayed by anything they said.

I had offered to represent the hospital myself at those meetings, not only because I wanted to go myself, but to save him the time, but my offer was always declined. It was control that he didn't want to give up. Plus, well, it was Paris. No one passed up a trip to the City of Lights.

"Well, fine. But don't make a habit of this, young lady." He stormed off, ignoring Miss Taylor's leap in the tight space to get out of his way.

❧

I finally had a chance to go to Paris when the American Red Cross arranged a meeting for all the chief nurses in France. Not only would I be able to spend a few days in a city I had only dreamed about but I would be meeting my colleagues, most of them for the first time.

After several days of drilling Miss Taylor on all she would need to do in my absence, with notes left everywhere and frequent drop-ins to her office and room, she was probably only too happy to see the day of my departure come.

I was hoping to go by boat, as the Seine, of course, would take me all the way to Paris. Alas, that was a rather circuitous route, and the train was much faster. We all arrived on the same day and met at the hotel. There were a dozen other chief nurses there. About half of us had been with the British, while the newer six had come over with the American soldiers.

We BEF-experienced nurses had to suppress our amusement when our newly arrived nurses exclaimed how busy they were becoming, with over a hundred patients! We were having double that number just in admissions each night. In the tents with the less critical patients, we had only one nurse and one orderly for up to one hundred patients.

We met in small groups and large, over tea and at breakfast. The new chiefs had so many questions, and we more experienced chiefs were only too happy to share all we had learned.

A curious topic, which I thought to be not at all pressing, took up an inordinate amount of thought and discussion. That was the policies regarding the nurses dancing and going out socially with the doctors or other men. The British nurses were not allowed to drink alcohol nor dance, and many of the American chief nurses had followed suit. I had left it up to my nurses, who had decided yes to dances and no to drinking in public. But as I related my policy to the new chiefs, there was clearly disagreement. Miss Dunlop from Philadelphia thought the nurses drinking in public in France was no problem at all. She even waggled her flask of her favorite whiskey while winking at me. Apparently, my shipboard hospitality had been more successful than I had thought.

Mrs. Christy, the matron from New York Presbyterian, was less enthusiastic. "Not all women can hold their liquor like Miss Dunlop. It would only take one incident to shed a bad light on us all."

"And what is wrong with dancing?" I asked.

They all mumbled and demurred. It seemed half of the group believed that since we were in France on the invitation of the Brits, we should follow their policy. The others, including me, thought each unit should make their own decision.

I thought we were spending too much time discussing it and tried to bring us to some sort of agreement. "Both issues seem to be a question of control rather than questions on social expectations or international relations. Certainly, the French had no qualms regarding drinking in public. But of course as guests in the country, we can't risk any behavior that would seem unruly," I said. "I let my nurses decide. I presented both sides of the issue. But they have given up so much, I don't want to be one to take away the little fun they have. But they decided on their own: dancing is allowed, but no drinking in public."

I was proud of my nurses' decision. Yet I had a moment of doubt when Miss Dunlop said, "It's fine for them to choose as individuals, but you must not let the nurses set policy. It hampers your ability to lead."

We finally agreed to disagree and to table the discussion until our next meeting. Another topic of concern was uniforms. We had all arrived with nicely made uniforms, but some of their attributes didn't match well to our situation, like the tall, peaked white caps that Nora and Dorothy had complained about and the lack of a light jacket or cape.

"We find the gray uniform to be superior to the white for its ability to hide all manner of stains," Miss Dunlop offered.

"I have to disagree," I said. "The point of the white is to identify us as nurses, important to patients who may not see well or who are confused. Furthermore, we should not be hiding stains. We should be cleaning them. Perhaps if we had a gray apron to wear over our whites, which could be changed during the shift as needed?"

This led to a cacophony of discussion, and I just sat back and enjoyed the fireworks.

The final decision was to make a list of requests to send to the American Red Cross headquarters in Washington.

I leaned over Mrs. Christy, who was scribbling in the chiefs' requests. "Can we ask for a lighter, shorter cape? The long blue ones are wonderful for cuddling in during the cold months, but I need something cooler that leaves my hands free. And how about red? Wouldn't that be stunning?"

All agreed, and a request for a short, red cape was added to the list, right up there with more roller bandages and sharper scissors. Nurses were obsessed with scissors.

"And how about a lower, softer cap? One that doesn't get knocked off every time a nurse enters a tent," I said.

There was a collective gasp. One does not lightly consider changing a cap.

"But it's our cap!"

"The one thing that ties us together..."

"It's how they know we're not British..."

"Write it down," I told Mrs. Christy. "Let's just see what they come up with."

We discussed much more than dancing and uniforms, of course. We shared all manner of tips for dealing with things as physically perplexing as caring for quadruple amputees to emotional challenges such as writing to families of the fallen. I think we all felt a sense of relief to be able to share these things with others in the same situation.

After a meeting to update us on all the wonderful things the American Red Cross was doing both stateside and in theater, we had a lovely reception at the Lyceum Club. The club had been started in London a few years back as a space for women of the arts and literature to gather and support one another, similar to the men's clubs they were excluded from. The Lyceum Clubs had caught on, and now there were several worldwide.

They fed us all manner of delightful treats, even lobster and thin, delicate little pancakes they called crepes. But I found myself longing for the simple rations of Base Hospital 21, which was now more home than was anywhere else. I missed my nurses and the constant swirl of activity, so after three days, I was eager to leave Paris.

The Paris train station was a huge affair, with long rows of metal and glass roof to let in the sunshine. Pigeons swooped and cooed at us and strutted around, picking up all manner of crumbs, a self-appointed cleanup team. I was lulled to sleep on the train ride, dreaming of a land of beautiful cathedrals and crepes and peaceful flowing rivers, with not a bomb or hospital tent in sight.

The British staff had warned us of the deep, bone-chilling cold that would descend upon us as winter fell over Rouen. Back in sultry June, it hardly seemed a pressing matter, but I did order plenty of wool blankets, sleeping bags, and some woolen underwear for my nurses. They were terribly scratchy at first, but we found with several washings with castile soap, they softened enough to be bearable.

When mid-October arrived and the nurses were already wearing their woolies night and day and still complained of cold, I knew we had a problem. Our wood-framed canvas tents did not hold in much heat. There had been plans for the engineers to make them into more proper wooden huts, but the construction was postponed several times. In the meantime, the deluge of rain that Rouen was known for began.

At first, it was pleasant, a nice steady rain that kept down the dust. The nurses ran out in it and collected rainwater to wash their hair. They said it made it softer and prevented lice. But after three days of steady storms, the enchantment had worn off. The soil in our area was fairly sandy, so at least we were spared the terrible thick mud that we heard swallowed entire farm tractors and trapped ambulances and soldiers alike.

But our lovely grassy areas were soon riddled with rivulets, and one could not venture outside without a heavy raincoat, rubber hat, and boots. Even so, we would still be entirely soaked down to our undergarments after a few minutes outside.

It was during this time that I started to have problems with my legs. Whether it was the rubbing of the woolies, the constant dampness, my lack of time and access to hot water to thoroughly cleanse them each night, or a combination of these, I wasn't sure. But ulcers opened up, first around my ankles, then climbing ominously up my lower legs. I knew before long they could get infected, so I cleaned and dressed them carefully and took my temperature each night.

I vacillated on whether I should consult one of the doctors. At home, I could be hospitalized, and they would clear up with attentive care. But here, the sores would be judged a liability. I simply had to take care of them the best I could.

I thought of Benjamin and his pig bladders. Could that possibly work for me?

I summoned him to my office and shut the door.

"I'm about to show you something quite disturbing, but you must not tell a soul. Do you understand?"

"Of course, Matron."

I brought a lamp closer. He might as well see exactly what we were dealing with. "This is not something new. It is what we call a chronic condition. It has happened periodically my whole life. But here, it presents a few more challenges."

He stood firm, arms across his chest. There wasn't much that shocked him anymore, I supposed. I raised the hem of my dress over one leg, the worst one. Then I peeled back the wooly, exposing roller bandage covering my entire lower leg. I removed the little metal clasp that held the end of the strip in place and slowly and painfully unwound the gauze.

I heard him gasp as the angry red skin and yellowing craters appeared.

"Good God, Matron. Why are you showing that to me? Have the doctors looked at it?"

"Remember you are sworn to secrecy. Trust me, I know more about the condition than do the doctors here, even though that isn't much. And I know how to treat it."

He stared at my legs with wrinkled brow, then at me, a questioning look in his eyes.

"They would simply send me home, you see. And I wouldn't go willingly." I started to wrap the bandage around my leg again. "I was thinking about the pig bladders you used for your trench foot. Seemed it was not only protective but perhaps therapeutic. I know if I can just get something between my skin and…"

"Say no more. I'll get you some."

In early November, the weather turned blustery. The last wisps of fall color were stripped from the trees, and they stood naked and vulnerable to the nightly frosts.

The moss-covered bell tents were slowly being replaced with wooden huts, but even they were little protection from the wind and cold. The small oil heaters barely kept temperatures inside above freezing. I fretted about what would happen when winter arrived.

I ordered more and better heaters and bargained for workers to install some sort of insulation, at least in the patient tents. Still, one early morning, Charlotte appeared at my door, her hands red and raw.

"I don't mean to complain, Matron, but I'm having difficulty. I need to introduce an intravenous needle, but find I have no feeling in my fingertips."

I took her hands in mine; they were two blocks of ice. "Charlotte, are you not wearing the fingerless gloves that have been knitted for us?"

"When I can. But that's not possible first thing."

"Why not?" I continued to inspect her hands. They were not just chapped. The swelling, red blotches, and blisters indicated chilblains.

"Because I have to thaw the IV bottles and water for the patients. I put them in water from the oil heater. My gloves would get all wet."

I closed my eyes and sighed. "I'll see about getting thick rubber gloves and more heat in the storage room. And I'm afraid I'll have to take you off ward duty until your hands heal."

"No, please, Matron. We're shorthanded as it is. I can't do that to my sisters or patients. I'll be more careful, I promise."

"You're a brick. But those blisters put you at risk for infection, and that wouldn't be good for you or your patients."

It soon became clear that even the woolen vests under our uniforms, woolen socks up to our knees, and fingerless gloves would not be enough to warm the nurses sufficiently.

I decided to go on a mission into town to search for more heaters.

I took Dorothy with me, as a good chance not only to catch up with how she was doing but to get reliable information about the rest of the nurses as well. They rarely complained, the dears, so I always wanted to head off trouble if I could.

She met me outside the grandstand at 9:00 a.m., the appointed time. Nearly as tall as I, she seemed to have the same problem with too-short sleeves. But hers had long white cuffs added to bring them to her wrists. She was rolling them up to fit under her coat.

"Night shift is the best shift for working," she said. "You have some quiet time, when you can actually get to know the patients. The docs aren't around so much, mucking things up."

I laughed. "That's true."

"But the worst part is adapting to the nonvampire world. Like Dracula and Miss Lucy, we have no power in daylight." She was quite the comical sight, with a broad-brimmed hat to protect her face from sunlight, her eyes appearing smaller behind her thick spectacles.

We had matching boots. Men's boots. When Dorothy bent to retie a bootlace, I commented, "Aren't we lucky to have feet big enough to wear these?"

"Gosh yes. Far sturdier than anything that can be found for women. The poor things with daintier feet wear out their soles in a week."

I had also taken to wearing puttees over my stockings. As if I didn't already resemble a man with my stature, wrapping my lower legs in these long narrow strips of cloth from my boots up to my knees didn't help the image. But they protected and supported my vulnerable legs, and I simply didn't care what others thought. It seemed Dorothy hadn't yet taken up the use of them, but she was sure eyeing mine.

Benjamin was waiting, along with Charlotte, who had asked for the day off. I had granted it, not knowing the reason why. This became quite apparent, as the two were very chummy with each other, exchanging glances when they thought no one was looking. The Ford was warmed up and ticking. Once the two others who were also doing errands in town arrived, we set off.

I always enjoyed the drive. We followed streetcar tracks up to the downtown. Along the way were many homes and shops, all built with a pleasant combination of stone and bricks. Sometimes the gray stone walls were accented with red brick, and sometimes it was the other way around. The windows were neat rectangles, sometimes with an eyebrow arch. The roofs were nearly all slate shingles. The structures seemed so stately and permanent, much unlike our own tent city. Perhaps that was a very good thing.

The small farms and houses soon gave way to narrower streets, filled with shops and cafes, as we entered the city center. Soon, we arrived at the quai, the flat area that ran along each side of the river. It was a busy area, with trucks loading and unloading the riverboats, fishmongers selling the day's catch, and people milling about, strolling along the river. The truck let us out here, and we dispersed to our separate duties. Dorothy wanted to buy a sewing machine for the nurses. "For sewing patches and alterations and such." She tugged on her sleeve cuff, which I could now see had been hand-stitched on.

"First, we must go to the bakery and coffee shop," I said. "If my favorite shopkeepers find out I came and didn't drop by, they'll be upset."

After having a treat and buying some to take back for the nurses, we wandered the narrow streets, which were paved with gray cobblestones mixed with red stone and brick. The nail heads on the soles of our boots made a distinctive tapping sound on the cobblestones, which frequently turned heads. We then got strange looks from the French, as they no doubt expected to see soldiers. Between the various hospitals and a supply depot, the city had had a large military population for several years now. I'm sure Dorothy and I presented another puzzle for them, as we towered over the petite mesdames. But they all smiled and nodded at us before huddling off, chattering and sniggering.

Dorothy, always a good sport, offered a group of children a closer look at her boots. How I wished I had a camera to capture the moment!

We found the supply store and ordered the stoves we needed. The buildings in that area were made mostly of limestone blocks. Many had ornate carvings around the windows. There were also many, seemingly the oldest ones, that were of the half-timbered style. Dormer windows popped out of the mansard roofs. Coal smoke puffed out of the brick chimneys, although it was a fairly mild day.

One stop we had to make was the cathedral. I had seen it from the road, but this was my first chance to go inside. I had no head covering with me, aside from my rain hat, and I hoped it would not offend. Upon entering, the soaring Gothic arches immediately lifted the spirits. The panels of stained glass were so detailed, it was apparent that each was telling a story, although we did not have time to figure them out. There were only a few silent worshippers, kneeling in the pews or lighting candles in front of the main altar or along the smaller side altars. They were all women, ghostly figures dressed in black, with dark veils on their heads.

In one of the naves, there was a choir of about a dozen men and women rehearsing. Their voices melded in beautiful harmony, as candles they held cast a warm glow on their faces.

As Dorothy wandered about, mostly admiring the marble statuary, I went to a pew and said a prayer.

Dear Lord, even in the midst of this terrible human tragedy, I feel your presence. I don't know why mankind continues to fight, or if we will ever learn to live in peace. Please grant me the courage, wisdom, and strength to continue this mission, on which I believe You have sent me. Amen.

After the cathedral, it was nearly time to start heading back to the quay, where Benjamin would be waiting for us. But I had one more stop I needed to make. One of my favorite streets, rue de Gros-Horloge, had a carved stone Renaissance archway going over and across it, with a slate-roofed building on top of the arch. The face of the building had a one-story-tall astrological clock. It featured a brilliant sun on its face against a blue background with stars, and a golden hand pointed to the golden Roman numeral hour. At the bottom of the face, rotating scenes represented each day of the week. Above the numbers was a sphere, representing the moon, that spun in coordination with its phases. I had never seen anything like it.

It seemed to be some kind of miracle that the beautiful city had not been bombed when so many had. It made me feel the loss, not just of so much human life but of history and culture. I was happy that so far, Paris had also been preserved.

As Dorothy and I stood, both staring at the wondrous clock, it seemed that her thoughts were similar to mine.

"Do you think it will survive the war?" She set down her packages. We were taking turns carrying the heavy sewing machine.

"It has survived since the fourteenth century, so we can be hopeful."

Fat rain drops began to fall, and as if orchestrated, black umbrellas popped up all around us. Knowing we would have too much to carry, neither Dorothy nor I had brought one. We ducked under the archway for cover and were treated to deeply carved scenes of shepherds and their flocks on its ceiling.

The rain only grew harder, and we prepared ourselves for a wet rush back to the quai. It was a fitting end to our little journey, a lesson to enjoy the beauty before it is suddenly taken away.

❧

Upon our return, I was still peeling off my wet outerwear when Fred appeared in my office door. There were also several nurses waiting in the hall to see Miss Taylor, whose office was next to mine.

"Shall I take a number?" Fred asked.

"Queueing is never necessary for you. Do come in." I led him to my small table. "Coffee?"

"That would be most welcome. But it's not just your fine brew for which I come."

I scooped the dark brown grounds into the percolator. The aroma alone could get me out of bed even on frigid mornings. "Why do I have the pleasure so late on a weekday? Has the war come to a glorious end, or at least paused for intermission?"

"It's good news and bad news. Good for you, I suppose, but bad for me." He produced his own coffee cup.

"Good news first, then." I took his cup and wiped off some drips.

"Your unceasing requests to be sent afield have been approved. Our unit's rotation to the CCS occurs in two weeks. The Wednesday before Thanksgiving, to be precise."

"That is good news." My mood brightened as I warmed myself by the coal stove. I hadn't noticed how chilled I had become during my journey. Manning the CCS was difficult, somber duty, but I needed to do it, not only for myself but as an example to my nurses. In addition, the firsthand look would give me much information. We had come far, but further streamlining of the process could only be a benefit to our soldiers. And they likely would be some of "our" soldiers, as Americans were increasingly in the fight. "And the bad news?"

"We are to have an extra surgeon, plus a nurse or two from the Australian unit meeting us there. It's to be sort of a demonstration of best practices to be used internationally. That's why you've been given the assignment, approved by God and Country."

"And Colonel Fife? That's hardly bad news." I opened a tin of biscuits, then adjusted the flame under the percolator. I could tell by the smell that the coffee was almost ready.

He rocked back in his chair as he accepted a biscuit. His mouth stretched into an evil grin. "Guess which surgeon has been assigned with you. Not his choice, I assure you."

The medical staff each popped into mind. I thought I had a good relationship with all of them, and none would hesitate to go. Except perhaps Dr. Valentine. But I didn't want to call him out. "Colonel Fife? He's so critical here…"

"No, he's not the unlucky one."

I poured two cups of coffee. "Unlucky to pull difficult and dangerous duty or to have to go with me?"

His grin told me it was the former; his phrasing was just a tease. "It's me. Colonel Fife said you could teach me a few things."

"And why is that bad news? Careful. I have boiling hot liquid at the ready."

"It's not ideal for us both to be gone at the same time. And because our little village would like nothing better than to have fodder for gossip, the two of us traveling together and working in close quarters. They're probably out there chatting about us right now. Not that I care, but you might." He glanced at the closed door. "As if such duty could ever be anything but hard work and emotional pain."

"And as if there were anything unseemly between the two of us." I didn't add how much I wished there were.

"There's another piece of news that may change things for you and me."

"Oh?"

"You know it's been a bit awkward for me, being the commander in reality while Colonel Fife is technically in charge."

I tried to remember indications of this. If there had been, I had been obtuse about it. "Actually, no. I'm afraid I had my head in the sand on that one."

"Well, that's good actually. It means we've managed to keep our infighting contained to the medical ranks. In any case, the army has seen fit to move Colonel Fife to another command, and soon, I will be commander of the hospital, both in name and practice. He will still be in our chain of command, so you'll see him from time to time."

"Congratulations. I'm truly happy for you."

"Thank you. It's a title is all. Nothing will change." He rose. "Thanks for the coffee. So 6:00 a.m. on Wednesday okay with you?"

I wanted to ask so many things. Had he actually heard gossip about us going around? Would more than just his title change? Was he apprehensive about going on this assignment with me for these reasons? Or did he request the assignment himself and was creating some sort of cover? It was all too confusing, and I simply needed to do my job and not be drawn into a sideshow. "Six o'clock it is."

I had thought it an impossible task to recruit sixty-four American nurses to go to an unspeakably awful war. Then, upon arrival, we inherited not the five-hundred-bed hospital we were prepared for but a hospital outfitted for thirteen hundred patients. Thankfully, our daily census averaged below that, but it was clear we needed more staff.

Early on, a few extra nurses had appeared, but I requested at least another forty nurses to be sent from the States, plus staff such as X-ray assistants and orderlies, or those who were willing to be trained for these tasks.

My first group of thirty-one new nurses and other staff arrived on November 13. Ned, the clerk who had helped me screen the nurses, had driven to the train station to pick them up, along with some supplies.

While the new nurses were getting settled after their long journey, I was most delighted when Ned came to my office to present me with a small package.

"It's from Washington," he said.

Ever the nosy one, he loitered a bit while I opened it and pulled out some pretty red silk.

"Ooh. Now, that doesn't seem regulation," he teased.

I unfolded the silk to reveal that it was a short cape, just as I had requested at the chief nurses' meeting. There was also a gray apron, and a rather slouchy white cotton cap, which I liked but suspected would not pass muster with the nurses. I searched for a note explaining if more were on their way, but nothing else was in the package.

～

We only had a few hours' notice of the new nurses' arrival, so we had quite the scramble to feed and house them. They would be replacing some of the British assistants who had been left behind but were now leaving, so some huts would open up, but others were assigned to hastily erected tents.

We had learned so much in our six months. My nurses grew and changed in ways they could never have expected. I wanted to share these things with the wide-eyed new nurses. They were full of energy and eager to work, having been through months of training and weeks of travel to get here. I wanted to help them find a way to keep that enthusiasm while adapting to an environment that was foreign in many ways and could be heartbreaking enough to crush a delicate soul.

So I gathered them in our meeting room, cozy with oil stove heat, and brought in some warm soup for their bellies. My original nurses filtered in and out as their duties allowed. As we broke bread, I introduced Fred and other staff.

Then I spoke of not the rules and regulations, as they were posted for all to read, but about our experiences. I watched the faces of my original nurses as I recounted the difficulties we had faced. I saw tears come to the eyes of Margaret when I told of how hard it was to deal with the cheeriness of our soldiers, with their battered and broken bodies. Charlotte nodded when I told them of the soldier who was so badly burned, we could only touch the back of his neck. I looked carefully into the eyes of the new nurses as I told them we had three nurses away in the Contagious Hospital with diphtheria. My worry was replaced with a warm glow when I saw them neither flinch nor look away.

"The most important thing, when you wake up each morning, is to remember the big picture of why we are here. I want you to remember how you felt at the cathedral in London, when the congregation was praying for you and thanking God for you. I want you to remember the parades on the streets of St. Louis and New York. That you are called to a purpose higher than yourself, to ease the suffering so that peace can reign once again on this continent.

"We who came here five months ago have surprised ourselves. Sure, we came here out of a sense of duty or patriotism, or maybe for the adventure. We came, willing to give up our bigger salaries, our comforts, the predictability of life for a few months, perhaps a year. But now, as we see no clear end in sight, we realize we are committed, that we don't want to leave until the job is done. Our future plans don't count. A certain peace has come over us, because we will stay as long as we are physically able. Our hopes, dreams, families, our whole lives deferred, for however long it takes."

The room was silent, except for the ticking of the oil stove. My words seemed inadequate for the transformation I knew I had felt and witnessed in the others. "I'll give you some examples. When we first arrived, I was asked many times a day, how long would our assignment last? After a few weeks, those questions ceased. When we were approaching six months, I requested discharge for two nurses, one to get married and the other to return to her husband, whom she had married just as we left St. Louis. The discharges were denied, and I tried to break it to them gently.

"But there was no need for that, you see, because they both took it like champions. They acted like it was entirely their idea to stay. So you see, my dears, this will be the hardest thing you have ever done in your life. At the same time, it is the most rewarding. It is a great honor for me to be here, and I shall forever hold each of you in my heart."

My old nurses wiped their eyes or nodded solemnly. The new nurses stared at me with open mouths or studied their feet. It was not possible to explain all this, I realized. It must be lived.

Then it was Fred's turn to address the nurses, and I seated myself in the back of the room. Once again, I admired his skill at keeping their attention, as every pair of eyes focused on him. His message was simple and heartfelt. I hardly listened as I took in his physical strength, his soulful eyes that every so often sought me out. When he said, "You have one of the finest nurses I have ever had the pleasure of working with as your leader," I demurred, shaking my head.

The nurses all turned toward me and clapped politely, furthering my embarrassment. Maybe there were knowing nods and smiles; maybe I imagined them. But I feared that the feelings Fred and I had for each other were becoming stronger and more noticeable by the day. I was also certain that if my superiors at Red Cross headquarters caught wind of it, I would be swiftly transferred to another base hospital or perhaps even sent home.

Somewhere in the four-inch-thick rules manual, there was a paragraph addressing just such a situation. However, I had a serious lack of curiosity to look it up. Instead, my answer was to push my feelings for him aside and throw myself even more deeply into my work.

One evening, after a full day of hundreds of admissions, I was in my office well after midnight, writing letters to the families of our seriously ill patients.

Miss Taylor, dressed in a nightgown and carrying a kerosene lantern, appeared in my office doorway. "Where will we all be when you collapse from exhaustion?" she scolded. "I don't care what you are doing, it can be done in the morning."

"You're right. Thank you, Miss Taylor." I packed up my pen and paper and bid her good night. Then I resumed the work in my own room.

CHAPTER 11

November 1917

M y plan for the CCSs had been put into place by late summer, and by November, it was proving to be a tremendous success. Although the British had had first aid provided by medics at the front all along, the CCSs, which were a short distance away, had been growing in number to the point where they were sparsely manned. As the front moved, so did the CCSs, although in the early years of the war, the front moved slowly, back and forth over the same areas. They were staffed with whatever medics could be spared and some brave nurses. In some cases, a single nurse was forced to make life-or-death decisions and perform care normally done by a surgeon.

They were always in danger of being overrun by the enemy, but they usually had enough warning to pull back in time. It was an ever-changing balance of having shelter, equipment, staff, and mobility.

Our goal was to organize the CCSs by geographic area and have teams from the stationary hospitals on a continuous rotation. The teams would consist of one or two surgeons, one to three nurses, and an orderly. Base Hospital 21 shared the duty with several other medical units in the Rouen area, so the loss of hospital staff was kept to a minimum. Due to the screening and treatment so close to the front, the most urgent cases were transported more quickly to the most suitable facility, while ambulatory patients requiring only first aid were returned to their units instead of taking a long, unnecessary trip to a hospital.

This did have the result of our unit receiving the most severe casualties, but our team of surgeons, nurses, and lab technicians and our advanced X-ray capabilities could process hundreds in a day. We didn't have the capacity to treat them to full recovery, so we established a system of sending them on to other hospitals as soon as they were stable enough.

When my nurses returned from duty at the CCSs, I grilled them to learn as much as I could about the process in order to keep improving it. One of the first to go was Dorothy. This fearless nurse pretty much demanded the duty, and I sent her with my own demand of a full report afterward. As requested, she reported to my office, where I offered her tea.

"What you should tell the next team is to be prepared for hell. A cold, soulless hell," Dorothy said.

I tapped my pen on my opened notebook. "Go on."

"Have you ever looked at the moon through a telescope?" She took off her glasses, wiped them with a handkerchief, and went on without waiting for a reply. "The landscape looks like that. Barren, full of craters. The only difference is that the countryside once held life, verdant hills and valleys where cows roamed and children played. There's none of that now. Just mud and rubble and long lines of weary soldiers trudging through it, their eyes staring blankly ahead at nothing at all."

Dorothy dabbed at her eyes. It was the first time I had seen any sign of emotion in the stoic woman.

"And your work at the clearing station?" I shoved the precious sugar bowl toward her, but she stirred her tea without putting any in.

She looked me straight in the eye. "That was the best work I've ever done. The cases seem to never end. I did intake—name, rank, unit, chief complaint. Ambulatory patients told their own story. Some really wanted to go on about it, but I had to move them along. I always promised to come back to let them talk when I could, and I did as much as possible. The stretcher cases, they had the carriers with them usually, and they gave the report. Sometimes they couldn't wait around, so they pinned a tag on the wounded's shirt. I made them form a separate line so I could get to them first."

"What kind of injuries were you seeing?"

"Lots of shrapnel from artillery. Head wounds from sniper fire. Usually greenhorns who couldn't resist peeking out the top of the trench. Pneumonia. Gas cases. Everything we see here, plus some lighter cases…and some that never make it here."

She tapped a finger on my notebook. "Here's something I didn't expect. About half the gas cases were from British canisters. The wind shifted after firing, and a bunch of their own got caught in it. It had happened a few days earlier, but the blisters showed up slowly. They only reported to the medic when the pain got unbearable.

"I saw it too. The mustard gas, a yellowish-green cloud out on the horizon." She shook her head. "They tell me the Jerries are combining the chlorine and phosgene gases. 'Best of both worlds,' they joked. The phosgene doesn't stink like the others and does its damage by first numbing the respiratory system. So the soldiers don't feel it and don't put on their gas masks soon enough and don't cough it out. When the chlorine hits, they cough mightily, feeling like their lungs are on fire. Then, their bodies try to put out the fire by pouring fluid into their airways. If they survive, that's when they get to us, drowning in their own secretions. But we haven't seen the hell they went through before that."

My nights of walking the wards, trying to comfort men coughing violently and struggling with each breath, attested to this. I patted her hand. "If something good could ever come from this war, it would be the outlawing of gas attacks forever. What else did you see?"

"Lots of trench foot. The terrible rains this summer made rivers of the trenches and wet feet for months. Sometimes we can clean them up, treat them with chloride of lime, and send them on their way with fresh socks and foot powder. But usually, if they're reporting to the station, it's beyond that. I got good at diagnosing with one whiff. The stench of a fungal infection is bad enough, but let's just say gangrene gives itself away."

I was interested in all the details of course, and it was important to allow Dorothy to talk about her experience. But the information I most needed was of a nature that no one else could gather for me. I had to get to the clearing station myself. Of course, I had requested the assignment straightaway, but it was denied due to the danger involved and the difficulty they would have in replacing me if something were to go awry. But I had persisted, and now, due to the international interest and with the American Red Cross's blessing, my chance had come.

As I walked to my rooms that evening, I had an attack of nerves. What if Colonel Fife had been right, and it was too dangerous for me to go to the CCS? Would I be overwhelmed by seeing the casualties, outside the security and comfort of the base hospital? What if I was gassed, or worse, captured?

My unease abated, however, when I entered my rooms. The air was perfumed with the scent of fresh flowers. There, on my little table next to the coal stove, was a vase of white lilacs. They were a favorite of mine, and the scent took me back to my childhood, when I had the honor of crowning a statue of Mary, Mother of Jesus. The flowers always appeared the same month as the crowning, which was held in her month of May. How on earth did lilacs appear in November? Leave it to the French to make that miracle happen.

There was a note with the flowers:

*Rare flowers for a rare and special woman. I look forward to
our adventure tomorrow. Apologies for any sense I may have
given you that I felt wise otherwise.*

Fred

I wondered how Fred knew I loved lilacs. Had he written to my
family? I thought that unlikely. Perhaps a lucky guess. But I let the
scent fill me with a deep sense of peace. I got to crown Mary because
I was the smartest girl in the class. And because I was brave enough
as a six-year-old to climb the ten-foot ladder to do it in front of the
whole school.

I was still smart. I was still brave. And I was loved and trusted and
wasn't about to let anyone down.

6:00 a.m. rolled around mighty quickly when I'd been up until five. My
bravado of the night before began to fade. Although I had a pretty good
idea of what to expect at the clearing station from Dorothy's report,
unexpected enemy advances putting us within the reach of German
artillery was always a threat. Their aircraft were getting better and
better. Soon, none of France would be safe from aerial bombs.

Then there was the uneasiness regarding my changing relationship
with Fred. Ever since our walk along the river, when he had confided
about the breakup with his girlfriend, I'd realized I had romantic feelings toward him. And the lilacs seemed to show that he felt the same. I
had to keep this to myself, as any hint of it getting back to headquarters
would lead to my swift departure and probable job loss at home.

I had heard snippets of gossip from the nurses when they didn't
think I was in earshot. Any attempt to quash the chatter wouldn't
accomplish anything, so I studiously ignored it. Maybe going off to the
CCS with Fred was a bad idea. But it wasn't my idea after all. Deciding

I was too concerned with the whole issue, I took the flowers to the mess tent for all to enjoy. Minus the note, of course.

Our assignment was to last three days, including travel time, so I packed a small suitcase, some refreshments for the road, and a nice bottle of French wine. In my silly, younger days, when I decided I didn't favor the taste of alcohol, I had not yet experienced a French wine. Who knew if I would have time to drink it, but one should never travel in France without. It had gotten quite chilly in the past week, so I brought my warm wool cape and rubber boots—wellies, as the Brits called them—as well.

Fred was waiting in front of the grandstand. He was smoking a pipe and reading a newspaper, leaning on our modified Tin Lizzie, a truck that had been built on a Model T frame. He glanced at his wristwatch, making me glad I was right on time. It still seemed strange to see a man wearing a wristwatch. Before the war, only women wore them. But field soldiers had too much to carry already without a pocket watch, and now it was becoming the manly thing to wear, even by men who carried nothing but a pen in their pockets.

"Don't you look snappy in civilian clothes," I said.

"Probably against regulation, but what the hell." He opened the passenger door for me. "I think it makes me less of a target for sniper fire."

I looked down at my uniformed self. "You're kidding me, right?"

"Uh, yeah, sort of."

"Should I change?"

"No, I like you just the way you are."

"Fred, I can't tell if you're serious or joking."

"Oh, I'm just trying to put you at ease. And failing miserably. Let's go. That is, if you're still game for this adventure." He glanced at my bottle of wine. "Well, it does seem you're prepared."

"Wouldn't miss it."

"Good." He picked up my bag and tossed it into the back. "Hope you have good warm clothes. The gas lamp doesn't put out enough heat."

☙

After stopping for petrol and lunch, we arrived at the clearing station, outside Albert, just before two o'clock. There were no lines of wounded soldiers, just a few men on stretchers being tended to by medics. The first thing Fred did was ask the medics to radio our expected French and Australian observers and postpone the planned visit. We needed a full-on casualty evacuation to demonstrate our methods.

The British had won an offensive up near Cambrai but were just now digging in and tending to the wounded. We received a report from the team we were relieving, then settled into a routine of intake, assessment, first aid, then queuing them for transport, either back to their units or on ambulances for further treatment. It was rather like duty at Base Hospital, except we were in the open air, and we had no warning by wireless before patients arrived. The low, booming thud of artillery fire was much closer. I could feel it in my bones.

The clearing stations moved with the front lines, some existing for a few months, others for years. This particular station had been set up recently, and there weren't enough of the large bell tents for the staff to sleep in, so they used small conical tents that had been left behind by the Germans. A few, those that had transportation, were scattered about in nearby private homes and farms.

Fred and I were to be housed on an all-but-abandoned farm. It stood a kilometer outside what I was told was once a charming village. There was nothing left of the village except narrow cobblestone streets and piles of rubble along them. We passed a few elderly women, dressed all in black, carrying baskets of what appeared to be walnuts.

Where they had gotten them was a mystery, as it seemed not a tree was left standing.

We could see trenches crisscrossing the landscape. Rows and rows of barbed wire stretched as far as I could see. Occasionally, we got out to inspect a crater or an opening to a tunnel, which were still framed by lengths of wood and protected by sandbags. We came upon a huge crater, nearly perfectly round, hundreds of feet wide and about a hundred feet deep. It was lined with chalky white earth.

"I can't imagine any artillery could have made something this large. And surely airplanes can't carry a bomb big enough," I said.

As Fred was officially in the army, he knew much more about such things as the latest weaponry. "No, you're quite right. Not artillery or aerial bombs. This was created from explosives set from underground mines.

"The front was right here for a good year or so. As you can see, there are long, low ridges and shallow valleys. No place to build a stronghold, so each side built underground fortifications. No doubt we're standing upon a maze of tunnels this very moment."

Even though we could see the effects of the war in the ruined villages and pockmarked landscape, there was a whole other world of ruin beneath us. I shook my head at the massive crater. Here and there, some tufts of brown grass bore witness to nature's effort to recover.

As we headed back to the truck, I wandered a few steps off the rocky path to examine what looked like a patch of mushrooms. Fred yanked me back by my elbow and gave me a stern warning. "You must not step off the path. There are unexploded shells everywhere."

I sighed. Those mushrooms were so close. I could just taste them, cooked in a little butter. Even with the extra rations Alice brought me, my stomach growled between meals. But I couldn't let my hunger get the best of me. The image of erupting in a plume of smoke and flames kept me on the path.

We had to carefully go off the path at one point to go around a bomb crater about fifty feet wide. A creek ran nearby, and the crater had filled with clear water. There was a large collection of objects at the bottom. I was taken aback when I realized what they were—helmets of several different types: British and French and German. There were rifles and bayonets and something that appeared to be parts of an artillery gun. "Is that a…" I didn't want to say it, but there appeared to be a skull among the muddy, rusting objects.

"God knows how many died here." Fred bent to scoop up a fistful of dirt and tossed it into the water. "May they rest in peace."

We were silent during the brief remaining drive out to the farm. I think we were both exhausted and aching for a world that once was. The setting sun streaked the sky with red, then purple bands, a signal that the world still spun, no matter the damage the foolish humans committed to it.

It was late when we arrived, and a note on the farmhouse door requested we stay in the nearby barn. It was hard to tell at night, but loose stones and debris around the house indicated it had been damaged.

Slightly disappointed but grateful to have somewhere to lay my weary head, I gathered my travel bag and walked behind Fred, who lit the way with a kerosene lantern. He unlatched the large barn door and pulled it open. The barn was constructed of yellow and gray stone and wood. Its interior appeared in better condition than the house, although there didn't seem to be any source of heat. Each side was lined with unoccupied animal stalls, and a couple of bales of hay bristled on the center of the dirt floor.

"How's this one?" He lit a second lantern for my straw-lined stall. "You should be nice and cozy in all that straw."

"Where will you be?" I cringed at my question. It made me sound either weak or wanting romance. Either one would be awkward.

His smile and raised eyebrow hinted that he thought it was the latter. "How about two stalls down." He pointed toward the back of the barn. "Far enough to give you privacy but close enough to protect you if a wild animal comes after you in the night."

"Like what, for instance? Do you think there are mice and rats in here?" I peered into the dark corners of my stall.

"Probably. You're not exactly a country girl, are you?" The eerie light cast by the lantern did not disguise his smug smile. He warmed my shoulders with his hands. "Don't you worry. The rats and I will take good care of you. And the hedgehogs. You're not afraid of them, are you?"

I wasn't sure what a hedgehog was, but I was too tired to worry about it. I crawled into my cozy stall and promptly fell asleep.

The second day at the station was busier, and lines formed, stretching out for half a mile. We hurried the process along as much as possible, ever aware of the suffering of those still waiting. When I could get someone to relieve my position at intake, I walked down the lines, doing quick assessments to find the most critical cases.

Some of the men who were able to speak wanted to share the story of what caused their injury. Just as Dorothy had warned, it pained me to put them off, but I simply had to. "I'm sorry. We'll have time to talk later," I told one after the other as I grasped their hand oh so briefly, then moved on to the next.

Fred came rushing up to me. "There's been an explosion at an ammunition depot. A whole trainload of men will be arriving."

"Okay, where do you want me?" I could feel the adrenaline pumping through my veins. My heart quickened, and I actually felt relieved to move on from the emotionally draining lines.

"Go out and help unload the train. I'll follow shortly, after I collect the French and Aussies. We'll be glad for their help after all."

There were two medics, one French doctor, and myself to meet the train, but there were four carloads full of badly burned men. After the quick ride in the ambulance, I jumped on the first railcar and found a British VAD (a member of the Voluntary Aid Detachment, like a nurse's aide) in charge. She was moving frantically from one patient to the next, applying water to cool compresses. There were no tags with condition and identity pinned to any of them.

"Where are the priority cases?"

"No time to triage them at the site and unnecessary, since they all have similar injuries," she replied.

An orderly arrived.

"I'll stay in the car. You two start loading the ambulance," I said. The VADs didn't commonly move stretchers, but she seemed sturdy enough. She jumped at the new responsibility, probably relieved to escape from the railcar, crammed with burned and groaning men.

I made a quick round of the twenty or so patients, some in chairs, a few leaning against the sides of the car, and the rest sitting on the floor or in stretchers. Most had burns to the hands and singed uniforms and hair but nothing life threatening. Then I came upon a soldier, lying on a stretcher, his uniform melted into his stomach. His eyes were bulging, and he looked at me pleadingly as he gasped for breath. He could make no sound, and his nose and mouth were badly burned.

The memory of something similar flashed through my mind. Fred and his lesson to the nurses before we left the States. "What do you do?" he had insisted over and over. This was real life, and this soldier needed to be intubated very quickly. Or lacking the equipment, a tracheotomy. I could do it. I had sharp, sterile scissors wrapped in cloth in my pocket.

I hesitated and yelled for help. I felt the soldier grab my arm; he was pulling me toward him with more strength than he should have been capable of.

I looked back at him. Bubbles formed on his lips, his color growing grayer by the second. I felt for my scissors.

Then I ran to the door and shouted at full volume, "Doctor! I need the doctor here immediately!"

At first, the hustle and bustle and screaming stopped, and there was silence. Then there was a chorus of "Doctor, Doctor!" with all arms pointing to me and the soldier. With the vocal arrows pointing at us, it wasn't more than a minute before the French doctor arrived.

He was an administrator, so I feared he wouldn't know what to do. But some instinct kicked in after I showed him the problem.

"Have you something sharp? " He ran his finger down the middle of the soldier's neck. Then he pulled a pen from his pocket and dismantled it.

I handed him the scissors, and he quickly made an incision with them and placed the outer pen housing in place just below the thyroid cartilage. Then he blew breath through it into the now unconscious soldier.

After a minute that seemed like forever, the soldier blinked his eyes open. His hand went to his neck in a reflex action, but I caught it in time.

"You're going to be fine. We'll secure this for you and get you to the hospital straightaway," I said.

By then, the medic had arrived, and he and the doctor were getting the pen taped in place. After that, we gave morphine as needed and moved all the injured soldiers onto the ambulances headed straight to hospitals.

CHAPTER 12

The next night, we had dinner with the farmer. I felt bad eating his meager rations, but he wouldn't hear otherwise. We did bring gifts of apples and carrots and, much to Fred's pride, the bottle of wine. The food was simple but delicious. Potatoes in browned butter, pork belly, some brown bread. Fred helped himself to two plates full, but despite my growling stomach, I took just a few bites of each.

After suffering through our attempts to pronounce his Flemish name, the farmer asked us to call him Tony. His village had been caught in an exchange of artillery, just before a British advance. "Mostly friendly fire. But what is the difference? The fields are ruined. And to think, I came here from Flanders to escape the destruction."

He told us a bit about the village he left near Passchendaele, Belgium. He grew more somber as the bottle of wine grew empty, talking about the loss of his family and his farm.

"What do you grow?" I asked, hoping to raise his spirits.

"Sugar beets and potatoes, mostly. Still one pile of beets out there, but I can't get to it."

"Why not?" Fred had been unusually quiet, one leg constantly jiggling.

I made a mental note to ask him what was bothering him.

Tony picked up our plates. "Too dangerous. How do you say it? Underexploded ordnance? It's everywhere. Just last week, a little girl of five years…"

"I'm afraid we've had a long day. Permission to hit the hay?" Fred wiped his mouth on the coarse napkin and pushed back his chair.

"Why, of course." Tony stood. "I'm sorry to have kept you, filling you with my sorrows. And I regret to only have the barn for you. You see, the roof has collapsed over the better part of the house."

Fred had seemed rather rude, but I went along. "Don't be sorry, Tony. Thank you for your gracious hospitality. But the doctor has a point."

As we headed out to the barn, the lantern cast eerie shadows on the wasted turf. Knowing there could be bombs hidden just below the surface kept us on the narrow path.

"Is there something you want to talk about, Fred?"

There was no answer for several paces. Then a great sigh.

"We, or rather I, have a tough decision to make."

"If I can help…?" I offered.

"You know we're to work the morning shift tomorrow. Our relief should arrive around lunchtime."

We entered the barn. He lit the second lantern and peeled off his coat and boots.

I took off my wool cape, then put it right back on again. No way I'd be warm enough without it.

"And then we head back to base."

"Has there been a change? I can stay a little later if necessary." I was enjoying the work at the clearing station, and staying in the barn was growing on me. There was something about being so far from anyone else, yet under Fred's watchful protection, that I found both exciting and comforting.

"Here, take my blanket."

"No, I couldn't. Silly of me not to bring one, but my cape will do just fine. So what is the tough decision?"

"I insist." He arranged a pillow and blanket for me. "Before we left the station, a messenger brought a report from London. A bad storm is running down the coast. First fierce winds and rain, then temperatures will drop, followed by sleet and snow. If we leave first thing in the morning, we can probably make it back. We could avoid it by going inland, but that puts us too close to the front."

"But what about the clearing station? Our replacements won't come until—"

"I know. Chances are, they won't risk the travel. If we stay, we could be stuck here for days."

"And the Base Hospital can ill afford to lose us for that much time. Especially you."

"We'd both be missed." He leaned against the wood post of the stall, patted his shirt pocket for his pipe tobacco.

The barn door, which we had apparently not secured, blew open in a gust of wind. It rattled and bits of hay and straw blew about until Fred pulled it shut again. When he came back into the light of the lantern, I could see his shirt was speckled with raindrops.

"So it's already started. Does Colonel Fife know? Surely he'll advise one way or the other." Tomorrow morning might be too late, I thought.

"He said to take shelter tonight and reassess in the morning. But of course, we have no communications here, and we'll have to make the decision on our own."

"I wonder if we need to go back, if it would be wiser to leave now." The thought of heading into that bleak landscape in the dead of night wasn't at all appealing, but I wanted to consider all the options.

"And if it all blows over, we will have left our duty station and disobeyed orders. Go on. Get ready for bed. I won't look." He winked. "Oh,

I almost forgot." He produced a small package from his pants pocket. "It isn't much, some sort of pumpkin bread. Happy Thanksgiving."

I slept fitfully. The temperature seemed to be dropping by the minute. I could see my breath, even in the weak light of the lantern. The tip of my nose was like ice, and my feet were getting numb. I decided to get up and walk a bit to get my circulation going. I checked on Fred, worried because he had given me the only blanket. But he was softly snoring under a pile of straw. The lantern was dimming, and I pumped air into the fuel tanks to raise the pressure.

I was about to curl back into my little nest of straw when the walls started to shake. I climbed the ladder into the loft, where there was a small window. It was too dark to see much, but the light from the farmhouse revealed trees bent into the wind, and a mixture of snow and rain and possibly hail pelted the window. Nothing to do but wait until morning. I did some calisthenics and unwrapped the little loaf of pumpkin bread. My stomach was growling after the meager dinner. I had intended to share it with Fred but greedily ate every last bit. It was fresh and spicy and tasted sublime. Thanksgiving indeed.

My body warmed and my stomach sated, I returned to my stall and soon drifted into a peaceful sleep.

"Julia, wake up. We need to go."

I fought off the sound of the impatient voice and snuggled deeper under the blanket. But Fred found my shoulder and gave it a healthy shake.

I groaned. "Is it snowing?"

"Yes. About four inches on the ground. The truck started up, no problem."

I raised myself up on my elbows and blinked the fog from my brain. "Which way are we going? Clearing station or base?"

He offered a canteen of water. "It's a fifteen-minute drive to the station. I think we need to head out there, see what's going on. Hopefully, the storm will start clearing, our replacements will arrive, and we can head home. The internationals got a good lesson yesterday and won't be back.

"Does that sound like a good plan? After we have some breakfast, of course. Tony dropped this off." He held up a small basket of bread and cheeses.

❧

The snow soon changed to rain, but the fifteen-minute drive turned into an hour, as we had to stop frequently to push the truck out of ruts. I was getting thoroughly soaked, but at least the physical activity kept me warm.

We arrived at the station to find a lone medic. He had no casualties to care for. "Seems even the Jerries don't like to fight in this weather."

Indeed, there was no booming of artillery fire. The world was cold, quiet, and desolate. I could see why Dorothy had compared it to the moon.

Our replacements sent a message by wireless; they were still four hours away. After a couple of hours of idle hands and stomping our feet to keep warm, Fred had had enough. "Seems our work here is done. It's going to take us longer to get home. I suggest we head back."

We gathered some rations from the first aid tent and headed back out onto the half-frozen, rutted mud road. Just as we did, artillery commenced its familiar booming in the distance.

"And the war carries on. No peace, no rest," Fred said. "The best we can hope for is to be back at base by dinner."

We had to stop frequently to clear the windshield from the driving rain and snow, and it was hard to tell the road from the surrounding fields. I continually wiped the mist from the windows, but even so, Fred had to pop his head out the window just to make sure we were still on track. Luckily, we came upon no opposing traffic, but we were not far down the main road when Fred swerved to avoid a pig. The truck went into the ditch, full of water two feet deep. I was jarred against the door, which flew open. Only Fred's quick action to grab my arm saved me from falling into the ditch myself.

"Are you okay?"

"Fine, but I don't think the truck is."

He tried to reverse out of the ditch, but it was no use. We would have to push it out, a very unpleasant thought in the mud and pouring rain.

"You stay in here and steer. No use both of us getting soaked." Fred was being magnanimous but not too realistic.

"It took both of us to push it out of smaller ruts." I was already changing into my wellies.

After ten or so shoves with all our might, Fred came up with a new idea. "We'll rock her out."

"Come again?" I pictured cradling the truck between us and alternately pushing from either end.

He walked back to the front of the truck and opened the door. "You get in the driver's seat, and when I yell, open the throttle while I push. Then let off and on, and she'll rock right out of there."

I looked at the three pedals on the floor and various sticks protruding from the steering column and center floorboard. The pedals were helpfully labeled, each with a capital letter. I assumed *B* was for *brake*. But how do you see that from the driving position?

Luckily, I had been watching Fred's elegant dance with all the pedals and knobs and sticks, and I had some idea of what to do. I climbed into the driver's seat, and he went over it all with me.

"You only need one gear—low—and the steering wheel and the throttle." He reached over me and wiggled the rod nearest my right hand.

We tried and tried, with me spinning the wheels and him pushing, until Fred finally yelled "Stop." He came around to my window, and I had to stifle a laugh. He was covered in muck from head to toe; his glasses had more speckles than clear spaces. I had the urge to put him in a warm bath.

After he used a rag to clean up as best he could, we sat in the truck cab, steaming up the windows with our breath. I was soaked to the bone, and my legs were starting to tingle—not a good sign.

"It's no wonder that soldiers die in this mud." He shook his head. "I hate to bother Tony again, but he's our only hope. Or we can wait here for help."

"How far would you say we are from the farm?"

The rain beat harder, pattering the roof like a bucket of marbles.

"Three miles, maybe. We should make it in an hour, hour and a half." He glanced at his wristwatch. "We've got another four hours or so of light." Fred wiped off his window. "But it's probably wiser to stay put, lacking proper rain gear."

"But not a soul is out in this miserable weather. We haven't passed a single one. We'll freeze just sitting here in wet clothes. I think it's better to keep moving." If given a choice, I always preferred to keep moving, even if it was in the wrong direction.

"We did pass a pig."

"I can't feel my toes."

He turned from the window, apparently no pig owner coming out of hiding. "That settles it then. We walk. I think there's an umbrella in here somewhere."

After the first mile, we gave up on the umbrella, or rather the wind forced us to, making it all but useless and slowing us down. We trudged on, arm in arm for support when our boots got stuck in mud.

"Remind me not to book a vacation in the Somme." I tried to keep up some light conversation to keep my mind off my frozen feet and empty belly. The early morning bread and cheese hadn't filled me up, and now, aside from a few scones we grabbed at the first aid tent, we had missed two more meals. I was about the same height as Fred, and even though he was a muscular former football player, I estimated I weighed just as much with my large frame. And yet I gave him the bigger portions.

I was usually hot-bodied, with energy to spare. But without enough fuel, my muscles were cramping and my mind was getting sluggish. Another mile to go, one step in front of the other. The tingle in my legs had been replaced with shooting pain, followed by numbness. I needed to get them cleaned up and medicated soon, or the dreaded ulcers and infections would return.

❦

"I think I see the farmhouse!" Fred shielded his eyes from the rain, which was once again mixed with snow. The mud on his clothes was washing off like watercolors off a paintbrush. How I would have liked to paint him if I had the talent: a strong figure, bent forward into the elements, heading toward a place of warmth and safety in the distance.

I had fallen back a few steps behind him and given up on conversation, so I had difficulty getting my lips to form a response. "L-lead the way."

He waited as I caught up, then looked at me with concern, took my hand, and held the back of my hand against his cheek. "Not a moment too soon. We've got to warm you up." He looped his arm through mine, and we trudged the last fifty yards to the farmhouse, a faint wisp of smoke coming from the chimney.

There was no answer at our knock, but since the door was ajar, we went in out of concern and desperate need for warmth and rest.

Tony was nowhere to be found. The last of the firewood, a charred remnant of a log, smoked in the fireplace in the keeping room next to the kitchen. Snow had drifted in from the door and through a broken window.

"I hope he's safe." I picked up the scattered glass shards.

"Me too. He probably got too cold and abandoned the place. Probably no fuel to heat water either." He checked, but there was no oil or kerosene anywhere. "Without firewood, it's going to be hard for us to warm up."

I collapsed on a kitchen chair. Fred busied himself, finding scraps of food, removing a dead mouse, while I sat, overcome by shivers. I missed being back at base. As hard as the work was, it beat this slow descent into a shivering heap of worthlessness. Darkness came, and we ate the last bits of cheese and some stale bread. Thankfully, there was a lantern with fuel, as we had left ours in the truck.

"I think we're better off staying in the barn for the night. It's warmer with all the straw and no windows. Besides, it's practically home."

His attempt at humor failed to raise my spirits. I nodded and started to layer back on the clothes I had placed by the pitiful fire. They smelled deeply of smoke but were barely any drier.

The barn did seem a bit more homelike. At least it was somewhat less drafty. I tried to get moving. To force some blood into my muscles, I helped Fred gather straw and hay and made a deeper nest in my usual stall. My brain increasingly foggy, I just wanted to lie down and sleep. He helped me remove the wettest of my clothes, my fingers too stiff to work the buttons. I was too numb and sleepy to be embarrassed, and he was a doctor after all.

"Oh Jesus, you're shaking." He spread a sheepskin he had found in the house upon the straw, then helped me down into the bed and covered me with my cape, the blanket, and another layer of straw. But it was no use. I continued to shake violently. At the same time, I felt as if I was burning. I started pushing away the straw, throwing off the blankets. I could no longer put a sentence together, but knew I was in trouble, and the world turned white despite the darkness.

I felt the weight of straw come off, then my boots. There was a strange pressure against my numb legs. My long hair was released from its bun and swirled around my face and neck. Then my clothes seemed to rise and fly in the wind, replaced with sunshine. I closed my eyes and let the warm sunshine wrap me in its loving grasp.

~❧~

Early morning light streamed through the cracks of the barn. The sweet smell of wet hay hit me. Then, the gnawing hunger in my belly. Next, I was aware of warmth across my back and bottom. I was lying on my side under a heavy pile, and for a moment, I had no recollection of how I got there. I ran my fingers down my chest and stomach. From what I could tell, I was naked. Panic and confusion rose in me until I heard a soft breath behind me.

Then I remembered. It was Fred. He was curled up behind me, no doubt naked, or nearly so, himself.

His arm pulled away from its position around my shoulders, and I rolled toward him.

"You're back among the living. You had me worried." He pulled away. "I'm sorry for this, but you were hypothermic."

"I understand." My body felt warm again, even the tip of my nose. But with the loss of numbness, my lower legs were on fire. I wanted Fred to huddle up next to me once more, liking it more than I wanted to admit. Silly of me, but my most pressing thought was how I would get up without Fred seeing my hideous legs.

Being a gentleman, he slipped out of our little haystack and into his trousers without another touch or glance at me. "Your dress is still damp. I've got some trousers you can borrow in the meantime."

"No thanks. My dress will be fine." I had worked myself into a sitting position and donned my blouse, which was neatly folded next to me. I peeled off my leggings, which had stuck to my now ulcered legs. No way did I want trousers touching them.

"Jesus, Mary, and Joseph!" Fred stood above me, gawking at my exposed, gauze-wrapped shins.

"That's not a very professional reaction from a surgeon." I tried to recover the hideous things with my blood-tainted leggings.

"What the hell, Jules? Why didn't you tell me about this?"

"It's a chronic condition I've had since childhood. I get flare-ups now and then."

"Let me take a look." He removed the soiled-through roller bandage and examined my legs. "This is serious under these conditions. You need treatment, maybe even skin grafts." He opened his first aid bag and took out antiseptic and rolls of gauze. "What caused it?"

"No one has ever been able to figure that out, despite many hospitalizations."

"Well, what did your uncle Lewis say?"

"He wasn't consulted." An old, bitter wound of a different sort was reawakened.

Fred stopped rolling on the bandage. "How can that be? He was the top in his field of surgery, and weren't you both in New York?"

"It's deep in the past, and I was but a child, so who knows? He was a very busy man, and it's not like I didn't receive care."

He finished bandaging my legs.

"Thank you, Fred. And for saving me last night. You won't tell anyone of this, I hope?"

"Tell them about our night together or your legs?"

I studied his face, trying to determine how he felt about the former. Was it, as he said, merely a clinical decision, like donating blood? But his face gave away nothing. If anything, it seemed he was slyly trying to determine how I felt about it as well.

"Both, for sure."

"Your secrets are safe with me. As long as you promise you'll let me know if your legs don't heal."

"Then we have a deal. I guess it's a heal deal."

"I'm holding you to it." He slipped on his coat. "I'll see what I can scrounge up for breakfast." A streak of light entered when he opened the barn door. "Hey, I see a horse and buggy. I think Tony is back."

We finished dressing, made ourselves as presentable as we could, and headed over to the farmhouse. Tony had been busy, collecting firewood and other provisions from the surrounding vacated farms. He also brought back two tabby cats (alive) and two scrawny pheasants (not so alive).

He emptied shotgun shells into a glass bowl. "Lucky shots. Two shells, two birds. Got seven shells left. And best of all, there's a pig frozen solid down the road. If you help me get him into the truck, we eat like kings tonight."

"We'll help, but I'm afraid we'll need to head back to base after that," Fred said.

"Too bad. But we shall feast this morning, no? Julia, can you clean and dress the birds?" He pointed a knife at the limp pile of feathers, beaks, and claws.

My eyes widened as I thought of how to gracefully decline the task. I hadn't a clue what to do.

Fred came to my rescue. "Ah, she's a city girl, but I've got some knife skills."

The men had the birds cleaned and defeathered and into a baking pan in no time. I was relegated to chopping apples and root vegetables. Tony roasted it all in the wood-fired oven, creating a warmth and aroma in the kitchen that filled me with homesickness. One of the scrawny cats curled up in my lap, completing the picture of how things should be.

When the birds were nearly done, Tony poured us all a glass of red wine, then tossed the rest of the bottle over the pan to deglaze it. My stomach rumbled, and I merely sipped at the wine, afraid of quickly getting tipsy on my empty stomach. Not to mention that wine with breakfast wasn't my usual habit.

This time, I ate as my appetite dictated. If either of the men noticed, they didn't mention it; they just kept heaping more food onto my plate. With our bellies full and some spunk in our step, the three of us set out in the horse and buggy to dislodge the pig, then rescue the truck.

The pig had already been claimed, leaving a long crater in the road, so we moved on to the truck. We found it just as we had left it, in an icy ditch. It took some cracking of ice, backfilling with sand under the wheels, and a lot of pushing by the men while I steered, but we raised it out of the ditch. Lucky for me, I had watched the throttle and clutch routine on the way up, as prior to this trip, I had never driven. The Tin Lizzie alternately stalled and bucked like a bronco in my far from expert hands, but we got her back on the road.

We were quiet on the way back to Rouen; the softly rolling hills covered in snow were a lulling comfort. We passed a few small towns. It was obvious which ones had been bombed, with buildings shattered and craters in the earth. There were fresh cemeteries everywhere. In some, there were boxes—I assumed caskets—piled several high. Perhaps the ground had become too frozen to bury the dead.

"No poppies now," I said. "Do you think they grow here too?"

Of course, Fred knew to what I was referring. Everyone had read and probably memorized the poem "In Flanders Fields" by John McCrae. McCrae was a Canadian physician who wrote the poem after he lost a dear friend in the Second Battle of Ypres, Belgium.

Fred recited the first stanza, just above a whisper. "'In Flanders fields the poppies blow, between the crosses, row on row, that mark our place; and in the sky, the larks, still bravely singing, fly, scarce heard amid the guns below.'" He looked at me and patted my hand. "I imagine they do grow here."

"And I imagine I will never see a poppy without thinking of this war. This terrible war. It's a hopeless, awful waste of life." I stared at the bleak landscape. We were passing what appeared to have once been a forest. But now, the trees were burned and broken, the ground littered with dead branches poking up from the snow.

"It is terrible. But the poem is saying to carry on. To have the strength and the courage to carry on, no matter what, because some things are more important than an individual's life." He slowed the truck as we came upon another, half-loaded with sugar beets, which looked like giant dirty radishes, passing by on the narrow roadway.

In some ways, the world still looked normal. Farmers tended their fields. Babies were born. Old people died.

"I know. That's why I volunteered to come here. But witnessing the inhumanity of it, seeing what humans are capable of doing to one another..."

"The world will right itself. The evil nature of a few will eventually be overcome by the goodness of the many." He squeezed my hand. Something *had* changed. Although this felt natural now, he hadn't done it on the drive up or any other time that I remembered. "It is not like you to lose faith. What is it?"

"Oh, I've always questioned God, my choices. I worry if I've brought sixty-four innocent women to hell on earth. I worry for my brother who followed me over here."

He pulled back his hand as he needed to pull back the throttle while he shifted to low gear. A gust of wind blew a smattering of snow against the windshield. "And now, you feel differently?"

"Same worries, same hell. But now I have someone I feel I can talk with about these things. I have to always put on a brave front to the others."

"You can always be forthright with me."

I thought about what a tremendous gift that was. "As you can be with me."

As the engine tut-tutted down the road, snow swirling cloudlike around us, I felt relaxed and warm inside the truck. Fred's steady hand was on the wheel, and his comforting words were in my heart.

～

We arrived back at base camp not a moment too soon. Casualties from battles outside Cambrai were pouring in as the Germans made a desperate push to save their supply lines.

As I did my rounds, Margaret rushed up to me. "Matron, can you please come see a patient? Dr. Valentine wants to amputate, but the poor fellow is refusing."

The patient was in bed, surrounded by Dr. Valentine and two orderlies holding a stretcher.

"Do I have a say here?" The patient looked at me. "Nurse, help me!"

Dr. Valentine sighed. "Of course you have a say. You can agree to lose part of your leg and live, or be buried right across the street." He pointed his thumb behind him.

The soldier spoke with a unique accent that sounded like a combination of German and French, which I had learned was Belgian. His right leg was bandaged from above his knee down to his foot. Fresh blood from his shin had soaked through, and I detected the ominous, putrid odor of gangrene. Margaret waved us back so she could change the dressing. As she cut the soiled one away, I could see the angry red, partially sutured wound running from just below his knee to his ankle.

"We've done all we can, lad. Your wound is deep, nearly to the bone, and we need to amputate. I can save your knee, so we can get you set up with a good prosthesis. Right, Matron?"

Dr. Valentine passed the last of the convincing on to me. But I was not convinced myself. The soldier clearly did not want the amputation.

"Can we try a few more days to save his leg?" I said.

Dr. Valentine whirled to face me; this was clearly not the support he was expecting. But the anger in his face faded, and he gave a little nod. "Why no, we can't. Gangrene has already set in, and as you can see, we haven't quite controlled the bleeding. This is no light decision."

The patient looked from me to Dr. Valentine, weighing the matter. I knew I should say something in support of the doctor, but I just couldn't. It seemed to me that the gangrene wasn't that far along, and the bleeding indicated there was still good blood flow near the injury. I'd seen patients with worse wounds wait for days before they amputated and a few others who, given more time and a lot of care, were able to heal.

"If I may offer a compromise? Can we delay the surgery by a few days, watching him closely, of course?" I asked.

"Not my preferred thing to do. He'll only get worse, and right now, the operating theater is open. Who knows what could happen in a few days' time?" Dr. Valentine was getting louder and more insistent. "We could have trainloads of patients arrive, needing immediate surgery. He could be waiting in line until it's too late."

"We can irrigate with Dakin's around the clock. Take him outside and expose the leg to fresh air."

Dr. Valentine turned to the patient. "It's freezing out there. Is that what you want?"

"Yes, yes! I'll do anything. Please give my leg a chance!"

"Thank you, Miss Stimson." The daggers in his eyes didn't match Dr. Valentine's stiff but polite dismissal of me.

The other thing that happened while I was away was that a number of our own staff had taken ill. Two of my nurses had been sent to the

Sick Sisters Hospital in Étaples with pneumonia, and my dear Ned, now a sergeant, had also come down with the lung infection.

As if my nurses hadn't already sacrificed enough, and were already in physical and emotional danger—now they must also face exposure to a mysterious illness. Stealthy and invisible, it could wipe out my staff in weeks if we weren't careful.

Pneumonia had become such a problem that I had campaigned to have one tent dedicated to patients and staff who suffered from it. Dr. Valentine had begrudgingly agreed to it, after I made it sound like his idea, of course.

∽

The following day, I was heading to the new tent for the infectious respiratory patients when I saw Dr. Valentine wheeling a cart of supplies.

"So we meet again. I think you're sweet on me, Miss Stimson."

His cheerful demeanor surprised me, so I didn't want to bring up our last encounter. I did manage a small chuckle, then turned to the chalkboard with the list of patients in the tent.

"Looking for Ned? He's confined to barracks." He pointed to his cart. "We've got to do a better job with isolation. I don't want to save a man's leg just to have him die of pneumonia."

Although pleased with his turnabout to my position, I wasn't about to show it. "Yes, I'd like to check on Ned. We go back to St. Louis days."

"Me too. A fine young lad."

The cart was laden with face masks, an oxygen tank, and folded cloth dividers we sometimes hung between cots for a modicum of privacy and germ containment.

"Can I help you with that?"

"No, I'm just setting them here for now. This whole tent will become a separate ward."

I waited, expecting some kind of barb aimed my way. But there was none, which only made me suspicious.

I went to the enlisted barracks where Ned had been sent to rest. His dark blond hair was a frightful mess, and his crooked teeth only added to a comical look. My big sister instinct kicked in, and I had to restrain myself from fixing him up. He seemed chipper enough in between bouts of coughing, joking with me about his buddy Benjamin. He told me how his friend sometimes wandered over to the wrong side of the road while driving.

"Benjamin says that Napoleon got it wrong, and it's France that drives on the wrong side. You hold your sword in your right hand, so it's better to be on the left side of the road to protect yourself. And you get on a horse on the left side. Who wants to mount a horse in the middle of the road?" Ned laughed. "Swords and horses. You got to love those crazy Brits."

I laughed with him, then shared my ditch driving escapade. "I'm just happy to keep all four wheels on the road, so either side will do." I stayed only a short time, and as he had no requests, I hurried back to the wards.

Very early the next morning, there was a quiet rap on the door to my private rooms. Thinking it was one of my nurses with something unusual to report at change of shift, I opened the door while trying to pin on my new slouchy and uncooperative cap. But it wasn't a nurse. It was Dr. Valentine, looking especially disheveled.

"Dr. Valentine! You look like you haven't had a wink of sleep. Come in."

He stayed in the doorway, still dark at this early hour. "Bad news, I'm afraid."

My mind went immediately to Phil. I hadn't taken the time to see him since I returned from the CCS. "Is my brother all right?"

"Your brother? I…no…he's fine." Dr. Valentine shook his head. "It's Ned."

I waved him into my sitting room, and he plopped down into a chair. He covered his face with his hands.

"Ned? He seemed fine last night. What's happened?"

When he removed his hands, I could see his face was raw with despair. "My fault probably. I just didn't see it. Or hear it, more likely. How could a young buck like that have lungs fill up so fast?" He looked up at me, still standing with my nurse cap in my hand. "I'm sorry, Miss Stimson. We've lost him."

Grief and fury rose in me, but seeing his absolute devastation, I spoke in an even, measured tone. "When? And why didn't someone come get me?"

"It all happened very quickly in the middle of the night. Your night shift leader—Nora, I think—hauled me out of bed. But it was too late." He rubbed his fist into his other hand. "Even so, I don't think there was anything we could have done. I suspect it's a beast we haven't seen before, an influenza. Unpredictable and sometimes deadly, even for the most strapping of young men."

I was torn between consoling him and screaming into the watery, pitiful light of an early winter dawn. Now we had a new battle to fight. "Influenza? I thought he had regular pneumonia."

"That's what I suspect. There've been reports of a new influenza. Seems like a bad cold, then develops rapidly, especially in young adults. It's the only thing I can think of that would take a healthy young man so quickly." Gone was the insufferable, bombastic surgeon. He looked at me with true sorrow in his eyes. "We thought we'd let you have another couple of hours of peaceful sleep. But I wanted to tell you myself."

"Oh, our sweet Ned." I set aside my nurse's cap and sat down. I was angry, but no longer at the doctor. He vexed me, for sure, but maybe that just made me try harder.

He took a folded piece of paper out of the chest pocket of his white coat. "I was going to report your insubordination to the medical committee." He tore the paper and tossed the shreds, then tapped his fingers on the table in between us. It seemed the closest he could come to a hug, which I suspect we both badly needed.

This was the first loss of one of our own. Not only Dr. Valentine and I but the rest of the staff took it very hard. An elaborate funeral was planned at the nearby cemetery and memorial chapel. The nurses, all fifty who could get away, put on their dark-blue dress uniforms, and the rest of the staff who were able wore their finest as well. It was just under a mile from our hospital to the cemetery, and it was lined nearly the whole way with mourners. They had hired a French hearse, and it was covered with wreathes of pine and laurel.

The cemetery was an expansion of one that had served the community for hundreds of years. There were large stone monuments, mostly laid horizontally and darkened by the ages, and elaborate walk-in crypts for the wealthier families. There were rows and rows of new marble gravestones for the fallen from many countries. They were mostly British, but I spied a few Australians, New Zealanders, and even Africans. As Ned was the first American, he was laid to rest in a newly prepared area. It was disconcerting, to say the least, to see all the empty space they had set aside for future casualties.

A number of local French villagers came by to witness the ceremony. As there were burials nearly every day when it was warm enough from all fourteen hospitals in the area, I wondered if the villagers came every day. But from my experience, those burials were quick and efficient, with few mourners present, if any.

Even though I knew Ned and his passing was painful to all of us, I also felt it was wrong somehow to have this elaborate service for one of our own, when all the Tommies and others were buried without.

Sometimes families would travel from England when they were informed that a loved one would likely perish. They would stay for the service. Sometimes, if I had had contact with the deceased, I would attend the short ceremony with them. This became harder and harder as the months wore on, each death adding to my emotional pain, but I was determined to continue the practice and somehow not become too numb to feel the loss.

After everyone else was gone, Fred and I shared our own time of remembrance. We lit candles in the little chapel, then sat in the small wooden folding chairs.

He blessed himself, then offered a prayer. "Dear Lord, take our dear Ned and keep him. His life on earth was much too short, but we give him now unto You."

"How well did you know Ned?" I asked.

"Not very. He would come to my office now and then. He was the first to congratulate me when I officially took command, back in October." He looked at me, an odd look on his face.

"While I didn't, you seem to be saying."

He waggled his head. "It was as if you didn't even notice. When we first arrived, I had a steady stream of our people from St. Louis coming to me to complain about Colonel Fife did this or that."

"I'm sure they did."

"There was a lack of what the army calls a *unity of command*. They were used to reporting to me, trusted me. But he was put in charge. It was like that." He paused and pointed to the flickering shadows from the candles. "I felt like a shadow on the wall. So when the army finally saw fit to put me in command, it was a big deal to me and, I think, the unit."

"I'm sorry, Fred. Sorry to be naïve about these things." I leaned my head on his shoulder. "Sorry to be so caught up in my own duties and not more attuned to your challenges. And your triumphs. And my own position—sort of part of the army, but without rank—leaves me rather out of tune with the command structure."

"Maybe I've overestimated my importance in your world. I suppose that's the real issue."

"Don't say that. The only thing you've overestimated is my innate sense of others' sensitivities. I seem to be severely lacking in that territory, especially for a nurse."

"Maybe it's because you are a nurse. How can you possibly concern yourself with all the emotions of the people you have to deal with every day? I imagine you need sort of an emotional wall." He looked over the prayer card with Ned's name carefully printed on it. "And not only for the patients. Ned was the first of us, but I imagine not the last."

"It's a narrow path we both have to navigate, between caring too much and too little." I stood, then went to blow out the candles. "In the future, don't assume I've noticed things that concern you, and bring my attention to them if I should."

We had not brought up our odd night together, my bout with hypothermia, or my wrecked legs. Maybe admitting to my frailties would force us to address them, and we both knew that would likely end in me being returned stateside. So Fred and I continued our close professional relationship, and I tried to be especially observant of his moods.

This was not an easy or natural thing for me. I was having dinner with him some days later and had made up my mind to listen to everything he said—and everything he wasn't saying—with every bit of my attention. My habit with anyone, not just Fred, was to listen enough to garner any important new information while sorting out some other issue in my head at the same time. So I forced myself to change that habit.

As a result, I found myself picking up so many nuances, things that led me to ask more insightful questions, and indeed, learning things I never would have. I felt myself drawing closer to him on an intellectual level. I always knew he was brilliant, but really listening helped me to focus and even share more of what was on my own mind. After the dinner, my burdens felt lighter, and I had answers to things I hadn't even directly thought about.

But more time spent in these intent conversations was more fodder for the rumor mill, due to our audience of curious, prying busybodies. Gossip was an inevitable part of any medical community, and Base Hospital 21 was no different. Perhaps it was the long, stressful hours, the close physical proximity to one another in our working space, or just human nature, but there were always rumors going around.

The discussions with the chief nurses in Paris regarding how to handle dances and outings and such between the men and women hadn't seemed of personal import to me at the time. In fact, I remember my feet doing a quiet tap dance under the table as I tried to hide my exasperation over the prolonged and what I thought unnecessary discussion. But now I was glad that our hospital hadn't seen the need for strict limits on relationships. For surely, Fred and I would be breaking them. There was still the matter of Red Cross policy, but so far, we had only skirted around the edges without intentionally breaking them.

CHAPTER 13

December 1917

Early in the month, we had a string of days filled with sunshine, even if it was the weak, watery sunshine of late fall. I checked on our Belgian patient, who so far had avoided leg amputation. Margaret was just about to wheel him outside for his daily dose of fresh air.

"*Goeiemorgen*, Matron!" the patient greeted me.

To which I replied in both languages, "*Goeiemorgen* and good morning to you. How are you feeling?"

"*Goed, dank u.* And that's thanks to you and my girl, Margaret."

Margaret beamed. "The doctors say if he keeps doing so well, he won't lose his leg after all. That big, bad infection slid off in one slough." She wrapped a blanket around his shoulders. "You're a lot of work but worth it."

As they headed out of the tent, I took a moment to feel something I hadn't experienced in some time. Joy. Sometimes good things happened.

Just as we seemed to have gained some control over the new procedures for isolating respiratory patients, a new challenge presented itself. Or herself, I should say.

Madame Curie had chosen late fall as a good time to check back on how our new X-ray equipment was performing. Although it was a great privilege to meet with her, I had tried to dissuade her from coming.

Dear Madame,

I received your letter and wish to assure you that your improvements to our X-ray machine and the addition of the radon tube are working fabulously well. We are triangulating bullets and other fragments with such accuracy that our men are up and back to duty in no time.

As we are experiencing an influx of patients with what seems to be a contagious influenza, I regretfully advise you to postpone your visit until a safer time.

Respectfully,
Julia Stimson

The response came back just two days later. Madame Curie must have had friends within the French postal system.

Dear Miss Stimson,

I assure you I have faced much larger threats. I will arrive next Thursday. There is much to discuss.

—MC

Letter in hand, I rushed over to speak with Captain Ernst. He was just finishing up with a patient, and two men in hospital pajamas were preparing to roll the patient out on his gurney.

"Are we short of orderlies?" I asked Captain Ernst.

He slid the heavy lead apron from his shoulders, and it fell to a steel table with a *thunk*. Waiting until the men had left the room, he said in a low voice, "Those guys are shell-shocked. It's good duty for them."

"I see." Even though it seemed like a good idea, I bristled at not being consulted. Orderlies were under my jurisdiction. But I tamped down that matter for the moment. After all, if Dr. Valentine could admit when others might have better ideas, so could I. "We're to have another visit from Madame Curie."

His face brightened. "Is Irène coming?"

I couldn't resist a little ribbing. "She's half your age."

He folded his arms across his chest and nodded to the letter I carried. "What does she want?"

When would I learn that Dr. Ernst had no discernible sense of humor when it came to the Curies? I cleared my throat and unfolded the letter. "She's coming next Thursday, just to check up on us. But then she mentions having 'much to discuss.'"

He motioned for me to walk ahead of him as we exited his space. "Well, thank you for the warning, but there isn't much I need to do to prepare." He surprised me with a little chuckle, and I turned to see him rub his stubbly cheek. "Except maybe a clean shave, in case a certain someone shows up."

On the next Thursday, on the dot of eight in the morning, the large white panel truck emblazoned with a red cross rumbled into the receiving area in front of the old grandstand. I tucked my hair into its tight bun and checked over my uniform. Not much made me nervous, but somehow this small, intense woman made me feel like a child in her presence. Irène was in the driver's seat, and Captain Ernst greeted her while I went around to open the passenger door. There was Madame Curie, sitting up stiffly and staring ahead, a small leather bag clutched in her hands.

"Madame?"

Slowly, she turned to me, then seemed surprised to see me. "Don't you have people for this?"

"For what, Madame?"

"To receive arriving supplies and guests, of course. And please, for you, I am Marie."

"You are no ordinary guest." I offered my hand to help her down from the truck, but she scampered down without my assistance. Although she was about fifty years old, she was as agile as someone half her age. "Would you like to rest first or tour the X-ray room straightaway, er, Marie?" Using her given name felt wrong somehow.

She handed me the leather bag and a large binder, bulging with paper. "Irène is fully capable of that. Let's be off to your rooms, then."

❧

Once we were settled with cups of tea and some biscuits, I tried to update Madame on the numbers of patients who had been X-rayed and the additional shielding we had put in place. She nodded politely but tapped her spoon on my small table with impatience.

"You are a very busy woman, Madame, and you come at a time of considerable risk." I let the unasked question linger in the air.

She stirred her tea with a tinkly-tink, even though she hadn't added any sugar.

"It's a delicate matter, young lady. I must find the proper English words to say something to you."

My mind whirled. What could she possibly need to share that would give her pause? She hadn't seemed to be one to mince words before. I reviewed the possibilities. Had she found grave danger in the radiation we were using? Was this critical tool about to be yanked away from us? Was Irène sent to advise Captain Ernst of this in private, out of respect?

"And it's personal."

So not radiation. "Personal for you or for me?" I got up to fetch more tea.

"You, of course. I wouldn't come here to burden you with my own personal issues. Although I do wish you to learn from them."

Despite her insistence that I call her Marie, I preferred the more respectful Madame. Perched on my little metal and green leather chair, masses of graying curly hair caught up in a messy bun, she reminded me of a cockatiel. "Madame, what could be so pressing as to take you away from your work?"

"My work? Good gracious, don't you know it is all shut down?" She looked around my small office as if someone might be hiding in a corner. "We've hidden it, you know."

"Hidden what? From whom?" I scraped my chair closer; she had my full attention now.

"The radium, of course. We can't let it get into enemy hands. There's no end of the destruction they could do with its power."

My stomach started to flip like a landed fish. "You can't hide something like that just anywhere. It would have to be very secure, far from the enemy, and where they aren't likely to look. And what of the radon?"

I thought of the tiny amount of radon gas we had for the X-ray machine. She had said that she had extracted it from radioactive rocks. How could they possibly gather and store all those?

"We are speaking of an amount weighing no more than this." She fished into a small bag hung around her neck, brought out a centime coin, and tossed it onto the table. "It is easy to hide."

I stared at her reddened, chapped hands. Madame's rather carefree attitude with the dangers presented by radioactivity worried me. At the same time, I was in awe of her; she had the power and knowledge to further science to benefit humanity in ways I could only imagine. I had to tread lightly, but still, the safety of my patients and nurses came first. "I understand. And I'm sure it's securely locked away, far from posing any danger to anyone."

"Away from Paris, I can tell you that much." She tilted her head, her intense gray eyes bearing down on me. "But that isn't why I came here."

"It's not? But you said… Well, why did you come?"

"I wanted to talk about you, dear."

I shook my head. "Me? Fine. Anything you want to know. But first, I need to know one thing. Have you hidden your supply of radium in my hospital?"

She threw her head back and laughed, the first time I had seen her laugh, and it wasn't a pleasant sight. She crowed and cackled, reminding me of a scene in a performance of *Macbeth*, when the witches chant, "Double, double toil and trouble; fire burn and cauldron bubble."

"I take that as a no." I looked at my watch. I needed to make rounds at the end of the shift.

"I want to discuss the nature of your relationship with Major Murphy."

"How so?" I could feel a knot developing in my throat, along with a desire to walk off in a huff. And I would have if this were anyone but Marie Curie sitting in front of me.

"It is a small world we live in, no? Such as it is, Irène has brought back some, how you would say, gossip."

I held up my hand as if stopping traffic. "Madame, please don't concern yourself."

She grasped my hand, pushing it back onto the table. "You should know. That is all I'm saying. Small minds, or perhaps minds seeking a diversion, like to relish in these things. And these small minds are saying that you are in a relationship with the commanding officer here.

And no good will come of that. You won't be able to hide your feelings, and it will affect your work. Believe me, I know this."

"Truly, not much has happened. Not that anyone else could be aware of anyway." Heat was rising in my face. Of course, I had heard a few wisecracks and giggles here and there but thought nothing of them. How could a perfectly normal and healthy relationship between two adults possibly be harmful? We had been ever careful not to allow our friendship to affect our work. I needed to think this through alone and then discuss it with Fred. I glanced at Madame, and she seemed to read my thoughts.

"It doesn't matter if you've done nothing wrong. It doesn't matter if it's love or lust or flirtation." She picked up her centime from the table, tucked it back into her bag, and rose from her chair. "What matters is the important work you're doing. Soon, you will have to make a choice. There is more to my story, but you will have to trust me for now." She touched a crooked forefinger to her temple. "Think. Because there is no going back."

My nurses started planning for Christmas directly after Thanksgiving. They wrote home for fun things to put in the men's stockings, which they had started knitting and sewing. We already had a choir of sorts, and I wrote home for some music for us.

It felt strange to be planning a joyous celebration in the middle of a war. When the nurses were having a stocking sewing session, I joined them one evening to see how they felt about it.

We had one hundred nurses now, and they planned to make ten stockings each, so we would have enough for a thousand men. Our admissions had fallen off lately, so we all hoped that should be enough. Since I could knit a bit, I settled myself next to Nora, who was using bright red and white yarn.

A pile of completed stockings was in a basket next to her. "If you can sew a white cuff on those, that would be most helpful," she told me.

After chatting a bit about all the Christmas plans, I asked her straight out how she felt about the celebration.

"It's a wonderful thing, really. An opportunity to show our men how much we care about them and how much support they have from back home."

"Do you think it makes them sadder though, makes them miss home even more and resent all they've lost?" I used a yarn needle to attach the white cuff to the red stocking.

"No. The only thing that could be worse is if we neglect to celebrate at all." She put down her knitting needles. "Come. I'd like to show you something you may not have noticed."

We put on our coats, and she led me outside the hut to a dark corner across the racetrack from the lines of tents. There was a blanket of freshly fallen snow that seemed to hush any sounds. I pulled up my collar to protect my cheeks from an icy wind.

"Look up," Nora said.

It was a moonless night, and clouds obscured most of the stars. There frankly wasn't much to look at.

"Here it comes."

A white spotlight appeared against the clouds and circled around us, then over the field. It made the clouds glow for a moment, then lit the dark space in between.

"It seems like it helps us see into heaven," Nora said. "I know it's man-made, but I like to think of it as a halo of protection over us. Out there, beyond it, is God and all the universe. But under that halo of light, we share a place of safety. A place where we love and take care of one another, even as terrible things happen outside it."

The light circled around again. I breathed in deeply of the night air as I imagined being under the light's protective watch. "Thank you, Nora."

On Christmas morning, we had about eight hundred patients, and the nurses delivered each of them a stocking. They were filled with candies, nuts, tobacco, and a little gift such as a small book. A group of ladies from a church back in the States had made bookmarks with Bible verses on them. They were colorful and sweet, and the men treasured them.

Later in the morning, we got word that two trainloads of patients were arriving. The nurses who were off duty got busy making and loading up some more stockings.

We had a special dinner for them. I had requested turkey or chicken, but with all the other special things we wanted for them, pork was what met the budget. They didn't complain a bit.

Garlands of pine and fresh holly decorated the nurses' mess tent, and we had a wonderful dinner, joined by the doctors. Then I gathered my choir, now fifty strong, for a last rehearsal. We bundled up, and each carrying a candle or a lantern, we made a procession outside to the last line of tents. I played a note on my violin to tune them up, then we went through our repertoire.

We sang familiar hymns: "O Come, All Ye Faithful," "Silent Night," "It Came Upon the Midnight Clear." Soon, officers and patients joined us, and our crowd grew as we moved up each line of tents and sang a few songs at each stop. There was some laughing and jostling, as the British patients had different lyrics and tunes for some of the hymns. Patients who couldn't come out were wheeled or walked to the tent openings, and they too joined in song.

The singing took on an ethereal sense. I felt warmed inside and joyful to be a part of it.

After warming up with some hot cocoa and cookies, we settled back into the mess hall, where the tables had been moved aside and a simple stage set up. We had a small actors' troupe, and they performed skits they had seen in London or made up themselves.

My big part was to read a poem written by two of my nurses as they acted it out. I had not had time to read it beforehand, so I was laughing and tearing up, even as I read it out loud.

It was titled "The Army Alphabet," and there was a line or two for each letter. One of my favorites was "U is us, as we used to be." My nurses strutted across the stage in wildly colorful civilian clothes, with outrageous hats and feathers everywhere. It garnered quite a laugh from the audience.

That was followed by a much more somber Y:

Y's for the years and years before we're done,
When we've healed every Tommie and killed every Hun,
Then old and decrepit and wrinkled and gray,
To America's shores, we'll wend our way.

How proud I was of my nurses. Just when I thought they could no longer surprise me, their creativeness and spirit once again over-whelmed me.

❧

The next day, I set out with Fred and Dr. Valentine to deliver gifts for charities in Rouen.

First, we visited a boys' home. It was a pretty dreary place, with sparse furnishings and not enough light. But the boys were clean, had adequate if shabby clothing, and were oh so happy to see us. The nurses had taken up a collection and had purchased toys, candy, socks, hats, and mittens for them. The boys accepted the presents with yelps of glee, and I was hugged again and again. As I bent to kiss each one on the top of his head, I felt I wanted to bring them all home with me.

I spotted Dr. Valentine sitting in a chair across the room, looking like St. Nicholas with a child on his lap. Fred had a circle of boys around him as he played a game of catch. Again, I had a moment of doubt: *Was it fair to come visit just this once, then disappear forever?* For I doubted we could find the time to come back.

Fred must have been thinking along similar lines, as on the ride back, he said, "We need to do this again. What do you think?"

To which I answered, "Absolutely. And next time, maybe have one or two of my nurses come as well."

"You're right. Probably best to cycle the nurses instead. I haven't a hope of getting away with any sort of regularity. And it's a selfish venture for me."

"How so?" I asked.

"Being with the children fills my heart. Sometimes I imagine playing catch or opening presents with my own. Having a good influence and raising a child right are some of the most important things one can do, don't you think?"

"Of course" is what I said. But what I was thinking was *But it probably won't happen for me.*

CHAPTER 14

January 1918

With the extra coal heaters I had ordered, bartered for, or otherwise managed to obtain, piles of woolen blankets, and donated knitted items, it seemed we might get through the winter. A lovely women's group in St. Louis had knitted woolen mittens for all my nurses, and I encouraged them to wear them whenever possible instead of gloves. "Your fingers keep each other warmer when they're together," I explained, once again feeling like a mother hen.

At first there were protests that they didn't look professional, but by and by, even my staunchest nurses, Nora and Dorothy, were spotted wearing them, at least when they weren't directly caring for patients.

❧

The cases of influenza, or "flu" as the British called it, increased with the colder weather. Dr. Valentine and I had reached a good agreement on reserving both the space and equipment we needed to care for them as well as we could. Which was not very well, I regretted. It was a perplexing disease, and we had no medication that helped. We had

THE WAR NURSE   183

to be very careful when giving cough syrup to the poor souls who were racked day and night with coughing spasms, lest it made them too sleepy to fight off the disease.

⁓

My nurses earned fifteen days of leave every six months, and I was determined to see they got them. It took five separate forms to organize everything, and if I didn't get everything just right, a nurse could be stranded at the port without proper authorization, or worse, misdirected to the wrong area. I was in my office, carefully filling out these forms, when I heard the tick-ticking of Sam's paws coming down the wood plank hallway. This raised my spirits, especially since he was usually in the company of Fred.

But it was not Fred but Dr. Valentine walking Sam.

"Miss Stimson, if you have a minute?"

"Of course. Come in."

"I won't be but a moment, but I have an idea to discuss."

Now, this was new. It seemed our shared loss of Ned had softened him toward me.

"As you know, tuberculosis, pneumonia, and now what seems to be a virulent influenza are filling up beds that we sorely need for the wounded."

"I'm not aware of a bed shortage. Our patient census is under a thousand, and we've got a full tent dedicated to respiratory conditions, and it isn't nearly full."

"Yes, but what happens after the next big battle? Things won't stay quiet for long."

"Indeed. What is your idea?"

"I'm thinking that we work on a protocol here. Put a physician in charge. Then, we seek approval to open a dedicated hospital, somewhere farther from the front. In Paris, perhaps."

"Seems reasonable." My defenses were up. "You certainly don't need my approval, but you would have it, of course. What do you need from me?"

He looked at his wristwatch. "He'll be here in a few minutes. We thought it best to include you in the discussion, out of respect. Major Murphy is on board."

"For heaven's sake, what are you talking about? Am I to be transferred to this new project?" I had a sinking feeling he was trying to get rid of me, like a stone in his shoe.

He looked toward the door, but whomever he was waiting for had not appeared. "Why, I hadn't even thought of that. Might be a jolly good idea." He gave a wry smile. "But no, it's about the physician to be in charge."

Just then, my brother Phil appeared in my doorway, grinning ear to ear. "Sorry to be late, but I've just received a wonderful phone call." He nodded toward Dr. Valentine.

Dr. Valentine got up to shake Phil's hand. "Then it's settled. Miss Stimson, meet the new head of infectious diseases, Dr. Philip Stimson."

So much for wanting my input. "Congratulations, Brother. Does this mean you will be leaving this cozy place for the big city?"

The two men looked at each other and laughed.

"Why no. I'll be right here to keep an eye on you."

"Dr. Stimson is still under treatment here. But we see no reason we can't use his brain while his body further recovers." Dr. Valentine was as jovial as I had ever seen him. A smile looked rather unnatural on his face.

They walked out, clapping their arms on each other's shoulders. I was happy for Phil, but this murky position between patient and staff at my hospital worried me. And I was wary of this newly minted alliance.

My next visitor was Fred. Of course, he was already aware of Phil's new position.

"So I hope we've made up for not accepting Dr. Stimson for the unit back in St. Louis." He ran his hand through his hair, something he tended to do when he was quite pleased with himself.

"Hmph." I hadn't quite made up my mind on how I felt about this plan. Of course, it really wasn't my decision to make, and Dr. Valentine had made a small effort to inform me, but it seemed there was some other reason I wasn't part of the discussion. "Why do you suppose Philip never mentioned this to me?"

"Oh, I forgot. You hate surprises, don't you?"

✍

In late January, I received a letter from the chief nurse in Étretat. I didn't know her well, even though she was perhaps the closest to me geographically, outside Rouen.

Dear Miss Stimson,

I regret to inform you that we have lost one of our nurses, Amabel Roberts. We believe she is the first American woman to lose her life in this conflict. She contracted a severe infection during her work with the wounded, and nothing could be done to save her.

I recall from our meeting that you were a graduate of Vassar College, as was Nurse Roberts. I am very sorry...

So we nurses had lost one of our own. I did not know Miss Roberts, but still, it was a punch in the gut. It was inevitable, of course. One couldn't place so many women in hazardous conditions and not expect casualties. I thought of my own dear nurses. I recruited them, trained them, convinced them to come. Of course, most didn't take much convincing, but still, they had entrusted me with their lives.

I thought of each of their young, innocent faces. They always put themselves last. The thought of losing even one of them tore me apart. And what if our hospital became a target, like the ones farther north? I put my head down on my desk and allowed myself a few tears. Not the slobbery, howling wails I wanted, but a slow drip of sorrow and a hug from my own arms to hold myself together.

CHAPTER 15

February 1918

S pring came slowly to the wet river valley. In early February, we had some unseasonably warm days, giving us a hint that winter was finally loosening its grip. The breakup of river ice started upriver, then the chunks flowed steadily downstream. By the time they hit Rouen, the chunks had amassed into craggy hills on the banks, with open water appearing in the middle.

In my teen years, I had seen a painting by Monet of this very scene. I remember thinking how cold and desolate it looked, the gray-blue ice reaching up to the blue-smoke mountain, with the dull sky above. Seeing this place in person (or very near it anyway), I found the artist had captured not only the colors but the mood of the place—of waiting. Now we were waiting for spring to come, for life to burst forth, for an end to the biting cold and the drab weariness, not only of winter but of an awful, exhausting war.

It was at this time of breakup in 1918 that I traveled to the village of Amiens with Fred, Benjamin, and two of my nurses—Charlotte and her roommate, Rebecca. The trains transporting our patients from the CCSs to Rouen had been compromised. We weren't told exactly what or where, but rumors held that there was so much unexploded ordnance between Cambrai and Amiens that the trains were at risk.

I saw this as an opportunity; I hadn't left Rouen in several months and was itching to relieve the feeling of being cooped up. We took three ambulances, as there was a particularly large number of sick and wounded to transport back to Base Hospital 21.

The ride out was ordinary enough, giving me time to chat with our driver, Benjamin, as the miles of brown fields passed by, some with a hint of green in the plowed rows. We crossed the still mostly frozen River Somme at Amiens, then continued east. I had hoped to have a brief stop in the town, but sadly, there wasn't time. There was a thirteenth-century Gothic cathedral there, much like ours in Rouen, that I would have liked to see, but it would have to remain a picture in my mind.

"I hear you've taken quite a shine to one of my nurses," I teased Benjamin.

He squirmed in his too-large overcoat. "Ah now, I've got a shine on all the Yank nurses, Matron. I'm hoping one will stuff me in her suitcase when it's time to go home."

"Not any one in particular? Perhaps our little Charlotte, who blushes and rushes to the loo whenever you pop in?"

"Does she now? Well, that's bloody well good to know."

"Always volunteering for extra duty, that one. Especially when it involves a ride in the truck."

"She must like trucks."

I smiled to myself. It was refreshing to see young love bloom.

"Sorry about the cathedral, Matron. But there's something up ahead that's quite amusing. And I'm afraid it's the only place around to offer a bit of privacy, should you need the loo."

"Who could resist that combination?" I assumed "the loo" was the clump of trees ahead, but it would have to do.

Benjamin pulled over next to what appeared to be an abandoned encampment. Spent shells and dented canteens littered the well-worn ground. It may have been my imagination, but I swore the smell of gunpowder still lingered in the air.

After following the helpful sign to *la toilette*, which was a hole inside a dugout inside a trench, and after witnessing the unhelpful rats that seemed unperturbed by our presence, the other ladies and I took to the clump of trees instead.

The other attraction turned out to be a depot for spent items. In no apparent order lay a shot-up tank surrounded by spent machine gun ammunition belts, rotted out boots, and other paraphernalia. I was quite unimpressed until Benjamin took me around to the least battered side of the French tank.

Written on it, in chalk, were messages in German, then French, then German, then French again, and finally one in English. Each message had a date. As I tried to translate it all, Benjamin helped, pointing at each message in turn. *Captured by Germans, 1 July '16; Captured by French, 8 July; Captured by Germans, 15 July; Captured by French, August;* and, finally, *Assigned to BEF, September '16.*

My fellow passengers all thought it was quite amusing, as did I. But I couldn't resist rubbing my finger on the lettering. How could the messages possibly have survived the weather, not to mention all those battles, when the tank itself was in ruins? It turned out the chalk did not rub off very easily, somehow having become one with the tank's coating.

Back on the road, signs soon appeared that we were approaching the railhead—a cluster of worn, shanty-like buildings next to two sets of tracks emerging from the forest. Soon, we pulled up to the rally point, with the other ambulances not far behind. We were just in time, as I heard the whistle of the approaching train.

We could hold eight stretchers in each ambulance, stacked four on each side, plus a few ambulatory patients sitting in chairs down the middle. It wasn't the best setup, but it was the quickest way to get them to base hospital in reasonable comfort. As the train pulled up, I counted the railroad cars. There were the usual supply cars, a coal car, and four for passengers. Unless ambulances were coming from another hospital, it appeared there might be too many patients for us to carry.

We had a well-rehearsed system, getting a report from a caregiver on each car, then ensuring each stretcher patient was tagged with identification and the nature of his injury.

As soon as the train stopped, I hopped on my assigned car. Upon seeing the groaning, doubled-over patients holding handkerchiefs to their faces and hearing the violent coughing and labored breathing, a wave of dread passed through me. They appeared to be victims of a gas attack. Yet I had not heard of one in recent months, both sides seeming to have come to the conclusion that they were ineffectual weapons, that using them injured as many on their own side as the enemy's.

They were mostly Tommies, but there were a number of Americans mixed in. Our troops were starting to arrive, and many were assigned to British units until there were enough in number to form their own commands. I found the caregiver, an American corporal. He was so young, I doubted if he even had to shave, his smooth face untouched by time.

"Seventeen," he responded to my question about the number of his charges. "Respiratory distress," was his equally laconic response to my next question.

"All of them?"

"Yes, ma'am."

"Was there an attack of poison gas?"

"I'm not at liberty to say, ma'am."

I blinked. This was a most unusual answer. "Corporal, it is essential for us to know the nature of the injuries to properly treat them."

"I understand, ma'am. Respiratory distress of undisclosed nature is all I can say."

Charlotte appeared in the doorway. "We're ready to unload, Matron."

A soldier on a stretcher in the far corner began to cough violently and retch.

"Charlotte, can you please do what you can for that patient?"

As we unloaded the ambulatory patients, I checked each one for urgent conditions so that Fred could see them before the long trip back. Finding none, we crowded them into the ambulances. I consoled myself that they weren't much more cramped than they had been on the train, and they certainly didn't complain.

But still, my mind turned the corporal's words over and over. Why was there a mystery about these injuries? Was there just a lack of communication between the field station and transport, or was something else going on?

I decided the best way to find out was from someone who was there. Late that evening, I went to the ward where Amiens arrivals had been assigned. Most of them were asleep. The room reverberating with the sound of loud snoring didn't seem to disturb them in their exhausted states. But midway down the center row of beds, I found a soldier sitting up, his legs dangling over the side of the bed.

I picked up the clipboard attached to the foot of his bed, noted his name and last vital signs. "How are you feeling, Private Riffle?"

He was hunched over, reminding me of elderly patients suffering from emphysema. He twisted his head around to see me. "Can't complain."

An American accent. I looked again at his flow sheet to confirm. "Where are you from?"

"Iowa originally. But we deployed from Fort Riley, Kansas."

A coughing fit interrupted the symphony of snoring. Then, one after the other, the patients fell into coughing fits, as if they were passing them along like a baton. Private Riffle coughed as well and wiped a suddenly bloody nose.

I gave him a towel, but it seemed the issue resolved quickly on its own.

"Has this been happening often?"

"Yeah, off and on." He peered at me over the brown towel. "I mean, yes, ma'am."

He was so green, he probably just got out of high school.

"Can you tell me more about what happened to your unit? I understand you may have been attacked by some new type of hard-to-detect gas."

"My unit?" He looked around at his fellow patients. "No, I don't know any of those guys. I just arrived in country and got real sick after a few days. Don't know from what. Maybe a sneak attack, something random." He hacked, then wiped his mouth.

I unwrapped the stethoscope Fred had lent me from around my neck. He had been coaching me on breath sounds. "Can I have a listen?"

From the rales and rhonchi, the bubbling and low whistles I could hear through the stethoscope, I knew his lungs were quite wet. The lower portions of his lungs had no sound at all, not a good sign. He probably had pneumonia, and from the sounds of the coughing and wheezing in the rest of the crowded ward, so did most of them.

"Thank you, Private." I helped him into bed, with an extra pillow to raise his head.

It seemed we were sent not a trainload of injured soldiers but a group of men probably infected with a contagious disease. I needed to put the entire ward on respiratory isolation. And what about Fred, myself, and the others who had come into contact with them?

It was eleven o'clock at night, after a very long day, but I would have to wake Fred.

CHAPTER 16

changed to a fresh uniform, then brushed and twisted my hair into the French knot I had seen local women do, telling myself the whole time I would freshen my appearance for any doctor I needed to consult in the middle of the night.

As I approached the door to Fred's hut, I could hear a soft snore and couldn't help my mind from wandering back to his warm body cuddling me against the bitter chill of the barn. Shaking off those thoughts, I rapped on his door.

A snort and a groan.

I rapped again. "Dr. Murphy, it's Matron."

"Jules?"

"Yes. We need you in the respiratory tent."

"Come in here."

I looked down the path both ways. No one was about, but still I couldn't risk someone seeing me entering his hut. "Um, I... Why don't you meet me in the mess tent? I'll make some coffee. It's urgent but not an emergency."

"For God's sake, just get in here."

If I left the door open, it shouldn't be a problem, I thought. "Okay, coming in."

Fred was sitting up in bed, wiping his glasses with a cloth, his hair a wild mane. He was undressed, at least from the waist up. "About time." He must have sensed my tension. "What has you so riled up? I don't think it's a patient going south. You're acting too strangely."

"Well, two things, actually. I'm uncomfortable coming in here, and we've got a pressing problem with a group of men just admitted before their first battle."

His eyes followed mine to his hair, and he ran his fingers through it. "I'm quite the sight, I'm sure, but you've seen worse."

"It's not that, and you know it." I looked toward the door I had left open. "We can't let prying eyes see me here and make the wrong assumptions."

"I don't give a crap." He pushed aside his covers, revealing, thankfully, a set of boxer shorts. He waved in the general direction of the lone chair in the room, where a pair of slacks were slung.

"Well, we can discuss that at another time." I grabbed the slacks and set them next to him. "We've just admitted thirty men with respiratory symptoms. Fever, cough, some short of breath."

"Gas attack?"

"No. These are all new arrivals. Haven't been close to the front."

"That doesn't rule it out. Bastards could have spies sneaking canisters aboard troop ships."

The strange reports I had received from the corporal on the train with the patients and the American private had made me suspicious of the nature of their conditions. "I don't think so. No burns, and fever isn't—"

"Let's go take a look." He had slipped on his pants and was fishing about the wooden wardrobe that occupied a corner of the hut.

On the way to the intake ward, I filled Fred in with what I knew.

"I think I know what you're thinking, and I agree," he said.

"Something contagious."

He nodded. "If it's tuberculosis, there's little we can do but isolate them and keep them hydrated. If it's a virus, pretty much the same treatment, but they should bounce back more quickly. We could try quinine, I suppose, if we have any."

We had arrived at the entrance to the newly designated respiratory tent. From a table just outside the door, I picked up two face masks the nurses had fashioned from some gauze and rubber bands so as not to deplete the supply for surgery. I handed one to Fred, then slipped one on myself.

There were two rows of fifteen men, lining the long outside walls of the tent. Most were sleeping. One of my nurses was holding a basin under the chin of her patient, who was in the midst of a coughing fit.

"So we'll give support, but it will have to run its course. Do you think we have enough space between patients?" I asked.

He fidgeted with the rubber bands encircling his ears. It certainly wasn't a comfortable feeling. "It would be best to put each of them in their own tent. Is that possible?"

I huffed at his rhetorical question. But he had a point. What choices did we have? There was some space in the postoperative tent. But to put the respiratory cases in there seemed a dangerous combination. "The only way to do that would be for the doctors to double up in their huts. Nurses are already two to a hut, but maybe we can stack them, like on the ship. We'll all bunk together."

"I'd be okay with that if I get to choose my bunkmate." His eyes crinkled above the white gauze.

Ignoring his attempt at humor or flirtation, I pressed on with my official duties, mindful that there were thirty-one sets of ears that might appreciate a tidbit of gossip. He had turned to exit the tent, and I double stepped to keep up with him. "I'll need written orders for the isolation, quinine, and whatever else you might want to try."

"Respiratory isolation and comfort measures." He yawned, blinked back the sleep I had interrupted. "Write it up, and I'll sign. Also isolation from anyone who has had contact with them without mask and gloves." He stopped walking. "Wait, you were at the CCS today. Were you exposed?"

I bit my lips. I had anticipated this question but still had not thought it through. I needed to review the whole day in my head. "Probably."

"Jesus. If you get so much as a sniffle, I want you to report to me."

Thankfully, although I was down for a few days with bronchitis, I bounced back quickly, and I watched my nurses like a hawk, but so far, they had remained healthy.

CHAPTER 17

Poison gas was unquestionably an atrocious weapon, but it did provide a tiny glimmer of light. It helped us learn how to care for the ever-growing number of victims of the respiratory condition we now believed was influenza. The two groups needed similar care, but this led to a perplexing problem.

When I did my initial rounds one frosty morning, I found Nora, the night supervisor, just going off her shift, having an argument with Dr. Valentine. She had her arms crossed over her chest in a defensive position, but there was no mistaking the fire in her eyes. "Yes, he may be your surgical patient, but I'm telling you he's not being assigned to this ward."

"Good morning," I greeted them. "What seems to be the problem?"

Dr. Valentine had dark circles under his eyes and appeared more rumpled than usual. "I just spent four hours in surgery saving the life of a man who your nurse doesn't feel is fit for her ward. He needs respiratory isolation, and this is the respiratory tent you insisted on."

"Indeed it is. What is your concern, Nora?" I asked.

"In addition to the burns Dr. Valentine has operated on, this poor soldier has been exposed to mustard gas. There is little we can do for his poor burned lungs, but we must at least keep him away from the influenza patients."

"But that's the point of this ward, isn't it? All the masking and gloves and extra room? To protect them from one another and to protect the staff?" His voice was hoarse with fatigue.

"You both have a point. But this isn't an issue to decide now, when you're on the brink of exhaustion. We'll put the patient in the officers' tent for now. It's nearly empty." I gently steered Dr. Valentine out of the tent by his elbow. He was too tired to resist.

Dedicating two tents to respiratory isolation was out of the question for the moment. We hadn't the supplies, the room, or the staff to manage it. But Nora was right. We had seen the havoc the flu caused on healthy lungs. There was no telling what would happen to the gassed patients if they contracted it. So I had the tent divided by heavy canvas drapes, added a handwashing station to each end, and advised the supervisors to assign the nurses to one side or the other. Likewise, the patients were assigned to the flu side or the nonflu side.

~

The gassed patients had seemed to do better with a daily dose of sunshine and fresh air. Each day, we bundled them up and rolled their beds outside. The men always enjoyed the outing. The sight of them, some wrapped in white bandages from head to toe, lying with their arms outstretched as if to capture the healing rays of the sun, at once raised my spirits and put a lump in my throat.

When the weather was cold, it wasn't safe to bring them outside. But they became more and more restless, needing more pain medication, and generally irritable. Skin infections increased at an alarming rate, and the coughing grew worse by the day.

It seemed to me that the influenza patients would also benefit from fresh air, and a less germ-infested working space would be of benefit to the staff as well. I came up with a plan to bring some of the healing powers of the outdoors in. We needed more beds, and tents were being added. When it came time to place the tents, I requested their direction be changed so that the large flaps on each end could be opened to the prevailing winds.

Summer would be the most important, and the cooling winds came from the north and west in the summer. In the winter, we had the westerlies and also a warming wind from the south. So we placed the tents with their flapped sides open toward the west.

The first new tent had just been set up and the beds and equipment placed as a trainload arrived with dozens more influenza patients. I went out to the receiving area to help unload the ambulances. I opened the back door of one and found twelve men in American uniforms, sitting on the floor or standing against the walls, playing cards or making bets.

"What are you fellows doing?" I asked rather rhetorically. They looked at me rather sheepishly, then all started talking at once.

"Wait. You." I pointed to one who had the stripes of a corporal.

"We're all fresh off the boat, ma'am. Barely got to our unit when one guy started coughing his lungs out. So the LT sent our whole platoon to the CCS. They didn't know what to do, so we got sent here."

"Are any of you ill or injured?" A chorus of nos and shaking of heads, and one "this guy here is not right in the head" with a friendly shove.

"So you've been exposed but not sick." It appeared they were sent to be quarantined, but we weren't set up to do that. And neither were the units. "Okay, guys, seems you're pretty comfortable here for now. I'll get you some food and water. Just stay put."

A quick tour of the other ambulances showed me much of the same thing, but mixed in with the healthy soldiers were a few with fevers and coughs. We separated them out straightaway, and I hurried off to check with the doctors for what they wanted to do.

I hastily arranged a meeting with Fred and Dr. Gross right there in the receiving area. We also sent for my brother Phil, as he was steadily increasing his work with infectious diseases.

Our little group went up to the ambulance full of poker-playing soldiers.

Fred asked, "You guys don't really want to be here, right?"

They just laughed. "Beats the front," one said.

"How about we set you up in a *chambre d'hôte* for a week or so? I got a friend in Rouen with some rooms."

They all cheered, and with a few words to the ambulance driver, Fred had them on their way.

As I steered the doctors to the next ambulance, I asked the obvious. "That's a wonderful solution for them, but how many French hoteliers do you know?"

"Ah, the lady asks too many questions."

The three doctors laughed and cheered.

"You know what I mean. And how will we pay them?"

"Let's just say they're returning a favor. And this is just temporary. I'll get on the horn and find some space in neighboring hospitals. Beyond that, it's headquarters in Paris's problem, not ours."

"Good, because running a quarantine for healthy, rambunctious soldiers is not something I want my nurses involved with."

"How much room do you have in the tent for respiratory cases?" Dr. Gross asked. His specialty was ophthalmology, but he frequently treated patients with facial burns and gassed patients as well.

"It holds thirty all together, and there's maybe a dozen patients in there now. A few gassed patients, one suspected TB."

Phil winced. "We really need to get the TB case out of here. As for the gassed—"

Fred interrupted. "This isn't Barnes. We can't have a separate ward for every diagnosis."

"What do we do then?" I asked. "We have the one tent for all of them. The staff wear masks, sometimes gloves, and we pushed the beds farther apart, but that's about the only difference."

Fred used his thumb to point at the soldiers in the trucks behind him. "Separate out the soldiers suffering from flu symptoms, clean them up, and admit them to the tent for infectious respiratory conditions. The healthy ones can wait here until we find a place for them."

"How far apart should the beds be?" I asked.

Fred shrugged. "Just spread them as much as you can within the space."

He was not forthcoming with how much distance was needed, probably because no one really knew. We knew that people in the same household were likely to infect one another but didn't know if that was because they breathed the same air, touched the same things, or were close enough to cough their germs at one another.

Phil couldn't give a concrete answer either. In fact, he merely added to our worries. "I imagine the germs are spreading hand to hand, maybe survive in the air, long after someone has left the room," he said.

"We can manage keeping them from contaminating things with their hands, but what about the air? How far could a sneeze carry the germs? A cough? Do we need to wash their bedding and clothes individually, like with smallpox or lice?"

"I'm sorry, Jules," Phil said. "We just don't have those answers yet. Run some electric fans, and do the best you can with what you have."

The more I thought about it, the more I felt sucked into a vortex of never-ending worries. There was, in fact, only so much we could possibly do. We couldn't put the men, or those who cared for them, in protective bubbles. We had to use what we had, which was bleach, rubbing alcohol, and a disinfectant that we aerosolized during surgery. Since we only did emergency surgery at night, it occurred to me that I could borrow one of those units from an idle operating theater. My mind buzzed, and I began to feel more hopeful.

That was until I met with the roadblock of Dr. Valentine, just as I thought we were making great progress.

❧

"What the hell do you think you're doing?" Dr. Valentine stopped me as I wheeled a cart out of the operating tent.

"Borrowing this equipment from an unused space to use where it is vitally needed."

"And where is that, I might ask, and by whose authority?" He was slipping on his white doctor's lab coat. All the other doctors had given them up as too impractical to keep clean.

"Is there some higher authority that guides the use of needed equipment? After all, I or one of my staff orders it, supervises the training for it, cleans it, and runs it." I hadn't had enough sleep the night before. I knew I was being testy, but I couldn't seem to stop myself. "But if you want to take over some or all of those duties…"

"Don't get smart with me, young lady. That is surgical equipment. We can't have nurses trotting off with it willy-nilly."

I took a breath. Challenging him would be of no benefit. "We need it for the new respiratory tent."

"Since when is listerizing a treatment for gassed patients? Who ordered that?"

He had caught me in the undefined middle ground between what nurses could do within their own practice and what required doctor's orders. I needed to tread carefully. "It's not an individual treatment. It's part of maintaining as sterile an environment as we can. And it's not for gassed patients. It's for the newly arrived men with respiratory conditions."

"I've heard more about that. They've not even seen battle. Why are we giving them special treatment? A sterile environment? Have you lost your mind completely? Or noticed we're in the midst of a war?"

"If we don't control the spread—"

"Listen to me, Miss Stimson. You get back to work saving the lives of the men who've been fighting. That's what we're here for. They've run out of strong men in Blighty. They're sending over the weak and the cowards now."

"They're Canadian." I couldn't seem to help myself.

His face reddened, and he yanked the cart out of my hands. "You haven't heard the last of this." He rattled away, his white coat flapping after him.

CHAPTER 18

The good news was American combat units were arriving in theater in increasing numbers. The bad news was the enemy was stepping up their attacks, sensing a need to weaken the Allies before they could establish more strongholds.

And still, our beds were filling with influenza patients. I could see Dr. Valentine's dire prediction heading toward us like a locomotive. Phil was traveling back and forth to Paris nearly every week, causing me to worry he would collapse from exhaustion. His damaged tissues and muscles had not had time enough to heal.

We needed to simultaneously care for our current patients, plan a new place to send the influenza patients, protect our staff, and prepare for the oncoming wave of casualties. It was my nature to worry about every possibility, but I couldn't, or I would spin my wheels and get nothing accomplished. And I had to be careful not to tread into areas that were not my responsibility.

Although I was invited to the medical staff meetings, I was a guest. Whenever I offered opinion outside my official duties, I got cold stares. Even so, at the last staff meeting, I had requested time at the next one to discuss that hazy line between what I or my nurses could do without first getting a doctor's approval. To function more smoothly, we needed better ground rules.

After that, the only way to succeed was to divide and conquer the tasks: first determine if I or my staff was responsible, then prioritize according to urgency, then assign to the most appropriate people. Of course, that all sounded simpler than it actually was.

Over the next few weeks, trainload after trainload brought a mix of casualties. Thanks to Fred's work in identifying places for quarantine, we weren't getting still healthy soldiers. But the numbers of soldiers with pneumonia and influenza were increasing steadily, sometimes outnumbering the wounded.

Squarely in my area of responsibility was to protect my staff from injury and illness as best we could. As I lay on my bed, not sleeping due to the images of coughing men spewing clouds of infection toward my nurses, an idea dawned on me. Our dwindling supply of face masks would never be enough for all these patients or for our nurses to change even once a day for very long. We were two weeks away from our next shipment, possibly a week if I got on the phone to London several times a day to beg for a rushed order.

My pleasant trip to downtown Rouen and meeting with the baker inserted itself in my dreams. Then the ladies chatting in rapid French in the fabric shop next door. As I tried to enjoy my mind's seeming distraction, I realized there was a connection my sleepy mind was trying to make. I sat bolt upright.

The townspeople were always eager to help, and there seemed not much we could ask of them without stripping them of their own meager supplies. But pretty fabric was one thing that was in abundance. Paris may have been the fashion center, but Rouen had been producing wool and cotton fabric for centuries. During my visit to a fabric shop, the eager proprietor had shown me bolts and bolts of cotton fabric, with tiny flowers and other designs. She waved at the fabrics, then waved disparagingly at the rather empty streets. From what I could determine, she was telling me *no one is buying.* The fabric and sewing trades were large, but the demand for their goods was low.

So when it seemed to be a respectable enough hour in the morning to summon Benjamin, I made a cup of tea to take to him. I rapped lightly on the door of the hut he shared with several other men. After a few tries, I got some groans in response, and I cracked the door open. "Benjamin? It's Matron. Can you come to the door?"

Within a minute, the young man slipped out into the dark alley, lit only by the kerosene lamp I carried.

"What's wrong?" He was hopping on one foot as he slipped a sock on the other.

I felt embarrassed; this was no emergency. It was simply my need to push forward with my idea as soon as possible. I held up the teacup, which Benjamin looked at with suspicion. He took the cup but coughed at the awkward moment.

"Can you take me into town? I want to be there when the shops open at seven o'clock."

Benjamin took a sip of the hot tea. "Of course, Matron."

"I should explain... I need to—"

"There's no need to explain." He checked his watch. "If you say you need to be there at seven, then I'll be ready with the Ford at six thirty."

My embarrassment ebbed. Indeed, outside medical staff meetings, my word carried some weight. It would have been too easy to abuse it, and I vowed to not squander any influence with selfish requests.

❧

We arrived on the dot of seven, but to my chagrin, the fabric shop was not yet open, despite what the posted sign said. Apparently on *lundi* (Monday), seven o'clock arrived closer to eight. Happily, the bakery next door was open, and the scents of fresh bread and croissants lured Benjamin and me over for a treat. During the drive, I had explained to

Benjamin that I planned to ask for help from the women in town to make face masks for our nurses.

We sat in delicately twined wrought-iron chairs. "Do you have a pattern for them?" Benjamin had switched to coffee, possibly to simplify the order by holding up two fingers. He made a funny face as he took a swig.

"Here, try with some cream." I pushed the small carafe toward him, then pulled a little diagram from my leather pouch. "It's not a true pattern, but I think they can figure it out from this."

Benjamin examined my drawing. "If I can make a suggestion? Instead of a rectangle, make it smaller on each end. Then when you gather the folds, it will be less bulky to sew. The straps should connect here—"

"How do you know so much about making face masks?"

"You Yanks have been here only a year and arrived with shiploads of supplies. We've been at this for nearly four. We've had to sew patches on uniforms with thread cannibalized from other uniforms. We learned from the locals to wear cloth over our faces when the spring winds come. Otherwise, you're breathing in some fine cow manure dust."

"I'm sure you've done much tougher things."

He looked at me, then away, in that misty-eyed stare I'd seen in so many of the soldiers. "I've been on the front lines, behind, and in between. Been shelled as an infantry bloke, shot at as an orderly carrying stretchers, and have driven through minefields. So yeah, I've seen my share."

"Anything you want to tell me about?"

"I've got some interesting scars on my chest." He rubbed above his sternum.

"From shrapnel?"

"Righto. Shrapnel in my heart."

That got my attention. "Oh my. That's not usually a survivable wound."

"Guess I was one of the lucky ones. They opened me up, cut out a piece of my rib, peeled back the lining of my heart, and plucked out that piece of lead. Sewed me up, and I was good for a while. But my hands and feet kept turning blue, and I couldn't catch my breath. They wanted to open me up all over again, but I didn't want to go through that bollocks twice."

I glanced at his fingernails, a telltale place to assess how well someone's blood was oxygenated. They were nice and pink and normally shaped, with no clubbing of the fingertips, which could indicate low blood oxygen over a long period of time.

"So what happened?"

"This was in a hospital in Belgium, and those nice doctors said they'd let me be. But then the British took over, and I had no choice. They said the first operation was dodgy, so they whipped me back into surgery. When they opened me up, they found a piece of my skin had gotten stuck on my heart, keeping it from beating properly. So they sliced it clean off, and here I am today." He took a swig of the coffee and winced.

"But I guess they didn't want to send you back to the front."

"No, ma'am. They made me an orderly at the base hospital, and when they found out I could drive like a demon, I did that too." He nodded toward the window. "Hey look, Matron. The fabric store is opening."

It seemed he was done storytelling for the moment. How painful it must have been to remember and share such an ordeal, but also hard to live and move on without expressing it. I was glad to have been the ear he chose.

⁓

The shop was small, maybe ten feet by fifteen. It was stuffed to the ceiling with bolts of colorful fabrics, and an entire wall was covered with notions: needles and thread, all manner of buttons, and lengths of cloth tape I hadn't a clue how to use.

Benjamin needn't have worried about a pattern for face masks. As soon as I pantomimed a mask over my face, the elderly but spry proprietor took me to a back room, where there was a stack of fifty or so masks, made from colorful fabrics.

"*Combien?*" she asked. How many?

I was startled that any would already be available and hadn't yet calculated the number I needed. I did some quick mental math: number of nurses working each shift times number of shifts per day. If they all wore them, 130, which I thought was best for now. But they would need to be laundered each day, and there would need to be a second set while the first was laundered. We needed at least 260.

"*Deux cent soixante.*" I was proud that at least I knew my French numbers.

The frail woman, dressed in a white dress with tiny blue flowers, clapped her hand to her mouth. "*C'est impossible!*"

I had reached the limits of my French and asked Benjamin to translate a question. "How long would it take to make that many?"

The answer came, and Benjamin translated, "The girls, a dozen or so, can each make one or two a day after school."

"Girls? *Filles?* How old are they?"

I was especially sensitive to seeing children put to work. In Harlem, we had little boys as young as seven admitted to the hospital with frostbite from being outside all night selling newspapers. And at Barnes Hospital in St. Louis, we had seen dozens of boys who had been recruited from orphanages to work at the many glassworks factories across the river. These child workers were shipped from all over the Midwest, arriving in boatloads on the Mississippi and trainloads into East St. Louis, their small hands valued for cleaning glass bottles.

Although the newspapers and factories claimed the children had a better life than where they came from, it still broke my heart when I saw their injuries.

A federal law passed in 1916 finally put limits on children working in factories, but there were still industries where it was allowed. I fully intended to find a way to support more protections for children in the United States.

But my reaction in the French shop was out of place. The woman waved me off and turned her back. Chagrined, I realized I had insulted her and her culture. Indeed, France had had child labor laws in effect for fifty years before they started being adopted piecemeal by some states back home.

"*Désolé*." I'm sorry. "Benjamin, can you please order enough fabric and thread for the project and offer your pattern if she wants it? And let's take some fabric back with us to get started with."

The revised admission process became routine. We got the influenza patients through the bathhouse and settled into beds in the newly designated ward in quick order, as they didn't require X-rays or evaluation by a surgeon. There was some griping among the nurses, which was unusual for them.

"Why don't they just put these crybabies back on a ship home? They haven't even dirtied a pinky, and they're taking up beds needed by the heroes out there fighting," said one to the nods and scowls of the others.

This attitude displeased me greatly and came as rather a surprise. I called together all the nurses on duty for an impromptu counseling session. "Ladies, we have newly arrived soldiers who have been stricken before they even set foot on a battlefield. This is through no fault of their own, and I can only imagine the discomfort they must feel at this circumstance. If they recover, they will go on to serve. If they don't, they will have given their lives to the effort, the same as any other of our fallen." I looked at each one of their faces, not singling any of them out.

"You will treat them with the utmost respect. They will receive the same care, that is, the best care possible from us. If you cannot do this or doubt your ability to protect yourself while caring for them, you may ask your shift leader to assign you to a different unit. Is this understood?"

They sheepishly murmured, "Yes, Matron."

It was the only time I ever had to make such a statement.

∽

My little Charlotte had been assigned to the respiratory tent and was her same dedicated self, bringing books and little treats to the men, who were feverish and coughing but otherwise unharmed. Apparently, she had an elderly uncle back home who had a huge personal library. He was sending his treasures to her, a few at a time.

She borrowed a metal cart that was used to pass medications and loaded it up every time she received a shipment of books. Then, she went down the ward, spending time with each patient to find what might suit them. Many asked her to sit on the chair next to their bed and read to them.

Between her long shifts, then the book sessions, I was becoming worried. She was just a slip of a thing when we started, and now her cheeks were starting to hollow.

When she reached the end of a row of beds and was about to roll her cart down the other side, I pulled her aside.

"Miss Cox, are you getting enough sleep? When was your last meal?"

"Oh, I'm just fine, Matron. Don't you worry about me."

"I am worried. If you don't take care of yourself, you can hardly take care of the others, and they need you."

"If I can't do this for the men, I will surely break down. It is such a relief from seeing the burned and bleeding and…" She shook her head. "Not that I mind that work, you understand. But I need this"—she waved toward the pale but otherwise whole men—"more than they need me."

"That's all well and good. But this is a special situation in here." I pointed to a quarantine sign and then to my own face mask.

"I'm being careful, Matron." She held up her gloved hands.

"You think you are. But I saw you lean in close to a patient and pull up your mask."

Charlotte reddened, and she looked away. "He couldn't understand me. It was just one moment."

"It only takes one moment." I let this sink in.

"Yes, Matron. I'll be more careful."

"All this work you're doing would be over. Not only that, you could become another burden to be cared for. Do you want that?"

I knew I had hit home by the way her eyes watered. Maybe I had been too harsh; she was such a delicate soul. But I shook off my doubts. It wasn't my job to coddle.

CHAPTER 19

I barely had time to make a quick round of the wards before a meeting scheduled to discuss the limits of our nursing practice. I was hoping we would be allowed the use of aerosolized antiseptics whenever we saw fit. It was foolish of me to take the equipment from the operating theater, even though it wasn't being used. That was apparently an overstep of the boundaries I sought to make more clear.

I had already written to my uncle Lewis for some guidance. Of course, his experience was limited to use in operating rooms, but I thought we should at least explore the idea for our respiratory patients.

On my rounds, I first went to the intake "lounge." We had adopted the French word, as it sounded so much more pleasant than *tent* or *ward.* There was the usual assortment of men in dirty uniforms, with bandages wrapped around heads or arms or chests. One of them greeted me by name.

"Matron Stimson!" He looked all of nineteen years old, with closely cropped sand-colored hair, deep blue eyes, and red and silvery burn scars around his nose and mouth. I had no recollection of him. My eyes drifted to the rank insignia pinned on his collar. A Canadian private.

"Good afternoon, Private. Are you being treated well here?"

"You don't recognize me, do you?" The soldier laughed and proceeded to lift his shirt. "Maybe this will refresh your memory."

His stomach was red and crinkly, scarred from burns. I still didn't remember him.

"I'm sorry. Perhaps you can remind me how we've met before?"

"You saved my life, you did. Maybe this will help." He opened his collar, revealing his heavily scarred neck.

It came back to me in a flash. It was the soldier who had been badly burned at the explosion of the ammunition supply depot, whom I had encountered still in the railcar near the CCS.

I looked at the soldier's neck, and sure enough, there was a horizontal scar, just below his Adam's apple, amid the bumpy burns. "Yes, I remember, you had some difficulty breathing."

"Difficulty? If you hadn't found me when you did, I would be a goner. This"—he pointed to his freshly wounded left shoulder—"is nothing. Thank you for saving me."

"I was just doing my job, as you are yours."

Little did the soldier know how I had struggled within the limits of my job, even as he struggled to breathe. In this case, the system had worked. But the thought of what could have happened if the French doctor had not arrived just seconds before it was too late haunted me.

After ensuring intake was properly staffed and equipped, I moved on to the surgical lounge. It, too, seemed to be in order, so I moved on to the respiratory lounge. I had left this for last so as not to contaminate the other wards. I donned a new mask from the pile the cooks were making in their off-duty time.

It would be several weeks before we received our order of masks from the French girls. Sometimes I felt bad about asking the cooks to do even more work after they had sweated over hot stoves and steamy sinks all day. But they had told me they enjoyed the different work, sitting at a sewing machine. They enjoyed talking to the staff, asking how they could be improved.

One evening, when I was clandestinely returning my dishes from my special snack to the kitchen, I ran into Fred, chatting with Alice while emptying his pockets of pipe cleaners.

"Don't tell me Alice has taken up pipe smoking," I said.

Alice sat behind the sewing machine with a pile of bright print fabrics next to it. She proudly held up a mask she was working on. "Oh, now that would be a sight. No, we're going to cut the pipe cleaners in half, then slip them into the top of the mask so's it fits better around the nose. That's how we made them back on the farm for when the tractor kicked up too much dust."

"Well, aren't the two of you clever," I said. It seemed I wasn't the only one who enjoyed visits with humble, cheerful, and wise Alice.

In the respiratory tent, I found Dr. Valentine supervising orderlies who were dismantling the disinfecting aerosol contraptions the nurses and I had put together.

"What is going on, Doctor?" I asked as I pinched my face mask over my nose. The piece of pipe cleaner worked just as Alice said it would.

He turned to me, his watery eyes barely visible through smudged glasses and the rest of his face hidden by a blue gauze mask. I made a mental note to advise my surgical nurses to add eyeglass cleaning to their presurgical duties. For all surgeons—we wouldn't want to single him out.

"What does it look like? I'm repossessing vital surgical equipment that someone has stolen."

"It wasn't stolen. I requisitioned it. We took nothing from you."

"Don't give me that asinine rubbish. As if all supplies are free and unlimited. And as I believe I have already warned you, this is still a completely unauthorized use, even if you requisition it."

"I'm in charge of the"—I waved my arms—"air in here, aren't I? And the air needs to be disinfected."

"You can't disinfect the air, you fool. The solution is heavier than air and simply drops to the ground, causing a slippery mess. And how do you know you're not damaging the lungs with whatever solution you've come up with? Fortunately, every time someone opens a tent flap, the air is changed. Which you would see is a good thing if you had any sense."

"Pardon, what did you call me?" My lioness instinct awakened. "You may refer to me as Matron or Miss Stimson. This is your first and only warning. Any derogatory term toward me or my nurses will be henceforth reported."

I let his shock of being spoken to by a nurse in such a way sink in. He worked his jaw up and down, and his eyes bulged, but he had no ground to object.

"And in answer to your complaint, aerosolized disinfectant has been used in surgical suites for a long time."

"Are you a surgeon, Miss Stimson?"

"Fortunately not."

"Well, stop thinking you can extrapolate the closed environment of a surgical suite to a ward full of patients." He motioned for the orderly, who was watching all this with an amused look in his eyes, to leave. "I'll see you at the meeting. Just in time for this decision. We need to clip your wings a bit, young lady."

It was an uncomfortable reminder of my next task. The meeting to clarify the nurses' roles and the limits to their duties. I rushed back to my office to pick up the notes I had been keeping on the situations that had caused conflict. I had mimeographed them and put them in the medical staff correspondence cubbies a few days previously. There were dates and brief descriptions, such as:

```
26 patients suffering from unknown gas
   admitted. No orders for removal of
   contaminated clothing.
```

```
14 patients admitted in respiratory distress.
   No oxygen tanks in wards. One patient
   expired while awaiting transport to
   operating theater.
Night shift nurses unable to obtain order for
   morphine.
Recommend standing orders for pain medication,
   isolation procedures, decontamination
   procedures. Request oxygen tanks be
   available, training for nurses, and standing
   orders.
Additional equipment needed on ward when
   supply tent and operating theater are closed
   at night.
```

The list of requests concerned me in that once something became a nursing responsibility, then it added to their already overwhelming duties. For example, giving oxygen had always been a doctor's procedure, but it was nearly always the nurses who determined a patient needed it. How much I wanted to transfer from the doctor's area of responsibility was a perplexing question.

When I arrived at the meeting room, a carved-out corner of the currently empty mess tent, all the doctors were already gathered around a table. The sudden silence when I walked toward them was not a good omen. It was 5:00 p.m., so I was right on time, but they must have decided to meet earlier, as they were certainly free to do. I tucked away a smidgen of hurt nonetheless. Fred was at his usual place at the end of the table, with Drs. Ernst and Gross on one side, Dr. Valentine on the other, and another I didn't recognize on the other end. I took a place between Fred and Dr. Gross.

Fred tapped a pen for attention. "Welcome, Miss Stimson. I'd like to introduce our guest, Dr. Heinz. He is an observer from the American Red Cross."

I nodded to Dr. Heinz. He was a thin stick of a man, with olive skin and dark curly hair. Curious I didn't know in advance of his arrival.

"Good to finally meet you, Miss Stimson. Your reputation precedes you."

"In a good way, I hope."

The other doctors chuckled.

"Absolutely. I come here with guidance from headquarters regarding the question at hand, the role for nurses." He slid a thick document toward me.

I noticed the others already had a copy, still closed in front of them. I opened mine and glanced at the headings. There were chapters for expected dress and behavior, followed by a section outlining care for each bodily system: digestive diseases and injury, skin disorders and injury, trauma of the head and neck, and so on. A brief skim of the pages revealed up-to-date practice. In fact, from what I could tell, it was the same document I had been given back in the States before we recruited the first nurse for this mission.

"I'll need to take time to read this thoroughly, especially any updates."

"Indeed, we expect that. I will leave my contact information if you have any questions."

"I have one now."

"Of course she does." Dr. Valentine had been rising from his chair but plopped back down.

"When was this written and updated, and by whom?" I asked.

"Why, it was written especially for us, by the experts at Johns Hopkins and other fine institutions," Dr. Heinz replied.

"You didn't say when," I pushed, because it seemed Dr. Heinz had been invited so that our own medical staff wouldn't have to make the decisions we needed. Fred, the ex-football star, would call it a "punt."

Dr. Heinz opened the heavy paper cover and ran his finger down the first few pages. "Looks like June 1916. Very up-to-date."

"Interesting. What does the section regarding nursing care of poison gas patients say? What does it say about caring for one hundred severely injured men who all arrive at the same time? I have a list here—"

"Thank you, Miss Stimson," Dr. Valentine interjected. "We get the point."

"Do you? You knew these were the questions, and yet you bring this…administrator straight from another world entirely to answer them."

Fred spoke up. "Thank you, Dr. Heinz. We will summon you if we have further questions."

But Dr. Heinz was not dismissed so easily. "I understand your frustration, Matron. It would be most helpful for you to create a nursing manual more relevant to your situation. I suggest you work with a member of the medical staff." He looked around at the mostly scowling doctors, who were donning their jackets, eager to get away. "Perhaps Dr. Valentine, since he has shown so much interest, could help you."

Dr. Valentine and I fairly glared at each other.

"I'd be delighted to work on this myself." Fred looked at me with an unmistakable twinkle in his eye.

"Even better." Dr. Heinz scraped back his chair and rose to leave. "Gentlemen," he said in the way of goodbye, then corrected himself. "And lady, I bid you farewell."

My strange discussion with Marie Curie came back to me. I hadn't had much time to think about it. She had said that my relationship with Fred would interfere with my ability to do my job. If anything, it seemed Fred was being even more careful, seeking an outside opinion, when he could have simply made the rules himself. Was this an example of what she meant?

I returned to my office, where, thankfully, there was no line of staff waiting to see me. I needed time to make sense of the strange remarks of Marie Curie and the obstacle of Dr. Valentine. And now I had a new task to accomplish: the assignment to create an all-new policy manual. We had one for the unit already of course, based on the hopelessly vague one Dr. Heinz had brought.

I actually looked forward to working on a thorough update, especially as Fred had seen fit to work with me on it.

My time of quiet reflection was short-lived. I had barely returned from the meeting when my head late-shift nurse, Dorothy, burst through the door without first knocking.

"Matron! Come quickly!"

I hesitated only long enough to grab my stethoscope and sterile scissors. "What is it?" I followed her as she rushed back to the wards.

"It's a leg wound. He seemed fine, then we were turning him over, and he just crashed."

I double stepped to keep up with her. I was pretty quick on my feet, but darn if Dorothy wasn't quicker. "Who is the surgeon on duty? Is he needing backup?"

She didn't answer but broke out in a dead run. I followed. It was about fifty yards to the farthest ward, and it seemed that was where we were heading. Finally, we arrived at the tent. Dorothy lifted the flap, and I could see four or five nurses and orderlies crowded around a bed. There was no doctor in sight.

I pushed through the crowd to see the patient. His color was pale, his lips bluish. Clearly not enough oxygen in the blood, or sudden loss of blood pressure. His breathing was rapid but not labored, so it didn't seem to be an airway issue.

"Where is—"

Dorothy interrupted. "The surgeons are all in theater. Ten casualties arrived all at once. This one seemed stable."

I remembered Fred showing me the oxygen tank in the operating tent and had seen it in action since.

"Rebecca, go to surgical supply. Bring back an oxygen tank and the tubing and cannula that should be near it. Take an orderly with you; it will be heavy. Dorothy, go get a doctor who is off duty. Now!"

"We've already sent Margaret to do that. I don't know why she isn't back yet. That's why I came for you."

I continued my assessment of the patient. His head and neck seemed intact. He was lying on his side, so I could get a good view of his torso. A few shrapnel wounds of the chest, but none seemed to be sucking air or bleeding heavily. I quickly worked my way down his body.

"You." I pointed at an orderly whose name I didn't know. "Go bang on doctors' doors until you find one. Then drag his behind over here."

I pulled my stethoscope from around my neck and listened to the patient's heart and lung sounds. His lungs were clear. His heart rate was 140 beats per minute. Much too fast, but its steady rhythm meant it probably was not a cardiac issue. Where was that doctor? I checked the patient's back—nothing there.

"What is his name?"

"Dempsey. Private Dempsey."

"I see nothing, but he has to be losing blood somewhere. Maybe an abdominal wound with internal bleeding. Help me turn him onto his back."

"Private, we're gonna figure this out. Don't you worry," I reassured the patient. He had lost consciousness, but I had learned that sometimes they could still hear you. Patients had told me that the comforting words they heard when no one thought they were listening meant everything to them.

I palpated his stomach. It was soft, indicating no internal bleeding, and the few wounds were superficial. Yet we were rapidly losing him. A trickle of blood between his legs caught my eye. I pulled up his undershorts. There was an entrance wound on his upper left thigh, and a hematoma was forming. He had been lying on this side, which was probably enough pressure to keep the blood from pouring out and us seeing it but not enough to stem the bleeding.

"Set up a blood transfusion. Do we have any citrated type O blood?"

"We can't do that without a doctor's order," Dorothy said.

"Where is the goddamn doctor? Get it set up. One of you go to the operating suite and get a verbal order. Now."

Blood started pulsing from the wound, which was directly above where the femoral artery was located. He would bleed out within minutes. "Give me a stack of gauze." I applied direct pressure, but it wouldn't be enough. We needed a surgeon, or this young man—he looked to be no more than twenty—was going to die. "Tourniquet!"

"We need a doctor's—"

"Then give me a nice clean hair ribbon. I'm just going to tie it around his leg for decoration."

My snarkiness seemed to work, as a piece of rubber tubing appeared. It had probably only been two minutes, but it seemed like an hour since we had sent for help. But still, what was the surgeon doing, strolling to the tent like it was the Easter parade?

"Blood is here, Matron."

"Dorothy, can you start an intravenous?"

"We're not supposed to… Yes, I can."

The orderlies returned, lugging a green oxygen tank, a gas mask, and rubber tubing on a gurney. "How do we…"

"I don't know. Just piece it together and open it up a little at a time." I tried to remember the different valves in the mask from my brief lesson from Fred, but it was too hard to concentrate on that at the moment. "Put it on yourself first, and make sure there's a good air flow."

Margaret came rushing up, breathless. "Dr. Gross is on his way. He's so slow with that limp." She panted, hands on her thighs as she caught her breath.

"What about any of the surgeons in the operating theater?"

Margaret shook her head. "They said ten or fifteen minutes at least."

The orderly arrived. "Major Murphy ordered two units of O negative."

"We've only got the one." The orderly opened a wooden ammo box and extracted a full bottle and some tubing and needles.

"Who here is type O? Anybody?" I said.

All who gathered shook their heads.

"Anyone know how to cross match?"

Again, silence.

Finally, my little Charlotte held up her hand. "Me, Matron. I'm type O. They collected some from me nearly two months ago and said I could give again in six weeks."

She couldn't have been one hundred pounds soaking wet with a monkey on her back. Six weeks as a rule for much bigger, stronger men made sense. But not for her. "Thank you, Charlotte, but that won't be necessary."

I could see from the blood-filled gauze and the pooling of it under the soldier's legs that my direct pressure was not enough. I estimated he had already lost over two pints.

I considered making a small incision, finding the femoral artery, and clamping it. It wouldn't be too hard. I could feel its pulse, although it was steadily weakening. This was far, far outside my scope of practice. Direct pressure, yes. Tourniquet? In a life-or-death emergency. Incision and basically exploratory surgery? Not on your life. Or this soldier's life apparently. He was probably only a minute or two from expiring.

Once again, the lesson Fred had taught us back in St. Louis pushed into my mind. We couldn't just make up rules as we saw fit in the spur of the moment. People were going to die; we couldn't help that. We had to work with the skill and equipment we had, and if we did the absolute best we could and what a reasonable person would do, we were doing our job.

But I had already exceeded the limits of my practice by ordering oxygen and a blood transfusion and requesting orders from a doctor for a patient he hadn't even seen. How much further should I go? What was the example to set?

I looked toward the tent entrance. Dr. Gross was still nowhere in sight. "Give me a scalpel."

CHAPTER 20

had just removed a sharp piece of shrapnel, which no doubt had severed the femoral artery, then had clamped the artery, when Dr. Valentine appeared, trailed by a limping Dr. Gross.

Still groggy and with gray hair wild about his head, Dr. Valentine hoarsely yelled, "What's going on here?"

I quickly brought him up-to-date.

"The tourniquet should have worked."

"Should have but didn't."

He listened to Private Dempsey's heart. "He's still with us. But you sure have made a mess of things."

I bit my lips.

He examined the thigh wound, now larger after my intervention. "Stable enough now. Let's get him to the operating room before he loses his leg, or worse."

❧

When I got back to my office, I had to pace for several minutes as I resolved in my mind that I did the right thing for Private Dempsey. No doubt my actions would be frowned upon, not only by Dr. Valentine but by Fred as well.

My gut told me that had I not acted, the patient would have died. And Fred himself had said that we sometimes had to make decisions in the field that weren't what was found in policy manuals. Needing to clear my mind, I made myself a pot of tea and settled myself at my table with a stack of letters.

I found a curious note from Marie Curie:

My dear Julia,

I hope you will think about what I said. There is more to the story, which I don't care to put into writing for the nosy to later find and judge.

Yours,
Marie

But I wasn't in the mood to answer her, as my mind kept return-ing to Private Dempsey. It was only a matter of time before word got around regarding my foray into medical practice. The fact that I undoubtedly saved the man's life would not be an excuse and could very well be challenged. I had to reconcile with myself first if I was to defend my actions and keep my job.

There was no doubt that my primary goal, going back to my college days, was to be a physician. I had the analytical thinking abilities, the drive, the stomach for it. I was less suited to the role of a nurse. To follow orders, to observe, to comfort. Indeed, I enjoyed training the nurses, loved them dearly, in fact. I relished seeing them grow, learning new skills. I enjoyed the physical giving of the care. What I didn't relish was the restrictions put upon me to provide care that I knew perfectly well how to do. It irked me to stand and guide a greenhorn doctor through a procedure that I wasn't allowed to perform myself.

Was my ambivalence toward my suitability for nursing causing me to be a bad nurse? Was I a poor example to the other nurses under me? That thought punched me in the gut. Clearly, I needed to talk this over with someone. My senior nurses, Dorothy and Margaret, came to mind. But as their leader, I thought it inappropriate. The obvious answer came to me—Fred. He had even suggested it when he offered to work together to develop a manual of nursing protocol.

I tucked Marie's letter back into the envelope. She seemed to be warning me about just such a thing—meeting privately with Fred. But her reasoning seemed shallow, and I sensed some bitterness that could be affecting her judgment.

The next morning, after a fitful sleep, I looked at my watch. Fred should be off duty and hopefully not still asleep. I gathered a pen and a notebook and headed over to his hut.

I knocked in the "shave and a haircut" rhythm, our little signal. His answer came: "Two bits!"

I pushed through the flimsy door and found him busy polishing his shoes.

"What brings you to my empire, Two Bits?"

"Is that my new name?"

"Well, you're worth at least that much." He leaned over and gave me a peck on the forehead.

"You might not think that after you hear what I did last night."

"Oh, I've already heard." *Swish swish swish*, his brush blackened the toe of his shoe. "We've got faster communication here than Ma Bell does to AT&T."

"Well then, let the tongue-lashing begin."

"Mmm. Tempting, but no." He dipped the end of the brush into a tin of Shinola. "Not my place."

"Do you think I was wrong to do what I did? The soldier survived. And probably will keep his leg too."

"You already know what I think."

I flopped into the only other chair in the room and held up my notebook. "I came over to start on the policy manual for the nurses that Dr. Heinz wants us to work on. But maybe I'm the last person on earth who should be writing it."

He poured a few drops of water from a pitcher into the lid of the shoeblack, dipped a rag into it, then started vigorously rubbing the tip of his shoe. A little too vigorously—a sign that he was upset with me. That, and his clipped answers to my questions. "Why would you say that? You are certainly the most qualified in this camp, probably about anywhere."

"Because I don't practice what I preach. My father was a preacher. Did I ever tell you that?"

"Interesting. But not relevant." He put down his shoe, wiped off his hands on a clean rag, then dragged his chair next to me. "What is going on?"

Once I got started, I couldn't stop. I told him about wanting to go to medical school and how that dream was crushed. I told him how I loved nursing with every fiber of my being but thought maybe I was unsuited to it. "How am I supposed to create guidelines for nurses when I struggle deeply with them on a personal level? I don't have the necessary perspective. In fact, I think..." I shifted uncomfortably; this was something I hadn't even admitted to myself. "I think after this is all over and we return to the States, I won't continue in nursing. Sometimes I think I might even return early. Let someone less pigheaded serve in this role."

I glanced over to see his reaction. But his face was open, intent, and unreadable.

"Go on. What do you think you'll do?"

"Well, it's far too late in my life to go into medicine now. And I have no hope for marriage and children. But I'd like to go back to taking care of them. Maybe I could go back to Barnes." A lump formed in my throat. I breathed deeply to remain in control of my voice.

"Julia, none of that is true. You're still young enough to do whatever you want to do. God knows you are brilliant and driven enough to accomplish anything you put your mind to." He nudged closer. "You could go back to Barnes if that's what you really want. But in all these years I've known you, you've never traveled backward. You mentioned preaching? Is that something you feel called to?"

"God no." I laughed. "Oops, that was probably an inappropriate answer, but there you have it."

"I'm not going to tell you what to do now or after the war. I won't agree that you aren't suited for nursing. I think you are exactly what nursing needs. If the boundaries are wrong, then you have to explore that. And I think you have enough good judgment to know where those boundaries should be, even if the rebel in you always wants to flout them. You are an extraordinary nurse."

He gave me a handkerchief for the tears I didn't realize were collecting. I dabbed at my eyes, then squeezed his hand. There was no one else I could talk to about these things. He made it so easy, I revealed more to him than I did to myself.

"Two Bits, can we change the subject?" He leaned closer.

I could smell his shave soap, the pleasant lilac scent mixing with a bit of the earthier shoeblack. I couldn't help wondering if he chose the soap with me in mind.

"Something tells me you didn't come here just for my words of wisdom. At least I hope not."

My heart quickened, and my body tingled. I wondered if his door had a lock. But before I could get up to check, his lips were on mine. And I welcomed them, pulled his shoulders toward me, even after voices in my head told me this was wrong. Marie Curie bounced into my brain, and I forced her out as I welcomed the warmth and comfort and excitement of Fred.

CHAPTER 21

March 1918

H alf of my respiratory patients had recovered and were being sent back to their units. The other half, eighteen or so men, were struggling. This was definitely not like the normal influenza that came around every fall. That affected everybody about the same: sneezing, coughing, muscle aches, and fever, all of which these patients had. But the men remaining in our hospital after two weeks had all developed pneumonia.

Dr. Valentine approached me as I was checking the clean utility room for supply needs. Clipboard in hand, I was adding up boxes of syringes. The last time I had seen him was at the bedside of Private Dempsey. At least his hair was combed now, and he had what might pass for a smile on his face.

"You seem to vacillate between other people's jobs. What's next, ambulance driver?" he asked.

"Good afternoon to you, Dr. Valentine. Our supply sergeant has taken ill, and it is easier for me to do the duty of inventory rather than to explain to someone new how to navigate the confounded British system." I didn't want to bring up the Private Dempsey incident. That would all shake out soon enough.

Apparently, he hadn't come to discuss that. "I've had communication from the field commanders. They are anxious to have those men, fresh from training, to join the lines."

"The respiratory cases?"

"Correct. I was hoping you would have a moment to do rounds with me. With this peculiar disease, the nurses sometimes see things we doctors don't."

Was this some kind of trick? Dr. Valentine was a surgeon. This was not anything close to his specialty. I straightened a row of boxes that didn't need straightening. "You want to see flu patients?"

He puffed up in umbrage, his tone suddenly hostile. "Certainly. We all have to work outside our favorite areas, now, don't we?" He pointed to the rack of supplies. "And some of them might require chest tubes. For once, do you think you could focus on your own work?"

I shrugged. Since I was mentally preparing myself to move on, his tone and underlying accusation didn't bother me one iota. "In my own work, I see at least a third of your chest tube patients die right after surgery. Maybe you should think about that before you go cutting into pneumonia patients."

"This isn't the time or place for that argument," he said. "We have regular meetings to discuss such observations."

I tried to soften my tone. "You might want to leave that white coat here."

"Why is that?"

I desperately wanted to roll my eyes but maintained full control of them and my oh so noncondescending voice. "Because it might be a bit bulky under the smock you'll have to put on for isolation procedures."

Then I chastised myself. Where had I gotten this terrible attitude? Perhaps it truly was time to move on.

My foray into the realm of thinking I should do anything else but stay right where I was lasted twenty-four hours. I woke up the following morning with a clearer head, having had a straight six hours of rest, practically a record for my time in theater.

I dressed quickly and hummed on my short walk to my office. Nothing was going to deflate my good mood. In fact, I was looking forward to consulting with Dr. Valentine and apologizing for being short with him. I dawdled, wondering if I should do that first thing, when I noticed the door to my office was already open.

I could smell coffee brewing, and upon entering, there was Fred, helping himself to a cup.

"Well, good morning, Fred. What brings you here so early?"

He held out the coffeepot. "Fancy a cup?" He poured, not even waiting for my answer. "It so happens that you are one of the few creatures on earth who is pleasant to be around first thing in the morning. Thought I could learn from your example."

I accepted the coffee. Whoa, it was strong. "It isn't me. It's the magic coffee beans. Once they wear off, you best keep five paces back."

"Duly noted. I did want to clarify my...um...what I said." He lowered his head so I couldn't read his expression.

"About what?"

"I don't wish to put pressure on you if this has all become too much for you. And whatever you decide, about staying or going, you know I wish you only the best." He brushed back an errant lock of hair, then took a couple of agonizingly slow steps toward the door.

"Fred."

"Yes, *Miss Stimson*."

It seemed Dr. Valentine had enjoyed retelling that little story, and it had been making the rounds all week. It was beginning to irritate me, which I supposed was Dr. Valentine's goal.

"I'm not going anywhere. All I really needed was to blow off steam and get a good night's sleep. There's no way on God's green earth I would leave my nurses. They'd have to drag me away with four horses."

"I'm glad. Because you're needed here. And I'm holding on to the slightest of hopes that there is one other reason to stay on with our merry band of men."

"Of course, with Phil here…" I teased.

"Okay, two other reasons."

The scent of coffee about to burn drifted toward us. I held up a finger to signal *wait a moment* as I took the coffeepot off the heat. It gave me the moment I needed. "Fred, do you think anyone saw you come over here at this most early hour?"

"I don't know. Who cares?"

"I do." I nodded toward the door. "They do. I'm already in enough hot water." I debated whether to tell him of Marie Curie's strange warning. "And if we have feelings for each other…"

"I do have feelings. And you won't convince me that you don't."

"I won't deny it. But we have to be careful. I've been reading through the manual. The Red Cross has pretty specific rules about relationships between people assigned together."

"Do you really think we can hide this? I'm two feet off the ground every time I'm with you. Others will surely notice, whether we're 'careful' or not. I say let's just get it out there, and let the chips fall where they may." He finally stepped away from the door, back to where I was standing, a hot coffee cup in my hand. "There are things that we can't control. I'm falling in love with you, Julia."

CHAPTER 22

I didn't return Fred's sentiment for two reasons. Letting the chips "fall where they may" might be an option for him, as he wasn't at risk of losing his position. A nurse, even a chief nurse, was much more expendable. The second reason was that I wasn't quite sure of my feelings toward him. I loved him, yes, and had for a long time. And I was attracted to him. But I didn't think the picture in his mind of our future matched mine.

I knew I couldn't be the stay-at-home, sweet doctor's wife like his first one. Not that he had come even close to proposing marriage. But it definitely seemed he was heading in that direction, and that made me want to dig in my heels before he became too attached to the idea. I feared I would only be a disappointment to him, and I knew that if I expressed that, he would brush it away as nonsense. In my mind, I could hear him say, *I wouldn't expect or want you to be like Cornelia.*

But surely I would be tempted to try to be the wife he really wanted. And how long would that last? Again, I saw nothing but disappointment for him. And I loved him too much to let that happen. Sadly, it wouldn't be right to share that with him.

So I persevered in the notion of having a strong friendship without pushing for more. We agreed to treat each other with the ultimate in professionalism and no favoritism on his part when I wandered astray of my ordained duties, as I was wont to do. Any insinuations, questions, or sidelong glances from others were to be dealt with either by a stony silence or "I don't know what you are talking about."

We would permit ourselves to get the occasional pass to leave the compound together and to go on walks when we had simultaneous time off, but there would be no public displays of affection. We would allow one dance with each other at the Monday evening socials with BEF Hospital No. 10 next door. Of course, there would be chatter in the rumor mill, but we would just laugh it off as a necessary diversion in their stressful lives.

It wasn't too hard to do, for my waking hours were so full. I did rounds in all the lines of tents and in the respiratory tent during each change of shift. Miss Taylor and I wrote letters to the families of every admitted seriously or dangerously ill patient.

Lately, we had had to write letters to families of some of the nurses. We had to admit three to the Sick Sisters Hospital in downtown Rouen within a week. One needed surgery on her arm after aggravating an old injury, another had diphtheria, and still another was suffering from a combination of exhaustion and a bad reaction to the smallpox vaccine.

Smallpox had been rearing its ugly head once again. The entire city of Rouen was under stay-at-home orders until the population could be properly vaccinated. We enjoyed a short respite from incoming casualties, as they were routed elsewhere due to the quarantine.

The smallpox vaccination caused a wound the size of a quarter on the upper arm, and the entire arm became quite sore. Most of my nurses were working one-handed for several days, which was tough to do. But they were bricks and never complained. I had received the smallpox vaccination as a child, so with full use of both arms, I filled in shifts for nurses who needed a break.

During our lull, I managed to read all my letters from home and to write quite a few as well. I tried to sound cheerful and minimized the strain we were all under. I didn't want to add to their worries, especially now with Phil in theater as well.

I decided not to tell my family about Fred and me. Of course, I casually mentioned him in my letters, but to have them fussing about that from three thousand miles away would just make the situation more difficult. I also endeavored to shield them from the infighting and territorial battles I was facing. Let them think we were one big happy family, working well together for the common good. Which, for the most part, we were.

Dearest Family,

I began this letter last evening but was interrupted by having an orderly bring me a huge bunch of sweet peas, mignonette, etc. from a nice colonel commanding a neighboring base. Of course, I had to stop and put them in such vases as we have. I brought some down to the officers' mess, where they were just finishing dinner and where I had to stay and chat a bit.

We feel now as though we have been here forever. If you have not read Lord Northcliffe's new book At the War, do get hold of it, for it describes just what we are in the midst of. If you should mail a good novel once in so often, I believe it would reach us easily, and it certainly would be appreciated. Another thing we would love to have is some music. Popular new dance music or songs and a hymnbook. We have some good singers, and we need some good popular airs. I believe I told you about the twelve-franc violin some of my girls bought me. You'd be surprised what sweet tunes it can play!

I told them about preparations for the deep cold of winter we were warned about by the British and the small coal and oil stoves and sleeping bags that sustained us. I even told them how the hospital tents would remain tents and not hutted like we had hoped. I didn't tell them of the men who had lost feet not to anything the enemy had thrown at them but by simply not having proper boots and dry socks. I told them we had a good supply of rubber boots, hats, and coats. I didn't tell them that the unrelenting dark days and steady downpours led me to designate a room for nurses to cry in.

The single thing I was completely open and honest about was my unending love and admiration of my nurses.

I have such splendid people here with me. They are loyal, affectionate, and entirely to be depended upon. Other hospitals have had difficulty forcing the nurses to forgo drinking and smoking, at least in public, lest they present the wrong image to our host nation. I told my nurses I would leave the decision up to them. They have decided themselves not to partake while they are over here. Their fine reputations have spread all the way to England, and I couldn't be prouder.

Despite my own insistence on not planning a future, I found myself daydreaming of a time after the war, where Fred and I could return to St. Louis and Washington University. Oh, how lovely it would be. We could take our lunch walk through Forest Park. In one daydream, I was even pushing a pram.

Then, a distressing realization. We would have the same restrictions even then. The chief of surgery and the chief of nursing could not be together. The stink of nepotism would destroy any credibility we could muster, especially for me. Once again, I would have to choose between my heart and my career.

Maybe I was overthinking. Maybe our relationship, or even we ourselves, wouldn't survive the war. It felt like steel bands were wrapping themselves around me, caging in my emotions. I thought of Phil. I should ask him to help me sort this out. He understood me like no other. But I knew what he would say without even asking. *Follow your heart, Jules.*

❧

Our wondrous smallpox lull ended abruptly when the Boche resumed gas attacks with a vengeance. There was an attack in a town only one hundred kilometers from us, and an American nurse at a CCS was injured. She wasn't one of mine, but still the threat was growing ever nearer.

With the warmer weather, our influenza patients improved, and the numbers of new cases dwindled down to one or two a week. Phil continued with the planning for a new infectious disease hospital, but it was to exist only on paper until and unless the threat reappeared.

I decided we needed to supply the nurses with gas masks and train them in how to use them. As the doctors had all received some combat training due to the possibility to be called to bear arms, I went to Dr. Valentine, who was now second in command, to request the same for the nurses.

I made an appointment to see him instead of just dropping by. I wanted to underscore how serious I thought the matter was.

He was sitting at his gray metal desk, glasses perched on the tip of his nose, in a pristine white coat with his name embroidered in blue thread over the chest pocket.

"Ah, Miss Stimson." He took off his glasses and stared at my empty hands. "I assumed you were bringing me the completed nurse procedure manual."

"No, this is another matter."

"Are you not taking that assignment seriously? Do I need to remind you of the thin ice you are treading upon?"

"Exactly why Major Murphy and I are taking our time and carefully vetting each and every policy and procedure for nurses. I'm sure you expect nothing less."

"Hmph. Well, what is it then?"

"I want my nurses to be fitted for and trained to use gas masks. Recently, a nurse in a CCS was—"

"I'm fully aware of that."

"Then you wouldn't disagree with the need for training."

"Of course not. In fact, somewhere around here…" He made a show of sorting through the various piles of papers and books on his desk.

But he didn't fool me. It seemed he was fine with the training, as long as it appeared to be his idea.

"Splendid," I said. "I'll work with the training officer right away. Why don't I add it to the new nurses' manual, which you will need to sign off on anyway?"

"Yes, yes, fine. No need to create more paperwork."

So I had easily gotten what I wanted and now had the key to getting more of it. I kept the smile of self-satisfaction to myself. "Thank you, Dr. Valentine."

On the scheduled day, I went with the first set of six nurses to be trained for gas attacks. They drove us in a large, open truck out to a wide hayfield, where small wooden huts leaned in the sunshine. There was one longer hut with no windows, but it was the only one with actual doors. It was apparent from its more modern structure that it was not part of the original farm.

"What is that one for?" I asked the sergeant who accompanied us in the back of the truck.

"That's the final testing center. If you survive that, you get your certification."

His tone was half-serious, half-playful. I was about to ask him if they had had any casualties during training, but the truck came to a halt with a jolt, and the door was opened for us.

We were led to an area where a group of about thirty soldiers were already gathered. Some were on chairs—officers, it seemed—and the rest were sprawled about the grass as if on a picnic. There was a set of six empty chairs reserved for us.

A stocky sergeant marched to the front of the group and yelled, "Attention!" Hands on hips and with no notes or any assistance whatsoever, he proceeded to speak for an hour about the preparation for, detection of, and action during a gas attack. Of course, we nurses had seen the effects of it firsthand and simply nodded as he outlined the horrific damage it did to a body. Some of the soldiers, however, seemed to turn green; indeed, a few walked a short distance away and retched.

"It was the most interesting and barbarous lecture I ever heard in my life," I wrote to my parents. "It is at one and the same time the refinement of science and civilization and of hideous barbarism."

After the talk, we were taken to one of the larger huts. It must have been used to store hay, as there were still several bales inside. It had been transitioned to a sealed room, as treated canvas sails lined the walls. We were each measured for masks, and then one was chosen for us. The sergeant demonstrated how to quickly put on the mask. He then barked the order, "Masks on!" and we all fumbled with the straps and rubber and nosepieces. Over and over again, we put them on and took them off as the sergeant timed us with a stopwatch.

"Too long," he barked as Margaret, who was sitting next to me, struggled.

I reached over to help her; the strap had been caught up in the bun in her hair.

"No! She must do it herself." He knocked my hand away.

When he was finally happy that everyone in the group could put on the mask in the required time, we moved on to the next step.

"We will now fill the room with a lachrymatory gas. It is not dangerous but will be quite uncomfortable for you, as you will feel your eyes burn and tear uncontrollably, and your nose will run and possibly bleed. However, if you have applied your mask properly, you should feel no effects."

After we had passed this test, we were taken to a trench where we had to put on the masks on a signal before we were sprayed with the same gas.

The final test was in the long hut I had seen previously. This test was to be with chlorine gas. Not the exact same as the weaponized chlorine gas but strong enough to enable us to learn its smell and learn to deal with wearing the mask in a more threatening situation. We formed separate lines, the six of us nurses in our own line. Then, three officers joined us.

At the signal, we put on the masks. By now, I was accustomed to the strange sound of my own breath echoing through the chambers, the pressure of the tight straps around my face and head, and the acrid, rubbery smell. Seeing my fellow nurses in the strange things no longer seemed as alien. The officers checked each of us for a proper seal, pulling hair away when necessary, as it would interfere with a tight fit. For this reason, soldiers were required to shave their faces closely each day, even while living in trenches.

There was a hiss as the chlorine was fed through tubes into the long hut. Two groups of soldiers went through before us nurses.

When they came out the other end, they tore off their masks and took deep breaths. Some were laughing and joking. It seemed the stress was more mental than physical.

Once the officers were satisfied that our masks were secure, it was our turn. One officer went to the head of our line, another in the middle, and the third at the end. No nurse was any more than two people away from a trained set of eyes.

The door squeaked open. The room looked like the inside of an icebox, lined with perhaps zinc. There were benches along either side of the room. The most disturbing thing was the large levers that bolted the doors in place. Undoubtedly to keep someone from accidentally opening them from the outside, they still made me shudder with the feeling of imprisonment.

There was a cooling feeling as the tubes above our heads began to hiss. Then the odor hit. It was fairly strong, but not more than the vats of diaper-cleaning solution we had used back in Harlem.

There were some muffled oohs and some coughing, but my nurses handled it well. We had to stay put while the gas was cleared through vents, but then the door was opened, and out we rushed into the fresh air.

When I got back to my office, the ink on my gas mask training certificate not even dry, Fred was there to greet me. Excited, I practically knocked him over with a hug.

"Whoa there, Two Bits."

I pulled back and could see in his drawn face that something was wrong. "What's up? Another bad trainload on its way?" I was already mentally preparing myself for another long shift, even after training for the better part of the day.

"No, it's quiet at the moment. Which is why, I imagine, Colonel Fife decided this was a fine time to present this." He tapped a large binder on my desk. It was the procedure manual we had completed and turned in a week or so previously.

"I take it he was not 100 percent on board?" I opened the binder, which had large sections crossed out and notes written in every margin.

"Sheesh. Why doesn't he just write it himself?" Colonel Fife had been promoted to headquarters, but he still remained in close contact with Base Hospital 21.

"Because that's not his job." Fred plopped down in my guest chair. "It's not all that bad. He has some good suggestions, and some of that scrawl is actually compliments."

Numbers started running through my head. Numbers of hours it would take to redo this project that I had thought done. In fact, we had already been implementing the policies and had refined some of them. "Well, I was hoping to finally have a smidgen of spare time to catch up on correspondence, but there are some updates I can add. And the other chief nurses and the American Red Cross are most interested in seeing this as well."

"It won't be time wasted." He produced a dark bottle of wine. "In fact, I thought we'd celebrate your successful training today, then get some of this work done."

❧

The revisions didn't take as long as I had feared. After a week of meeting with Fred for an hour or two after dinner, we had gone through all of it. As we checked over our work one last time, I actually began to feel a little disappointed that our sessions would end. I had enjoyed bouncing ideas around with him. He was quite clever at solutions and gifted with describing procedures step-by-step. He was always a perfect gentleman, and if I got distracted during the work, it was only due to sometimes wishing he wasn't.

We met in my office, always with the door open, and during the week, I think every one of my nurses, not to mention orderlies, doctors, and walking patients, had some need to drop by. They usually came to the door, apologized for interrupting, then went off whence they came. Except for that one time, when someone could have gotten a wrong idea in their head.

We were nearly at the end of our last review of the manual and feeling mighty relieved to have it close to done. Fred had brought a nice bottle of champagne in anticipation of the moment.

"Don't you want to wait until it is completely done?" I asked as he unwound the metal wire restraining the cork.

"This is the best moment to celebrate. When we can see the end of the drudgery but can still enjoy our special time together. I'm going to miss it."

"Miss it? My office is ten steps away from yours."

"You know what I mean. I've been thinking of that time when we spent the night in the barn."

"I think about that too. I don't think I would have made it through that night without you." I kept my voice hushed. Someone could be just outside the door. *Maybe I should go check*, I thought.

He pulled his chair a little closer. "I was so worried. Even back then, I knew you were special, irreplaceable." He lowered his voice as his eyes followed mine to the door. "But enough about that." He gently tapped my knee. "How are your legs holding up? Anything I can get for you?"

Relieved to have a change in subject, I cheerily announced, "Oh, I have the best stuff. But you must keep it a secret." My legs had vastly improved thanks to Benjamin's help.

"What? Why? Have you found a witch's potion?"

"Something like that." I pointed to the puttees that were visible between my boots and uniform hem. "You'll never guess what I have under these."

"I wouldn't hazard a guess." He laughed.

I was about to explain that I had a set of thoroughly scrubbed and disinfected pig bladders wrapped around my legs when I heard a cough coming from the hall outside my door. Darn it, my instincts were right; someone was listening. No doubt our conversation would be misinterpreted. "Well, another time," I said.

I was summoned to the telephone on the first evening that Fred and I were no longer meeting. I was expecting a call from Miss Dunlop. But it was not her.

There was quite a bit of static, then a familiar voice. "Marie Curie here. From Paris."

"Yes, Madame, what can I do for you?"

She seemed to have a four-month rotation of the major hospital encampments. I counted months on my fingers; she was not quite due to return.

"I'm heading up to Le Havre. Thought I could spend the night in Rouen along the way if it wouldn't be too much trouble."

Buzz. I missed her next sentence.

"I'm afraid we don't have the best connection. Of course you are welcome here. When should we expect you?"

The line went dead before I got an answer, but two days later, late in the afternoon, Benjamin appeared at my office door.

"Matron, they're all running around like chickens at the Pointe. You have an important guest."

The Pointe was our receiving area, in front of the grandstand. Over the months we had been there, it had grown more and more organized so that there was always a receiving team at the ready.

"Who would that be?" Although I was pretty sure it was either my cousin Henry, the former secretary of war and now a colonel in the artillery, or Marie Curie. But Henry would presumably have given me notice.

"It's Madame Curie." Benjamin was a mess of nerves. His uniform, always two sizes too large, was twisted at the waist as if he had tried to shore up the excess.

"Wonderful. You may bring her to my private room." I quickly stashed away my work and hurried to my room.

246 TRACEY ENERSON WOOD

Darn, she was quick. I had barely the time to tidy up a bit before she led poor Benjamin over to me. He trailed behind, carrying something quite heavy. I could only hope it wasn't radioactive.

We double kissed in the French fashion, although of course she was Polish. "France is my adopted country, and I must adopt its customs," she had told me. It was rather late when she arrived, and I settled her in the empty room of two of my nurses away on leave. But bright and early the next morning, she was at my door.

There was a boom of distant artillery. Although we didn't fear we were in danger in Rouen, the front had become uncomfortably close. But the sound didn't seem to concern Marie, who took her customary seat in my sitting room. Although there was absolutely no physical resemblance, something about her reminded me of Emily Warren Roebling. Somehow, I had merited a lick of attention from two of the bravest and most remarkable women of my lifetime. It felt like Emily was conspiring with Marie from heaven to make sure I was fulfilling my promise.

"So, my dear, I have but a few moments. I have been training women to be radiological assistants, and you will be receiving some excellent ones soon. I am hopeful you will take them under your wing with the nurses. Captain Ernst is competent, but I don't think he'd be suited to this."

"Thank you. I'm sure they will be most welcome. I'll see to it they are each matched with a nurse to help them get settled."

"Yes. Also, I have heard about the new procedure manual and would like a copy."

"This can be arranged. Although it doesn't pertain to radiological procedures."

"Hmm. And I'm told you wrote it with the help of Major Murphy. Which proves you haven't considered my advice. Have I not told you to keep your distance?"

Now my feathers were getting ruffled. How did one politely tell someone of this stature to mind their own business? "Madame, surely you shouldn't concern yourself."

"Young woman, are you not a student of history?"

"Umm…"

"How old were you in 1911?"

"Er…thirty?"

"Then certainly old enough to have known they nearly took the Nobel Prize away from me."

I scratched my head. "But they didn't, did they?" I searched my brain for a clue as to what had happened. I had only the dimmest awareness of a scandal that had long since faded away.

"No, they didn't. And they wouldn't take them back when I offered the medals for the war effort. I guess that means something."

"Your Nobel Prize medals? You offered them for scrap?"

Marie was more fidgety than usual. She had never before spoken of her awards. Why now?

She waved off my question. "So long ago, it doesn't matter. What does matter is this. After my beloved Pierre died, I was adrift. He wasn't just my husband, the father of my children, and the man I deeply loved. He was my partner in science. My partner in discovering objects and principles in chemistry and physics that will change the world, for the better I fervently hope.

"And then, in an instant, he was gone. For years, I merely existed. Can you imagine, one day, we were at the peak of our careers, award-winning scientists, with plans to build a science institute like no other."

"You still are, and you have."

"But in 1910, it seemed all would be lost. Oh, I had friends, of course. And my beautiful daughters, who are the only reason I managed to breathe. And of course, there was Paul Langevin. Certainly you've heard of him?"

I shook my head. "Afraid not, although perhaps I've forgotten."

She sighed. "This is to be more difficult than I had imagined. Paul was Pierre's protégé. The three of us worked for years in any space we could claim. A shed, a borrowed lab. It was Paul who fed me tea when my kidneys failed. Paul who brought the girls to school when I couldn't get out of bed. He had been so totally devoted to us and the work that I'm afraid his wife could not bear it, and I don't blame her."

"So his marriage was troubled, and that was blamed on you and Pierre?"

"Yes, but that happened first, you see. It all began before Pierre was gone. Then, as Paul helped me through those awful years, his wife, who never understood the importance of our work, divorced him."

The water kettle whistled, and I poured the steaming hot water over the tea leaves in my teapot. I was beginning to see where her story was going, and I didn't like its direction. "And you and Paul continued to work together."

"We did, and more." She slipped her hands and forearms up each opposite sleeve of her long black dress. "It is not that I regret what we did. Without Paul, there would have been no second Nobel. Probably no Curie Institute, although it isn't clear that will ever open." She looked at me, her eyes moist, the first time I had witnessed anything but stolid confidence from her. There was a caring, feeling being under that efficient, stolid shell.

"Then what is it you regret?" My stomach rumbled; I hadn't had the chance to have breakfast. I banged around my single cupboard for some biscuits.

"Oh, child, I regret we didn't burn the letters. Burn the evidence of our affection so that it couldn't be used against us."

"He was divorced, and you were a widow. You wrote affectionate letters. What on earth could be used against you? You published your research; it wasn't a secret."

"The scientific world is small but complicated, with big egos and jealousies. I dared to be a woman in a man's field. I dared to present myself as more suited to an important position than a man. These things do not come without cost."

I found some lemon drop candies; they would have to do. "And the price you paid had to do with Monsieur Langevin."

"The letters were stolen and mimeographed. Copies given to reporters and mailed to everyone in Paris who mattered, the Nobel committee, and so on. I was asked to stand down from accepting the prize, and the position I sought was given to someone else. I didn't give in, of course, but mobs started to collect outside my Paris flat. Eve and Irène were just young girls, and they were petrified.

"We had to escape, and we went to live with friends. This went on for a year before everyone grew tired of the charade. But my girls, they suffered so. Perhaps it made them stronger, but none of it was their fault."

"And Paul, did you stay together?"

"Oh no, my dear. There couldn't be any of that. He *worked* for us, you see. As if it wasn't bad enough he was married, at least at first, but he was our employee. That is a line that cannot be crossed. We wrote now and then, but my work was too important. My daughters too vulnerable." She untucked her arm from her sleeve and plopped a lemon drop into her tea.

"That's sad then. It seems he was important to you as well."

"I had no choice really. Which is why I've come here and shared this with you. I'm afraid you are or shortly will be in a similar situation."

"That hardly seems true. I am no famous scientist, just an ordinary nurse."

"Don't underestimate yourself. You are a female pioneer, as was I. But in addition, you are a leader. Whether you realize it or not, the eyes of the world are on you. The future for women in science will be carried, in part, on your strong shoulders. Do not throw this away for a dalliance."

"You're speaking, I presume, of my relationship with Major Murphy." The gray light of early morning had brightened. I doused my kerosene lamp.

"Of course I am." She nodded toward the heavy box she had Benjamin set on my small table. "Open it."

I did as she requested. Inside the box was a dozen or so books. "Why, thank you. The nurses always beg for more reading material. Sometimes it's their only escape." I checked to ensure they were in English and looked at the authors and titles. Shakespeare's *Othello*, Jane Austen's *Mansfield Park*, Flaubert's *Madame Bovary*. I was sensing a theme.

Marie looked toward the small, dingy window as a faint light appeared and a low rumble could be felt even more than heard. "A thunderstorm?"

We both knew it was not.

She pushed her teacup and saucer forward. "Storm or no storm, I need to say *adieu*. But I leave you with this. The choice will be yours. Do not underestimate the harm that can be done. It happened to me, and from what I hear, all the way in Paris, there are things in motion that will hurt you as well."

I wanted to ask what the "things in motion" were, but since she clearly needed to be on her way and I was aware of rumors, I didn't press her further. It would be better to discuss with Fred in any case.

❧

The perennial flowers the British had sown were starting to peek through the warming earth. Grass had already popped up between the rows of tents. I decided to take my afternoon walk alone, telling Fred I needed to sort some things out. But it wasn't Fred that my mind seemed to want to focus on.

Now that the Americans had arrived en masse, the tide of the war was turning. The Boche had not taken new ground, and although there were still horrific battles, they seemed more desperate attempts by a steadily weakening enemy.

In my pocket was a letter from Dean Herbert Mills at Vassar College. He was setting up a summer camp to train nurses and had invited me to have an important role, perhaps even to become the dean of the camp myself. It was quite the honor, of course. The summer camp was to be followed by two years of training at highly regarded hospitals in New York and Philadelphia.

It was just the position I had always aspired to. In addition, the training would be designed so that the women could continue on to a career in medicine if they so choose.

I grew excited at the possibilities. Dean Mills was emphatic that I would have a free hand in determining recruitment and curriculum. It was the perfect opportunity, and yet I vacillated.

Although I adored teaching and administering, I was doing that in my current position. Taking the Vassar position would require me to leave the war effort by late spring. I was sure I could negotiate a release from the American Red Cross and army, as I would be heading up a program that would provide urgently needed trained nurses.

As I walked up and down the rows of soft green grass, I weighed the pros and cons of leaving or staying. There were many more pros for heading back to New York. And yet my heart would not go along.

Lost in thought, I didn't hear Benjamin calling for me. I finally noticed him, breathless as he chased after me down a hundred-yard-long row.

"Matron, Matron, please come quickly."

This was odd, as trainloads of critical patients could now be arriving, and our smooth-running hospital would not need to call me to help. Phil was healing well and about to leave for some meetings in Paris. "What is it?"

"It's Charlotte. Nurse Nora told me she hadn't shown up for her shift and thought she was with me. So we went to her room." His voice shook, and he grabbed my arm. "She's sick, Matron, real sick."

My darling little Charlotte. My mind got fuzzy; my only thought was to get to her quickly.

❦

She was alone, curled up on her side in her bed, a mountain of blankets over her even though the kerosene stove was keeping the temperature quite warm.

Benjamin and I quickly peeled back the blankets. Charlotte groaned as we turned her onto her back.

"Charlotte. Charlotte, honey, can you hear me?" Benjamin gently rubbed her shoulder.

Nora entered the room, carrying some wet towels. "She's got a hell of a fever, I'll tell you that."

Charlotte responded with another groan. She was pale, and her skin was too warm.

I always kept a clean thermometer in my pocket, so I slipped it under her tongue and held her mouth closed. "Hold this," I told Benjamin. "Can I borrow your stethoscope?" I asked Nora.

After we had pulled off most of the blankets and two sweaters, I was able to get the stethoscope head onto her chest. Although her breathing didn't seem labored, her breath sounds were bubbly on the top and diminished on the bottom. We would need the doctor to confirm, but I was sure she had pneumonia.

"One hundred four." Nora shook down the glass thermometer, then applied the cool towels to Charlotte's skin.

"Prop her up, and see if you can wake her enough to get her to drink some fluids. I'm going to get Major Murphy."

My first thought was to find Phil, but he was due to leave for Paris.

So I quickstepped all the way to Fred's office, hoping he was there and not in surgery. All the way, I begged God to watch over our sweet Charlotte. She was young, I told myself. She should be able to fight this off. But I thought how she had looked the last week or so, the circles deepening under her eyes, her sallow skin. Why hadn't I put her off duty, sent her away for a rest? I alternated castigating myself with little prayers until at last I ran into Fred, in the hall between our offices.

❦

Fred concurred with my suspicions; Charlotte had pneumonia. We were able to get her to take a few sips of water and gave her aspirin for her fever. I sent her roommate and Benjamin away, as they had had too much exposure already. I donned a face mask and stayed by her side. There wasn't much I could do but try to keep her comfortable while her body fought.

I turned her every two hours so gravity could help clear her congested lungs. I comforted her as she shivered when her temperature rose, held her sitting up during her coughing spasms. I read to her during quiet times. I told her to fight, to fight with all her might. I tried to imagine what she would most want to fight for. "You want to be with Benjamin, don't you? Would you like to be strolling along the river right now, hand in hand? He is here, waiting for you, pulling for you. When you open your eyes, I will let you see him."

I sat in a hard chair next to Charlotte, having a difficult time keeping my own eyes open.

Nora stuck her head in. "Shift's up, Matron. Get yourself to bed. I'll watch after Miss Cox."

"You seem to have a soft spot for our little Charlotte." I started gathering my few things. I held out the book I had been reading out loud, Dickens's *Great Expectations*. "I've been reading to her. Would you like to continue?"

"No, not that one. It's always been a little too close to home."

"You were an orphan too, weren't you? Sent from England to a farm in Canada?"

"Sent to be a slave to farmers at age seven. That I was." She nevertheless took the book from me and shooed me out the door with it. "Now go. This little girl is the daughter I will never have."

"Only if you promise to come get me if something changes."

I left, my heart heavy with worry. Those nasty demons that worried me in weak moments and filtered into my dreams set about me like shadowy weights upon my shoulders. *What have you done? Why have you used these women to fulfill your own dreams? Haven't you been given enough in your life? You had choices. These women didn't, and you took advantage of that.*

I quietly slipped into my room so as not to awaken the nurses in the adjoining rooms. Exhausted, I fell into my bed fully dressed. But my mind wouldn't rest. It went around and around, seeking something else to do to help Charlotte. Something else to prevent my other nurses from falling ill. How contagious was this pneumonia? I tossed and turned, longing to pad down to Fred's room for comfort. I knew he wouldn't mind.

I had just drifted off when I heard Fred's voice, calling my name softly. At first, I was confused; had I walked down to his room? I fought the cobweb of sleep and opened my eyes to see him, in a nightshirt, standing next to my bed.

"Julia, wake up."

I knew that tone. In an instant, I popped up. "What? Is it Charlotte?"

"I'm sorry, Jules. She's taken a bad turn, I'm afraid."

I followed him, a dark shadow behind the light of his lantern. He led me where I desperately didn't want to go but where nothing on earth could stop me from going.

I heard the Cheyne-Stokes breathing before we even reached her room. A cycle of irregular, choppy breaths, followed by deep, noisy breaths, then falling into a too-long silence. The sound of impending death.

Nora was there, and Benjamin, who was hunched over Charlotte, holding her hand and whispering into her ear.

She had the face of an angel. Clear skin, golden hair fanned about her head. I couldn't imagine why God would create a girl so loving, so unselfish, only to snatch her away before she had even had a chance to really live.

I felt Fred's arm around my shoulders. But I didn't want comfort. I wanted to scream at an unjust world, to scream at an uncaring God. I stepped away from him and knelt next to her. Nora dangled a mask toward me, but I ignored it. I kissed the girl's cheek, felt the soft, fading warmth against my lips. I tried to pray, but all that would come to me was *God damn it*. God damn it all.

CHAPTER 23

Late March 1918

T he answer to Vassar was overdue. The dean had sent a second letter, presuming the first had gotten lost or at least giving me the benefit of the doubt of having been too busy to answer.

None of that was true, of course. It was a matter of a battle within myself. Although I was sure my nurses would deny it emphatically, they no longer needed me there. Miss Taylor had learned all I could teach her, our little hospital running as smoothly as possible given the still-difficult assignment.

Phil was receiving ongoing care for his newly healed wounds and to strengthen the muscles that had been damaged, so he was still technically a patient. But he had also been studying and experimenting and had become quite the expert in infectious disease. Together, we had sorted out the symptoms of the strange trainload of men who had come in a few months earlier and Charlotte's illness and death shortly after. We had concluded it was influenza.

There were a hundred or so cases after that and several more deaths, then it seemed to disappear as the weather grew warmer. But Phil and I were still concerned. In his last year in his pediatric practice before being conscripted, he had been intensely studying infectious diseases, which claimed the lives of so many children. He studied the teachings of Louis Pasteur and dreamed of working on vaccines for measles and other deadly childhood diseases.

When Phil and I had a chance to chat, usually in the evening after supper, it was almost always about the excitement of a promising new vaccine or disappointment when they failed. Shortly after Charlotte died, our conversations turned more toward influenza.

"Unfortunately, the experiments with vaccination have not been successful. They don't know why exactly. It seems the germs are rather rascals, changing their colors, so to speak. It's like chasing a mouse that turns into a cat. And when you catch up with the cat, you find it is now a leopard."

This was why, I realized, I was vacillating with the dean's wonderful offer. Why it didn't feel quite the thing I ought to be doing. I felt I was still needed in theater, if not at Base Hospital 21, then with some sort of work to prevent another awful influenza outbreak.

Fred had been in no hurry to officially discharge Phil, as our hospital was greatly benefiting from his knowledge, and everyone, especially I, enjoyed having him around. But we understood that a discharge would mean that he would be assigned elsewhere. But by the end of March, he had completed treatment and there was no way to justify his status.

Phil and I had been having supper together his last few nights after he was officially discharged as a patient, as he awaited orders. We were late that Monday night, and the crew was already pushing tables aside for the weekly dance when we gathered with our bully beef and wax beans to have a chat.

He pulled out a folded sheet of paper from his chest pocket and tossed it on the table. "So I have orders."

I grabbed the paper. The top half was a bunch of numbers that meant something to army sorts but was gibberish to me. I followed down until I saw *Permanent Change of Station: Report to Paris Station soonest*. "Well, you poor devil. Paris."

"I can hardly believe it, Sis. I mean, I've spent the war lagging about, and I get this?"

"I'm very happy for you. Truly. You deserve it." I probably wasn't hiding very well the tiny bit of envy I felt.

"The best part is I get to continue my work on infectious diseases. Self-appointed expert and all." He grinned, his boyish face lighting up. "There are some astounding developments at the Institut Pasteur. Phages, tinier even than bacteria, may be the answer to eradicating disease. But still a long way off."

"I shall miss you around here."

"Any decision? Does this mean you're turning down Vassar?" he said.

I pushed the food around on my plate. No longer holding back on my portions, I wasn't as obsessed with food as I had been. And wax beans were an evil substance. "Haven't yet. But I believe I'm going to."

"I'm a bit surprised. You haven't seemed to have the same passion for this place since…"

He didn't have to say it. Since Charlotte died. It was true but not something I wanted to admit, even to Phil. And it wasn't only Charlotte. It was also the game I had to play with my relationship with Fred. I was tired of it all. I looked up at Phil and shrugged my shoulders. He seemed to read my mind.

"And what does Fred think of this? Is he another reason you want to stay? Is that the choice then?"

I cocked my head and raised my eyebrows.

"Don't think everyone doesn't know." He carefully folded his napkin. "Why don't you just admit it and go on with it? This"—he waved a hand toward the room—"won't last forever."

THE WAR NURSE   259

"Yes, and what of that? What happens when we return to St. Louis and he is chief of surgery or medicine or whatever? And if they will have me back, I'm chief of nursing. The situation won't change. Or I go to New York and he goes to St. Louis. What then? It's impossible in any case."

"Don't be ridiculous. Last time I checked, it was a free country."

"Realistically speaking, any way you cut the cake, I would need to give up my career."

"Has he asked you to do that?"

"No. In fact, we haven't even discussed it."

"Well, don't you think you ought to?"

I pondered whether I should discuss Marie Curie's warnings with Phil. I was sure he would just wave them off as the ramblings of an out-of-date and slightly erratic personality. I gathered my plate and eating utensils, even as Phil dug into his dessert: blueberry pie.

"Congratulations on Paris, Phil. I'm truly happy for you."

❧

At long last, a meeting was scheduled among the doctors and myself, the agenda being whether I was to be disciplined for performing a procedure outside my practice when I clamped the femoral artery of Private Dempsey. I was actually surprised they still wanted to address this, as after a number of weeks, it seemed to be moot. But the timing of it made it awkward, for I was about to tread upon their guarded turf once more.

Colonel Fife had returned due to the importance of the issue in the entire theater and called the meeting to order, with Drs. Valentine, Ernst, and Murphy and two new doctors also in attendance. The American Red Cross representative was invited but had declined to travel from Paris to attend. *We will accept whatever decision is made by the local board*, they had written.

I wasn't apprehensive in the least. I arrived last, and all the men popped up in a chivalrous show, Colonel Fife even pulling out my chair for me. It wasn't that I ever minded these customs, but I wondered if they weren't perpetuating a schism between male and female workers that we were trying to mend.

"Miss Stimson, we have concluded the medical business early so as not to waste your precious time. Therefore, we should move on to the matter directly involving you. That is the performance of a surgical procedure, namely a venous cutdown. We have exchanged considerable discussion, including the possibility and, to some, the probability that the soldier would have died if not for your efforts. Dr. Valentine, your findings, please."

Dr. Valentine wiped his glasses and straightened his small stack of papers. He then loudly cleared his throat. Oh, the drama. I watched it as if in the audience of a particularly dull play. I wanted to be found not guilty, of course, but the emptiness I had been feeling inside ever since we lost Charlotte prevented me from experiencing any emotion either way. It wasn't that I didn't care, really; it was more a gut feeling of the futility of it all. I almost wanted them to tell me to go home. Then I wouldn't have to make the difficult choices I had been steadily avoiding.

"Gentlemen and gentle lady, we have taken serious consideration to the events of March 10, 1918, and have the following findings."

I glanced at Fred, hoping for a sign of support. But he stared at his fingers, his face arranged in a neutral position. He wouldn't give anything away. I realized we hadn't even spoken of the matter just between the two of us, and I didn't know on which side he fell.

"That the chief nurse, Miss Julia Stimson, did exceed her authority by performing a procedure that is clearly the purview of the medical staff.

"That the procedure was performed after a reasonable effort was made to provide medical staff for the event.

"That medical staff, in the person of a medical student, was in attendance.

"That the chief nurse was acting under duress, without adequate time for careful evaluation of the situation.

"That policies and procedures have since been clarified." Dr. Valentine then looked at me, giving me the first eye contact since I had arrived. It seemed a good sign.

"We, the medical board of the BEF General 12 and AEF General 20, find that although we cannot condone the action, we do not recommend a reprimand, and we find no further action necessary."

At this, several in the group cheered. Fred, in particular, remained silent.

Colonel Fife tapped his fist on the table for attention. "Can I see a show of hands. Are we all in agreement?"

All raised their hands. I breathed a sigh of relief. I suppose I was more concerned than I realized.

"Thank you, Miss Stimson. Please continue your important work here."

At that, they all stood, and I realized I was being dismissed.

"Thank you, doctors, but if you don't mind, I do have an issue to address."

There were groans and shaking of heads as they eased back into their chairs.

I opened my satchel and took out a document I had mimeographed. I circled the table, giving each of them a small stack of papers. "So as not to take up too much time, I've written my findings for you to review later. But here is the summary. As you know, we have experienced the tragic loss of one of our nurses to influenza. In addition, we have had a number of deaths of soldiers and the incapacitation of an even larger number.

"My request is simple. I wish to notify the other units in theater of our measures of containment. Although not perfect, as even modest concessions are difficult in our conditions, we do what we can.

"Furthermore, I request that we create a united protocol to be presented to the medical community at large, our allies, and of course back home. As we know, this influenza has not been isolated here in Europe, and the constant movement between theaters creates further risk of spread."

I don't know what I expected their reaction to be, but I certainly didn't anticipate the silent, awkward exchanges of doubtful looks.

"Any comments, gentlemen?"

Fred stood up. "As this is not on our agenda and we've had no notice of this…this unusual request, I recommend we take our assigned reading"—at this, there were several chuckles—"and discuss at a later date."

They all stood and filed out of the room, avoiding me altogether. Except for Fred, who, bless his heart, rested a hand on my shoulder and said, "Congrats, Two Bits."

"Thank you, Fred. I'm not sure I'd still be here if not for you."

"Still authorized to be here or want to?"

"Both." I gathered up the stacks of paper that half of them had left behind.

The exact mechanism for issuing warnings regarding the dangerous influenza to the folks back home was not included in my recommendations to the medical staff. I had thought that I was already stepping out of my lane, and to go further would have alienated them from the idea. Some of that stemmed from my earlier lesson on the value of having it seem their own idea. But with the improper surgery accusation still hanging over my head, I had been doubly careful.

But this issue was too important to leave to the chance that they would agree with me and take the swift action necessary. And they certainly did not seem moved by my words at the meeting. I wanted to give myself a knock on the head; my timing was awful.

So I conjured up new ways to seek their support. My immediate thought was to get Fred involved. We had worked so well together on the procedure manual project, and of course it was enjoyable to work with him as well.

But Marie Curie's warnings nagged at me. The proper thing to do seemed to be to distance myself personally and professionally, no matter how sad that made me.

I thought about all this as I did busywork in my office. Many of my daily tasks—correspondence, ordering supplies, authorizing leave, completing pay vouchers—were routine, and my goal was to complete them all before lunchtime so I could spend the afternoon making rounds, checking in with the nurses, and helping out in the operating tent when needed. I desperately wanted to go back to the CCS, but we had enough staff to cover it and only one person to cover for me in my absence. It simply wasn't logical for me to go.

As we got further into springtime, the number of influenza cases dropped sharply. Thanks to careful hygiene and isolation, no more of my nurses became ill. The diphtheria cases also recovered, and my nurses were nearly at full strength.

The casualties continued to wax and wane with the movement of the front and the changes in weapons. We grew hopeful that the war was nearing an end when things slowed down and the enemy pulled back, only to be thrown back into a cycle of trainloads of casualties pouring in, all-night surgery sessions, then a busy recovery period.

We did not keep patients through their entire recovery and rehabilitation, whether they returned to their units or were sent back to England. We had become rather specialized; as we had a fine team of surgeons and excellent, experienced nurses, the worst of the surgical and neurological cases were sent to us. We got them through surgery and the first critical day or two, then we sent them on to other hospitals for longer recovery if they needed it.

So it was not surprising that the medical staff took little interest in a campaign to prevent another influenza outbreak. But losing Charlotte and the possibility of having lost many more if we hadn't acted quickly and had Phil present to guide us wasn't far from my mind. I rolled different ideas in my head. Posters in the cities? A radio campaign? Training at medical schools? Letters to Congress? The answer to that campaign eluded me, just as my own path seemed to become clearer to me.

I was loath to leave my nurses, but at the same time, I believed they deserved fresh leadership and direction. I had given them all I had to give. But what should I do?

I retired to my room and picked up my violin. I ran my fingers over its smooth wood, carefully tightened its strings into tune. I played a tune of my own making, letting the bow sing to its own rhythm. It was probably not music to anyone else's ears, but it was a soothing comfort to me. My violin was telling me I had to go my own way, find my own song.

I knew the direction had to be toward more power, more responsibility. If I was to begin making the changes that I had seen as necessary, I would need to leave the relative comfort of my known territory. Several positions with the Red Cross headquarters in Paris were opening. I would write a letter expressing my interest in the morning. It was time to move on.

CHAPTER 24

I had not cooked a single thing in over six years. My flat in St. Louis had nothing but a single kerosene burner and an icebox for which I regularly failed to acquire ice. There was a bakery along my walk home that offered wonderful bread, so my lack of an oven was no issue. Aside from building a lunch sandwich from tinned meat, I had taken all my meals at the hospital.

And since arriving in France, I always ate at the mess tent, except for the occasional outing in town. But my mother had taught all five of us girls how to cook, and it was a skill I thought I was in danger of forgetting completely. And so, for a break in routine and the unrelenting sorrow over the loss of Charlotte, I requested a group cooking class from our mess cook, Alice.

She was only too glad to help. I posted a notice on the bulletin board, and we were both pleased to have seven nurses including me, one orderly, and Fred sign up for the event.

Although they had separate dining areas, Alice and her staff fed not only the patients, who frequently numbered over one thousand, but all the staff and visitors as well. They did this in a remarkably small space, a tent similar in size to the ward tents, and some storage space within the grandstand structure.

I arrived at 7:00 a.m. to ensure all was ready for our class. There were huge steel pots and saucepans hung from hooks over the cook-stoves that lined both sides of the tent. At either end were clusters of sinks and crates of supplies. Down the center were two rows of tables for preparation. They formed an assembly line, with setups for different stages, such as peeling, chopping, and trimming.

At the appointed time, the nine of us cooking students gathered outside the tent, shivering in the early morning dew. Alice took us to her herb and vegetable gardens and pointed out the various crops. The vegetables were still just rows of tiny seedlings, but several herbs were ready for harvest.

She handed out several small baskets and pairs of scissors. "Pick you some thyme and chives," Alice said in her Alabama drawl. "You two." She indicated Fred and me. "You look like you can handle the potatoes." She pointed to a pile of potatoes in fifty-pound sacks. "Bring them inside."

Fred couldn't resist giving me a smirk and teasing bump of the elbow. To which I responded, "Oh, shut up."

Of course the orderly and my nurses rushed to help with the potatoes. The men threw sacks over their shoulders, and the women carried them in teams of two.

We gathered in a semicircle around Alice as she gave a brief tour and explained the meal preparation routine. "Raw meat is handled at its own station to avoid cross-contamination. Things to be boiled are gathered in the far corner from the dining room. We keep pots on the boil all day and night, for it would take too long to start them over again each morning.

"We will be making a potato dish today. Potatoes dauphinoise, a traditional dish, which I learned in the south of France." Alice, whom I had never seen without her full apron, paused for her audience to appreciate this. After a few nods and smiles (from her frown, it seemed a disappointing response), she continued. "This recipe will use knife skills, sautéing, vegetable prep, and baking, so a nice mix for you. And it's hard to muck up."

With that, she got a better reaction, as my nurses laughed.

Alice moved to the center table where lay a tray loaded with something the size of a turkey, hidden underneath a cloth. "Do you know the three secrets to French cooking?" Now that she had everyone's rapt attention, she pinched the top of the cloth and pulled it away with a flourish. "Butter, butter, and butter."

There were oohs and aahs, as indeed, the "turkey" was a huge mound of the creamy colored stuff. It certainly hadn't come from the British supply channels. There was no way I would ask how she came upon such a treasure.

Then she broke us up into groups of three, and we circulated between the tasks: washing, drying, then peeling a mountain of potatoes, sautéing mushrooms, asparagus, and green beans, and slowly warming a mixture of milk, cream, butter, and herbs to a simmer. Alice brought out a huge ham bone, which still had a fair amount of meat attached. This entered the rotation as we used surgical skill to separate the meat from the bone, then finely diced the meat.

My group of three included Nora and Corey, a young nurse from New York City who had recently joined us. We had divided up the ham assignment, with Corey cutting the meat off the bone, Nora separating the fat and gristle, and me attempting to slice the remaining meat into equal-sized little cubes. Alice came by and sniffed. "Smaller."

Nora said, "I'm thinking of what we can do to honor Charlotte."

"Oh?" I said. "What is your idea?"

"Well, there's no point in erecting some kind of plaque or monument here or even at Saint-Sever."

Saint-Sever was the chapel and cemetery that adjoined the racetrack and where Ned and many of our fallen men were buried while there was still space.

"Because this will all be taken away, thank goodness, once the war is over. And Charlotte is buried in the big American cemetery way out east."

"Then what should we do?" Corey piped in. "I believe she was from West Virginia. Maybe something there?"

Nora paused in her knife work. "I was thinking more along the lines of using her death…now I know that sounds awful…but somehow using it to benefit others. Like to spread the word about how bad this influenza is."

"It's not awful, Nora. And I agree. That's what Charlotte would have wanted. And I have an idea of something we can do. It may not amount to much," I said.

"Time's up!" Alice interrupted all discussion. "Move on to the next station."

Meanwhile, an idea that had been percolating in the back of my mind started to become clearer.

After our threesome reconvened at the potato-peeling station, Corey said, "Please, Matron, what can we do?"

"We can gather our stories, all us nurses who worked with Charlotte. Write down our observations of the healthy men cut down by this invisible foe. And"—I quieted, as it was too soon to have this be heard by everyone—"make a list of people to send letters to. People in the medical community, people in government…"

"I have a diary. I can look for examples," Nora said.

Corey picked up a fat brown potato. "I'll have to think about it. Should we tell the others as well?"

Alice admired my evenly thin potato slices. "Very nice. Now get them covered so they don't discolor."

As she stepped away, I quietly answered Corey. "Not yet. I want to figure out the list and our strategy before we start anything. If we step on the wrong toes, it will all be for naught."

Nora pretended to fasten a button on her lips, and Corey giggled and followed suit.

When all was ready, we buttered great roasting pans, then alternated layers of the hot cream mixture, thinly sliced potatoes, shredded gruyère cheese, and the sautéed vegetables, repeating until we reached the top of the pan. Then we sprinkled more cheese and some fresh thyme. Into the wood-fired ovens they went, and we all heartily congratulated ourselves on a job well done.

It felt so good to be building something, to do something different with my hands than holding a pen, a stethoscope, a bandage, or even the hand of a thankful soldier. It was good for the mind to be occupied with something so concrete, and it even helped us figure out a sticky problem.

As we started the cleanup process, Alice shooed Fred and me out the door. "I've got plenty of help here. You two had better get back to whatever it is you do."

Fred and I laughed and didn't argue with her.

"That was a great idea," Fred said.

"I'm glad you enjoyed it. And I think the nurses loved it. We'll have to do it again."

"Maybe graduate to a whole roast pig." He unrolled his sleeves. "What else is on your agenda today?"

"Nothing, actually. It's my day off, and Miss Taylor has forbidden me from entering or even thinking about entering the office." I kept my fingernails trimmed short, but still, there was something bright green under them. I brought my hand to my nose and was rewarded with the scent of thyme. "I might have a soak in Old Sorry, then read a book."

"Far be it from me to keep you from Old Sorry, but I was hoping you'd spend a bit of time alone with me."

It had been such a lovely day, and I would cherish some time alone with Fred. But I had recently made up my mind to do something different, something that would inevitably take me away from him, and hadn't thought it through enough to discuss it. Yet it would be awkward and impossible to hide from him if we were alone together. And I was not ready to share my thoughts on the letter-writing campaign.

All good reasons to beg off his invitation. But I couldn't say no to his earnest face. I felt my relaxing bath slipping away from me. "Old Sorry can wait."

CHAPTER 25

As it happened, Fred knew I had the evening off and had arranged for us to take the Ford into town. There were a few official errands to run, but then we would be free to have a nice dinner. I couldn't say no to such a proposition but found myself staring out the window even as Fred chattered about the cooking class and a training class he was planning for all the surgeons in the area.

"What's wrong, Jules? You've hardly said a word."

We had arrived at a butcher shop, where we were to pick up some hams for Alice. The shopkeeper had them already wrapped in brown paper, with white string crisscrossed around them. "*Merci beaucoup*," I said.

As we loaded the hams into the back, I confided, "Fred, I need to tell you something."

"I knew something was wrong." He looked at me, concern in his eyes.

"I'm fine. Everything is fine. It's just about, well, the future."

"Okay. But not here." He tilted his head toward the truck. "Get in. There's somewhere I want to take you."

My stomach was growling on empty. We hadn't gotten to eat the wonderful potatoes dauphinoise. But I didn't want to disappoint him. "Sure. Let's go."

We dropped off the hams, then set out on a route that followed the Seine, going toward Paris. As it twisted and turned, we enjoyed new, spectacular views. I spied a picnic basket on the floorboards that I had somehow missed before. I leaned over to peek under its cover. "Ooh, I'm famished. Please tell me there's food in here."

"There is. But you have to wait, just a few more minutes."

Stomach now loudly complaining, I was none too happy to wait. But as promised, we pulled off the road shortly thereafter. We bumped along a dirt road until we were at a clearing next to the river.

I followed Fred and the all-important basket to the riverbank.

"Here we are. Look."

I had been watching my steps, as it would have been easy to turn an ankle on the rough path. When I looked up, I saw the most magnificent view of towering cliffs. They shone a brilliant white in the late afternoon sunshine, almost glowing. Rather like the Palisades one could see across the Hudson River from Manhattan, except much more imposing. Off in the distance, I could see what appeared to be castle ruins at the top of the cliffs.

"That's Château Gaillard, in Les Andelys. I hiked up there once. Incredible view of the valley. We must go there when we have a whole day to spend."

He spread a blanket and had barely opened a tin of something unidentifiable before I pounced on it.

"Wild animal," he teased. "So what is it that you need to share with me?" He stretched out on the ground as if totally relaxed, but I knew better. The concern in his voice was so endearing, it made me even more hesitant to say what I knew needed to be said.

"Fred, I've become very fond of you."

He scrunched up his face. "Fond? I don't think I like where this is going."

"You might not." I put down the tin and wiped my lips.

"Is this about the nonsense Marie Curie is telling you?"

"What? You know about that? I didn't…"

"Of course. She's been working me over too. Listen." He leaned closer. "I will not let that brilliant but slightly deranged woman have any influence on how I feel about you or my actions. I've been patient because of our positions, but you're right. It's time to talk about a future."

Oh God, was he going to propose? I had to head this off. "No, love, it's not about Madame. There are things I need to do. What I'm saying is, I am going to ask for a transfer."

"You're going back home?" He sat up. "Jules, I mean, I can't blame you, but…"

"No, not home. I want to go to Paris. There's a position there, a more senior position…"

He drew up his knees and wrapped his arms around them. "And Phil will be there. Well, if you've been offered a promotion, you should take it."

"It hasn't actually been offered yet. But I think I have a good chance, with your blessing."

"Ah." His voice grew bitter. "I get it now." He started repacking the basket.

"Fred, this has nothing to do with how I feel about you."

"And how is that?" He rose, our dinner apparently over. "I know you're ambitious. I actually love that about you. I just didn't think that was what this"—he waved a hand back and forth between us—"was about."

"Stop it. Right now." I pushed my weary self up to a stand and followed him toward the truck. "That's not what this is about." I caught up with him and tugged at his sleeve to turn him around.

"All that 'we have to be careful, rumors,' all that crap. You've pushed me away and pushed me away for ages. Did you ever care for me at all?"

He yanked back his arm. "I'll give you my recommendation. And the key." He dangled the truck key. "You know how to drive, right? I'll take the riverboat back."

He walked away, and I called after him, but to no avail. Then I waited as the sun set, turning the white cliffs pink. I trudged back to the truck and sat, my head resting on the steering wheel, willing for him to come back.

Maybe this was some kind of test. What was I supposed to do, run after him? Instead, I primed the carburetor, set the choke, adjusted the timing, and, the hardest part, cranked the engine starter, running back and forth between the front of the truck and the driver's position. I was sure he was listening, even as he headed toward the river, for the telltale sounds of cylinders firing.

It was a long, lonely, and painful drive back. Each time I crunched through the gears, it felt like I was crushing my heart a little more. I reviewed my disastrous part in the misunderstanding. For I was convinced it was a misunderstanding. I hadn't been using Fred for my own gain. Or had I? Why was I so willing to accept the guidance of a veritable stranger who had no business interfering? Why was I so hesitant to allow myself to have feelings for him? Why was intimacy so hard?

꩜

Once back in my room, I undressed. I took off my boots and regarded my scarred legs and my feet, big enough to wear men's shoes. I stretched out in my bed, where the top of my head brushed on the metal frame. Why had God made me this way? How could Fred, or any man, be attracted to me?

Somewhere, deep inside, I knew the answer. I wasn't meant to be like any other woman. I wasn't a man, for whom the things I wanted to do would have been easy. I was meant to break down the wall in between.

The next time I saw Fred was at the weekly medical staff meeting. He was cordial and professional, as I knew he would be. I'm sure only I could hear the slight clip to his voice, see the distance in his eyes.

When it came time to present my regular update, I handed out more mimeographs, to the groans of all assembled.

"We must hide that machine," grumbled Dr. Valentine.

Ignoring him, I went right into my presentation. "I hope by now you've all had a chance to read my suggestions for communicating the importance of isolation procedures for respiratory diseases."

There was some nodding and some ceiling staring.

"After consulting with my nurses, they feel they want to honor our dear departed Miss Cox with a letter-writing campaign. I have given you a list of the pertinent contacts, both stateside and in theater."

"What is your expectation here, Miss Stimson?" Dr. Valentine said. "We hardly have the time to—"

"Glad you asked. For my proposal is this: the nurses and I will draft the letters and address the envelopes. I ask merely that someone from this committee approves the drafts and signs for all."

"Well, then, I think we can vote on that. All those—" Fred said.

Dr. Valentine interrupted. "Hold on a minute. As a senior member of the Philadelphia medical community, I want to handle those letters myself."

As Dr. Valentine seemed to have a rather cavalier attitude toward isolation procedures, this worried me some. But this was no time to rock the boat, when things were sailing my way.

"Miss Stimson?" Fred was clearly in a mood to approve and move on.

"That's a fine idea, Dr. Valentine. We will take Philadelphia off our list. Anyone else prefer to do the same?"

After a pause with no takers, Fred repeated, "All those in favor?"

The motion was passed unanimously. I had gotten exactly what I wanted. I stood up to leave, my business being done.

Dr. Valentine held up his hand. "Hold on a minute, Miss Stimson. We need a committee member to review and sign these letters, correct? Any volunteers?"

It was awkward standing there while they looked around at one another. Of course no one wanted to take on more work. I had planned to ask one of the doctors privately so as not to put any one of them in an awkward spot. Just as I was about to ask him right then, Fred cleared his throat.

"I'll do it. Be happy to." He smiled at me, rather unconvincingly.

"Yes, sir," said Dr. Valentine. "Dr. Murphy and Miss Stimson, you are quite the team."

It suddenly felt like the air had been sucked from my lungs. I quickly gathered my things and stepped out of the room.

Once alone, I heaved a sigh of relief. Somehow, the germ of the idea that Nora and I had envisioned was becoming my main focus. Somehow, this project needed to be developed further, and somehow, it needed to relate to my next position. Even though it wasn't clear what that was.

After a quick round of the wards, noting nothing out of the ordinary, I headed to my office. There, I took the cover off my typewriter and fed it some paper. I had much letter writing to do.

Soon, I had a draft letter to share first with Nora.

Dear XXXX,

It is with much regret that we inform you of the recent passing of one of our nurses, Miss Charlotte Cox. She was a fearless and dedicated young woman who gave her life to caring for the sick and injured men. At the time of her death, she had been exposed to patients with symptoms of pneumonia and influenza, and it is presumed this awful disease was her cause of death.

We are writing with great urgency to inform you of the transmission of this disease despite normal prevention protocols. This influenza, unlike in previous outbreaks, is much more contagious and deadly. In addition, it seems to affect a different demographic group, that is healthy young adults. As this is precisely the group who are fighting this great war and are therefore placed in situations of unhygienic and close living quarters, we must consider additional screening and prevention measures, such as temperature taking, frequent handwashing, and facial masks for all medical personnel.

Enclosed please find a list of other preventative measures to consider.

As I clacked away at the typewriter, I didn't hear anyone come in. As I pulled the paper from it with a loud spin of its roll, I felt the presence of someone behind me. I turned to see Fred, standing quietly, arms crossed across his chest.

"Well, hello there. I didn't hear you come in." I assembled two pieces of paper with carbon paper between them.

"Didn't want to disturb you, being so hard at work." His voice revealed nothing of his feelings, as if nothing at all had happened. "In case you're wondering, I volunteered to help you as sort of an apology."

"Oh? For what?" I busied my hands, rolling the next sheet of paper into the typewriter, the *zip zip zip* a comforting sound.

"Jules, I have no right to expect anything more than a professional relationship. It is what you've said all along. Well, maybe not all along. But fairly consistently." He sat in my guest chair.

I tiptoed behind him to close the door. Gossipers be damned. "I'm sorry about that. It must be confusing. I'm confused myself." I turned my second guest chair to face him and plopped in it, knees to knees. Tenting my hands, I said, "I wish things were different."

"That's what I don't understand, among other things. You wish what were different?"

How could I explain? "My career is my calling. I have a sense of duty, a sense of being a leader and role model. I was brought up to put the needs of others first and to accomplish something important in life."

"I know all this. I just don't see the problem." He pulled his pipe from his pocket and rubbed the small carving on the wood. It had been given to him by his father. "Why are you making this harder than it needs to be? Unless our feelings aren't mutual. If they are, tell me now."

It would have been easy to fall in love with him. Surely, I already had. Easy enough to give up nursing and become a wife. Although the possibility of children was diminishing, there was still that chance.

But he was right. If we wanted each other and careers, we could fight to make that happen. There would have to be sacrifices made and boundaries broken, but when had that ever stopped me?

But there was something else. And it was physical.

"Stand up." I took his hand and rose from my chair, as did he. I stood toe to toe, chin to chin, and nose to nose with him. "What do you feel?"

"Confused?" He chuckled nervously.

"What do you see?"

"A beautiful woman, who at once confounds me and attracts me like no other."

"Really?" I unbuttoned the top buttons of my blouse and pulled it down to reveal my too-broad shoulders. "How about now?"

"Shoulders I want to kiss? Where are you going with this, Two Bits?" He put his hands on my bare shoulders. "I assure you all my parts are in working order."

"I don't think I need to remind you of the state of my legs."

"Is that what this is about? I don't care…" He slipped his arms down and circled my waist.

It felt so good to be held by him. But after years of deprivation, would it feel good to be held by just about anyone? I closed my eyes and imagined it was a movie star. No. Dr. Valentine. God no.

He leaned close and whispered in my ear. "Is this telling you what you need to know? Because it's definitely telling me something." He kissed my cheek, and I turned and met his lips with mine. A warm feeling spread throughout my body, and I longed to disappear into him. Longed to leave everything behind and just fade away into this moment as he pulled me impossibly closer, and my doubts floated away like wispy clouds of spring.

"Fred?"

"Mm?" He moved on to nibble my ear.

"I didn't get to ask my question."

"The answer is yes."

"Well, the question is, if these were normal times and you had your pick of the hundred prettiest ladies in St. Louis, all who were just dying to become Mrs. Dr. Murphy, would you still think I was attractive?"

There. I had said it. It was hard, and I didn't even really mean to ask it, but now it was out there, like a naked man at a funeral. I pulled back to read his face. It would tell me everything.

But he laughed. Not a little nervous *ha-ha*, but a rippling laugh, a gut-holding bender. I wanted to cower in a corner. No, to run. Run fast, faster than all the boys, who could never catch me. Run and then hide like the hideous freak of a woman I was. But I stood there, hurt and confused and pretending not to be.

Finally, he got a hold of himself. He grabbed both my arms and squeezed. "What, you think I'm that shallow? I'm crushed." More laughter.

"Fred, I'm serious."

"Jules, they could parade the world's most beautiful women naked in front of me, and I would only want one of them. I would want the tallest, the brightest, the most challenging and, yes, attractive woman I have ever laid eyes upon." He adjusted my blouse back into a presentable position. "It is not a war that has kept me away from a world of marriageable women. It's a war that has brought me to the only one I want."

CHAPTER 26

April 1918

P hil had been taking trips back and forth to Paris, ever since he had been selected for his new position, but it wasn't clear when exactly he would be moved. It had been hard to say goodbye when we didn't know which trip would be the last. But then, in typical army fashion, he received official orders to leave in two days' time.

The night before his departure, we had a little send-off party, with a cake and paper streamers and a big farewell banner signed by all the staff and many patients as well.

Phil had become a brother to all, reading to the soldiers with bandaged eyes, pushing ones with no legs in their wheelchairs or stretchers. As he always had a fondness for children, he had arranged for some from a local school to come sing for the soldiers. They came back to sing for Phil on his last night as a surprise for him.

And Phil had a surprise for me as well. He presented me with a small brown box. Upon opening it, I found a beautiful glass pendant. Inside the teardrop-shaped glass was a tiny red cross.

As he looped the chain around my neck, he said just above a whisper, "They want you to come to Paris."

"Who does?"

"The army. They want you to come and be the director of all the Red Cross nurses in Europe."

I clapped my hand to my mouth. I had written the letter to the headquarters some time ago, offering my services should they be needed there. But I never presumed such a vast leap. "Are you pulling my leg, Brother?"

"Much as that is my job, not this time. Think about it."

Someone started playing a tune on the piano, and Phil was pulled away by his fans. We didn't get to speak about it again that evening.

～

The next morning, as I walked with Phil out to the truck that was to take him to the train station, he clapped me on the back. "Will you be all right then, Big Sis? How much should I worry over you?"

"None at all. You can see I'm hale and hearty as always."

"Ah, but it's not your physical stamina that concerns me. And while you're probably the strongest woman I know, the pressure you've been under would reduce the best of us to a blubbering pile of goo."

"I wouldn't have wanted to be anywhere else. I draw great strength from making a difference."

"Have you considered what my contact in Paris said? You only have to nod your considerable head, and they will put an offer in writing."

"My head isn't that big."

"Pretty big. And you could probably still out arm-wrestle me." He held up a twiggy arm as proof.

"To answer your question, if you think they're serious, yes. You can tell them I'd be honored to head up all the nurses." As I said the words, it just about knocked the wind out of me. My hand went to my chest, where the glass pendant hung. When I had sent my regrets to Vassar, I didn't know why exactly I was turning down such a prestigious posting. But it seemed there was a good reason after all.

The problem, of course, was how to present this possibility to Fred. Just as we were sorting out our feelings for each other, we had this complication. A complication I foresaw the entire time, of course, but that didn't make my predicament any easier.

I wrestled with whether I should even mention my possible promotion, which would require a move to Paris, before it was even a written offer. What if I brought it up, with all the ensuing heartache and questions with no answers, and then it didn't come about?

But perhaps even worse would be to have the offer in hand and have him ask, as he certainly would, how long this had been in the works. I could already see the look of having been deceived in his eyes. I had seen that before. Even if it had been unfounded, I didn't want to see it again.

After checking the surgical schedule and seeing he would be off rotation, I wrote a note to him to slip into his pocket during rounds.

Meet me in the officers' mess for a private dinner. 7:00. Bring your best apron.

If Fred was going to be mad at me, we might as well have a nice dinner together. After our cooking class with Alice, we had met several times at the smaller officers' mess and made simple meals for ourselves. Maybe it was a bit of a dress rehearsal for domestic life, or maybe it was just an escape to some sense of normalcy, a trial to see how we might function in a noncombat environment.

He arrived at the appointed time, and I was already there, helping to clean up the last of the dishes from the staff's dinner and setting out the ingredients for ours. I had gotten permission from Alice to gather some fresh vegetables, and I had some gorgeous red radishes, thin green asparagus, mushrooms, and nice firm carrots.

He gave me a peck on the cheek and plucked a carrot from my pile.

"Aren't the colors pleasing?" I was so proud of my freshly picked and scrubbed vegetables.

"Sure." He chomped on the carrot. "What's for dinner, love?"

He had recently started referring to me as *love*. I wasn't sure I was comfortable with it. Sounded rather forward…and British.

"Well, there's these, and some bread, and maybe we can cook up some beans?"

He was already on the hunt for something else. "They will take too long, an hour or so. Ah." He pulled down a wire basket from the shelf. "Eggs."

We settled into a nice routine, with me chopping vegetables and him scrambling eggs and sautéing the vegetables as they were ready.

"I have something I need to tell you." As soon as the words were out and he twitched, I knew my phrasing was all wrong. I winced. "Sorry. Forget I said that."

Too late of course, his slow glance at me told me he knew something unpleasant was coming.

"Well, out with it, Jules. What arrows are you going to sling at my heart this time?"

"Now, don't go jump in the trenches yet. You know how you keep saying you support my career and us?"

"I'm listening."

"What if my career required me to move, not far away, but somewhere where we couldn't see each other every day?"

"We don't see each other every day." He dropped the last of the vegetables, the asparagus, into the hot pan, which smoked and sizzled. It smelled heavenly.

"Six out of seven."

"How far are you talking about? And what do you mean by 'if'? Is this a hypothetical situation or what?" He scraped the fluffy yellow eggs onto plates.

"Nothing's official yet. But Phil seems to think it's a good possibility I might be promoted and sent to Paris." The thought lifted my spirits. Or maybe it was the smell of the fresh vegetables he was piling on top of the eggs. "Isn't that wonderful?"

"Phil? What does he have to do with this?"

"I think the proper answer is, 'How wonderful for you. Congratulations.'"

"Sorry. I'm happy for you, of course. You deserve it. But I feel rather left out in the rain."

I dug into the hot eggs but didn't taste them. "It only came up last night. He told me at the party."

"Oh, it came up, just like that. Out of the blue."

"I don't understand. You seem displeased." Of course he sensed something else had to have happened to initiate the move, and I'm sure he suspected it was me. But his reaction chafed at me, my inclination to push away renewed. "You speak of supporting my choices, of understanding that I have chosen an unusual path for a woman. And yet here you are, not happy that my hard work might be recognized and rewarded but hurt that you weren't involved."

He put down his fork, wiped his mouth with his napkin, and let out a big sigh. "I'm not sure you're 100 percent on board with this relationship. Distance doesn't matter. How tall you are or how successful isn't the point. The point is the sharing. It's an emotional bond that ties two people together, forever. I'm not the one jumping in the trench, Julia."

❧

I might chalk that dinner up in the failure column. But as it happened, I considered it a timely warning. It seemed I wasn't ready for the type of relationship that Fred wanted, even as much as I longed for one, longed for a sense that I wouldn't be alone until the end of my days. I could still imagine us together. There was so much we had in common, and we really enjoyed each other's company. But still, I knew my mind could not make the transition necessary to be as fully committed to him as he deserved.

An invitation to come to Paris for an interview appeared. Awkwardly, it was Fred himself who delivered it. There was no mistaking what it was, with *Director, American Red Cross Nursing* emblazoned on the return address. He tossed it onto my desk and eased himself into the guest chair without saying a word.

I picked up the envelope and tapped it against my hand rather than ripping it open in front of him.

"Go ahead." He nodded toward me. "See what it says, although we both know."

"I could just toss it away," I said, more to see his reaction than with any real intention of doing so.

"You could."

I ripped it open. "It's not an offer. They want me to come for an interview. On Tuesday." I glanced at the calendar on my wall. "Good gracious, that's in three days."

"I'll go with you." He got up and headed for the door.

"That's not necessary." When I saw his frown, I added, "But of course, I would be honored to have you along."

The next week, Fred and I set out by train to Paris. It was early April, and the trees were beginning to bud with that light, almost glowing green. The rains had stopped, and the sharp winds of winter had given way to softer breezes.

We were dropped off at the train station just moments before our train departed, having had a flat tire along the way. It was a British train, with the large letters R O D painted on its side, for Railway Operating Division of the Royal Engineers.

We shared the car with several Tommies and many crates of food and ammunition. Indeed, the trains were arteries of the war effort, bringing the lifeblood of supplies to the front.

Fred and I had agreed not to discuss our current situation. *Détente* was the word he used, and I was only too happy to oblige.

We were only an hour or so into the trip when I was feeling peckish, despite a good breakfast. I fished around in my travel bag for the piece of dark bread I had squirrelled away.

But Fred was more prepared. "If experience serves me, you're famished by now." He pulled small, oblong tins from each of his chest pockets.

"Sardines?" I was probably one of the few people who would eat the small, oily fish right out of the tin, but still, it was an odd snack.

"No, tuna." He wiggled the key off the bottom of the can and proceeded to peel away the metal strip to open it.

"Hurray!" Canned tuna had just started appearing in our markets before we left the States. I had tried it a few times. "What a nice break from bully beef."

I was quite enjoying the fish, spread on some crackers, when the conductor announced, "Next stop, Vernon." Some fellow passengers fairly leaped from their seats. Apparently the tuna smell wasn't quite as endearing to them as it was to me.

Fred started packing things up and putting on his wool uniform jacket.

"We still have quite a way to go." I poked at some crumbs on my lap. This was not the neatest of snacks.

"I thought we might take a bit of a side trip. This is a lovely village; I think you'll enjoy it. I checked the schedule, and another train will come by in less than two hours."

I ran the numbers through my head. "That will put us in at…"

"4:00 p.m. Plenty of time. Will you trust me on this?" He was already standing, prepared to disembark.

"The name is familiar. Oh, I went to an art show in New York several years ago. There were six or so artists, and I believe they lived here."

"Hush. You'll spoil my surprise."

The station was just a covered walkway, and we were the only passengers to disembark, confirming my suspicion regarding the smelly tuna.

I could tell immediately that it was a special place. Fred led me down a narrow road where we hired a horse and buggy, as there were few automobiles here.

We traveled across the small village, then across Pont Clemenceau, a small stone arched bridge over the Seine. The buggy pulled up at a small hotel, apparently the end of his tour.

"It's a mile or so farther. Would you like to walk? Or I'm sure we can find another ride."

It felt great to be stretching my legs, and I had on my good sturdy boots. "Let's walk." I took his hand in mine. Surely that would be allowed during détente.

It did me a world of good. Birds chirped from the treetops, flowers were poking up here and there, and there was not a sign of an ammunition dump, nor a burned-out tank, nor lines of wounded soldiers. It would have been one of the best of my days, just enjoying the walk. But as promised, Fred had another surprise in order.

We came to an ornate iron gate. Fred checked his watch, then pushed right through it.

"Fred, this looks like private property."

"Indeed. My friend has obtained permission from the owner to explore the grounds."

He led me on a narrow path along a small, bubbling creek. The area was thick with vegetation, with many trees, including willows that seemed to be leaning to drink from the stream. The creek soon forked, and in between was an amazing stand of a tall reedlike plant.

"Bamboo," he said.

"You've been here before?"

"Yes, once before."

As we came around a bend in the path, the vegetation thinned, and a beautiful small pond appeared. Spanning the far end of it was a single arched, green wooden bridge, as I'd seen in a Japanese-style garden. Even though it was still early spring, there were blue irises and delphiniums and multitudes of white and yellow flowers ringing the pond. Although there were not yet flowers, lily pads floated on the surface. The trees and flowers reflected in the rippling water between the lily pads.

With a start, I realized exactly where I was. "Oh my word."

I tore my eyes from the incredible view to look at Fred. He wore a huge grin.

"What do you think? Worth a stop?"

"This is le Clos Normand, isn't it? Claude Monet's garden." I could hardly catch my breath.

"The very same. Come. The house is just around a few more bends."

"The house? *His* house?"

Fred laughed. "Yes, but don't worry. He's not currently here. But we can take a look from the outside."

We passed through garden after garden. One was surrounded by an unusual shrub, trimmed as a short, straight hedge, like a boxwood, but the leaves were larger. Taking a closer look, there were fragrant flowers and here and there some fruit, just starting to develop.

"Do you know what this shrub is?" I asked. "The fruit looks like little cherries."

"Believe it or not, those are apple trees. When Monet bought the land, it was an abandoned orchard. I guess he wanted to preserve some of them."

We came to a crossing of the paths, and looking to the right, I could see the house. It was two stories tall, pale pink with green shutters. At least I thought it might be pink. The front façade was nearly covered with ivy.

I stopped in the middle of the intersection of the paths and closed my eyes. I willed my brain to capture everything about the moment. The trees, the flowers, the birds, and even the bugs singing. The orchard rescued from destruction and given a new way to thrive—I wanted to remember it all. I breathed in the scents of the blossoms, held out my hands to the breeze that rippled the pond and caressed my face. I let it fill my heart. Then, I felt the comfort of Fred next to me. Felt his pleasure, knowing how much joy it was giving me.

"Well, my darling, what do you think?" he said.

"It's perfect. Absolutely perfect. I'm afraid I'm going to have to kiss you now."

"If you must." He took me in his arms, and as the breathtaking world swirled around me, I knew I was right to forever capture the moment.

We arrived back at the train station only minutes before the train came huffing into the station. It was time enough to grab a quick croissant and slice of *jambon*. Once aboard, feeling relaxed, I rested my head on Fred's shoulder and fell promptly to sleep.

In what seemed like seconds, he was jostling me. "We're here."

Sure enough, we had arrived at Gare Saint-Lazare. As we stepped from the train, I had the feeling of déjà vu. The black train threading through the station, with its roof a web of glass and steel, looked familiar.

"Another of Monet's favorite subjects." Fred answered my question before I could ask it.

There was a line of taxicabs outside the station, and we hopped in one and handed the driver the address. It had recently rained, the cobblestone streets glistened, and the raindrops clung to the trees lining the wide boulevards. Rouen was quaint, with its small alleys and stone and brick buildings. But Paris was magnificent. It was like comparing a girl in a summer frock to an elite woman in a sumptuous ball gown. We drove around traffic circles, sometimes several times. I wasn't sure if the driver missed the correct street to exit or was just giving us a bit of an extra tour. Looking down the roads that spread from the circle like spokes on a wheel, it seemed you could see for miles.

Fred advised me that the long, straight, and wide streets were designed that way to protect Napoleon from artillery or snipers. I wasn't sure if he was kidding me, but they certainly made the city beautiful.

Upon reaching the building where my interview was to be held, I parted with my travel partner. It wouldn't do to seem to need an escort. I met with the director of medical service, but the overall chief of nursing was away on business. As I waited for my appointment, I nervously worried the edge of my cuffs as I ran my credentials through my head.

But it turned out there wasn't any actual interview. My appointment seemed a forgone conclusion, and I was simply asked when I would like to begin—how about next week?

I was still reeling from the quickness of it all when I met up with Fred, who was sitting at a sidewalk café. He had pointed out the red-and-white awning beforehand, and I was glad not to have to concentrate too much to find my way.

"How did it go? Are congratulations in order?" He stood as I approached, always the gentleman. He had a bottle of champagne in his hand.

"It seems you've already decided they are."

"If you got the job, we celebrate. If you didn't, we celebrate having more time together." He pulled out a black wire chair for me. "But I'm sure you got it."

"Yes, it's rather more an order than an offer. The Red Cross says the final decision is up to the army. And that their policy is move up or out."

Pop went the cork.

❦

Back in Rouen, I fretted over how to tell my nurses. By now, there were over a hundred, plus dozens of nursing assistants and orderlies, all under my supervision. I was closest to my original sixty-four, of course, and I wanted to tell them privately of my leaving.

By the whispers and glances, I knew they were already aware something was up, and I was pretty sure they knew exactly what. So I couldn't delay the announcement.

I put a note on the bulletin board that there would be a meeting of squads 1 to 8 that evening and squads 9 to 16 the next. This fooled no one, for when I arrived for the first meeting, my original crew were all there, stood up simultaneously, and applauded.

"Sit, sit, my ladies." I waved them back to their seats. "It seems you have news for me?"

They laughed, and I could feel my shoulders relaxing as I started feeling better about the whole thing. "You know how much I love you all. But it so happens the overall American Red Cross chief of nursing deserves a well-earned rest. I will be going to Paris to replace her."

Despite my best efforts to contain them, tears welled up in my eyes. "This doesn't mean I will be forgetting you. Quite the contrary. I will be able to oversee your needs and get you the supplies and support you well deserve. And you will always, always"—I placed my hand over my heart—"be with me."

Dorothy was the first to rush up and give me a big hug. "This is for the best, Matron. You must go where you are needed."

Miss Taylor was next, her hand outstretched rather than a hug. "I will always be grateful for your leadership."

"You have been appointed the new matron," I said and shook her hand.

Nora came forward. "Congratulations, Matron, and Little Matron."

With that, the whole group was upon us, hugging and jostling and whooping. It was time to move on, and yet I never wanted to be with them more.

My preparations were fairly simple. I had paperwork to finish up, but since Miss Taylor had proven herself competent in my absence numerous times, there was little training that needed to be done. I planned to stay with Phil, as he had already acquired a nice flat in Paris, and my belongings could fit inside two steamer trunks.

The most difficult task by far was sorting out what this meant for Fred and me. I had not changed my mind; I still thought he deserved someone who could fill the role of dedicated wife and mother to his children. As much as I loved him, I knew that couldn't be me. But every time I had tried to explain this to him, he sulked off like a rejected suitor. I couldn't seem to get through to him that it was my love for him that guided me.

My date for leaving, April 10, was fast approaching. Each night, I spun and spun, bedsheets wrapping around me like a cocoon, as I wrestled with what to say to Fred. Finally, I knew, and on the afternoon of April 9, we escaped together to one of our favorite spots along the river.

We sat on a wooden bench under the shade of a plane tree. Rabbits stared at us as they munched on fresh spring grass. The Seine, its usual grayish tan, was swollen from recent rains, and there wasn't a sound except from the chirps of birds. It would have been the idyllic place for two lovers to meet, but my heart was filled more with trepidation than lust.

"I know you'll be overwhelmed at first. It's a big job you're taking on."

"No harder than running a field hospital in wartime."

"Just the same, it's different, all sorts of people and routines to get to know." He patted my thigh. "Not that I have any doubt whatsoever that you'll ace it all. They picked the right person, at the right time."

"Thank you for your confidence in me. I don't know what I would have done without your support."

"You'll still have it. In fact, that brings me to my big question—"

I turned my head sharply toward him, my eyes widened.

He laughed. "No, not that. Don't worry. But I was wondering when you might have things in order well enough for me to come to visit. A week, I'm hoping. I'm not sure I can go a whole month." His arm reached around and rested on my shoulders.

I stared at my hands, which traced the lines on my serge skirt. "Fred, do you want children someday?"

He pulled back his arm and was silent for a few moments. "Julia, I have a son."

My mind raced through all our discussions. I was sure he had never mentioned a son. "Since when?"

"Since '05. Cornelia died when he was barely two. He's been mostly raised by his aunt."

"My God, Fred. You never told me this."

He covered his face with his hands. "I should probably tell you we also had a daughter."

I'm sure my jaw dropped as I waited for him to explain, his entreaties to *share* emotional pain niggling at my mind all the while.

"Her name was Helen. Died in infancy. Cornelia never recovered, and then I lost her too."

I blinked back tears, both for him and for the disappointment. Clearly, he was not as close to me as he claimed. "I'm so sorry."

He held up a hand. "It was so long ago. I have long since buried that sorrow. But if it's God's will, I would like more children."

That was another punch to the gut. I took a deep breath. I was heading into more unguarded territory. "My dear man, do you know how old I am?"

"Early thirties? Why?"

"Thirty-seven on my next birthday. By the time this war is over… I'm afraid I'll never be a mother. And I'm not sure I'd want to be."

"I see. There's also adoption." He glanced at me. "Or being childless isn't the end of the world."

"For me, no, it isn't. But clearly, you want more children. I've heard you talk about that." I took his hand in mine. "Don't you see how impossible this is?"

He let out a deep sigh. "I don't care, Julia. I love you."

"I know. And I love you too, deeply. But I'm not sure I can separate the circumstances of our love—the endless support you've given me and my nurses, the wonderful you that I've come to know so well here, from the everyday bangers and mash for dinner kind of love."

He looked at me quizzically.

"What I mean is, everything is heightened here. Love, life, it's all in an artificial emotional state. Will we still feel the same way when life returns to normal?"

"I will."

"You say you can't go a month without seeing me. I think you'll be surprised how easy it becomes. You'll miss me, but life will fill in the empty spots."

"Of course. We'll adapt. But I'll always be happier with you than without." He bent to pick a blade of grass, then smoothed it between his fingers. "I know this because I was married before."

"Not to me." I chuckled. "I'm a handful."

"Nonsense."

"Tell me about Cornelia. She must have been very special."

"It was a good marriage. But we only had a few years together." He looked at me, his soft brown eyes sad.

"I'm sorry."

"Do you know we've known each other longer than my marriage? In some ways, I know you better than I did her. Of course, you and I also share professional interests."

"But in other ways, you knew her better. You were married, after all."

"There is knowing someone. Caring for them. Loving them." He played with the blade of grass, wrapping and rewrapping it around his finger. "But there is something else. Something deeper. It's being vulnerable enough to share things that you wouldn't share with anyone else."

"Fred, I hope you feel you can share anything with me."

He took a deep breath before answering. "I do. I've laid my heart out to you more times than I can count."

I could think of one giant exception but didn't mention that. "But?"

"But I don't think you do the same. There's still a band around your heart. An emotional distance, if you will."

"I guess I was brought up that way. We didn't exactly sit around the dining table discussing our feelings and such. I've not been married, other than to my work. And maybe my emotions are just not that deep."

"You're making fun of me."

"I'm not, truly. And I'm willing to learn to be more open. You have to remember all we've been through together, and it's only rather recently our relationship has taken a distinctly different turn. There's so much we need to explore about each other. I need time."

"There isn't any rush. I just need to know if you push away because you don't share the same feelings or because, as you say, you need more time."

I didn't really know the answer to that. "I have a proposition. Why don't we take advantage of this separation? Make no plans to see each other until we both just can't stand it any longer." I stopped to let the birds chime in. "I'm sure I'll be the first to cave in."

"Okay." He surprised me with his easy acceptance. "But on one condition."

"Uh-oh," I said lightly.

"That we make our last night memorable."

CHAPTER 27

April 10 dawned with unsettled weather. The days were growing ever longer, so the sun rose well before breakfast, breaking through the rain clouds and giving hope of a pleasant day.

After dinner the night before, my nurses and the doctors held a grand send-off party for me, along with a reception for Miss Taylor as the new matron and her new assistant, Miss Claiborne. The officers gave the three of us bouquets of beautiful and fragrant roses, along with a crystal charm from Tiffany's for my watch chain. The doctors escorted the three of us being honored to the mess tent, which had been decorated with many French and American flags, along with the Union Jack.

Then the three of us formed a receiving line, and every one of the nurses, assistants, and officers came through and shook our hands or gave us hugs. Each one had something wonderful to say: best wishes and good luck and how much they'd miss me. Some told me a quick story of something they would never forget. "Thank you for teaching me how to listen" or "You set an example I'll follow the rest of my life" and words of support for my new role: "We love you, but you must go where you are most needed."

I got through it by burying my emotions, smiling and hugging, and thanking them in return. But when I got back to my room, I had myself a good cry before heading over to say goodbye to Fred.

As I had hoped, the clouds scattered during the train ride to Paris. Alone this time, it gave me the opportunity to review the rather scant instructions regarding my new job and to mentally transition to the role. The scope of it both excited and overwhelmed me. Within it, I could effect real change, make policy that was based on real-world experience, rather than administering from a distance.

But the staggering responsibility of it all felt heavy upon my shoulders. As I watched the scenery go by, the whole world out there waiting to be discovered, I wondered if Fred was right. He hadn't actually proposed marriage, but he wouldn't do that until he was sure of the answer. And I had yet to come up with one. He was a perfect gentleman in our last night together, neither pushing for more than I was ready for nor brushing me off. We spent the evening chatting over too many glasses of red wine and nibbling at a tray of cheeses that Alice had made for me.

It was oh so normal. Something we had never had before.

Would it be so terrible to be the wife of a doctor? To spend my days not under the weight of a thousand demands but to do things of my own choosing? I could certainly volunteer for the Red Cross and make a contribution in that way. The conversation I had with my nurses soon after our arrival came to mind. "What will you do when the war ends?" they had asked one another.

The train clicked as it rolled steadily toward Paris and my immediate future. At this moment, that was what I needed to focus on. It seemed the more Fred pushed, the more I instinctively shied away. The challenge ahead was enormous. I needed 100 percent of my attention to be on the job I had accepted. There were many lives depending on me.

The first two months were a whirlwind of learning a new role, mostly without the help of the previous director. She had been called away, and her assistant had taken ill. Instead of having to learn the strange British system, as I had in Rouen, I had to learn the system of the American Red Cross, which was just as foreign.

But I found that since the role was so new, I could forge ahead with my own way of doing things, which delighted me. I soon had a regular routine and a trained and able staff to assist.

It didn't take long for Marie Curie to learn that I had been reassigned to Paris. An invitation soon came to visit her in nearby Sceaux. After a month of nonstop work at the Red Cross offices, I was excited to take a day off, do some exploring, and see my friend.

She and her daughters had lived, on and off, at her late husband's family house. It was not a place visited by anyone outside the family, so it was quite an honor to be invited. When I arrived, Marie was tending a flower garden in front of her home.

"Aren't they the most wondrous gift from nature?" she said without any other greeting. And she was wondrous, all five feet of her, surrounded in a sea of yellow, white, and lavender.

We kissed the air on both cheeks in the European fashion. It occurred to me how much I would miss living on the Continent when the time finally came to return to the States. "Good morning, Madame. You look well."

She waved my compliment off, as I knew she would. "Come inside. I've baked us some goodies."

As we sipped chamomile tea and gobbled the wonderful pastries, it seemed Marie was in an extraordinarily good mood. "It's nearly over, you know. I'll be able to get the Radium Institute running full bore. And to think of all the new uses."

"Indeed. The X-ray machines have saved so many lives and limbs. I think history will treat you kindly." I wiped my mouth, sure that it was encircled with fine crumbs.

"What of the radon gas–filled needles? Have they proven useful for treating diseased tissue?"

"To tell you the truth, we had limited experience with that in Rouen. We focused on emergency surgery and immediate effects. I can contact the convalescent hospitals for more information for you."

"Yes, that would be most helpful. I rarely get out to the field these days." She poured more tea. "I hear congratulations are in order, my dear. And why did I not hear of this great honor from yourself?"

My face warmed. Marie had a way of making me feel a child again. "I'm sorry. It all happened so quickly. But you are the very first person I came out to visit."

"Mm-hmm." Her lips set in a straight line. She did not seem convinced.

"My brother is here as well. We live together—"

"Yes, yes." She waved her hand. "Now, I have to apologize."

"What on earth for?"

"In my time I have learned a few things. Some lessons come harder than others." She collected her china cup and plates, and I followed suit. "I'm afraid I gave you terrible advice." She glanced at a framed portrait resting on a side table. It was a photograph of her and Pierre and their bicycles.

"No, Madame. All your advice was well intentioned and from the heart. I was and am always free to apply it to my own situation as I see fit."

"Yes, it was well intended. But you see, my life was devoted to my work, as I suspect is yours. And Pierre's life as well. We were together always, night and day. Now, as each year passes, I realize more and more how lucky I was to have that precious time with him. We were fortunate to share great joys along with our many sorrows. When I first met you, I was blinded by the urgent need for our work to be of benefit to the French people. I knew you were of a mind to see to that, along with all the wondrous things you and the Americans were doing to save us."

She beckoned me to a flowered chintz settee that sat in front of a window. Tall flowers—delphiniums and gladiolas—grew just outside the window, giving the impression of a continuous sunlit garden flowing from the inside out. As she sat, her hair glowing in the light, I thought it was a scene perfect for Monet to capture.

"I've only done my small part, and it has been a great privilege." I sat down beside her.

She gripped my wrist rather firmly. She may have been built like a squirrel, but she didn't lack for strength. "Listen to me. Forget what I said about rumors and not mixing love and work. Love is the more important thing." She released my wrist and picked up a packet of old letters, tied with string. "These are letters from my beloved. Not Pierre, mind you. Paul Langevin." She walked her fingers through the stack. "I was fortunate to have two great loves, but I bungled them both. I should have pushed aside work for a time each day and just enjoyed life with Pierre. And Paul…"

I swallowed. It was painful to watch her suffering such regret. I wanted to put her mind at ease. "You did what was best at the time. Who's to say that you and Paul would have had anything close to what you had with Pierre? It's easy to imagine it, but regrets do nothing for the soul."

She slid her fingers between the letters, looking for something. "He left his wife because of me, you know." She sighed. "But that was probably for the best as well."

I looked at my watch chain. The train only ran once an hour. "I'm afraid I will have to leave you now. But we will get together again soon."

She stood. "Will you promise me something?"

"Of course, Marie."

"Promise to put love first. Without that, nothing else matters."

On the train ride back, my parting words notwithstanding, I had the feeling I wouldn't see Marie again. It seemed she was telling me goodbye forever. Indeed, even though we now lived much closer to each other, we both had taken on even larger responsibilities. But it wasn't only that. It seemed that being with me forced her to rethink her choices and caused her emotional pain. I didn't want her to think that she had hurt me or my life choices in any way.

I had learned that outside family, people came into our lives and stayed a while, as we learned and grew with each other. But mostly, they left again, as we inevitably moved on, as we each needed different people in our lives.

CHAPTER 28

June 1918

These were very busy days, with tens of thousands of American troops arriving every week. The number of nurses was growing exponentially as well. If I thought about Marie Curie's words at all, it was late at night as I drifted off to sleep. Her reversal was curious; I wondered what had happened to inspire it. Had she been speaking with Fred?

Not that it mattered in any case. He was consumed with running a hospital back in Rouen and had just been promoted to lieutenant colonel. I was sure he was as occupied as I was, and we could safely tuck away our mutual attraction until a better time.

I had to coordinate with the training hospitals back home, to recruit and train what we needed on a timely basis. The front, after over a year of stalemate, was finally starting to push back toward Germany. There were a few times when the Germans developed a new weapon or did a desperate attack to recapture ground, but the overwhelming feeling was that victory for the Allies was near at hand.

I could no longer hear the distant thunder of artillery, except for one time when there was an explosion near our office. But this sound was different. It was a sudden, sharp sound, rather than the deep ground rumbling I had become accustomed to in Rouen, or the louder, pounding sounds we could hear from the CCSs.

I went outside, because it had sounded close by. A few French men and women were pointing up the street, but I couldn't quite understand what they were saying. *The front was too far away* was all I could decipher. Finally, an American supply sergeant came hurrying up.

"Everything okay here?"

"Yes, but do you know what that was?"

"The Boche developed a long-range artillery gun, and a round landed not far from here."

There was some English-to-French babbling as the word spread among those gathered.

This knocked the wind out of me, as surely as if I had been punched in the stomach. "They can reach Paris?"

"Not to worry, ma'am. The explosives are too small to do much damage. Until they fall right on top of you, that is."

His answer hardly soothed me or the gathered crowd. If their guns could reach Paris with small rounds, it was only a matter of time before they could reach us with larger ones. Just when it seemed the enemy was on its last legs and peace was at hand, it could all tumble into an even more terrifying conflict.

And of course, Paris was the grand prize. The Germans had blazed through Belgium and Luxembourg and were ripping their way through northeastern France, not just for the industrial cities, ports, and raw materials, but to capture the beating heart and nerve center. Because to control Paris was to control France.

I needed to get back to my office. It was time to make evacuation plans, should they be necessary. I was fortunate to have a telephone in my office, and I made quick work of calling a meeting with the other senior department leaders.

The next day, we met in our conference room, which was dominated by a large square table at its center. In addition to the overall director of the American, French, and British Red Cross organizations, there was a colonel who reported directly to General Pershing in attendance. Upon this table, we had a dozen maps, of all the countries in Central Europe plus North Africa and Mesopotamia. They were marked with red and blue arrows, indicating the movement of the military divisions on both sides.

It was not up to me when and where to move the people and resources. It would be my job to coordinate with all the chief nurses and communicate the plan to them. I was glad to have met most of them several months back. I knew which ones could be told once and would execute perfectly, which ones would need to argue about why it couldn't be done, and which ones would need lots of hand-holding.

I was madly taking notes as the colonel spoke. He seemed to think we had time, several months at least, to formulate and test our plan. But the tension in the room was palpable. These were all people who had seen the devastation of war firsthand.

A messenger came to me as I was straining to hear one of the quietest members of the group, the head dietician, who was responsible for all food supplies. The messenger handed me a folded note, then excused himself.

Important visitor. Please go to lobby.

Unless it was General Pershing himself, I could hardly think of a visitor important enough to take me away from this meeting. But then I thought of Phil. Oh my God, had something happened to him? Those new bombs…

I excused myself and rushed to the lobby, my heartbeat pounding in my temples. I made the usual twenty steps down the central corridor in fifteen, then skipped every other stair down the winding staircase.

I held a firm grip on the brass handrail; this was no time to trip. My boots tapped a quick rhythm on the terrazzo floors, and I made no attempt to step lightly to quiet them.

Finally, I reached the heavy mahogany door and pulled it open. At first, I saw no one in the wood-paneled room. The majestic windows that went nearly to the ceiling let in plenty of light, and I had to blink at first. Then, I saw him.

Fred was in a corner, absently pulling pamphlets from a rack. I was instantly grateful to see him but horrified at what may have brought him there so suddenly. My throat felt like it was closing.

I rushed up to him. "Fred, what's wrong?"

He took a step back. "Who told you… What do you mean?" He replaced a pamphlet as calmly as you please. He held out his arms to me. "Are you not happy to see me?"

I panted, still catching my breath. I was tempted to pull my dress away from my now damp underarms. "Is Phil okay? My nurses?"

"As far as I know, yes. What's happened?"

"I… Well, I thought… You do know about the new German artillery reaching Paris?"

He scratched his head, still wearing a look of confusion. "We know. Nothing to panic about."

"So there's no emergency?"

He shook his head.

I looked at my timepiece. The meeting was scheduled to end in fifteen minutes. "Fred, of course I'm happy to see you, but please excuse me. I am in the middle of something. I'll meet you at Phil and my apartment in two shakes of a lamb's tail."

I followed that up with an awkward kiss on his cheek and scurried back upstairs.

It was nearly 9:00 p.m. before I could break away from the office. The director was in my office, still wanting to review the plans we had made so far, when I realized my brain was so foggy, I wasn't taking in what he was saying.

"Can we possibly continue tomorrow?" I asked, a question I should have asked hours before.

Luckily, our flat was only a couple of blocks away, and it was a refreshing walk home. I let myself in and found Phil and Fred in the sitting room with full glasses of brandy and a nearly empty bottle.

"Jules! Look who the cat brought in!" My brother gave me a big hug, then fetched me a glass.

"I know. We've—"

Fred interrupted, squeezing me with a big hug. He even lifted me off the ground, not something many men can do. "Ah, but she's too busy for me." He smiled, his breath forty-proof.

"I'm leaving you two to your own devices." Phil winked, then left with his brandy in hand.

Fred and I clinked glasses.

"If I had known you were coming… Forget it. There was nothing I could do to rearrange my day today." I took a drink of the deep amber liquid. It was god-awful strong. "What is this stuff?"

"Calvados. Apple brandy from Normandy. You remember Normandy, don't you?"

"It's only been a couple of months. And we agreed—"

"To wait until we couldn't stand to wait any longer to see each other. And I did," he said.

I don't think I had ever been with him after having that much to drink. His emotions seemed to be right on the edge. I wanted to ask him if he'd been communicating with Marie Curie. It all seemed a bit fishy to me. But it seemed wrong to bring her up at the moment. And after all, her message was to treasure love, experience it fully, and not let others bully their way into it.

"And I'm glad you did."

"Ah, Two Bits, I've missed you so." He took my glass and put it aside. "And I've got wonderful news. I've been promoted."

"Oh yes, I've heard. In all the excitement in seeing you, I forgot to congratulate you."

"There's more, love." He slipped his arms around my waist. "I have to go away for a month or so with a unit up at the front." He seemed to be reading my eyes, which probably registered fear. "But don't you worry. After that, I will be reassigned someplace quite safe."

I let out my breath in relief. "Where would that be?"

He grinned broadly. "Paris."

"No! Are you kidding?" When he shook his head, I grabbed his hands, and we twirled about the room like two teenagers at a dance. Then he took me in his arms. I let his happiness and his strength envelop me, felt love in his touch. The world could go on fighting, maiming, and killing, bent on destruction. But at that moment, that was far, far away, and there was only him and me.

It was a moment to treasure, to bottle up and place in the heart forever. From the warmth of his arms around me to the sound of his voice whispering in my ear and even his brandy-soaked breath, I wanted to remember it all. I wanted to push aside any fears for his safety or doubts that we could be together and let the future unfold as it needed to.

For whatever happened, wherever the winds would take us, we would have that time together. I had learned from him how to let someone in, how to share the deepest parts of me. I had learned it wasn't enough to share a meal or a conversation or a bed. To share the secrets of one's soul was the true love that surpassed anything else.

AUTHOR'S NOTE

When I thought about a topic for my second novel, I wanted to stay in the same vein as *The Engineer's Wife*. That is, to focus on a woman in American history who accomplished amazing things, yet whose story has been lost to time.

Since I had practiced as an RN for many years and knew how challenging and unheralded that work is, I wanted to write about a nurse. Then I considered time frames. Although the World War II time frame is fascinating, there are already many novels written about the era, including many featuring female heroes. But at least in the United States, there hasn't been many written about the World War I period. This particular time was a watershed era for nursing and medicine.

In my research, I learned of Julia Catherine Stimson. Although I had studied the usual leaders of the profession, such as Florence Nightingale and Clara Barton, I had not heard of Julia. And since she was from the same geographic area and social strata as my previous heroine, Emily Warren Roebling, I could easily imagine them meeting and passing the torch of advancement for women.

So with a person and era in mind, I delved into the fascinating history of medical care in France during World War I. I was fortunate to be living in Europe at the time, and many of the places have remained unchanged through the years, with many monuments to mark them. The racecourse in Rouen that was the location of several stationary hospitals is now a park. Sadly, there is no commemoration of the hospitals there at this time, but as the park is under renovation, my hope is that some kind of permanent monument will be installed. I found it interesting that despite the vast efforts at renovating the area, a Google map still shows faint lines of the former tent city, like scars on the landscape. Perhaps that is the only monument necessary.

The Saint-Sever cemetery mentioned in the story is still there and has been lovingly maintained.

Many readers of historical fiction enjoy learning which aspects of the story can be documented as true, which are solely in the authors' imaginations, and which are somewhere in between. For that reason, I submit the following:

Julia Stimson, Fred Murphy, Philip Stimson, Colonel Fife, Dr. Ernst, Marie Curie, and Annie Goodrich were real persons and served in roles similar to this story, although their specific thoughts, actions, and dialogue are imagined. Nurses Charlotte Cox and Nora W. were World War I nurses who served at the time but in different units. I discovered the story of Miss Cox upon visiting Meuse-Argonne American Cemetery, and Nora W. was my husband's great-aunt.

Although the characters of Benjamin, Ned, and the Belgian patient are fictitious, the illnesses and injuries they suffered were like those described in diaries of real war nurses, or in the case of Ned, the first real casualty in the unit.

In the story, Julia and her nurses go through Grand Central Terminal in New York City on their way from Saint Louis to their ship. In reality, some of the nurses met them in New York City, and it isn't clear where they all met up. At the time, a train from Saint Louis could also have arrived at Penn Station, or in New Jersey, to be ferried to the ship. I chose Grand Central to simplify, and because it was and is a fabulous building.

An interesting tidbit, the original aboveground Penn Station was destroyed, and Madison Square Garden was built over the remaining underground tracks. There was such an uproar over the destruction of the beautiful architecture that laws were passed to preserve many historical buildings, Grand Central being one of them.

Marie Curie and her daughter Irène did in fact travel across France and Belgium, providing radiological services. They visited hundreds of field and stationary hospitals, mostly French, but some of the Allies' as well, bringing equipment and training staff. I did not find documentation of which hospitals they visited and when, but as AEF Hospital 21 was known to be at the forefront of radiological services, I imagine it was on their list. Madame Curie's troubles due to her love affair with Paul Langevin are well documented.

The relationship between Julia and Fred is also one of those somewhere in-between aspects. They did both arrive at Barnes Hospital/Washington University in St. Louis in 1911. Letters to others attest to conversations between them, but I did not find letters directly to each other. It is documented that Philip Stimson did try to join the St. Louis American Red Cross unit in 1916, and Dr. Murphy apologetically declined, mentioning Julia several times. It is documented that Dr. Murphy was a widower at the time of the story and that he and Julia were both reassigned to Paris within a few months' time. So they were in close proximity, worked together for seven years, and moved twice with each other.

In addition, in the collection of her letters home found in the book *Finding Themselves*, Julia is quite effusive in her praise for Dr. Murphy, especially early on. She mentions having dinner with him and how much the nurses love him. Toward the end, he gets a more passing reference, almost like she was hiding their true involvement.

After the war, it seems they went their separate ways, as Julia started moving up the ranks, ultimately being in charge of all nurses in the European theater, then head of the Army Nurse Corps and the Association of Nursing, while Fred Murphy returned to his surgical practice.

Julia never married, while Dr. Murphy did remarry after the war. So although there isn't written documentation of a romantic relationship (and why would there be?), there is ample evidence that they were personally close, but then something happened. There is documentation that the members of the group continued to have reunions in St. Louis for many years after the war. Strangely, it seems Fred and Julia didn't attend in the same years. It may be coincidence or happenstance, or it may be due to a falling out or bitter regret. They took that secret to their graves.

READ ON FOR A LOOK AT

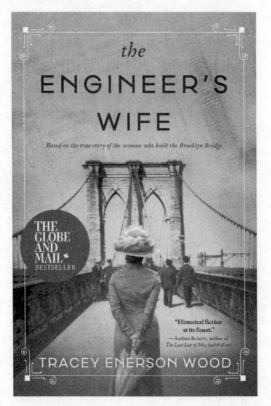

AVAILABLE NOW FROM
SOURCEBOOKS LANDMARK

CHAPTER 1

Washington, DC
February 1864

The light, sweet honey scent of burning candles did not quite mask the odor of blood and sweat in the makeshift ballroom. Not far from the White House, the room was tucked inside a military hospital, itself a repurposed clothing factory. Noise echoed in the vast space, with cots, machinery, and great rolls of cotton neatly stacked against the walls. Tall windows let in slanted rectangles of light upon women in dark uniforms setting out flower arrangements. I too felt out of place. Dressed in a ball gown, I was like a fresh flower in a room meant for working men.

Double doors opened from an anteroom, and chattering guests tumbled in. An orchestra hummed, tuning up as men clad in sharp Union dress uniforms gathered in conversation groups with women in their finery. Nearer to me, a line of men on crutches and in rolling chairs aligned themselves along a wall, each of them missing a limb or two or otherwise too broken to join the healthier soldiers.

I nodded my greetings, hesitant at first. Like most young women in my small town of Cold Spring, New York, other than a glimpse of a few limping, bedraggled returned soldiers, I had been sheltered from the consequences of war. Here, the wounded men clambered over one another, some in hospital pajamas, some half in uniform, reaching out to me, seeking to be included despite their infirmities.

I ignored the bloody gauze wrapped around heads and the stench of healing flesh as I shook their hands, right or left, bandaged or missing fingers, making my way down the line. One after the other, they thanked me for coming and begged me to dance and enjoy myself.

In the letter that had accompanied the invitation to the event, my brother had been clear: *The ball is intended to be a celebration of life, a brief interlude for men who have seen too much, and the last frivolity for too many others.* It pained me to look into their eyes, wondering who amongst them were enjoying their last pleasure on this earth.

"So pleased to meet you. I'm Emily." I offered my hand to a soldier with one brown eye, his face cobbled by burns.

He held my hand in both of his. "Miss Emily, you remind me there is still some joy in life."

I smiled. "Will you find me when it is time to dance?"

The soldier laughed.

My face flushed. It was too forward for a lady to ask a gentleman to dance. And perhaps he was unable.

"You can't tell from my pajamas, but I've earned my sergeant's stripes." He tapped his upper arm. "I won't be joining the butter bars."

The term *butter bars* rather derogatorily referred to the insignia of newly minted lieutenants. Belatedly, I recalled my invitation was to the *Officers'* Ball, and the sergeant had apparently come to watch. My cheeks warmed. I had gaffed thrice with one sentence. Not an auspicious beginning, considering my goals for the evening.

More women filtered in, each on the arm of an officer. In contrast to the men against the wall, the exuberance and freshly scrubbed skin of these officers made me doubt they'd seen battle. I felt rather out to sea.

I had insisted on arriving without a chaperone, as I had expected to be escorted by my brother, but he was nowhere to be seen.

His last letter had said the fighting had slowed during the winter months, but that could change at any moment. Even if it hadn't, he was a target. I shook the image of a sniper out of my head. Surely, if something terrible had happened, they wouldn't still be setting up for a ball.

The soldier still had a firm hold on my hand. I pasted a smile on my face and peeked about the room. Was it more awkward to mingle with the others, all in couples, or rude not to?

The sergeant jutted his jaw toward the center of the ballroom. "Go now. We'll be watching."

I nodded and slipped my hand from his, resisting a peek at my white silk gloves to see if they'd been soiled. My ball gown showcased the latest fashion: magenta silk, the skirt full in the back and more fitted in the front. My evening boots echoed the profile; with an open vamp and high heel, they reminded me of Saint Nicholas's sleigh. I smoothed the gown's travel creases and mulled its merits. *Comfort: adequate. Usefulness: very good, considering its purpose was to please the eyes of young men.* Mother had disapproved of the deeply scooped neckline, but she had sheltered me long enough. I was now twenty years old and craved amusement.

The handsome dress uniforms and elaborate gowns each guest wore suggested formality and elegance, but raucous laughter shattered the tranquility of the elegant piano music. Clusters of young men erupted in challenges and cheers, guzzling whiskey and fueling their spirits.

I stepped closer to a particularly animated group in which a tall, handsome captain held court among a dozen lieutenants. Perhaps he could advise me as to where I could find my brother.

"What will you do after the war?" someone asked.

"Rather the same thing as before. Build bridges. Blow them up."

The captain raised his glass, and the others followed, laughing and cheering.

A bespectacled, earnest-looking young man asked, "Sir, why would you blow up bridges in times of peace?"

The captain's smile faded, and he leaned into the group as if sharing a great conspiracy. "There are only so many places to build a bridge, and sometimes we have to blow up an old, rickety bridge to make room for a new one."

I stepped back, feeling awkward for eavesdropping.

The captain continued his lesson. "I'll be helping the country to heal, connecting Kentucky and Ohio with a long-abandoned project. And then we'll be doing the impossible. Connecting New York and Brooklyn with an even grander bridge. It will become one enormous city. If you want a job after the war, boys, come see me."

I shook my head. The captain didn't lack for hubris. But just as I was about to approach to inquire about my brother, he excused himself and hurried off.

Twilight had faded, and the candles and gas lamps burned brightly, as if the assembly's energy had leached out and lit the room. All the women seemed thoroughly engaged, so I wandered about, my worry for my brother steadily increasing. A tiny glass of golden liquid was thrust at me, and I took a sip, the burning in my throat a pleasant sensation.

The orchestra played a fanfare, and a deep voice rang out. "Ladies and gentlemen, the commander of Second Corps, Major General Gouverneur Kemble Warren—the hero of Little Round Top."

Relief ran through me like a cool breeze on a hot day. I should have known that the commander of thousands would need to make an entrance. Officers snapped to attention and saluted the colors as they passed, then held their position for my brother. My heart fluttered when I saw him, taller than most, shaking hands as he made his way through the crowd. Our family called him GK, as Gouverneur was a most awkward name. Thirteen years my senior, he was now in his thirties, with sleek black hair and a mustache that met the sides of his jaw.

After months of worry and cryptic letters from which I could only gather that his troops had won a major battle in northern Virginia, seeing my brother lifted me two feet off the ground. I waved as he scanned the room, his eyes finally finding me.

GK had been more surrogate father than older brother, our father having passed away several years previously. He was the closest to me amongst all our surviving siblings, no matter the time or distance that separated us. As he edged closer, my smile faded at the sight of his gaunt frame, the strain of war reflected in the streak of gray in his hair and the slump of his shoulders.

The young officer following behind my brother glanced my way. I looked, then looked again—GK's aide was the same captain who had been boasting about healing the country with bridges. His eyes landed on me for the briefest moment, then scanned the room as if the enemy might leap from the shadows.

I coughed to cover a laugh. While he tried to appear vigilant, his gaze returned to me again and again. Perhaps he had seen me eavesdropping.

I squeezed past the knots of guests toward GK, but the crowd was thick around him. He greeted the wounded men, exchanging a few words and shaking hands down the line. Next, he worked his way into the larger crowd, and I was pushed back by officers surging toward him as they jockeyed for his attention.

"Men of the Second Corps." GK's booming voice filled the room as if to assure them that he could be heard over the firing of cannons. "Let us welcome these fine ladies and thank them for honoring us with their presence."

He signaled the orchestra, and hundreds of young men in dark blue began to dance, their shoulders shimmering with gold-fringed epaulets, like an oasis after years in the desert. I danced with one handsome lieutenant, then another and another, each spinning me into the arms of the next in line. When at last I paused, gasping for breath, the officers gathered around me, helping me to tuck back the long ribbons that were losing the battle to contain my curls. While the other women sniffed their disdain at my exuberant dancing and frequent change of partners, the men laughed and vied for me. No matter about the women. I meant to keep my promise to my brother by providing amusement for his men.

A lieutenant came by with a tray of drinks, whiskey for the men, tea for the ladies, he said, although it was difficult to tell them apart. The guests emptied the tray save two. The lieutenant handed one of the glasses, filled nearly to the brim, to me. "For you, Miss…?"

"Just Emily." He needn't know I shared a surname with the general.

"For you, Miss Just Emily," he said, loudly enough to elicit chuckles from the crowd.

I took the glass and sipped. It was whiskey.

"No, all wrong." He took the last glass, swirled the amber liquid, and took a deep whiff of its aroma. Then he downed it in several gulps.

I poured the whiskey down my throat and held up my empty glass, pressing my lips together to stifle a cough. The group cheered and my spirits lifted, sailing on fumes of whiskey. I was no longer a fresh flower in an old factory. I was their queen.

The crowd grew louder, but this time, it wasn't me they were rooting for. A short, broadly built officer leaped into the air and landed with his legs split. The throng whistled and yelled "Just Emily!" for my response.

The group clapped a drumbeat, encouraging me. My competitive spirit outweighed my sense of decorum, and I spun, each step in synchrony with the clap, faster and faster until my dress lifted. Then I slid down into a split, one arm raised dramatically, my ball gown splaying in a circle of magenta folds around me.

As several officers helped me up, the crowd parted, revealing GK and his aide. My brother raised one eyebrow in warning, and the younger officer gaped at me. Heat rose in my face, but this time, it wasn't the whiskey.

"Moths to the flame." GK gave his aide a slap on the shoulder.

The aide then closed his mouth, his Adam's apple bobbing above his blue uniform collar. "Shall I escort the young lady from the dance, sir?"

My opinion of him matched that of the booing crowd.

GK rubbed his chin. "A generous offer."

The aide flashed a conspiratorial grin, but his smile faded when GK added, "But that won't be necessary."

Even though the captain had seemed a presumptuous young man, I was chagrined that GK was teasing him. GK slung his arm across my shoulders and led me away from the group.

"Emily, I trust you are enjoying yourself?" GK's face showed a mix of tenderness and disappointment. I wanted to curl up like a pill bug.

"Quite. It is my pleasure to offer a small bit of entertainment." I crossed my arms across my middle, feigning boldness. It had been a full year since I had seen my dear brother, and I wanted to show him how grown up I was and how much I cared about our soldiers. But despite my good intentions, I was a bit late to realize that my actions might reflect poorly on him.

One of the men called out, "Aww, let her stay and dance with us, sir."

"Not now. The lady needs a rest." GK maintained a grip on my arm, firm enough to tell me I was most certainly out of line.

The aide glanced wide-eyed from GK to me. His thick hair and neatly trimmed mustache were the color of honey, and his expressive eyes reminded me of the crystal water that filled the quarry at home.

"Miss Emily Warren, allow me to introduce Captain Washington

Roebling." GK lifted my gloved right hand and offered it to his aide. "I owe my life to this captain and my sense of purpose to this charming sprite. It is only fitting the two of you meet."

The captain cleared his throat. "You—your wife? I thought she was unable to—"

"Gracious no." GK laughed. "My sister. She and my wife happen to share a name. Now then, will you be so kind as to guard the honor of *Miss* Emily Warren?"

I felt sorry for the poor man; his eyes took me in, from escaping curls to rumpled hem, as he reconciled my identity. Perhaps trying to oust his commander's sister from the event was only slightly less humiliating than ousting his wife. My presented hand hung awkwardly in the air until the captain regained his composure and took it in his own.

"It will be my pleasure, sir." Then his first words to me: "Miss Warren, Captain Roebling, at your service."

READING GROUP GUIDE

1. How much did you know about nursing (particularly World War I-era nursing) before reading this book? What was the most surprising thing you learned?

2. If you were told that your entire workplace was uprooting to support a war effort, what would your first reaction be? Did Julia have a real choice when it came to shipping out?

3. Both Julia and the doctors she assists can be territorial about their authority. How does this affect their working dynamics? Are there any consequences for the patients the team treats?

4. Julia and Dr. Murphy discuss the ethical and procedural challenges of authorizing nurses to perform lifesaving procedures on their own. Compare the benefits and drawbacks of strictly following protocol to the consequences of a nurse performing whatever procedures she feels are best.

5. Dr. Murphy compares the doctor's role to that of a car mechanic

and gives the majority of the healing credit to nurses. What do you think is a nurse's most important role? How would you rank their importance next to doctors?

6. Julia hesitates in her relationship with Fred, not wanting to feed the rumor mill. How does outside opinion influence relationships? Compare the rumor mill of Base Hospital 21 to today's social media. How do their relative positions affect their willingness to "let the chips fall where they may" when they begin seeing each other more seriously?

7. What did you think of Julia's choice to keep her skin condition a secret? Do you think she was right to fear dismissal? What were the consequences of her decision?

8. How does the 1918 Spanish flu outbreak compare to the 2020 novel coronavirus? Are there lessons that can be learned from the way Julia and her nurses battle their pandemic?

9. Did Julia do the right thing by violating protocol to operate on Private Dempsey? What would you have done in her place?

10. What did you think of the final scene of the book? Can you think of a moment you wanted to bottle up and keep forever? What do you think is next for Julia and Fred?

A CONVERSATION
WITH THE AUTHOR

How did Julia Stimson evolve as you started to relive her story?

First, I read the collection of her letters in *Finding Themselves*. This gave me a good idea of her voice and perspective of the events. I realized that what she wrote home was probably censored, both officially and by her, so as not to upset her family too much with how difficult a situation she was in. So I continued my research, reading diaries of other World War I nurses, along with other historical references. One reference, a letter from one of the real doctors to his wife, spoke glowingly of Julia: her organizational skills and positive relationships. This enabled me to fill in the blanks and hopefully present a more realistic view of what Julia went through. She became a more three-dimensional person in my mind, with hopes and fears, regrets and insecurities—most of which she had kept to herself.

How does working with a true historical figure change the process of getting to know your characters?

I think it is more difficult to work with a true historical figure, because you are limited in many ways, such as time and geography. I would have loved, for example, to put Julia in more physical danger from the war, but that would be too far from documented facts. But in some ways, true characters are more rewarding to work with, because you have bits and pieces of their lives and true anecdotes that are fun to work into a scene.

When writing relationships like Julia and Fred's, how do you strike a balance between character motivations and historical accuracy? Do you have any rules for when to exercise creative license?

My basic rule is that what I write about the relationships—and other parts of the story—either happened or *could have* happened as far as I know. In historical fiction, we are filling in the blanks: the emotions, the dialogue, the motivations that don't get documented and therefore are not included in nonfiction accounts. But these very things bring a story to life and, for me anyway, make it more enjoyable to read.

There are times when I break this rule, and that is usually when I have to move events in time or place a bit to better fit with the arc of the story.

That said, it must be remembered that this is a work of fiction. There is no way to research every piece of documentation in existence. That is why I have the caveat *as far as I know.*

Like any historical novel, *The War Nurse* required a great deal of research. What kinds of sources did you rely on most? How did you find the resources you needed?

As previously mentioned, *Finding Themselves* was an invaluable resource. Another was *Nursing through Shot and Shell*, the memoir of Beatrice Hopkinson, a British nurse. Washington University in St. Louis has extensive online documentation of Base Hospital 21. Harvard and Vassar databases also provided insight on Fred and Julia.

But the most enjoyable and perhaps most important research was actually visiting Rouen and the surrounding area and taking tours with historians throughout Belgium and France. Not only did I learn a lot from them but they led me to other sources I wouldn't have found on my own. I found museum bookstores to be a treasure trove for finding obscure, narrowly focused information.

What were the most surprising things you learned while writing?

I guess the most surprising thing I learned was Marie Curie's involvement in the war and of the extensive accomplishments of her daughter, Irène, who, with her husband, also went on to earn a Nobel Prize.

I also noted how so many things never really change. Sure, we have better treatments for most illnesses and injuries, but the human body and its frailties are the same. And while we think we are seeing something new with COVID-19, we are not.

Were there any interesting facts that ended up not being included in the book?

I learned much about World War I history, but I purposely avoided including too much of it. There are plenty of books about wars, both nonfiction and novels. I wanted to focus not on the battles and destruction and weapons but on the personal experiences—the human story, through the eyes of Julia. I also underplayed the horror of it. I believe there is only so much gore my readers want to see. There needed to be enough to set a scene, but I didn't repeat the very unpleasant things the nurses were dealing with. As a nurse myself, I know how they learn to ignore what they need to in order to help their patients and get through the day.

Did the COVID pandemic change the way you wrote about the Spanish flu outbreak?

Since the Spanish flu would have been mostly a problem of fall 1918, slightly after the story takes place, I hadn't planned on it being as important in the story, other than the character arc of Charlotte Cox. But with the parallels of COVID, I realized its relevance to current events, so I made it a larger subplot.

The 1917–1918 pandemic killed at least fifty million people worldwide. In my research, I found an interesting comparison between how St. Louis and Philadelphia handled the Spanish flu pandemic. Philadelphia ignored the warnings and proceeded with a planned parade to raise funds for the war. Two hundred thousand people crammed the sidewalks to view it. Afterward, the city's hospitals were full, and there were soon 2,600 deaths. In contrast, St. Louis banned gatherings, closed businesses, and treated the sick at home. It was able to "flatten the curve," as we say today, resulting in a lower death rate than Philadelphia.

I didn't find an explanation for why the cities handled the situation so differently, but it certainly seems reasonable that they followed the advice of people at the war front, where the situation first became critical. Hence, this inspired the standoff between Julia and Dr. Valentine regarding sending advice back home.

What lessons from 1918 did you apply to your own life?

That just when things look the bleakest, change will come and some equilibrium will be restored. We ourselves will have grown and changed, become stronger and more resilient.

Which books are on your bedside table right now?

Kristin Harmel's *The Book of Lost Names* and advance reader's copies of Greer Macallister's and Marie Benedict's upcoming books, *The Arctic Fury* and *The Mystery of Mrs. Christie*.

ACKNOWLEDGMENTS

I would like to thank my friends and family who have put up with my protracted mental distraction as I follow my dreams and write books. They understand how I can be in the same room, possibly even answering their questions, while my mind is a hundred years and thousands of miles away. Most especially, my devoted husband, Dave, whose unending support has allowed me this privilege.

I would also like to thank the many historians from whom I learned so much and the people of Belgium and France who were so gracious during my visits.

I had the great fortune to have early input from the amazing novelist Stewart O'Nan and several other writers at Stewart's workshop in Tenuta di Spannocchia. To these wonderful writers, thank you, and write on.

But without the hard work of my editor, Anna Michels; line editors Sabrina Baskey and Heather Hall; as well as the entire team at Sourcebooks Landmark, this book would never have been completed.

And to my agent, Lucy Cleland, once again thank you for your support and for believing in me.

ABOUT THE AUTHOR

Tracey Enerson Wood is a published play-
wright whose family is steeped in military
tradition. This is her second novel, following
The Engineer's Wife.